A. M. Clarke

Life of Reverend Mother Mary of St. Euphrasia Pelletier

First Superior General of the Congregation of Our Lady of Charity of the Good

Shepherd of Angers

A. M. Clarke

Life of Reverend Mother Mary of St. Euphrasia Pelletier
First Superior General of the Congregation of Our Lady of Charity of the Good Shepherd of Angers

ISBN/EAN: 9783744749442

Printed in Europe, USA, Canada, Australia, Japan

Cover: Foto ©Raphael Reischuk / pixelio.de

More available books at **www.hansebooks.com**

LIFE OF THE REVEREND MOTHER MARY OF ST. EUPHRASIA PELLETIER.

ROEHAMPTON :

PRINTED BY JAMES STANLEY.

QUARTERLY SERIES.   VOLUME NINETY-TWO.

LA Rᴅᴇ Mᴇ̀ʀᴇ Marie ᴅᴇ Sᵀᴇ Eᴜᴘʜʀᴀsɪᴇ Pelletier

Fondatrice et 1ʳᵉ Supérieure Générale
de la Congrégation de N. D. de Charité
du Bon Pasteur d'Angers

LIFE OF REVEREND MOTHER
MARY OF ST. EUPHRASIA PELLETIER

First Superior General of the Congregation of Our Lady of Charity of the Good Shepherd of Angers.

BY

A. M. CLARKE.

LONDON: BURNS AND OATES, LIMITED,
NEW YORK, CINCINNATI, CHICAGO: BENZIGER BROTHERS.

1895.

PREFACE.

It will be a hundred years on the 31st of next July since the birth of Rose Pelletier, who became the first Superior General of the Congregation of Our Lady of Charity of the Good Shepherd of Angers.

It is, therefore, a fitting tribute to her memory that her daughters in England should publish a biography which will make her better known, and which, by setting forth the history of her inner life, will touch and instruct the hearts of many, who burn with love for the work of the Good Shepherd.

It is not so generally known that the Founder of the Order of Charity, or of the Good Shepherd, is the Venerable servant of God, John Eudes, who was one of the most distinguished priests among the French clergy during the first and middle parts of the seventeenth century.

It was not, however, till within the memory of living people, in 1834, that the Order of Our Lady of Charity was so far developed and consolidated as to require a Superior General. The choice of the Sisters fell upon Mother Mary of St. Euphrasia Pelletier, and she governed the Order with unabated zeal, tact, and prudence till her death, on the 24th of April, 1868, in the seventy-second year of her age.

God is often pleased to bestow upon the first Superiors of Religious Orders that are destined to fill the Church with the perfume of their virtues and to enrich it by the conversion of innumerable souls, signal and extraordinary graces. It is as though the efficacy and healing of the leaves were to be found in greater abundance in the root of the tree which He has planted. So it would seem to be in the present instance. The Order of the Good Shepherd, instituted for reclaiming sinners, was founded by the Venerable John Eudes, whose beatification is in hand, and its first Superior General is a woman who died in our own time in the odour of sanctity, and whose Process was actually commenced within twenty-one years after her death, in 1887. Many graces and miracles are said to have been wrought by her intercession, and there is little doubt but that the fame of her sanctity will be spread and augmented by the publication of the history of her Life.

The Sisters of the Good Shepherd have been fortunate in securing the literary services of Miss A. M. Clarke, who has made a very readable volume of the materials placed within her hands.

HERBERT, CARDINAL VAUGHAN.

September 2, 1895.

CONTENTS.

		page
CHAPTER I.—Birth and early years .	1
,, II.—Life at school	19
,, III.—Vocation .	36
,, IV.—Novitiate and Profession	51
,, V.—Superiorate at Tours	70
,, VI.—Foundation at Angers .	93
,, VII.—First idea of the Generalate .	109
,, VIII.—Establishment of the Generalate	125
,, IX.—Results of the Generalate	144
,, X.—Further spread of the Order	162
,, XI.—Rome .	174
,, XII.—Time of Trial	192
,, XIII.—Munich .	213
,, XIV.—London . .	231
,, XV.—The New World	251
,, XVI.—The Dark Continent	265
,, XVII.—Labours and Sorrows . . .	282
,, XVIII.—Glimpses of many lands .	303
,, XIX.—Devotion to God and the Saints	328
,, XX.—Personal Virtues .	356
,, XXI.—Last Illness . .	373
,, XXII.—Death	392
Conclusion	408

The writer of this biography begs to acknowledge her indebtedness to the authors of the following works for the assistance she has received from them:

1. La Servante de Dieu Marie de Sainte-Euphrasie Pelletier, Fondatrice du Généralat de la Congregation de N.D. de Charité du Bon-Pasteur d'Angers, sa Vie, son Œuvre, ses Vertus. Par M. le Chanoine Portais, Rédacteur des conférences ecclésiastiques du diocèse d'Angers. 2 tomes. Paris et Angers, 1893.

2. Vie de la R. M. Marie de Ste. Euphrasie Pelletier, Fondatrice et première Supérieure Générale de la Congregation de N.D. de Charité du Bon Pasteur d'Angers. Par M. l'Abbé H. Pasquier, Doyen de la Faculté catholique des Lettres d'Angers. 2 tomes. Paris: P. Lethielleux, lib. ed. 1894.

3. An Apostle of the Sacred Heart in the Seventeenth Century, and the Order of Our Lady of Charity of the Good Shepherd. By the Rev. Bertrand A. Wilberforce, O.P. London: Convent of the Good Shepherd, Finchley.

CHAPTER I.

Rose Virginie Pelletier belonged to a family which had for many generations been settled in La Vendée, and whose faith, handed down from parent to child, and securely fixed upon the rock of Peter, had stood firm against the stormy billows of the Revolution.

Her father, Julius Pelletier, was one of seven brothers, and made choice of the medical profession, in which he appears to have met with no inconsiderable success. He fixed his abode at Soullans, a town of La Vendée, in the diocese of Luçon, and became the right hand of the parish priest, whose post was not an easy one, on account of the conflicting elements which prevailed among the two thousand inhabitants of his parish. M. Guillon, for such was his name, was a man of no ordinary type. He had been sent to Soullans by Mgr. de Mercy, Bishop of Luçon, because of his unusual sanctity, wisdom, and prudence. Erelong his tact succeeded in gaining over all parties, and harmony reigned everywhere. In places such as Soullans, the mayor fills the foremost position. After him comes the priest, and the doctor forms no unimportant factor in what we may term a triple alliance, each member of which works in concert for the public good.

M. Pelletier, who was everywhere known to be a truly pious man, became an intimate friend of

B

M. Guillon, and in 1780 we find them labouring
together for the benefit of the bodies and souls of their
fellow-men.   A year later, M. Pelletier, having made
for himself a large practice in Soullans and its environs,
thought it was time to marry.   He chose for his future
wife a young lady named Anne Mourain, who was, like
himself, sincerely pious, and had been trained in every
Christian virtue by an admirable mother.   Being an
only child, she was, moreover, the heiress to a large
fortune.   The marriage took place on August 7, 1781,
the bridegroom being twenty-nine, the bride twenty
years of age.

Theirs was a pattern household, blessed by God,
beloved by man.   For a period of ten years their lot
was one of nearly unclouded happiness. Mdme. Pelletier
devoted herself to the care of the seven little children
who came, in quick succession, to adorn the family
hearth, and rejoice the heart of their father when he
returned home after a hard day's work.

In 1791, the devoted wife and affectionate mother
beheld with terror the heavy clouds which were gathering on the horizon, threatening to break, as they did
only too soon, into the revolutionary storms, which were
to sweep away her happy home, and deprive her for
several years of the free exercise of the religion she so
truly loved.   She was now thirty-one, and seems to
have experienced few, if any, sorrows.   But her time of
trial was to be both protracted and severe, extending
almost to the close of her life, in 1813.   She was,
however, far too good a Christian to shrink from taking
up her cross, or to fail in bearing it with courage.
Over and over again had she read the words of
à Kempis: "The Cross leadeth to the Kingdom.   Go
where thou wilt, seek what thou wilt, and thou shalt

not find a higher way above, nor a safer way below, than the way of the Holy Cross."[1]

Erelong M. Neau, who had succeeded M. Guillon as parish priest of Soullans, was proscribed and hunted down, as were the majority of his brethren who refused to take the oath of the Republic. He sought and found shelter, sometimes in one house, sometimes in another, repaying the hospitality accorded him, by celebrating beneath the roof of his protectors the adorable Mysteries of the Altar. In the spring of 1793, he was surprised by a detachment of the Republican soldiery, just as he had finished his Mass, and cruelly put to death by them, without a moment's delay, in one of the outlying farms which belonged to his parish.

We are not engaged in writing a history of the Vendean War, which derives its interest and importance chiefly from the fact that it affords proof how deeply rooted was the attachment to the Faith in the hearts of the French people. In the worst days of the Revolution, when anarchy, vice, and bloodshed were rife throughout the land, there lay beneath the surface depths of virtue, sanctity, and devotion, unseen by the multitude; supernatural faith inspired an heroic band of soldiers to rise in defence of their Church. Their deeds are as worthy of admiration as those of their adversaries are of reprobation. Intrepid, noble-minded, generous, merciful to their enemies, the Vendeans recited the Rosary on the way to the battlefield, and threw themselves on their knees before the crucifix, preparatory to charging upon the foe. Nor did they lay down their arms until liberty of worship was guaranteed to them, and their priests were protected by law. The history of this warfare cannot, however,

[1] *Imitation*, bk. ii. c. 12.

be otherwise than a sad one, on account of the excesses of the Republicans. M. and Mdme. Pelletier witnessed, with horror and apprehension, the terrible scenes which met their eyes on every side. Many of their friends and acquaintances were called upon to lay down their lives, as the penalty of having sheltered some proscribed priest, and assisted at his Mass. These martyrs displayed an heroic courage, worthy of the Saints of the early Church. A single instance may be quoted here.

Mdme. Petiteau, a neighbour and intimate friend of Mdme. Pelletier, had been left a widow with three children, the eldest of whom was only nine years old. She received into her house M. Neau, the parish priest of Soullans, in order that he might say Mass there on Easter Sunday.[1] For this pious and charitable action, she was dragged from her home, and thrown into prison at Challans, where she languished for nearly a year. In March, 1794, she was chosen to form one of a band of fifteen prisoners, who were destined to be taken to Noirmoutier, where their final sentence was to be pronounced by the Republican judges. No doubt could possibly exist as to what that sentence would be. The chief magistrate of the district was nearly related to Mdme. Petiteau, and felt extremely anxious to avert her approaching doom. He besought her to deny what she had done. "Never," replied the courageous woman, "will I try to save my life by telling a lie. I did give help and shelter to a proscribed priest, because he was persecuted, and a minister of God. If to do this is a crime, I am guilty." Numerous exertions were made in the hope of saving her, but they all failed. On

[1] This priest was shortly afterwards murdered, as has been mentioned above.

August 3, she was marched down to the beach, and shot together with twenty of her companions in captivity. She went to meet death with firm step and head erect, thus proving that the Catholic Faith can impart to weak women a fearlessness equal to that shown by the bravest of soldiers.

M. Pelletier felt that no alternative remained to him, except that of abandoning his home and his professional duties, in order to find a refuge in the island of Noirmoutier. He could not permit his wife and seven children to witness the scenes of horror which met the eye on every side. Churches were burnt to the ground, the soil was stained with blood, neither women nor children being spared.

Noirmoutier is an island, forming a portion of La Vendée. It is several miles in length, and is separated from the mainland by a narrow channel. Thither the family removed in March 1793. The journey was a slow and painful one for Mdme. Pelletier and her seven young children. A farmer, who was devoted to the family, accompanied and aided them. Whilst crossing the channel which, as we have just said, separates Noirmoutier from the mainland, he several times had to carry the mother and children by turns upon his back in order thus to enable them to traverse some portions of the channel which, even at low water, are never left entirely dry.

But alas! for the deceptive nature of human hopes and anticipations! Noirmoutier, beheld from afar, had looked like an oasis in the desert, but when it was reached, it was found to be no peaceful place of rest and refreshment, but a desert more scorching and terrible even than that which they had left behind them. The Republicans, infuriated by the resistance they met with, spread slaughter and devastation everywhere, and in the space of a few months only, twelve hundred victims were either shot or drowned, including every one of the priests who had sought shelter in the island. The church was well-nigh levelled with the ground, and during a period of seven years the exercise of public worship was forbidden under severe penalties.

The reader has already been made acquainted with M. and Mdme. Pelletier, and will therefore understand that this total privation of all religious privileges and outward means of grace was the heaviest of their many crosses. They could no longer hear Mass, or approach the Sacraments. It was during this period of special privation and trial that the subject of the present biography first saw the light.

Rose Virginie Pelletier, the eighth child of her parents, was born on July 31, the feast of St. Ignatius, in the year 1796, and baptized by her father the very same day. In less than a year, however, a priest, M. Gergaud by name, who had remained in hiding at Nantes during the worst days of the Revolution, ventured to journey as far as Noirmoutier, in order to administer the sacraments. He married a large number of persons, and baptized many young children. Mdme. Pelletier joyfully brought to him Rose Virginie, who was conditionally baptized, with all the ceremonies prescribed by the Church, as were at the same time two other little girls, destined in after-life to become her intimate friends. Owing to the state of the times, no formal record could be made of these baptisms. Hence Rose Pelletier never had any baptismal register. Nor was her infant cradle rocked by the usual nursery songs; the first stories she heard, while seated on her mother's knee, were tales of heroic deeds, of patriotic

courage, of sufferings cheerfully endured for the sake
of God and of Holy Church. Her quick intelligence
and warm heart understood and sympathized with all
she heard. At a very early age she learnt to look at
everything in view of that eternity to which we are
hastening, and in the light of which we ought to
live.

Lessons of practical charity abounded under the
parental roof. Her father not only bestowed upon the
sick poor the benefit of his professional skill without
payment; he distributed among them medicines, wine,
strengthening food, all, in short, that they could need.
Nor did he stop here. He hesitated not to receive the
sufferers into his own dwelling, when occasion required.
One day he came upon an unfortunate man who had
been terribly hurt through some grievous accident. He
lifted the poor mutilated creature upon his own
shoulders, bore him home to his house, and there
tended and cherished him until he was completely
cured. Sometimes in the course of his daily rounds
he met with children who had been abandoned by their
parents, and were consequently in a state of pitiable
destitution. He would bid them climb into the conveyance which he was driving, and take them home to
his wife, who never sent them away until they had been
suitably provided for. Sometimes whole families were
received at once. Mdme. Pelletier was the right hand
of her husband in all these undertakings. She exercised
Christian charity in no ordinary degree, and was a
mother to the poor around her. She made their beds
if they were sick, washed their sores, swept their
rooms, and did not refuse to render them the meanest
services. During a period extending over several
months, she did everything that was necessary for a

poor old man, who was completely paralyzed and utterly friendless. Whenever some hungry, ragged child knocked at her door, she used to say to her own little ones : " Here is a poor little sister (or brother), let us see what we can do for them." Nothing delighted Rose more than to help in these good works, she was always ready to give away anything of which she had the disposal. No sooner had she learnt to handle a needle, than she used to beg her mother to give her pieces of stuff, which had been put aside as useless, in order that, after her childish fashion, she might make garments for those who needed them.

In December, 1800, Bonaparte having, in his character of First Consul, restored liberty of worship, the Catholic clergy were once more enabled to exercise their sacred functions in peace and quietness. One of the first baptisms which were performed with all due ceremonies, was that of a little son, who was born to M. and Mdme. Pelletier on the feast of our Blessed Lady's Annunciation, March 25, 1101, and received the name of Paul. No one welcomed the baby brother with such eager delight as Rose, now nearly five years old. Not a thought of envy, not a cloud of jealousy troubled her pleasure in this new possession. She had hitherto lived with brothers and sisters who were older than herself, and she had from the very first a special affection for Paul. It was a pretty sight to see her clasp him in her chubby arms, when trusted to hold the precious burden for a few moments. Later on, she would guide his tottering steps, and she was always ready to make any personal sacrifice in order to please or amuse him. Such details can hardly be considered trivial in the case of one who was destined by God to be the mother of many souls, and who, at the early age of five years, showed that she possessed the germs of her future vocation.

As she grew older she was no less remarkable for piety than for charity, and throughout the whole of her life she was always ready to acknowledge how much she owed to her excellent mother, whose constant endeavour it was to instil into the hearts of her children a dread of sin and love of virtue; and who, moreover, taught them at an early age to examine their consciences, to be unremitting in their attendance at Divine worship, and ardent in their attachment to the Church of God and to His Vicar upon earth. Here we may relate an amusing incident which occurred at a much later period.

Rose had been taught as a child never to omit, at her evening prayers, to repeat some petitions for the intentions of the Church. Upon one occasion, Moïse, the faithful nurse who had brought her up and was much attached to her, went to the Good Shepherd Convent at Angers, to pay her a little visit. Moïse greatly amused the nuns by saying, in the presence of the former Rose Pelletier, then Mother St. Euphrasia: "If you only knew what a little *dévote* Miss Rose used to be! When I was putting her to bed of an evening, I could not get her to finish her prayers. 'Do wait a little while, dear Moïse,' she used to say, 'I have not yet said my five *Paters* and my five *Aves* for the Church.' Mother St. Euphrasia smilingly replied: "My dear Moïse, I am sure you will be glad to hear that since that time I do not think I have ever missed saying these five *Paters* and five *Aves*, for I have always had a deep reverence and love for Holy Church."

In fact, a love of prayer seemed to have been born

with Rose Pelletier. Taught by the Holy Spirit of God, she soon began to practise mental prayer after her own simple fashion, and delighted to place herself in a special manner in the presence of her Creator. While yet a child, she would subject her actions to a severe scrutiny, and consider how they would appear in the eyes of an all-seeing Judge. As a matter of course she loved the house of God, with its ceremonies and services. As the Feasts came round, they were to her a source of real joy, though much which captivates the senses and delights the imagination must have been lacking, at the outset especially. The sacred building had been, as we have said, more than half pulled down, the interior being completely wrecked, and all the fittings, plate, and vestments, sacrilegiously taken possession of. As is so frequently the case in England, at Glastonbury and elsewhere, in regard to churches ruined at the period of the so-called Reformation, the arches and some portions of the side-chapels had been left intact, so as to render the work of restoration comparatively easy. Nothing, moreover, could destroy the imposing effect of the unusual elevation of the high altar, so that, when giving Holy Communion, it was necessary for the priest to descend a double flight of stone steps, in order to reach the intending communicants. As soon as Rose had reached a suitable age, she was assiduous in her attendance at the catechetical instructions given by M. Moizeau, the vicar of the place. She distinguished herself by her quick intelligence, and the readiness with which she entered into the spirit of the Church's teachings. The parish priest, M. Bousseau, who had hastened to return from his exile on German soil, in the hope of resuming his former labours, found himself disappointed in his expectation, owing to a complication of diseases, which increased upon him year by year, and rendered him unequal to all active exertion. It was only rarely that he was able to say Mass. Occasionally he was carried to the church on Sundays, and when the services were over, he held a sort of reception in one of the porches. His affectionate and devoted parishioners used to press around him in order to kiss his hands and beg for his blessing. Rose Pelletier was invariably present at these touching scenes, and learnt in this way much of that profound respect for the ministers of Jesus Christ, which was one of the prominent features of her character.

When she was nearly eleven, she was prepared for her First Communion. Besides attending with the utmost care to the instructions that were given to her, no exertion was lacking on her part which could give practical effect to those instructions. She redoubled her prayers and good works, making in addition great efforts to overcome her faults, and discovering many ingenious methods of practising self-sacrifice, and at the same time benefiting her neighbour. When the solemn moment at length arrived, we are told but little of what passed between her soul and the Heavenly Guest Whom she was permitted to receive. And it is well that it should be so. Does not Holy Scripture assure us that, *Sacramentum regis abscondere bonum est*—"It is good to hide the secret of a king"?[1] Much later in her life, however, she confessed to her Sisters in Religion, that she had felt herself to be rapt as if in ecstasy, and had, from that day forward, never doubted for a single instant, that she was called to the religious life.

[1] Tobias xii. 7.

The following year she received the Sacrament of
Confirmation, and her preparation was no less thorough
and practical than it had been the year before. The
impressiveness of the occasion was increased by the
circumstance we are about to relate. Mgr. Paillon,
Bishop of La Rochelle, in the course of his pastoral
visitation, came to Noirmoutier in order to administer
the rite of Confirmation. Since the Revolution, the
bishopric of Luçon had lapsed, and was now merged
into that of La Rochelle. In order to show honour
to his Bishop, M. Bousseau, whose limbs were now
paralyzed, caused himself to be carried down to the
church porch. As soon as the prelate was perceived
to be approaching, he made an effort to rise from the
arm-chair in which he had been seated. Supported on
either side by one of his parishioners, he welcomed in
the warmest terms Mgr. Paillon, who had in former
times been his fellow-student at the Seminary. The
kind-hearted Bishop was moved to tears when his old
friend took leave of him in the following words: " May
you long continue, Monseigneur, to be a blessing to
your diocese! May your youth be renewed like the
eagle's! As for myself, my end cannot be far off, and
I can scarcely hope that I shall ever see your lordship
again in this life. But since God in His mercy has
permitted me to behold the Salvation of Israel, I shall
depart in peace." Contrary to all expectation, the
noble old man lived nearly eight years after this
memorable day. It was not until July 5th, 1816, that
he was called to exchange the cross he had carried so
long and so patiently for an eternal crown in Heaven.

Rose evinced, from her earliest years, a strong love
for the beauties of nature. She delighted to spend as
much time as she possibly could, in the open air, and

especially in wandering upon the beach, sometimes alone, sometimes in the company of her little friends. Doubtless the sea-breezes, by materially strengthening her constitution, did good service in preparing her for the toils of her after-life. Fearless and enterprising, she always exercised an ascendency over her companions, who submitted willingly to her control, allowing her to determine the direction of their rambles, and settle any dispute which might arise. Already she possessed a genius for command, and a power of organization, and already she strove to use her gifts for the glory of God.

St. Philibert was one of the first of the holy men who at once civilized and evangelized France. Born in Gascony, the scion of a noble house, he was in his early life the page of Dagobert, and the friend of St. Ouen. At a later period he founded the Benedictine Abbey of Jumièges, on the banks of the Seine. He was, however, compelled to fly from the wrath of one of the kings, whose vices he had, like the Precursor, fearlessly reproved. He sought refuge in Noirmoutier, and became the apostle of the island. He further taught its inhabitants how to manufacture salt, and how to resist the inroads of the sea by means of dykes. Thus, through the spiritual and temporal benefits he conferred upon them, he bound them to him by a double tie of gratitude. As generation after generation passed away, his memory continued to be held in affectionate veneration. One of the numerous caverns, which the action of the waves has hollowed out among the rocks, is known as St. Philibert's grotto, because popular tradition relates that it was a favourite resort of the Saint, who loved to retire thither in order to meditate and pray.

Brought up as she had been, it cannot appear surprising that Rose Pelletier should learn to share in this favourite devotion. She loved to make St. Philibert's grotto the object of her long rambles on the sea-shore, and would lead thither the steps of her young companions, and especially of her two most intimate friends, Sophie Duchemin and Clementine Viaud-Grand-Marais, who had received Baptism at the same time with herself. But her practical mind did not content itself with these visits and these prayers. *Laborare et orare*, she had even then unconsciously chosen for her motto, and she resolved to do something more for the honour of her beloved Saint.

. The chapel of St. Philibert consists of a crypt, situated beneath the choir of the church of Noirmoutier. This chapel, the architecture of which is extremely simple, is divided into three parts by two rows of pillars. Between the first four of these pillars is a tomb, formed of solid blocks of stone, its sole ornament being a raised cross, also of stone. Until 836, this tomb contained the body of St. Philibert, and also that of St. Viaud. At this period the Benedictines belonging to the Abbey of Jumièges, forced to escape from the violence of their northern invaders, removed the remains of these two great servants of God from one place to another, in order to preserve them from profanation, until they were finally deposited at Tours. The subterranean chapel, which had been for many centuries a celebrated shrine and the scene of numerous miracles, had been so roughly handled, and so rudely desecrated, during the Revolution, that it was absolutely impossible to say Mass there, as had been the custom in more peaceful days. Rose Pelletier and her little friend Sophie resolved to do all they could to bring about

a better state of things. With their childish hands
they swept out the crypts, and cleared the altar from
the rubbish which had been heaped upon it. Their
next business was to clean the tomb, and finally, having
ornamented the altar with flowers, they went to their
respective homes, and told the story of their labours.
It is scarcely necessary to add with what delight this
story was listened to. Gladly did their parents second
the efforts of their daughters, and supply everything
that was still lacking for the due celebration of Divine
Service. Before long it was re-established as in olden
times, and due honours were once more paid to the
Patron Saint of the island. The reader will imagine
the joy and gratitude with which the growing piety
of Rose filled the heart of her pious mother, who already
began to see the fruit of her early training. Frequently
did she remark to her intimate friends : "Rose will be
a real blessing to our house. It is wonderful to see her
love for religion, for hearing sermons, for attending
catechetical instructions in the church, and for every
work of piety and charity." As to M. Pelletier, his
clever, bright little daughter, who shed so much
brilliance and vivacity upon the domestic hearth, was
his special favourite, and peculiarly dear to his affectionate heart.

Much as Mdme. Pelletier would have wished it
otherwise, the numerous cares and occupations devolv-
ing upon her as the head of a large household, rendered
it impossible for her to do more than superintend the
education of her children. She regretted this all the
more, because it was at that time so difficult to find
suitable instructors for them. The Republic had upset
everything. For the enemies of God and of His Church
are, in all ages, fully alive to the importance of educa-

tion, since upon the training of the young depends the future of a country. Hence their unceasing efforts to prevent that education from having a Christian colouring. In the present case, the public schools had been closed, thus forcing the masters to seek elsewhere the means of livelihood. Religious communities had been dispersed or driven into exile, so that Mdme. Pelletier scarcely knew which way to turn. She finally engaged the services of a person on whom she could thoroughly depend, and whose high moral principles, kindness of heart and solid piety, atoned for her want of learning and accomplishments. In fact, she could do little more than teach the children to read and write, and impart to them the mere elements of learning. Rose became very fond of her governess, and never ceased to remember her. Later on, when she had herself left Noirmoutier, she used to send her former instructress little presents from time to time, in order to cheer and soothe her somewhat lonely and neglected old age.

To her parents, Rose invariably showed the utmost respect and affection, nor was she ever known to quarrel with her brothers and sisters. Yet, in spite of her piety and her many charming and attractive qualities, it must not be supposed that she was by any means faultless. Ardent and impetuous, vivacious and daring, she not unfrequently allowed the warmth of her feelings, and the exuberance of her animal spirits, to carry her beyond due bounds. She could not confine her mischievous tricks to the members of her family circle, but ruthlessly practised them upon strangers, whenever the fancy to do so took possession of her. For instance, an aged gentleman, distantly connected with M. Pelletier, one day took a stroll in the woods which are not far from Noirmoutier. It was the height of summer, and overcome by the heat, he lay down at the foot of a tree, and fell fast asleep. He had previously taken the precaution of removing his wig, and placing it, together with his hat and sun-umbrella, on a mossy bank close by. On awaking an hour or two later, he found to his amazement and dire consternation, that his wig had disappeared. After a vain search, he was compelled to return home without it, but as he drew near his house, no words could depict the feeling of astonishment with which he recognized his missing head-dress, nailed to the front door. Rose had been wandering in the wood, and, coming suddenly upon the sleeper, had crept softly to the bank where the wig was lying. Yielding to a sudden impulse, she snatched it up, and carrying it off in triumph, nailed it, as if it had been a trophy gained in battle, on the door of its unlucky owner. Many similar stories might be told, but it is only just to add, that whenever Rose thus forgot herself, she used to spare no self-reproach when the evening came and she began to examine her conscience. She did not hesitate to impose upon herself penances which were certainly very severe for her age. More than once she sentenced herself to stand barefoot for an hour at a time on the wooden floor. At such times she would say to her faithful nurse: "My dear old Moïse, whatever you do, don't tell mama about this!" She herself used often to relate this story to her penitents, as an instance both of the care with which the examination of conscience ought to be practised, and also of the necessity of atoning for even slight faults.

Hers was one of those strong, resolute characters, equally potent for evil or good, according as nature or grace prevails. Happily for her, the principles of faith were firmly rooted within her, and fervent piety enabled

c

her to combat, and finally to conquer, the rebellious impulses which, if not subdued and enslaved, might have led her to wander far from the paths in which her youthful feet had been led.   It is such characters as these that Divine Providence chooses as His instruments when a great work has to be done.   Have we not inspired authority for saying that it is " out of the strong" that " sweetness comes forth "? [1]

[1] Judges xiv. 14.

CHAPTER II

LIFE AT SCHOOL.

WHILST relating, in the preceding chapter, the history of Rose Pelletier's early years, we have, in order not to break the thread of our narrative, omitted the mention of some family events, which are of too great importance to be passed over. We must, therefore, retrace our steps for a while before taking up once more the story of her life.

Death had frequently visited the family circle, and on each recurring occasion the gap thus made was more painfully felt. Mdme. Pelletier lost in succession three of her daughters. On the 19th of August, 1805, Victoire Emilie was suddenly called away. She was just fifteen, and her loss filled with passionate grief the heart of her sister Rose, who was six years her junior, and looked up to her almost as to a second mother. Pious, charming, and intelligent, she appears to have been in every way worthy of the confidence reposed in her, and a fitting guide for her little sister. Heavy as it seemed at the time, this sorrow was light in comparison with that which the next year held in store for the once happy family. On the 27th of November, 1806, the household was bereft of its head. M. Pelletier died, at the age of fifty-four, leaving to his widow, who was, as the reader will remember, ten years younger than her husband, the weighty responsibility of the care and education of the six children who remained to her. An aunt, Mdme. Pelletier, who resided at Bouin, herself a childless widow, took charge of the eldest daughter, Anne Josephine, and gave her a home in her house.

Rose thus found herself the only girl left to console her broken-hearted mother, who stood in sore need of comfort. There are wounds which, in sensitive and affectionate hearts like hers, can never heal on this side the grave, and although she did not allow herself to murmur against the will of God, but bore herself as a true Christian should under this bitter trial, she could not rally from its effects. She was a changed woman for the remainder of her days. Rose grieved deeply for the loss of the wise and kind father, whose favourite child she had been. With the quick intuition which was one of her natural gifts, she understood that her mother suffered an acuteness of anguish into the depth of which her childish heart could not enter. While respecting the sacredness of that sorrow, she omitted no loving attention which could soothe or lessen it. She seems to have concentrated upon her remaining parent all the filial affection in which her father had formerly had so large a share. She became more and more attached to her mother, whose memory remained deeply engraved upon her heart.

In 1843, thirty years after the decease of that beloved mother, when an inhabitant of Noirmoutier enlarged upon her virtues, and spoke of the loving remembrance in which she was still held by all who had had the privilege of knowing her, her daughter, then Mother St. Euphrasia, who was present, burst into an uncontrollable fit of weeping, and it was some time before she could restrain her emotions. One of her children in Religion, who was an eye-witness of this painful scene, said to her : " Dear Mother, if you were so very fond of your departed parent, why have you never spoken to us of her ?" " Because," replied Mother St. Euphrasia, with a fresh outbreak of tears, " ever since I had the misfortune of losing her, I have never been able even to utter her name without renew- ing all the first intensity of my grief. I had such an immense affection for her ! When I received the announcement of her death, the news almost killed me ! " On this subject we shall have more to say in another place, and will therefore quit it for the present.

About two years after the death of M. Pelletier, the Ursulines, then recently founded by Father Baudouin, made a foundation at Noirmoutier. They opened a boarding and day-school for girls, and the inhabitants of the town were only too glad to avail themselves of the opportunity thus afforded for the education of their daughters, which, as we have seen, had been since the Revolution a matter of so much difficulty. Rose Pelletier was among the earliest pupils. At school, as elsewhere, she displayed her attractive qualities and her marked defects, for grace had as yet not overcome her natural imperfections. Lively and high-spirited, full of eagerness in the study-room and the play-ground, wilful and mischievous, yet withal extremely pious, she was a continual puzzle to the good nuns. They did not know what to make of the strange, brilliant, troublesome bird which had found its way into their quiet aviary. Little could they dream that a phœnix was in their midst ! Upon a certain occasion, when Rose had allowed her exuberant gaiety to carry her even further than usual, one of her teachers said to her : " My child, take care what you are about, you will be either an angel or a demon." " Oh, no," was the quick retort, " I shall not be either, I shall be a nun." " How can you think of such a thing with a character like yours ! " replied the teacher. " I know what I am saying," answered Rose, who had suddenly grown grave, " I shall have to be thoroughly broken in, but all the same I shall be a nun."

Gifted with no ordinary intelligence, and with mental powers far above the average, Rose made rapid progress in every branch of human learning, but her supreme delight was in her religious studies. Father Baudouin, the founder of the Ursulines, frequently came to visit their house at Noirmoutier. One day, when he was examining the pupils, he promised to give a prize to the scholar who should, when next he came, repeat most correctly the history of the Sacred Passion, as found in the Holy Gospels. Rose recited separately without a single mistake the account given by each of the four Evangelists. She received as her reward a prettily-bound copy of the well-known *Visits to the Blessed Sacrament*, by St. Alphonsus Liguori. She greatly valued the little volume, and kept it for many years. At last she parted with it, in order to gratify the wishes of a lay-sister, who had taken a fancy to it, and ventured to petition that it might be bestowed upon her.

Rose spent four years at Noirmoutier after her father's death. In 1810, her eldest sister, Anne Josephine, who, as we have said, had been under the care of an aunt, married M. François Marsaud, a wealthy landowner, residing at Bouin, the place where his bride had of late years found her home. This event caused great joy to the whole family, and Rose took her full part in the rejoicings. Yet an event in which, a few months later, she filled an important position, gave her a deeper and more lasting delight. A poor woman who lived at Noirmoutier, and had often received substantial assistance from Mdme. Pelletier, on account of her necessitous condition, now had the misfortune of adding twins to her already large family. Under these circumstances she was at a loss where to find sponsors for her new-born babies. Rose Pelletier and Sophie Duchemin, whose friendship had not cooled with the passing years, at once came forward and offered themselves as godmothers to the two little boys. They were fully alive to the responsibility they were taking upon themselves, and Rose never lost sight of her god-son. Long years afterwards, when Superioress of the Good Shepherd Convent at Angers, she sent for her *protégé*, and found an excellent situation for him. But her efforts to further his temporal welfare proved fruitless. The young man had been a sailor from his early youth, and erelong began to pine for the sea-breezes and the dancing waves he loved so well. He took a grateful leave of his kind patroness, and returned to Noirmoutier, there to resume the old life, which had become as a second nature to him.

Mdme. Pelletier had always regarded Noirmoutier as more or less a land of exile. After the loss of her husband this feeling grew upon her to such an extent that she at last resolved to return to Soullans, her native place, where she had many relatives and friends. She had never revisited it since her compulsory departure in 1791. Her decision was no doubt influenced by her wish to promote the welfare of Rose, whose naturally buoyant spirits were beginning to give way beneath the pressure of the gloomy atmosphere which had prevailed in her home ever since her father's death. She no longer cared to take the country rambles, which had contributed so much to her health of both body and mind. She alleged, as a pretext for remaining indoors, her desire to spend as much time as she could beside her bereaved mother. Her real motive was that she could not bear to see how her beloved father had, to a great extent, ceased to be remembered by those amongst whom he had lived and worked. Precocious as she had always been where matters of feeling were concerned, she experienced, though she could not formulate it, the sentiment which a great poet, but most miserable man, has so well expressed when he said:

> How can ye sing, ye bonnie birds,
> And I so weary, full of care.

And yet, with the strange inconsistency which is inseparable from human nature, Rose could not leave Noirmoutier without many a keen regret. Tears dimmed her bright eyes when she looked for the last time at the house in which she had been born, a simple white building with a high roof, only a few steps distant from the church where she had delighted to worship. Every nook and corner of the island was dear to her, the woods and fields where she had played with her companions, the sea-shore, the grotto of St. Philibert, his crypt which she had helped to restore. She never forgot her native place, and when Providence placed her at the head of the Order of the Good Shepherd, she desired to show her gratitude by founding a convent there. This happened as late as 1860. She entered into negotiations which had for their object the purchase of an ancient monastery, that had formerly belonged to the monks of St. Bernard. More than this, she journeyed herself to Noirmoutier, with two of her assistants, in the hope of thus furthering the end she had in view. But certain petty local interests stood in the way. It was not possible to overcome them, and the charitable project was never realized.

Towards the close of 1810, Mdme. Pelletier found herself once more settled at Soullans. The education of her two youngest children was far from complete. She placed Paul at the Little Seminary of La Garnache, which was under the superintendence of the parish priest. She might have sent Rose again to the Ursulines, who had a school in the vicinity; but she felt that a thorough change of air, scene, and surroundings, would be advantageous to the young girl, now more than fourteen years of age. She consulted several of her old friends, who confirmed her in this idea. Travelling was in those days a very different thing from what it is now. The distance is great from Soullans to Tours, and it cost the affectionate mother no small sacrifice to separate herself, perhaps for years, from her beloved Rose. However, it had been her habit never to think of herself, when the welfare of her children was concerned, and in the course of a few months after her return from Soullans, she undertook to take her to the school at Tours, where she had resolved to place her. The journey occupied three days and three nights. When the travellers at last reached their destination, and the time came to say good-bye, the reader will understand how bitter the parting proved. Yet it would have been a thousand times more bitter, could the mother and daughter have foreseen that from that day they were to meet no more, until they should be united in their true country, never to part again.

Before we proceed further with our history, we must give a brief account of the school in which Rose now found herself placed as a boarder. It was an establish-

ment remarkable in itself, and remarkable also because
of the influence there exercised upon the future life of
the new pupil.   Among the old friends who gathered
around Mdme. Pelletier, and welcomed her on her
return to Soullans, were several members of the
wealthy and noble family of the Chobelets du Bois-
Boucher.   They had been her playmates in her
childish days, three sisters being her more especial
friends.   Of these one had been married for many
years, while the remaining two had devoted themselves,
and their not inconsiderable fortunes, to the cause of
Christian education.   In the midst of the horrors of
the Reign of Terror, they had dared to open in Poitiers
a school where the name of Jesus Christ was openly
taught, honoured, and adored.   As a matter of course,
they were thrown into prison, and narrowly escaped
with their lives.   As soon as they had recovered their
freedom, one of them, Mlle. Pulchérie, directed her
steps to Tours.   She there purchased a convent,
formerly belonging to the Ursulines, and induced
several of her friends, who, like herself, were anxious
to devote their talents to the training of the young, to
join her in forming a religious community, to which she
gave the name of *l'Association chrétienne.*   She at once
opened a boarding-school, which proved so successful,
that in 1810 it numbered ninety pupils, belonging to
the best French families.   We cannot be surprised that
Mdme. Pelletier should determine to confide her child
to Mdme. Chobelet, who was, besides, so anxious to
take her under her wing, and who promised to watch
over her with the tenderest care.

Yet, though to an onlooker all things seemed so
fair and smiling, the homely proverb which tells us
that, "Great beginnings make small endings," was

never destined to be more fully exemplified that in the case of *l'Association chrétienne.* Mdme. Chobelet was pious, highly educated, and gifted with a talent for teaching, but she was destitute of the qualities necessary for the foundress of a religious house. Instead of following to the letter the admirable Rule which had been drawn up for her, she yielded to a real, though misguided desire after perfection, and incessantly introduced one novelty after another. For instance, when the life of a Saint was being read in the refectory, greatly struck by the record of some heroic act, she would desire her subjects to imitate it. Hence came to be practised fasts of extraordinary length and severity, together with various kinds of strange and new-fangled devotions, into the nature of which it is beside our present purpose to enter at length. It requires no special gift of foresight to perceive that these fanciful changes and additions must in the long run destroy the Rule altogether, just as parasitical plants, each one small perhaps in itself, unite their feeble stems and crush the life out of a noble tree. Erelong the Community split into two factions. This had a very bad effect upon the school, for it was impossible that some of the germs of discord, with which the air was full, should not now and then be wafted, by an unlucky breeze, into the midst of the pupils. In a short time matters came to such a pass, that ecclesiastical interference became necessary. Mgr. de Barral, Archbishop of Tours, forbade the taking of vows by any member of the Community, although these vows had never been binding for more than a year. Several of the best of Mdme. Chobelet's subjects profited by this opportunity and quitted her roof, which can hardly be termed a religious house, though she desired it to be regarded as such. Yet it was pervaded neither by a spirit of ready, cheerful, and implicit obedience, nor by a close and literal adherence to the Rule, and bore within itself the germs of decay and dissolution. The head teacher of the school, Mdme. Loisel, was among those who left, and her loss was irreparable. She was the life and soul of the establishment, which must inevitably, in this crisis, have been shipwrecked, had it not been for the rare gifts of the second mistress, Mlle. de Lignac, in whose hands the direction of the school was placed, though she was scarcely twenty years of age. She showed herself equal to the emergency, and sustained the prestige of the house, which to the eye of a superficial observer appeared at this time to be in the zenith of its prosperity. We must add that Mlle. de Lignac would gladly have left, but remained out of gratitude to Mdme. Chobelet, who had brought her up, and to whom she knew herself to be indispensable.

Such was the state of things when Rose Pelletier began her life at Tours. She could not understand the reasons which had induced her mother to send her so far away, and missed her grievously. Her character moreover, was one liable to be misunderstood at first sight, and this increased the home-sickness from which every school-girl on her first exile from the parental roof must suffer more or less severely. Besides this, her new confessor treated her with great harshness. He magnified her every-day faults into serious sins, and his ill-advised exaggerations confused and distressed her delicate conscience, so that she might have given way to permanent discouragement and depression, had not God sent a friend to console and help her. This friend was none other than Mlle. de Lignac, of whom we have so lately spoken. She had taken a great fancy to the new-comer, and perceiving her to be so much out of spirits, she sent for her into her room. Kind and gentle words soon opened the heart of Rose. Her friend sympathized in her troubles, helped her to make her examination of conscience, and cleared up her doubts and perplexities. Speaking of this wise guide in after-years, Mother St. Euphrasia says, in an address to novices: "She had suffered many trials and hardships on her own entrance upon school-life, and this stern apprenticeship had taught her how to combat and conquer the melancholy, sometimes despair, that children and young people often feel, when placed among complete strangers. Nothing escaped her keen glance, which read the souls of her pupils as one reads an ordinary book. Never did she fail to discern the special cause of the sadness she discovered."

A strong mutual affection quickly sprang up between teacher and pupil, which deepened as time went on. Their characters, radically different in many points, had yet a great similarity in others. Moreover, the parents of both had suffered for the faith. Mlle. de Lignac's father had perished on the scaffold; her mother had been imprisoned for a period of eighteen months. All that their children, like those of M. and Mdme. Pelletier, had seen and heard in their early years, had inspired them with an instinctive aversion to sin and irreligion, and a rooted conviction that no sacrifice is too great to be made with joy for the sake of God and His holy Church. Rose had the privilege of passing a considerable portion of her school-life in the class taught by Mlle. de Lignac. Nor was the teaching and example of her saintly instructress lost upon her. Her progress in every branch of secular learning was surprisingly rapid. Her bright, clear, quick intelligence, aided and supplemented by an accurate memory, enabled her to master with unusual success the various branches of study presented to her active mind, which literally thirsted for knowledge. Now, as during her childish days, her chief delight was in the study of religion, and the instructions given by Mlle. de Lignac were to her a source of real profit, as well as of much pleasure. This talented lady had the art of making her subject attractive in form and practical in effect. At the close of an explanation of some passage from the Gospels, she would bid her pupils choose the text which had most impressed each of them. " Now, my dear children," she would say, " tell me which of all these sayings appears most likely to promote your eternal salvation ? " Then came a series of questions intended to discover whether the lesson just given had been thoroughly understood. The most difficult of these questions was always addressed to Rose, whom Mlle. de Lignac playfully termed, " My dear little Doctor of Divinity." But the admiration aroused by the piety and interest in spiritual things which she displayed, was not confined within the walls of her school. The clergy and canons of the Cathedral, who frequently came to the house of *l'Association chrétienne* were much struck by her gifts, both of heart and head, and several of them prophesied that such fragrant flowers would in the future produce rich and abundant fruits.

Never had Rose for one moment relaxed her efforts to overcome her natural faults of character, and she had been triumphantly successful. She had learnt to tame her once undisciplined tongue, and to curb the mischievous propensities she had formerly been so ingenious in exercising to the annoyance of those around her. She had gained the esteem of her teachers, the affection of her fellow-pupils. On the feast of her patron, St. Rose of Lima, she always received a number of little presents. On one of these occasions a companion, who had a talent for painting, offered her a rose, copied from nature, and skilfully depicted in water-colours. Beneath was the following inscription : *We have found a rose without thorns.*

This proves how greatly she had profited by the teaching and influence of Mlle. de Lignac, who, if she erred at all, erred on the side of too great severity. So at least it appears to us in the present day, a day of laxity and over-indulgence, when, as the Holy Father recently remarked, "labour is regarded with abhorrence, and suffering of whatever kind a thing to be at any cost avoided."

As time went on, the relations between Mlle. de Lignac and her favourite became those rather of attached friends than of mistress and scholar. Both had one common rule of conduct, implicit obedience to the commands of God and of His ministers. Both viewed with distrust the virtues of those who revolted against authority, or who departed from the *via ordinaria*, in order to wander in strange paths of their own finding. Instead of describing vice in order to give her youthful charges a horror of it, Mlle. de Lignac strove to inspire their souls with a love of virtue, by depicting its beauty and charm, as exemplified in the life of our Lord, and of His saints and faithful followers in all ages. This was, at a later date, a prominent feature in the method adopted by Mother St. Euphrasia. Devoted as she was to the conversion of sinners, she made it her invariable practice to lead them to abandon vice by representing the loveliness of virtue. "Show them what virtue really is," she would say, "and vice will become odious in their sight. It is most undesirable that we should enlarge upon all its hideousness and horror."

It was not possible for Mlle. de Lignac to be so intimately associated with Rose without clearly perceiving the germs of her future vocation. Among those signs was her constant concern with regard to the spiritual state of her companions. Of this we will quote one instance, leaving Mlle. de Lignac to relate it in her own words: "During one of the years which she spent under the roof of Mdme. Chobelet (I cannot distinctly remember the exact date), Rose was much grieved to see the carelessness displayed by her schoolfellows respecting the solemn feast of Pentecost, then close at hand. She came to me, and begged me to give her permission to speak, during recreation-time, to those who appeared most indifferent, adding that she had confided her secret to two of her especial friends, and they were ready to help her. I felt that the idea must be an inspiration of the Holy Ghost, and I at once granted the request. Carefully concealing the admiration I felt, I seconded their efforts in every way I could. The result exceeded my warmest expectations. A marked change gradually came over the school, and on the morning of the Festival the whole of the pupils who were of suitable age approached the Holy Table in the best dispositions. Nor was this a mere transient effervescence of feeling; the amendment proved permanent, and the good resolutions then formed were subsequently acted out. From that moment I understood that Mlle. Pelletier would, later in her life, accomplish great things for God."

In October, 1812, death carried off Constant
Pelletier, one of Rose's brothers. He died at Soullans,
aged twenty-four years. The grief of his affectionate
sister was doubled by her distance from the beloved
mother, with whose tears she would fain have mingled
her own. The sympathy of her chosen friend, Mlle.
de Lignac, was of no small help and comfort to her.
How little did she know what far greater demands she
should make upon that faithful sympathy, in the course
of a few short months.

Mdme. Pelletier's cup of sorrow was now filled to
the brim. Her life, since she had left Soullans nearly a
quarter of a century ago, had been one long succession
of trials. Unwavering as she had ever shown herself
in submission to the will of God, and in readiness to
partake of the Saviour's chalice, her physical strength
was now utterly worn out. Nothing exhausts the
human frame like painful and protracted emotions, and
those for whom life has lost all its zest, cannot very
long continue to live. Mdme. Pelletier does not appear
to have suffered from any definite disease; her hold
upon existence gradually slackened, she grew weaker
and weaker, the doctors who were called in declared
they could do nothing for her. At length, on the 11th
of June, 1813, she died a peaceful and holy death, not
having as yet completed her fifty-second year. By her
express desire her mortal remains were taken to Noirmoutier, and interred beside those of her beloved
husband.

For Rose the blow was a crushing one. We have
already seen how deep and tender was the love she
bore her afflicted mother, and the tidings of her death
affected her all the more intensely because she had not
been able to be with her in her last hours, nor to attend

D

the Requiem. Her natural tendency to extremes now rendered her grief so violent and overwhelming, that fears were entertained for her life. Her brother-in-law, M. Marsaud, was appointed her guardian, and her sister, who was her senior by twelve years, might have become to her almost a second mother, had not her home been so far away. In her loneliness and desolation, Rose found comfort and help in the never-failing sympathy of her friend, Mlle. de Lignac, who was all the more able to share her sorrow, because she had, only a few months previously, lost her own mother. But Rose was early to learn the full meaning of the words, *Dieu seul.* At the moment when she most needed her beloved friend, this friend was to be taken from her, and she was to learn truly to understand and enter into the beautiful words of à Kempis, who, when speaking of the want of human consolation, thus expresses himself: " Do thou learn to part with an intimate and beloved friend for the will of God. And take it not to heart when thou art forsaken by a friend, knowing that at last we must all be separated one from another."[1] We are not referring in this quotation only to the period when Rose lost her mother. Much as she then needed help, she needed advice and counsel yet more when the time came for her to quit *l'Association chrétienne*, in pursuance of her vocation, the idea of which took a more definite and decided shape after the death of her mother, which, as she used herself to say, detached her from the world more than anything else.

Mlle. de Lignac had from the first foreseen that the house founded by Mdme. Chobelet could have no permanent existence. She herself left it in April, 1814, under circumstances which we shall relate in the

[1] *Imitation,* bk. ii. c. 9.

succeeding chapter, in connection with the history of the vocation of Rose.

Perhaps we cannot better close the present one than by giving a description of Rose's personal appearance at the age of eighteen. She was of middle height, and seemed taller than she really was, because her figure was so slight. Her features were not regular enough for beauty, but her face was very pleasing, lighted up as it was by two bright dark eyes, which expressed both intelligence and kindliness. Her manner and bearing had also an attraction of their own, being gracious, yet dignified, simple and frank, courteous and never haughty. No sooner did she open her lips, than her clear, well-modulated voice prepossessed her hearers in her favour. The favourable impression thus created was increased by her fluency and happy choice of words. In spite of the impetuosity of her character, she never allowed herself to fall into the habit of talking fast.

CHAPTER III.

VOCATION.

IT is impossible not to sympathize with the painfully isolated and solitary position of the young girl whose career we are engaged in tracing. It is rarely that any one, at the early age of eighteen, finds herself so utterly alone as did Rose Pelletier. Her beloved friend and guide, whose help and influence had been of so much use to her, had, as we have said, entered the Ursuline Convent. She did not forget her favourite pupil, but wrote to tell her of a vacant cell next her own, which was, so to speak, waiting for her. It would have seemed only natural if the affectionate heart of Rose had been powerfully attracted in this direction. The prospect of beginning her religious life in company with one whom she respected as well as loved, was certainly a pleasing one. Yet she never turned a single glance towards the Ursuline House. In her vocation everything was supernatural, the choice of the community she entered, and the grace and strength, the firmness and courage, which enabled her to weather the storms which were to assail her before she reached the port where God designed that she should at length cast anchor. It almost seems as if the words of the Wise Man had been expressly written for her, so applicable are they to her case: "When thou comest to the service of God, stand in justice and in fear, and prepare thy soul for temptation.[1]

Shortly after the departure of Mlle. de Lignac, one of the head pupils, a very superior and accomplished girl of seventeen, Mary Angelica Dernée by name, having completed her education, left *l'Association chrétienne*, in order to enter the Carmelite Convent at Tours. This was another bitter grief for Rose. Little could she foresee that the bonds of friendship, thus rudely snapped asunder, were in future years to be once more knit together, for the mutual benefit of those concerned, and the furtherance of the saintly desires which animated their souls and inspired their actions. The Carmelite Order had always been the object of a very special admiration on her part, yet she never entertained the thought of entering it. She appreciated the beauty of a life devoted to prayer and penance, with a view to the conversion of sinners, and later on, she wrote to the Prioress of the Carmelites at Tours, entreating her prayers and those of the other nuns, in order that she might succeed in her vocation. In this letter she said that, whilst engaged in mental prayer, she had been inspired by God to write it. The Prioress, on her part, was so delighted with the epistle, that she preserved it for many years, so admirable was the fervour which breathed in its every line, and so decided the desire it expressed to engage in active labours for the salvation of souls. Meanwhile the sky grew darker and darker over her head, and the atmosphere in which she lived more and more uncongenial. Her education was finished, she had no home to go to, and the school degenerated day by day. Its character had become altogether changed, a spirit of insubordination began

[1] Eccles. ii. 1.

to prevail, and the mischief produced by an objection-
able book which one of the elder pupils brought back
with her on her return after the holidays, and lent to
every one who would read it, was widespread in its
effects.   Under these circumstances Rose wrote to her
brother-in-law, M. Marsaud, who had, as we have seen,
been appointed her guardian, and earnestly requested
his permission to try her vocation.   Backed up by her
brothers, he peremptorily forbade her to entertain the
idea of entering upon the religious life, and expressed
annoyance at her desire to do so.   He added that if
she were so obstinate as to persist in going into a
convent, the Sacred Heart was the only Order to which
her family could tolerate the idea of her belonging.
When she told her teachers and companions of her
grievous disappointment, they only laughed at her, and
made it the subject of a petty persecution, in which
they were all the more delighted to indulge, because
her conduct was a constant, though silent reproach to
their own.   Indeed there were not a few who went so
far as actually to hate her, solely on account of her
virtue and piety, though she was scrupulously careful
never to give them any cause for offence.   She next
turned to Mdme. Chobelet, but here again nothing but
discouragement and opposition met her.   Mdme. de
Chobelet made every possible effort to keep Rose,
knowing her value.   She offered her the post of head-
mistress, left vacant by the withdrawal of Mlle. de
Lignac, and bitterly upbraided her for wishing to quit
the roof of her mother's old friend, especially as that
beloved parent had entrusted her to her care.   Poor
lady! let us not judge her severely, but rather remember
the bitter disappointment with which she must have
seen the house she had founded falling to pieces about

her ears. It was now passing through a fresh crisis, and the Archbishop had again to interpose his authority. To enter into details regarding the history of *l'Association chrétienne*, in these sad days of its decline, would be beside our present purpose. We only concern ourselves with it, in so far as it influenced the character and career of Rose Pelletier.

All this opposition only strengthened her determination, and heightened her dauntless courage, as is always the case in characters cast in a like mould. She wrote again to M. Marsaud, who persisted in his obstinate and arbitrary refusal. This appears all the more tyrannical and unreasonable, because Rose had no family claims, but was absolutely free to arrange her own plan of life. However, the utmost her guardian would concede, was that if she remain quietly where she was for three years longer, he would, when she had attained the age of twenty-one, "think over the matter."

This made Rose's determination irrevocable. Remain for three long years where she was, she could not, and she resolved to turn her steps at once towards the place whither God was calling her. But what and where was this place, the reader will ask? We will now proceed to tell how Rose was first introduced to it. Not far from her school there rose the walls of an ancient-looking convent, which was pointed out to the pupils in the course of their daily walks, and they were told that it was a Refuge for young girls who had been disobedient to their parents. This was enough for childish ears, but as Mlle. de Lignac's pupils gradually developed into womanhood, and ceased to be children, she allowed them to understand what this Refuge, conducted by the Sisters of Our Lady of

Charity, really was, and how great was the misfortune of those who had strayed from the path of virtue, and sinned against the angelic loveliness of purity. Sometimes the door was by chance left ajar, so as to afford glimpses of the interior. Sometimes again, on Feast-days, the older pupils were taken to Benediction in the chapel, and occasionally they were allowed to wait on the inmates at table, and bestow upon them any little delicacies they had been willing to set aside from their own dessert. All this was enough and more than enough to fire the lively imagination and generous spirit of Rose Pelletier. Erelong she felt and understood how sublime a vocation it is to devote oneself to the salvation of sinners, and as time went by, the call of God made itself more and more distinctly heard within her soul, until at last, as we have seen, she finally determined, in the teeth of the most obstinate and persistent opposition, that she would join the Community of the Sisters who conducted the Refuge, and devote her life to the service of the forsaken girls who had found shelter within its walls.

But how was she to see the interior of the house, and make herself acquainted with the nuns? For some months she prayed earnestly that a way might be opened to her, but her petitions remained apparently unheard. At last a happy thought occurred to her. One evening towards the close of October, when the days had already grown short, she threw a veil over her head, and, accompanied by one of the teachers who had evinced much sympathy for her loneliness, and who faithfully promised to keep her secret, she slipped surreptitiously out of doors, and succeeded in reaching the Refuge unobserved. The Superior, Mother Mary

of St. Joseph, received the truants with the utmost
kindness. She closely questioned the applicant as to
her age, family relations, the origin of her vocation, her
tastes and aptitudes. The keen and practised eye of
the Superior enabled her to discern the value of the
treasure which was offered her; she promised to receive
Rose into the number of her daughters, as soon as the
obstacles which kept her in the world could be overcome. The night was intensely cold, but Rose tripped
home with a glow at her heart which made her indifferent to the chill of the atmosphere. Alas! a glacial
reception awaited her. When the supper-bell rang,
and the pupils were gathered together, her absence was
at once apparent. It was easy to guess whither she
had gone, so constantly had she talked about the
Refuge. Her companion managed to elude notice, so
that the whole fury of the storm burst over Rose's
unprotected head. She was obliged to confess where
she had been, and Mdme. Chobelet loaded her with
bitter reproaches. "Bread and water for this young
lady," she exclaimed, in her wrath, "dry bread and
cold water!" Overcome with distress, Rose burst into
a flood of tears, and sobbed bitterly. This turned the
tide of general feeling in her favour, and secured the
victory for her. Her fellow-pupils, who had hitherto
been so unkind, and so unjust towards her, now took her
part. They revolted openly and cried out to Mdme.
Chobelet, who was sitting at the head of the table,
"What are you thinking about! How can you sentence
this poor little thing, who has never done any harm,
to have nothing but dry bread for supper? She
is a martyr, suffering persecution on account of her
vocation! If she wishes to be a nun, why cannot
you let her go to the convent?" Then they gathered

round the culprit, led her to the fire, and fed her with the best of everything that was on the table, loading her, meanwhile, with affectionate caresses. Mdme. Chobelet could only look on, powerless to control her angry pupils. The reins were fast slipping from her limp and nerveless hands, and scenes like the above became more and more frequent, much to the distress of Rose, who had no sympathy with this spirit of insubordination, even when manifested on her behalf.

Mdme. Chobelet now wrote again to M. Marsaud, in order to strengthen him in his opposition. Finding that she succeeded, she addressed herself with the same object to his wife, who was, as the reader will remember, the elder sister of Rose. On the other hand, all the Sisters belonging to the Refuge took a deep interest in Rose, and prayed constantly for her vocation. One of their number wrote her a letter in which she said that while she was engaged in mental prayer, the Blessed Virgin had made known to her that Rose must join the Sisters of Our Lady of Charity, unless she desired to run counter to the will of God, and thus imperil her salvation. This letter made a deep impression on the mind of Rose. From her earliest childhood she had cherished a filial devotion to that most amiable Mother, whose name she had learnt to lisp when seated on her nurse's knee. This love of Mary is universal in the land where she was brought up, and explains why she subsequently bestowed that dear and beautiful name upon all her daughters in Religion.

She felt that there was no time to be lost. The hour for parleying and temporizing had gone by. Conscious how much more can be effected by personal

influence than by the most lengthy correspondence
she resolved to try what she could do towards overcoming the prejudices of her family, since they had
really no valid reasons to allege. Circumstances, moreover, smiled upon her project. On the 30th of May,
the birth of a third daughter rejoiced the heart of
M. Marsaud, and softened it in regard to Rose, who by
his wife's especial desire stood godmother by proxy to
the new-born baby, her youngest brother Paul being
the godfather. Later on in the same year, probably in
the holidays, Rose went to stay at Bouin, in the house
of the kind aunt who had, as we have seen, brought up
her elder sister Anne, and from whose house the latter
had married. She afterwards proceeded to Nantes,
where the Marsauds were at that time residing. She
pleaded her cause with so much force, eloquence, and
tact, that, after passing through several painful scenes,
she at length obtained the long-desired consent. Taking
a final leave of her relatives and friends, she returned
to Tours, free to carry out the desire of her heart, and
greatly was she surprised at the reception which
awaited her. The world always smiles upon success,
and now that she came back triumphant, both teachers
and pupils received her with a show of affection, and
vied with one another in congratulating her, and
expressing every hope that her vocation might prosper.
Veering round with the rapidity of a weathercock,
Mdme. Chobelet, who had been, to speak mildly,
very unkind to Rose, and had left no stone unturned in
order to keep her under her own roof, now addressed
her as follows : " My dear child, I am afraid my line of
action had sometimes appeared to you rather incom-
prehensible. Believe me, my sole motive for doing
what I have done, has been a desire to promote your

real good. If I have been severe, it is because you are one of those strong characters which can bear reproof. Go now with confidence where the voice of God is calling you." We cannot but express our admiration of the perfect charity which Rose always showed when speaking of her former teachers. She never uttered the least complaint in regard to Mdme. Chobelet, at whose hands she had suffered so severely; she even avoided the mention of her name, when the difficulties which had overtaken *l'Association chrétienne* were made the subject of conversation in her presence. Yet her silence had an eloquence of its own. She would have been only too glad to speak, had there been anything praiseworthy to relate. We must here mention that there is a measure of doubt concerning the perfect accuracy of the chronological order in which the events we have just related occurred, since the principal details are drawn from an address which Mother St. Euphrasia delivered to some novices, in the course of 1866. The subject had always been a highly distasteful one to her, and she had never before yielded to the requests of her daughters, when they asked her to tell them about the latter part of her school-life. This at least is certain, that she made a stay of some length at Bouin, for she, towards the close of her life, asked one of her great-nieces to have a Mass said, in order to obtain pardon for the faults she had committed whilst staying there.

At last, free to go where her heart had long dwelt, she finally entered the Refuge on October 20, 1814. This day was specially kept there as a feast of the Sacred Heart. Hence she was regarded as a postulant dedicated to the Sacred Heart of Jesus. But before entering upon the story of her religious life, we must give some details with regard to the Refuge conducted by the Sisters of Our Lady of Charity.[1]

The Founder of the Order of Our Lady of Charity was the Venerable Servant of God, Father John Eudes, one of the most distinguished ecclesiastics in France during the seventeenth century. He was a native of Normandy, and was born in 1601, being, like the Prophet Samuel, the fruit of the earnest prayers of his mother. After a boyhood of singular virtue, he chose the ecclesiastical career, and received minor orders on September 19, 1620. Seminaries for the special education of priests did not then exist in France. He therefore studied first in the University at Caen, but finding his surroundings uncongenial, he sought and gained admission into the French Oratory. The house of this Congregation at Caen, though small in numbers, was fervent in spirit, and the Fathers were constantly employed in every kind of charitable work. Eudes was ordained in 1625, and afterwards sent to a quiet country house near Paris, where he spent his time in the study of Holy Scripture, and in mental prayer. He used to declare that at the foot of the crucifix God had given him all the light he possessed.

This peaceful life was erelong interrupted by an outbreak of plague in the diocese of Seéz. Terrible were the ravages of the disease, and Father Eudes determined to devote himself to the service of the sick and dying. During the time that the pestilence raged in Caen, he slept in a large cask which he had caused to be placed in a field near the Convent of the Holy

[1] *L'Association chrétienne* dragged on its existence for a few years. At last Mdme. Chobelet, finding herself compelled to give it up, sold the house, which was turned into a boys' school. She herself found an asylum for her old age in the house of the Ursulines, where she died about 1857, in the arms of her former pupil, Mlle. (then Mother) de Lignac.

Trinity. This he did in order to avoid carrying the infection to his brethren. The Abbess supplied him with food, and he spent his whole time in assisting the dying. After this novitiate of charity he began to preach missions, his apostolic ministry being blessed by God with an abundant harvest of souls. The origin of the Order of Our Lady of Charity was a mission preached in the city of Caen, in 1639, and during the Lent of the following year. A number of women who had been leading sinful lives were converted during these missions, and the question arose how their perseverance in virtue could be best assured. Father Eudes exerted himself to secure temporary homes for them in the houses of several charitable ladies, and some he entrusted to the care of an old woman named Magdalen Lamy, who, although poor, was full of zeal for souls. She it was who suggested the work that afterwards developed into that of the Good Shepherd. Standing one day at her door, she cried out to Father Eudes, who was passing at that moment with some of his friends, " Where are you going to now? Into the churches perhaps, to look at the images of the saints, for doing which you will consider yourselves very pious. You ought rather to work hard to found a house of refuge for poor girls, many of whom are lost for want of help." These outspoken words excited some laughter at the time, but they made a deep impression on Father Eudes. He never forgot them, and they increased his desire to found some permanent institution for the safe keeping of these lost sheep of Christ's fold. After some delay, he was enabled by the help of friends to hire a small house, opposite to the chapel of St. Gratian, which was the cradle of the future Institute. The first penitents were received on March 25, 1641 ;

and during the two hundred and fifty years which have elapsed since that time, the work has been steadily carried on in spite of every discouragement, and is continually extending itself in all directions. Father Eudes made a house-to-house collection throughout the town for the support of the work. Amongst other gifts, he received from the Carmelite Nuns an image of our Lady, which still stands over the seat of the Superior in the choir of the Religious of Our Lady of Charity at Caen.

As at first there was no idea of founding an Order, the house was called a "Refuge." At the outset success seemed certain, but before long opposition was aroused. The devil was destined to lose too much by the work thus started to allow it to proceed quietly. People began to criticize the new undertaking, and to declare that though begun with the best intentions, it was imprudent, and would surely prove a failure, since women who had been leading a life of sin, would never persevere, but would return to their evil courses. Father Eudes found the municipal authorities prejudiced against him, and was obliged, through Cardinal Richelieu, to obtain the royal authorization for his work.

Besides opposition from without, there was what is worse, division within the house. A lady named Margaret Morin had undertaken the superintendence and management of it, but becoming discontented, and not approving certain arrangements made by Father Eudes, she suddenly abandoned the Refuge, taking with her several others. Only a young niece of Father Eudes and one other lady, Mlle. de Taillefer, remained. It was then proposed that the Order of the Visitation, founded by St. Francis of Sales, should assume the direction of the house. After considerable difficulty, the Bishop was induced to give his consent to this plan, and the Superior of the Convent of the Visitation at Caen left her own Community to take charge of the Refuge. Father Eudes gave the inmates of his new convent the Rule of St. Augustine, to which he afterwards added Constitutions necessary to guide them in the peculiar work they had undertaken. He also desired to substitute for the simple name of the Refuge, the title of Our Lady of Charity, a change afterwards approved by authority and adopted by all the houses. To the three ordinary vows of poverty, chastity, and obedience, he added a fourth, whereby the Religious bound themselves to labour for the conversion of women who desired to reform their lives and who sought a refuge from the temptations of the world in their convent.

Until then, as has been said, no Religious Order had been established with the peculiar object which Father Eudes had in view, and it was necessary to proceed with the greatest caution. The Bishop of Bayeux, Mgr. Molè, who, on account of certain misunderstandings with Father Eudes on other matters, did not regard the Refuge with a very favourable eye, was at last, in 1651, induced to give a formal approbation, a result which was attributed to the fervent prayers that had been for years perseveringly offered for this end. Until some Sister of the new Institute was considered ready to undertake the office of Superior, the house was to continue under the government of the Religious of the Visitation. The training of the Sisters, both in their conventual duties and their work for souls, was confided to Mère Patin, the nun who had come from the Visitation Convent.

The effect of the episcopal approbation was to encourage several persons who felt called to the work, to join as postulants. The first Religious clothed with the habit was Mlle. de Taillefer, who had already given unmistakable proof of her constancy and other virtues. The nuns had to welcome the Cross, and among other trials they were so poor that sufficient food was often wanting to them. The house they rented was besides badly built, and quite unsuited for their needs.

Not until after twenty years of trial was the approbation of the Holy See granted to the new Order, with permission for the Religious to take perpetual vows. This was at last accomplished on January 2, 1666, by a Bull of Alexander VIII., to the great joy of Father Eudes, whose zeal and perseverance was thus happily crowned. Father Eudes is known as the first active propagator of the devotion to the Sacred Hearts of Jesus and Mary. To them he dedicated the Order of Our Lady of Charity of the Refuge, as well as a Congregation of missionary priests which he also founded.

At the epoch when the storm of the Revolution burst over France, the Order had seven houses. They shared the fate of the other Religious Institutions in the country, although the object for which they were founded might, it would seem, have appealed in their favour even in those terrible days of destruction. The Community at Caen was saved from dispersion by an act of courage on the part of one of the Sisters which deserves to be commemorated. The Mother Superior had been already arrested, together with several of her subjects, and thrown into prison. When all seemed desperate, an energetic young Sister hired a cart, placed

E

in it all the oldest and most infirm of the Religious, and drove with them to the Council-chamber where the revolutionary leaders were assembled. "I bring you," she boldly exclaimed, "all our infirm and aged Sisters. You have deprived me of all means of feeding them, as well as of the younger Sisters who helped to support them. Moreover, you have billeted soldiers on our house, and now that I am alone I can neither wait upon them nor earn bread for their support." "Very well," replied one of the Council, "we will send them to prison." "As you please about that," returned the Sister; "at any rate you must feed them there." Embarrassed by her ready answer, and pleased at her fearlessness, the Council answered: "Take home your poor old Sisters, citizen, and we will see to their maintenance." Accordingly the soldiers were removed, the nuns liberated from prison, and a sufficient sum was allowed for the support of the convent and its inmates.

When at last order was restored, the Refuge of Tours was amongst the first to be re-established. The Community consisted of a small number of nuns, aged more by sorrow than by years, and two or three young novices. One of these novices was Rose Virginie Pelletier, the commencement of whose religious life will form the subject of our next chapter.

CHAPTER IV.

NOVITIATE AND PROFESSION.

Rose Pelletier had long dwelt in spirit in the house she was now to inhabit in bodily shape. To her we may fitly apply the beautiful words of St. Augustine, when he says: *Ubi amat, ibi habitat.* The Sisters received her with warm affection. Her heart was filled with joy at seeing the desires of her soul accomplished at last. In order to test the reality of her vocation, and also in deference to the wish of her guardian, she was to continue a postulant for about a year, notwithstanding her zeal and the sense and judgment which, in spite of her youth, every one about her speedily discerned. During this period she continued to wear her secular dress, and spent her time chiefly in studying the Rules and Constitutions of the Order. The Superior of the house placed her under the charge of the Head Mistress of Penitents, in order that she might be initiated into the duties of her new calling. This nun, whose name was Mother St. Victor, thoroughly appreciated her pupil. She took her into her confidence, and taught her the art of governing souls. The idea of aiding in their salvation filled Rose with holy zeal. She was ready to make any sacrifice, even the greatest, and wished that such might fall to her share.

At last the period of probation drew to a close. When the time arrived for choosing the name which was to be hers in Religion, Rose, who had read with deep interest the Life and writings of St. Teresa, and had, moreover, as we have said, a special devotion to the Carmelite Order, desired to be called after her. When she made known her wish to the Superior, the latter exclaimed: " What is this I hear! How can you think of adopting the name of so illustrious a Saint? Do you fancy that you can ever be equal to her? Remember that you are as yet only an aspirant to the religious life. Go and look for some humbler Saint, one whose name is less known to the world at large." The future novice withdrew in confusion, and while turning over the pages of a large volume of the Lives of the Saints, lighted by chance upon the name of St. Euphrasia. Returning to the Superior's room, she humbly requested permission to be called after this comparatively unknown Saint. Permission was at once granted, and the matter was thus decided.

St. Euphrasia, whose family was connected with that of the Emperor Theodosius the younger, retired into a convent at a very early age. Her love of mental prayer, the severity of the mortifications she practised, and her preference for the lowest offices, acquired for her a reputation for sanctity. She possessed great power over the evil spirit, and had, in addition, the gift of miracles. Dying at the early age of thirty, she is specially honoured in the Greek Church. It is curious that Rose Pelletier should, without any definite reason, have selected her name, for Euphrasia means in the original, " One who speaks well," and assuredly the future novice was destined, not only to speak well

herself, but to make her Order well spoken of throughout the whole world.

The longed-for day dawned at last. On the feast of
our Blessed Lady's Nativity, September 8th, 1815, the
ceremony of clothing took place. It was performed by
M. Danicourt, the head of the Community. Rose
Pelletier, who will in future be known to us as Sister
Mary of St. Euphrasia, or, as we shall call her for the
sake of brevity, Sister St. Euphrasia, at length saw
herself clothed in the white habit, the sight of which
had stirred her youthful heart when she was still at
school under the roof of Mdme. Chobelet. The habit
and the symbolism attached to it originated with
Father Eudes. The dress, the girdle, the scapular,
and the mantle were all of white material, in order to
remind the wearers that they ought to strive continually
after a purity like to that of the angels, and endeavour
likewise to instil into the minds of the lost sheep
committed to their charge a love of the same virtue.
A small blue cross, worn over the heart, was to recall
to the thoughts of the nuns the Passion of our Lord,
endured for their sanctification and that of those given
into their keeping. It was also to teach them that in
the pursuance of their vocation they would meet with
many crosses, which they must accept in a spirit of
expiation. The blue colour was to speak to them of
Heaven, to which the Cross is the sure and only road.
Father Eudes added a silver heart to be suspended
round the neck. On this heart, executed in relief, was
a figure of the Blessed Virgin, bearing the Holy Child
in her arms. On one side of the figure was a stem of
lilies, on the other a spray of roses. In this way the
Sisters were to learn to keep Jesus and Mary constantly
in their hearts by means of the precious virtue of

chastity, of which the lily is the emblem, and by the fragrance of charity, symbolized by the roses. Nor were the thorns of these roses without a mystic meaning. They were to remind the novice that from thenceforward she was to attach herself to Him alone Whom she had chosen as her Divine Spouse.

The novitiate of Sister St. Euphrasia was long remembered at Tours. Docile, confiding, affectionate, and grateful, she soon won the heart of the Mistress of Novices, Sister Mary of St. Aloysius, who bestowed special care on a subject full of such rare promise. " Mary of St. Euphrasia will do great things one day," she said; " there is something quite unusual about her." What was most striking in her at first sight was her simplicity of manner, her absolute frankness, her charming ingeniousness and candour. Thoroughly and unaffectedly humble, she showed herself to be such in her simplest actions. She folded her hands in prayer, she accused herself of her faults and failings, in so lowly a fashion, that she was held up as an example to her fellow-novices. A great proof of her humility was her freedom from susceptibility, and from all tendency to take offence. She was never known to have any altercation with her companions, in regard to whom she always showed herself gentle, obliging, and kind. Ever ready to sympathize with any one in trouble of body or mind, her spirit of cheerfulness and content rendered anything like murmurs impossible in those around her. Her very movements were a lesson in themselves. So regular were her steps, so invariably downcast her eyes, that she seemed to be perpetually recollected in herself and penetrated with a continual sense of the presence of God. Absolutely detached from all which belongs to the earth, she never appropriated to her use even the smallest object without asking permission from the Superior. She was always satisfied with what-ever was given her, yet always ready to part with it. When the time of year came round for the Sisters to exchange amongst themselves, by drawing lots, various little possessions which they are not allowed to keep permanently lest they should become attached to them, no cloud was ever seen on the face of Sister St. Euphrasia. Her heart overflowed with charity towards her neighbour, and the hope of working for the conversion of penitents never left her. While antici-pating the time when she should be allowed to devote herself to this object, she did her best to further it by means of prayer and mortification, while labouring incessantly on the work of her own perfection.

Full well did she perceive that the true touchstone as regards the perfection of a soul, is the practice of obedience. Indeed, from the first moment of her entrance into Religion, she was conscious of a special attraction for this virtue. She observed with scrupulous exactness the Rules, Constitutions, and even the customs of the Order, doing this not from a spirit of fear, but of love, and from a sincere desire to please God. Equally ready to do what was difficult as what was easy, equally careful in great things as in small, she obeyed every command of her Superior, not only without a murmuring word, or even a discontented look, but in a spirit of gladness, for love of Him Who "humbled Himself, becoming obedient unto death, even to the death of the Cross."[1] Never did she hesitate to break off, at a moment's notice, any occupation in which she might be engaged, if ordered to do so. In a word, she saw, in the person of whoever might for the time be

[1] Philipp. ii, 8.

placed over her, the representative of our Lord, a Mother to whom filial respect was to be shown, a ruler at whose feet all self-will and private judgment were to be once and for ever laid down and renounced. But, since no one can be perfect here on earth, occasions must inevitably arise when even the best Superiors are found lacking in judgment, or exceeding their due claims. Such occasions are often the test of a vocation, the turning-point of a spiritual career. They expel from Novitiates in every Order all over the world subjects possessed of commonplace every-day piety and mere ordinary intelligence. Lacking what St. Teresa so well characterizes as *l'entendement*, they are not able to grasp the fundamental principles of the religious life, and so fail in it altogether. Out of such-like trials, Sister St. Euphrasia ever came forth triumphant, and she is said never to have failed in obedience, in spite of her strong will and impetuous character. The following anecdote bears upon this perfect obedience of hers, and may be fitly introduced here. One day when the Life of St. Dositheus was being read in the refectory, she was observed to be so deeply affected that she could not control her emotion. Tears ran down her cheeks, and saturated the bread she was eating. What more especially touched her, was the relation of a vision which one of the Fathers living in the same monastery had after the death of the Saint. This latter appeared to him surrounded with light, and enjoying a very high place in Heaven. His fellow-Religious was greatly astonished, and said within himself: " How is it that Brother Dositheus, who never practised any special austerities, but allowed himself to accept all the mitigations which the Rule permits, can have attained so great an elevation?" At once he heard a voice which

said: "It is through the perfection of the obedience
he practised when on earth, that this glory has been
granted to Dositheus. It is true that he did not perform
the exterior mortifications practised by many of his
brethren. But these dispensations were granted him
by his Superiors on account of his weak health, and he
accepted them with the greatest purity of intention,
and in a spirit of obedience and submission." The
companions of Sister St. Euphrasia perceived nothing
in this account likely to cause so unusual a display of
emotion, and they questioned her as to its cause. She
told them, in the presence of the Mistress of Novices,
that God had vouchsafed to her, during the reading of
the Saint's Life, so keen a perception of the beauty of
obedience, and so intense a desire to practise it in its
fullest perfection, that it had not been possible for her
to restrain her feelings. The Novice Mistress consulted the Superior in regard of the lights thus granted
to the Sister, and it was determined that she should be
permitted to pronounce her vow of obedience before
the appointed time. With what joy and gratitude this
permission was received, it is no difficult matter to
imagine.

Yet she was not without her trials. Of these the
severest by far, as she herself frequently related in her
later years, was the comparative inaction in which she
was left. Her ardent, active temperament thirsted
for some object whereon to spend its energies; she
could never be happy when not at work. Constant
occupation was with her a positive necessity, and she
suffered deeply for lack of it. Indeed, she not unfrequently passed sleepless nights in consequence, her
pillow in the morning being soaked through and
through with her tears. The only manual labour she

was allowed to perform, was that of dusting the thirteen stalls of the choir nuns. This she asked to do three times over, in order to create a vent for her super-abundant activity. One day an aged lay-sister, who numbered eighty years, greatly cheered her by saying: " Be of good courage, dear little Sister; the day will come when you will have more work upon your hands than you will know how to get through."

The wisdom of the Mistress of Novices, in acting as she did, must be apparent to all. Whilst feeling deeply for the sufferings of Sister St. Euphrasia, she felt that they were absolutely necessary to the forma-tion of her character as a Religious, both because they formed the most crucial test to which the reality of her vocation could be subjected, and also because it was indispensable that her tendency to over-activity should be curbed with a firm hand, and subjected to due restraint. In order to alleviate the lassitude which was beginning to affect her physical condition, intellectual activity was granted her. She was encouraged in the study of Holy Scripture, and made good use of the permission. The more she dwelt upon the sacred pages, the warmer grew her love for them, the greater her appreciation of their beauties. She committed many passages to memory, and made herself so thoroughly acquainted with the Old Testament stories, that she was able in after-life constantly to refer to and quote them in her instructions to her Religious. It is not too much to say, that so thorough a knowledge of the Bible has rarely been possessed by a woman. M. Alleron, her confessor, did not hesitate to say: " I must avow to my shame, that Sister St. Euphrasia knows Holy Scripture better than I do myself." She also gained much profit from perusing the Annals of the Carmelite

Order. Though she had been forbidden to take the name of St. Teresa, she was not prevented from drinking in her spirit. Her admiration for the illustrious Reformer of Carmel became enthusiastic, and for the life of prayer and penance, which has as its aim the conversion of sinners. While conscious that she desired to pursue the same end, she never for a moment faltered as to her vocation, nor ceased to feel that the path which God destined for her, was one of greater external activity, and more direct influence upon the souls to be saved.

Yet many hours still hung heavily upon her busy, restless hands, and she could not help lamenting this sometimes to the Mistress of Novices, while her bright eyes were dimmed with tears. It is very greatly to her credit, that in spite of her interior sorrows and trials she always preserved her cheerfulness of demeanour when in the presence of others, and especially during recreation. Some of the nuns who were bowed down by the weight of years and saddened by the griefs they had undergone during the Revolution, used to make room for her close to the place where they were seated. "Come and sit by us, dear little Sister," they would affectionately say. And when the young novice had complied with their request, they used to get her to talk to them, and thus refresh their weary spirits with her youthful vivacity and charming gaiety.

At a later period of her novitiate she was, as the Rule directs, brought into immediate contact with the penitents. The rare aptitude she evinced for this new occupation, caused her to be appointed Second Mistress. She comprehended at one glance many things which it takes less gifted souls long years to learn. She understood, as if by intuition, that the way to convert sinners is not to be perpetually lecturing them. " Such a course of conduct can only weary and repel them. The true method is first of all to gain their confidence, and if possible their affection also, by unwearied kindness and forbearance, thus inducing them to desire to amend the faults of their character, and by acquiring a soft and gentle demeanour, bring themselves into greater harmony with the atmosphere of love and charity by which they find themselves surrounded." We have quoted the words of Mother St. Euphrasia, as uttered towards the close of her life, in the course of the instructions she gave to her novices. In these instructions she goes on to mention several mistakes into which she fell at the outset, and more than one failure which she made in the management of those committed to her charge. These particulars are intended as admonitions to her spiritual children, as beacons to warn them off the rocks. To dwell upon them would be manifestly beside our present purpose, and if we allude to them in a passing manner, it is solely because it is so discouraging to those who desire humbly to follow in the footsteps of eminent servants of God, to find them represented as already perfect from the beginning. Even our Blessed Lord, in condescension to human infirmity, allows it to be said of Him : " Jesus advanced in wisdom and age, and grace with God and men."[1] Development is a universal law, both in the order of nature and in that of grace. Does not our Lord say : " First the blade, then the ear, afterwards the full corn in the ear "?[2] And how does the Wise Man describe the life of the children of God ? " The path of the just," he tells us, " as a shining light, goeth forwards and increaseth, even unto perfect day."[3]

[1] St. Luke ii. 52.   [2] St. Mark iv. 28.   [3] Prov. iv. 18.

The time of probation, and the two years' novitiate, drew to a close at last. Sister St. Euphrasia underwent the examination prescribed by the Rule. When the Superior of the Refuge addressed to her the customary questions, she, as the reader will already have anticipated, replied with a radiant countenance that she was perfectly satisfied and should pronounce her vows with a heart full of overflowing joy. Her profession took place on the 9th of September, 1817. The venerable M. Petit, parish priest of St. Saturnin, and confessor to the Community, received her vows. To the three vows usual in other Orders, those namely of obedience, chastity, and poverty, the Sisters belonging to the Refuge added a fourth, that of devoting themselves to the conversion of penitent women. It is a remarkable fact that almost immediately after the solemn words had passed her lips, one of the older among her Sisters in Religion stepped up to her, and whispered: "You will one day find yourself compelled to alter the formula of these vows." And so it proved in the sequel. It is not possible for mortal pen to describe what passed within the soul of the newly-professed Sister at the supreme moment when she consummated her sacrifice. But this at least we do know, that she offered herself to God in a spirit of absolute generosity, without making any reserve or holding anything back from Him. She even went so far as to renounce the privilege of disposing, according to her own wish, of any Indulgences she might gain, leaving them all in the hands of God, to do with them as He might see fit. This *Heroic Act* has been made familiar to us all through the means of the late Rev. Father John Morris, S.J. Doubtless, Sister St. Euphrasia never for a moment regretted what she had done. Yet her act exposed her, we are told, to a painful trial, when shortly afterwards her beloved eldest sister, Anne Marsaud, was called to leave this world. This incident affords a singular commentary on a remark made by Father Morris, not long before his death, to the writer of the present history. " People should consider well," he said, " before they offer anything to Almighty God. He is certain to take it, especially if the sacrifice involves what is painful to human nature."

Very marked was Sister Euphrasia's progress in virtue after her profession. Her perfect observance of the Rule, her deep humility, her ardent piety, her unruffled serenity of demeanour, her gratitude to all those who performed for her the smallest act of kindness, and above all, her extreme care never to say anything which could wound charity, made her an example to the whole House. In this last respect she is more particularly to be praised, for her sprightly and vivacious character, keen power of observation, and sharp and ready tongue, might easily have betrayed her into sallies, which if lively and amusing, might have wounded the feelings of those at whom they were remotely aimed. Sufficient proof of the truth of this description is afforded by the fact that a short time after her profession she was appointed to fill the important and responsible post of First Mistress of Penitents, although she was not much more than twenty-one years of age. Her zeal had now full scope, her time no longer hung heavy on her hands. On the contrary, she had the delightful consciousness of being engaged in the work God had appointed for her to do. Her marvellous tact, her cheerful temper, her striking fertility of resource, all became useful to her in their turn. Her sole cause of regret was the small number of those under her care. "If we could only have sixty penitents!" she would sometimes exclaim. "How your youthful imagination does run away with you, my dear child!" the older Sisters would reply with a kind smile. "It is vain to hope that these dreams of yours will ever be realized. You would not talk as you do if you had lived through the Reign of Terror and seen what we have seen." Nothing, however, damped the zeal of Sister St. Euphrasia. Her hopes were doubtless founded on the presentiment our Lord deigned from time to time to grant her, concerning the great work she was to accomplish for His glory and the conversion of sinners.

In order to illustrate what has been said of her virtues, and to show them in their practical exercise, we will give a few anecdotes and illustrations concerning the work which now engaged all her energies, and the manner in which she carried it on. And here we may remark, once for all, that we shall allow her to speak for herself whenever we can. Her instructions to those under her government are so judicious, so prudent, so full of affectionate sympathy and maternal care for their interests, their joys and sorrows, that her words well deserve to be quoted. Prominent, moreover, among her gifts is one which we have not yet mentioned, but which was no unimportant factor in her success, the undeniable charm of her epistolary style. Her letters are delightful in every way, and we shall hope to place ample specimens of them before our readers at a later period.

"During the time I was First Mistress of Penitents," she tells us, "I one day noticed that a large proportion of those who composed the class I was superintending, seemed to be in a very bad temper. They kept whispering together, and showed their ill-humour in various ways. Fearing they were planning some act of open disobedience, I took the first opportunity of sending for the Second Mistress, whom I requested to take my place for an hour. This hour I spent in prayer before the Blessed Sacrament, and then went back to resume my duties. Scarcely had I opened the class-room door, when the greater number of those present burst into tears. Some who had behaved the worst hastened forward to meet me, warmly expressing their regret, and protesting that they would try and never vex me any more !

"Another time I heard a confused sound of voices outside my door. I stepped promptly out into the corridor, and found a little group assembled. 'What do you want, my children, and why are you here?' I asked. No one dared to reply. At last the boldest spirit among them said that she spoke in the name of all the rest, and laid before me certain grievances, expressing herself in language which amounted to a menace. 'What nonsense you are talking!' I exclaimed. 'How can you be so foolish as to imagine that a daughter of Our Lady of Charity would allow herself to be influenced by threats! Return to your own quarters, and remember that I am ready to die, if necessary, rather than fail in my duty.' My command was instantly obeyed, and I heard no more complaints. Of course I was careful not to make the least allusion to the occurrence, which I treated as if it had been a bad dream.

"Great judgment is needed in choosing a suitable occasion when it becomes necessary to reprove. For instance, I never used to talk about penance on a day when the dinner had not been quite so nice as usual.

Rather would I say, 'Dear children, I wish we had had something better to set before you. I am really very sorry.' Those whom I thus addressed generally made some such answer as this: 'O Mother, pray don't talk in this way, our dinner is good enough.' Then, on a more propitious occasion, I used to strive to impress upon the minds of the penitents the tremendous evil of sin and the fearful nature of the sufferings awaiting us in Purgatory, in order that they might see how fortunate are those who, by practising mortifications in this life, can escape those cleansing flames.

"While still in the world, I happened to have heard the head of a large boarding-school enlarge upon the danger of allowing a spirit of dulness and *ennui* to prevail among the pupils. I felt that this principle was equally applicable to my present charges, but I found no small difficulty in carrying it into practice. One Sunday afternoon in particular I shall always remember. The heat was oppressive, the air sultry, the storm which was evidently gathering over our heads appeared to influence the moral atmosphere as well. The girls sat together in the shade of a large tree, talking among themselves, and refusing to enter into any plan I could devise for their amusement. I felt fairly nonplussed, and could only raise my heart to God in a fervent entreaty for help. Casting my eyes on the ground, I chanced to descry a grasshopper close to my feet. I picked it up as carefully as I could, and exclaimed, 'Come and see what I have found!' One by one my poor children came to where I was standing, but at first they only laughed in a mocking way, and told me it was scarcely worth while to go and look at a common grasshopper. I pretended not to hear what they said,

F

and went on making little plans for keeping the insect, constructing a cage for it, feeding it, &c. Before many minutes had passed the clouds were dispelled. One ran off to get something wherewith to fashion a cage, another volunteered to take care of the grasshopper, and the poor little creature served to amuse us during our recreations for some time to come."

Many and touching are the stories connected with the penitents over whom Sister St. Euphrasia exercised so great an influence. She shall relate two of these in her own simple words:

"There was one penitent whose face was literally disfigured by the abundant tears she shed. She scarcely ever spoke, and would not be consoled, so deep was her grief for having offended God, and for having been instrumental in teaching others to offend Him. 'O my God,' she would frequently cry out, 'is it possible I can ever hope to obtain pardon from Thee? My sins have been so many, and so heinous in their nature!' I felt the deepest compassion for her, and often reminded her that the mercy of God is infinite, and that she must have confidence in Him. 'Dear Mother,' she would answer, 'I shall not live much longer, I am certain. Death only can put an end to the piercing sorrow I feel for having sinned against so merciful a Saviour.' She was most grateful for every little attention shown her, and often said that she could not think how any one could ever speak to such a miserable creature as she was. But she was shortly removed from our midst. During the last days she spent on earth, and, indeed, during the whole of her illness, she experienced terrible assaults from the devil. He caused her to see a large open book, on the pages of which all her sins were inscribed with pitiless accuracy, and cruel minuteness

of detail. Yet when her end was evidently drawing
very near, she appeared so calm and placid that she
was asked whether her fears and apprehensions had
ceased. 'Yes, dear Mother,' was her answer, 'I am
dying in peace. I have hidden myself in the wounds
of our Lord, and trust to His infinite mercy, from
which I hope everything.' She retained her consciousness to the very close, her last words being, *In te,
Domine, speravi, non confundar in æternum.*

"Another of the penitents I had under my charge
was of a very different type. She seemed to have been
possessed by a positive hatred of God ever since the
day of her first Communion, which she had made in an
unworthy manner. She took delight in committing
mortal sins, for the mere purpose of offending Him.
She communicated daily, without having fasted up to
the time of so doing. Whenever she saw a flock of
lambs, she used to throw a shower of stones on them
and drive them away if possible, because the harmless
creatures reminded her of the Lamb of God. Nor had
she scrupled to injure her fellow-creatures, if opportunity
offered. Several crimes of arson were laid to her charge,
especially that of setting wheat-fields on fire. Yet at
last her hard heart was touched by grace. She came
to us, and implored us to take her in. Her conversion
was thorough, and she obtained the gift of such deep
contrition, that she scarcely dared to raise her eyes to
Heaven. For three years she dwelt among us, setting
an example of perfect obedience to every Rule of the
house. At the expiration of that period she was seized
with a fatal malady, prepared for death in a manner
which gave general edification, and expired in most
excellent dispositions. It is a singular circumstance,
that the evening before her death, she asked me to

accept a little picture of St. Euphrasia, occupied in erecting churches."

It cannot but be apparent to all how great must have been the interest of witnessing these wonderful transformations. How great, moreover, was the privilege of co-operating in effecting them. Sister St. Euphrasia remarks that in the case of the generality of penitents, a double conversion takes place. The first is more or less a matter of feeling. It is produced by the emotions which bring the wanderer to the convent, by the extreme kindness and charity of the Religious, by the good example set by her companions, by the order, quiet, and harmony of her new life, standing out in salient contrast to the horrors of her past existence. But this state of things seldom lasts long. A revulsion of feeling takes place. The remembrance of past pleasures and enjoyments, the thirst for liberty, the impatience of restraint, all assail the penitent, who is apt to sink into a state of depression and indifference. At this point the work of the Mistress becomes at once more difficult and more important. She has to call the reasoning faculty to her aid, to impress upon those under her charge the great truths of religion, the immortality of the soul, the tremendous alternative of spending eternity amid the ineffable joys of Heaven, or the unutterable torments of Hell. "The two greatest temptations of penitents are against faith and against hope." Therefore it is highly necessary to excite in them a spirit of confidence in God, lest when they awake to the true enormity of their past sins, they should fall into despair, and imagine there can be no forgiveness in store for them.

From the year 1819, about eighteen months after her Profession, Sister St. Euphrasia was called to endure interior trials of no ordinary severity. They lasted for twelve years, and were doubtless designed to teach her that those who work for God must labour in a spirit of self-abnegation, and aim at a total freedom from self-love and self-pleasing. She learnt, moreover, that suffering is the dew which renders good deeds fertile, and remained humble in the midst of success. At a future period she was able from her own experience to aid and counsel her spiritual children, who were called to undergo trials like her own. To these interior sorrows may be added those which were inseparable from her duty as Mistress of Penitents. There were times when she felt weary and depressed, and imagined herself to be effecting little or no real good. Can we wonder that her bright and courageous spirit was occasionally overshadowed by clouds and gloom, when even the illustrious Prophet Elias, in the midst of the great work he was achieving, and sojourning, as he did, upon the venerable heights of Carmel, half-way between earth and heaven, exclaimed, in the anguish of his heart: " It is enough for me ; Lord, take away my soul : for I am no better than my fathers." [1]

Yet God was about to lay upon the shoulders of Sister St. Euphrasia a far heavier cross, and a still greater weight of responsibility. Concerning the manner in which this came to pass, it will be our business to speak in the next chapter.

[1] 2 Kings xix. 4.

CHAPTER V

DURING the eight years (1817—1825) which had elapsed since the Profession of Sister St. Euphrasia, one important event had marked the external life of the Community, namely, their removal into the house they had occupied before the Revolution. A great part of it had been destroyed; the remainder had afforded a shelter to the Carmelites, when in 1805 they were allowed to return to Tours. In 1822, however, these latter had the joy of regaining possession of their own original convent, which had suffered but little damage. Thus the Sisters of the Refuge were enabled to acquire the locality which was left vacant, and which had been the cradle of their Order. But alas! how great was the havoc which had been wrought! The Carmelites had been obliged during their term of occupation to arrange as best they could the house formerly used for penitents, and to content themselves with the choir and sanctuary of the chapel, the nave having been entirely pulled down. Thus this house, and a portion of the chapel, were all that the Republicans had spared of the conventual buildings, the rest having been levelled with the ground, and the land divided amongst various proprietors. Mother St. Hippolyta, who was Superior of the Refuge from 1819 till 1825, had, by dint of great perseverance and incessant exertion, succeeded in buying back one portion after another of the land which had in bygone years been the property of the Sisters. By this means the way was gradually prepared for the return of her Community. As soon as the Carmelites were re-installed in their own convent, the work of restoration and re-building commenced. It occupied upwards of a year, and it was not until the feast of the Guardian Angels, October 2nd, 1823, that the Sisters found themselves once more settled in the home which was so dear to the hearts of the older ones among them. The Archbishop of Tours presided at the re-establishment of the regular enclosure, and in an eloquent address warmly congratulated the assembled Religious on an event so fortunate in itself, and so rich in promise for the future.

Early in May, 1825, the second triennium of Mother St. Hippolyta expired. The Rule forbids the re-election of a Superior at the conclusion of six years. Besides this, Mother St. Hippolyta was broken down by age and infirmities, which, even apart from the Rule just alluded to, rendered her manifestly unfit for the arduous post she had filled. All eyes turned to Sister St. Euphrasia. Her talents and virtues pointed her out as the fittest person to take the helm. Yet once again the Rule served to block the way. It ordered that no member of a Community should be elected Superior who was not turned forty years of age, and had not been professed for a period of eight years. Sister St. Euphrasia was scarcely twenty-nine years old, but so high was the regard in which she was held, not only by her Sisters in Religion, but by her confessor, M. Alleron, and also by M. Monnereau, the Superior of the house, that the latter determined to apply to Rome for a dispensation. His request was granted,

the election took place on the 21st of May, 1825, and
Sister St. Euphrasia was chosen Superior without so
much as a single dissentient voice.

Great was the surprise of the youthful Superior, and
greater still her consternation. In truth her post was
a difficult and an arduous one, from several points of
view.   The house she was called upon to govern
contained many distinct elements, and for this reason
required all the more skill and prudence in the hands
which held the reins.   Predictions of her success, both
in the present and in the future, were not lacking.
A Bishop who knew her well said: "If Mother
St. Euphrasia had been a man, she would have been
chosen Pope."   Later on, another prelate expressed
himself as follows: "The wisest head in Angers is
that of the Superior of the Good Shepherd." But we
must not, in relating her history, allow ourselves to
anticipate. Before, however, we commence the account
of all she did in her new capacity, we must make a
remark which applies to her throughout the whole of
the long and useful career which was opening before
her.

She always laid the greatest stress upon the
importance of small courtesies and acts of kindness.
Never did she fail to perform them, when opportunity
offered.   When little attentions were shown to her, she
was always ready to mark her sense of them, and
express her gratitude. Brought as she was into contact
with innumerable persons of every rank and position
in life, there is no doubt that her pleasing manners and
invariable politeness contributed in no trifling measure
to her success. She never received strangers, whatever
might be their errand, except with kindness and consideration, placing herself moreover at their disposal,

and never appearing to be in a hurry, however urgent were the claims upon her time. In this way she over-came many prejudices, obtained many concessions, and won for herself an army of friends. She laboured to impress the necessity of this line of conduct upon those under her, and was accustomed to say, that setting aside the higher motives of Christian charity, kindness and courtesy infallibly meet with their reward, even in this life. As an illustration of this we will here relate an incident which occurred soon after her election. We quote her own words:

"While I was Superior at Tours, a card was one day brought to my room, bearing a name absolutely unknown to me. I was told that a gentleman wished to see me, and I therefore went at once to the parlour. My visitor desired to consult me respecting some painful and embarrassing family matters, which were causing him no little distress and anxiety. I listened to his story, and sympathized sincerely with him, for the tale was a very sad one. I gave him the best advice I could, and, as it happened, I was able to render him real assistance through the medium of some old friends of mine. Years went by, and the circumstance had faded from my memory, when in 1830, after the Revo-lution which took place in that year, a second visit from the same gentleman was announced to me. He explained that he was now one of the principal authori-ties of the city, and that he hoped he had at last found the opportunity for which he had so long been watching, of repaying the service I had rendered him. He said that, were fresh disturbances to arise, he would take care that we should not be annoyed in any way, as we were to consider ourselves and our house under his special protection, adding that, in case of real

necessity, he would station gendarmes at our door.
Not satisfied with this, when the time came for us to
journey to Angers, our grateful friend took the trouble
to discover at what hour we were to start. To our
astonishment, he came to the door of our carriage, just
at the moment of departure was close at hand, and
said to a couple of officers who happened to be our
companions: ' I give these kind nuns into your keeping,
and beg that you will show them all possible respect
and attention. I shall consider everything you do for
them as if it were done to myself.' "

The first work undertaken by Mother St. Euphrasia,
after the reins of government had been placed in her
hands, was the realization of a wish she had cherished
almost from the very beginning of her intercourse with
the penitents, and which had grown and strengthened
with every passing year. Her penetrating eye had
discerned, among those committed to her care, a certain
number of souls whose conversion to God was thorough
and radical, and who desired to embrace the religious
life. Here, however, a difficulty arose, which might
have intimidated a less intrepid character. The Constitutions of the Order forbade the penitents ever to be
admitted into the number of the Sisters of the house in
which they were, nor into any other house, whatever
might be their talents or virtues. Mother St. Euphrasia
applied to several other Orders and Communities, but
in the generality of instances she was met by a point-
blank refusal. In the few remaining cases, where a
penitent was received, the attempt invariably resulted
in a dead failure, and the individual had to be sent
back to Tours. Nothing, therefore, remained but to
keep those who wished to become Religious at the
Refuge, under the care of the Sisters who had been

of wonder if even Mother Euphrasia's marvellous powers were taxed to the uttermost before she could succeed in breaking in these wild, wilful creatures, and inducing them to run in harness.

Her joy at returning to Angers was tempered by many trials. Great poverty still prevailed, the walls were not as yet thoroughly repaired and rebuilt, hence for several months the nuns had much to suffer from the nightly depredations committed in their gardens by a number of rough lads, who were in the pay of their enemies. Imaginary terrors were added to real causes of alarm. One Sister would fancy that she saw several men hidden under one of the trees at night. Another would imagine that she heard advancing footsteps, and mysterious threats, and so on. Mother St. Euphrasia did not herself know what fear is, but she found it no easy task to remove the apprehensions of those around her. The annoyances inflicted on the Community finally reached such a pitch, that she was obliged to appeal to the magistrates of the city, and obtain legal protection.

As a further proof of the truth of the proverb which tells us that "troubles never come single," an unusual amount of illness broke out in the house, so that the Superior did not know how to supply Mistresses for its various departments. She was compelled to choose the most able of the novices, and place them at the head of the classes. The one who was selected to superintend the penitents was Sister Mary of St. Vincent of Paul, whose enlightened zeal and unflagging devotion to the work of the Good Shepherd rendered her, at a subsequent period, a valuable supporter of the Institute.

In the midst of these griefs and perplexities, the Community was much cheered and encouraged by a

instrumental in their conversion. This necessitated
the founding of an Order for their especial benefit.
Mother St. Euphrasia proceeded with great prudence,
well knowing that: *Chi va piano va sano: chi va sano
va lontano.* After having consulted M. Alleron, her
confessor, and M. Monnereau, the Superior of the
Refuge, she assembled the Council, and said to the
Sisters who comprised it: "You have chosen me for
your Superior. I am conscious of my own unworthiness and unfitness for the post. But, since you have
called me to fill it, we will establish a Community of
Magdalens." As a matter of course, the new Community was to be devoted to penance. Mother St.
Euphrasia desired that its members should, as far as
possible, be imbued with the spirit of St. Teresa, of
whose writings she had herself made so thorough a
study, and for whose character and labours she felt an
ever-growing admiration. M. Monnereau agreed entirely
with her, and, as he was the Superior of the Carmelite
Convent as well as of the Refuge, it was easy for him
to make the Carmelite Prioress acquainted with the
wishes of the head of the Sisters of the Refuge. The
Prioress entered into the idea in the kindest manner
and did everything she could to help Mother St.
Euphrasia. She lent her a copy of the Rule and
Constitutions, and sent a habit for her to see. The
Rule of the Magdalens is founded to a great extent on
that of the Carmelites, certain alterations and modifi-
cations being necessary, as a matter of course. Their
dress is of the same colour and material. In fact the
serge employed in the fabrication of the habits worn
by the first four Magdalens was a present from the
daughters of St. Teresa. M. Monnereau drew up a
formula for the Clothing and Profession of the "Sisters

of St. Magdalen," which was duly submitted to the Vicar-General, and approved by him.

It was on the 9th of November, 1825, that the habit was given by M. Monnereau to four members of the new Sisterhood, who applied themselves courageously to the observance of their Rule. They rose at 4 a.m., and retired to rest at 9 p.m., their beds not being of the softest nature. Their duties included the recitation of the Office of the Blessed Virgin, besides certain special prayers, and the usual exercises of the religious life. Perpetual silence reigned everywhere, except during the hour of recreation which followed each of their two meals. As the Magdalens have no other means of livelihood except that obtained by the labour of their hands, their employment is principally needle-work.

It was not long before God manifested to His servant, by unmistakable signs, His approval of her zealous exertions. Among the earliest of those who enrolled themselves members of the new Sisterhood, four begged of our Lord the grace of a speedy death, so greatly did they fear to fail in fidelity to Him. Their prayer was heard and quickly answered. All the four were summoned to Heaven, according to the date of their Profession. Three of them had been converted through the instrumentality of Mother St. Euphrasia, while she was Mistress of Penitents. The fourth was a very young and perfectly innocent girl, who had entered the Refuge for the sole purpose of obtaining the conversion of her mother, who was leading a deplorably vicious life. As soon as the Magdalens were founded, she entreated to be received into the Sister-hood. She set an example of every virtue, especially that of obedience, and practised great austerities, hoping thus to procure the salvation of her unhappy parent. In fact, when this latter heard the story of her child's heroic sacrifice and holy death, she was so deeply touched that she forthwith forsook the paths of sin, went to confession, and persevered in leading a new life as long as she remained in this world.

During the night that succeeded the day on which the holy young Sister breathed her last, she appeared to Mother St. Euphrasia, shining with celestial radiance, and wearing the habit of the Sisters of Our Lady of Charity belonging to the Refuge. "Dear Mother," she said, "I am in Heaven, and I form one of the choir of the Religious of Our Lady of Charity. God has seen fit to assign me the place destined for one of the Sisters who lost her vocation and has just expired." During the course of the next day, news reached the Community that a Sister, who had not possessed the courage necessary for leaving the world a second time after the Revolution, had died quite suddenly the evening before, in a country house where she was residing.

The story of the last hours of another follower of St. Mary Magdalen shall be related in Mother St. Euphrasia's own words: "One of these dear children, who was evidently drawing near her end, exclaimed, when I entered the infirmary: 'O my true Mother and best friend! How much good you have done me! To you, under God, I owe my conversion! It is a consolation indeed to behold you, for I am sure that our merciful Lord Himself has sent you to my bedside to strengthen and comfort me.' In the midst of excruciating sufferings, her courage and patience never failed, and if she asked for anything which might alleviate her pain, she used to reproach herself afterwards. My mind was at that time much occupied by the wish of extending our good work, and one day I said to her: 'My child, you will probably die before very long. If, as I hope and trust, you are received into Heaven, promise that you will ask God to grant me some direct indication as to His will, with regard to my desire of founding houses for the reception of those who are anxious to quit the ways of evil.' 'I promise not to forget your request,' she replied. Only a brief period elapsed subsequent to her death, before I was called to found a house at Angers."

This incident occurred shortly after the re-election of Mother St. Euphrasia to the Superiorate, which took place in May, 1828, her first tenure of office having expired a few days previously. Devoted as she was to the care of her own Community, and to the formation of fresh plans for the benefit of the penitents under her surveillance, there was nothing narrow or exclusive about her. On the contrary, she was ever ready to acknowledge the excellence of other Orders, and to say how much benefit she obtained through the friendship she cultivated with their members. Of her admiration for the Carmelites we have already spoken, and one result of the frequent communications which took place, at the time when the Magdalens were founded, between the two convents, was that she renewed the friendships of her school-girl days with Mary Angelica Dernée, now Sister Mary of the Incarnation. The reader will doubtless remember the grief which her departure caused to her chosen companion, then known as Rose Pelletier. On account of the uncommon sanctity and virtue of Sister Mary, as well as of the esteem and affection in which she was held by Mother St. Euphrasia, she deserves some further mention in these pages. She was about the same age as the Superior of the Refuge, and came from the same neighbourhood. The innocence and purity written on her youthful countenance inspired even the municipal and revolutionary authorities with respect, and she was known in the town where her parents lived by the soubriquet of *La Vertu.* As we have seen in a former chapter, she was sent to the school connected with *l'Association chrétienne,* and left, when her education was completed, to enter the Carmelite Convent. In due time she was chosen Mistress of Novices, and filled this post for a series of years. She was called to rule over her Community from 1834 to 1857. Her business faculties were so remarkable, that she contrived, by dexterous management of the funds of the convent, to free it from the extreme poverty which had hampered it since the Revolution, and to erect a new and more commodious house, to which the nuns removed in 1846. Moreover, she gathered together from the other French convents all the books she could which treated of the Rule, the Constitutions, and conventual customs. From these various works she compiled a single volume entitled *Le Trésor du Carmel,* which is regarded as of no small value, and has proved very useful to the Order. Mother St. Euphrasia habitually consulted her, and frequently wrote to ask for her prayers. As years went by, the bonds which united these two holy women grew closer, and their mutual confidence more intimate and complete.

The other chosen friend of Mother St. Euphrasia was the Superior of the Ursulines, whose acquaintance the reader has already made in these pages under her family name of Mlle. de Lignac. Little, therefore, need be added here concerning her. She displayed in the government of her subjects the same qualities which

had distinguished her when a teacher under the roof of
Mdme. Chobelet, for she was essentially one of those
who are born to command. She had great difficulties to
contend with, but she overcame them all, and raised the
school connected with the convent to so high a place in
public esteem that more pupils were offered to her than
it was found possible to receive. As the Rule of the
Ursulines permitted them to walk out in the streets
of Tours, Mother de Lignac was able to visit the
Refuge, and thus the two friends had the consolation
of sharing, by means of personal intercourse, their
sorrows and joys, their successes and defeats.

We are now approaching an important era in the
life of Mother St. Euphrasia, and before we enter upon
it we must give some account of the good work which
had been going on at Angers, the spirit of which was
similar to that which pervaded the Refuge of Tours.

At Angers, previous to the Revolution, Christian
charity had not been inactive on behalf of women and
girls who had left, or were in danger of leaving the
path of virtue. The oldest institution for their rescue
was St. Magdalen's Home, founded in 1640, for the
reception of those who were repentant, and desirous
of forsaking their evil ways. The first Superior of
this house was Sister Teresa, a woman of humble
origin, but richly endowed with supernatural gifts, who
died in the odour of sanctity, and who is not yet
forgotten in Angers. Some twenty years after her death,
which occurred in 1674, her work was supplemented
by the formation of a Community which took the title
of Sisters of the Good Shepherd. They were not
enclosed; their object was to provide a Refuge for those
who, on leaving the House of Penitents, desired to
perfect their reconciliation with the God they had

offended. Neither of these good works had any
connection with the Refuges established by Father
Eudes. Like them, however, they were submerged
by the deluge of impiety that swept over France.
Submerged, but not completely destroyed, for when
the storm had passed away, a house was to arise on
their ruins, combining in itself the two-fold aim for
which they had been established, and carrying it out
on a larger scale and with greater perfection.

There was at Angers a widow lady possessed of a
large fortune, named Mdme. de Neuville, whose life
was given up to good works. For many years she
cherished the desire of resuscitating the former House
of the Good Shepherd, but in 1827 the hand of death
removed her before her project could be realized. Her
only son, the inheritor of her piety and benevolence
as well as of her name and fortune, felt it to be his duty
to carry out her wishes; with this intention he placed
in the hands of the Bishop the sum of 30,000 francs
(£1,200), which his mother had bequeathed to found
a House of Penitents. Mgr. Montault, who then
governed the diocese, had in the time of the Revolution the weakness to yield to his mother's entreaties,
that, instead of emigrating, he would accept the
bishopric offered him by the Government. Three years
later he redeemed his fault by resigning his see, making
a public retractation, and imploring the pardon of the
Supreme Pontiff. During the remainder of his life,
he kept the remembrance of it always before him,
speaking of it with bitter tears, and expiating it when
raised to the see of Angers, by forty years of unremitting
labour in the service of the Church. Every work of
charity for the spiritual or temporal welfare of his
flock, found in him a zealous patron and promoter,

G

and he welcomed M. de Neuville's proposal. Still he
thought it better to defer the enterprise for a time, as
the moment seemed hardly opportune for it. At that
juncture, however, an incident occurred which led him
to rescind his decision. He received a letter written
at the request of a young woman, formerly an inhabitant of Angers, who, having strayed from the
ways of virtue, had become an inmate of the Refuge
at Caen. There she died, and on her death-bed she
had entreated a lady, also a native of Angers, to write
and implore the Bishop to found a Refuge in his
episcopal city. Almost at the same time that this
letter reached him, the clergy of Angers severally and
collectively urged upon him the necessity of establishing a house for the reception of fallen women. A
suitable site for its erection was therefore sought for,
and in due course of time, as we shall presently see,
was happily found. But to meet with a lady both
willing and able to undertake the management of the
house, proved a more difficult matter. At length it
was resolved to entrust the work to Religious. One
of the priests who had taken a leading part in carrying
out the project, wrote to a lady of great experience
in Paris, asking her if she knew of any Community
there who would accept the direction of a Refuge at
Angers. The lady appealed to, Mdme. d'Andigné,
replied that it was not necessary to look further than
Tours, where there was a Community which would
exactly fulfil their requirements. She advised him to
apply to the Superior, Mother St. Euphrasia, a woman
of great energy and ability, whom she knew personally
and esteemed most highly.

In consequence of this information, M. Breton, the
priest above referred to, set out for Tours, on May 18,

1829, accompanied by one of his curates. He went straight to the Refuge, and asked to be shown over it, without, however, divulging the real object of his visit. Charmed with all he heard and saw, still more charmed with the winning manners of Mother St. Euphrasia, he requested her, before he took leave, to allow him a private interview. On hearing his proposal, her delight knew no bounds. God seemed to be about to grant the desire of her heart. " I fancied myself already in Heaven!" she said afterwards, in her bright, vivacious manner, when describing the visit of M. Breton. No time was lost. The very next day she set out with one of her nuns, Mother St. Victoire, and M. Breton, in a carriage hired by the latter, for the purpose of inspecting the premises intended for the reception of the Religious.

When after a wearisome journey of several days, she beheld Angers for the first time, she was deeply moved. The ancient city, called in former days *La ville noire*, on account of its slate roofs, can be perceived from a considerable distance, dominated as it is by the Gothic pinnacles of the Cathedral, and by the Roman tower of an old convent belonging to the Abbey of St. Aubin. These memorials of the faith of our forefathers cheered the heart of Mother St. Euphrasia. As soon as the immediate vicinity of the city was reached, M. Breton, whose character was not lacking in originality, alighted from the carriage, and invited his companions to follow his example, saying as he did so : " My dear ladies, you desire to be followers of the Apostles, and yet you think of entering Angers otherwise than on foot!" He marched on first, followed by the Religious, who had to walk all the rest of the way, though the heat was excessive. First

of all they went to the episcopal residence, to ask the
blessing of Mgr. Montault, and then M. Breton led
them to his presbytery. The next day was Sunday,
and they heard his Mass, which he said at six o'clock
in the morning. In the course of a brief address which
he delivered after the Gospel, he pointed to the two
Sisters from the Refuge, whose white habits had
already attracted the attention of all present, and told
his parishioners that these Religious had power to heal
every kind of infirmity, so that the blind, the lame, the
paralytic would do well to have recourse to them. He
was, of course, alluding to the diseases of the soul.
In quite another sense were his words interpreted by
his simple and unlettered hearers. They imagined
him to refer to physical maladies, and no sooner was
Mass ended, than they poured into the sacristy, bringing with them sufferers of every description, whom they
requested the Sisters to cure. When these latter explained the real object of their coming, some members
of the throng grew very angry, and even abusive. It
required all Mother St. Euphrasia's tact, courage, and
persuasiveness to pour oil on the surging waves of
excited feeling, and induce the crowd to disperse
quietly, while she herself and her companion re-entered
the presbytery by a private door. This ludicrous
mistake had one fortunate result: it brought the new-
comers under the eye of the public.

Later in the day, M. Breton and M. de Neuville
took the Sisters to see the property, the purchase of
which was in contemplation. It was called *Tournemine*,
and had formerly been an extensive manufactory of
cotton goods. Standing on the gentle slope of the right
bank of the Maine, in the very shadow of the Church of
St. James, it had on one side a suburb of Angers, on the

other wide stretches of meadow-land reaching far away into the open country. Forming altogether a vast enclosure, it contained spacious gardens and shrubberies, with numerous buildings of various kinds. Everything looked forlorn and dilapidated, but Mother St. Euphrasia's mind was soon made up. She was more than satisfied, she was delighted, for she saw how easily the place could be adapted for her needs. What gave her especial satisfaction, was that the buildings were isolated, and the grounds not overlooked. With a thankful heart she returned at once to Tours, requesting that the purchase might be completed with the least possible delay.

At the Refuge, the necessary formalities were speedily gone through, and such was her energy that on Wednesday, June 3rd, the fourth day after her return from Angers, she once more set out for that city, taking with her five Sisters from the Refuge, one of whom was chosen Superior of the new convent, though it was decided that all organization and arrangement should rest with Mother St. Euphrasia. This second journey was no pleasanter than the last. Again the heat was extreme, and a not too sober coachman allowed the carriage to jolt so incessantly, as to cause Mother St. Euphrasia great suffering from violent attacks of something like sea-sickness. Yet this was not the worst. At a spot where the road skirts the Loire, and is only separated from it by a belt of grass, the horses got off the track, so that the travellers thought they must inevitably be jerked into the water. It was midnight when at last they reached their goal, but Mdme. d'Andigné, who had accompanied them, thought it better they should rest for the night, before entering Angers. Close to the road stood a spacious house, called Mille-Pieds, whose directress, Mdme. Blouin, was an intimate friend of Mdme. d'Andigné, and had for years devoted herself to the training and education of the deaf and dumb. She was delighted to welcome under her roof the Sisters who were about to found a Convent of the Good Shepherd, and lavished upon them every kind and hospitable attention, thus earning the warm gratitude of Mother St. Euphrasia, who never forgot her benefactress, although the hand of death called her away in the midst of her charitable labours, a few months later. The next day they became once again the recipients of M. Breton's hospitality, and on Saturday, June the 6th, which was the eve of Pentecost, he conducted them to their new abode. The curious originality by which, as we have already said, his character was distinguished, induced him to take the Sisters through the most disreputable streets of the town. As they walked along, he said aloud from time to time, " I wish all the bad girls in the place would come to these ladies, and learn to abandon their evil ways." The following morning the little company of Religious heard Mass in the Church of St. James, and, on returning home, had nothing for breakfast except the scanty remains of the provisions they had brought with them to supply their need during their journey. Of dinner there was absolutely no prospect. But in the course of the morning, Providence sent them a visitor, in the person of the excellent priest of St. James', M. Vincent by name. He made many inquiries as to their resources, and finding that they were, at least for the moment, in a state of actual destitution, he sent them his own dinner, which, on re-entering his house, he found already served and awaiting him in the dining-room. This generous and charitable act was

the beginning of happy and cordial relations between
the convent and the presbytery. M. Vincent became
a valued friend and counsellor, while Mother St.
Euphrasia never ceased to feel for him the liveliest
gratitude and the fullest confidence. Nor did she
stop short and content herself with mere feelings.
By many delicate attentions and little gifts, she showed
from time to time, as soon as it was in her power to
do so, that she had never forgotten the self-denial
he had practised on behalf of hungry and destitute
strangers.

Since it had been finally resolved that the manufactory of Tournemine should be turned into a house
of Refuge, the priests belonging to the various city
parishes were indefatigable in their efforts to obtain the
funds necessary for the purchase. Their exertions met
with a success for which they had not dared to hope,
their appeal being everywhere kindly and liberally
responded to. Amongst his fellow-priests, M. Breton,
who had the cause of the Sisters most deeply at heart,
displayed a singular zeal. He made a house-to-
house visitation of his whole parish, and obtained a
sum proportioned to his efforts. The originality which
characterized him, together with a certain holy audacity,
if we may so term it, made him a first-rate beggar.
Having heard that the officers belonging to the 17th
Regiment of Light Infantry were about to give a grand
banquet in honour of their General, M. le Comte de la
Houssaye, he requested to be allowed to enter the mess-
room after dinner, in order to ask for alms. Having
obtained the desired permission, he thus addressed the
assembly: " My dear friends, I dare say you have all
been guilty of certain *peccadillos* at one time or another
of your life. I have come to propose to you a means

of atoning for them. A house is about to be founded in this city, for the reception of young girls who have yielded to temptation, and strayed from the paths of virtue. May I hope that you will kindly contribute towards the purchase of the buildings necessary for their reception?" All those present, without a single exception, promised M. Breton a day's pay. One day he chanced to meet M. de Neuville out of doors. "My dear Curé," the latter began, "I hoped that you regarded me as one of your faithful parishioners. Whatever have I done that you should treat me as you do? I hear that you are collecting everywhere in order to obtain the means for opening a house conducted by the Sisters of the Refuge. Why have you left me out in the cold?" "You have quite misunderstood me," returned M. Breton, with a smile. "If I have left you to the last, it is because I am so sure of you, and have kept you for a *bonne bouche*." "That is just as it should be," answered the Comte, "and to prove that your confidence is not misplaced, I will at once promise you 38,000 francs (£1,520). I am all the more pleased to help you, because I know how rejoiced my beloved mother would have been, had she lived to see this day. A foundation such as you purpose making was, as you well know, the object of her earnest desires and prayers." M. de Neuville may be regarded as the founder of the Convent of the Good Shepherd at Angers. At a later period, as he remained unmarried, he sold his estates, and bestowed on the house almost his entire fortune. Until his death he was its devoted friend and firm supporter. His heroic charity was but little known, since his humility made him desire to conceal it from the eyes of the world.

Since he was so closely connected with Mother

St. Euphrasia, and so highly esteemed by her, we cannot close our present chapter without saying a little more about him, even if by so doing we somewhat anticipate the course of our narrative. He was brought up at the Jesuit College of Stonyhurst.[1] He followed his teachers thither when on their expulsion from Belgium, during the time of the Revolution, they were compelled to close their establishment at Liège. This happened in 1794, when Mr. Thomas Weld generously made a gift to the exiles of his mansion and grounds, and Augustine de Neuville was one of the first pupils of the now famous College, which in the present year (1894) is about to celebrate its centenary. He always cherished a great love and respect for the Jesuit Fathers, and used frequently to speak in feeling terms of the kindness they had shown him, and the care they had taken to train his soul in virtue. His library contained all their works, not only in French, but in Greek, Latin, German, Italian, and English. He was a perfect master of all these languages, and wrote and spoke them with fluency and elegance. But English was his special favourite; he used to say that he preferred it to his mother-tongue. He often wrote in their own language to the Nuns of the Good Shepherd in England, and sometimes enclosed short poems of his composition for their amusement.

In spite of his innocence, and the sanctity of his life, he regarded himself as a great sinner, and several times conceived the idea of retiring to La Trappe, in order to do penance. He never allowed any mark of distinction to be shown him in the convent, and was seriously vexed when Mother St. Euphrasia desired to place upon the walls a shield with the armorial bearings

---

[1] At school he was known as Augustine La Potherie, or Lapotherie.

of the family of la Potherie de Neuville, as a mark of her gratitude. In fact, he induced her to abandon her project.

His humility was equalled only by his devotion to our Blessed Lady. Every day, at the hour of midnight, he was accustomed to recite the Office of the Immaculate Conception, having previously meditated upon the lowliness of the Divine Word. Nor, when overtaken by the weakness and weariness of old age, did he abate any of his pious practices. The sweet name of Mary was ever on his lips. He loved to call her his Queen, his Lady, his *Mater Admirabilis.* When the nuns tried to thank him for all his benefits, he would say : " Do not thank me, I entreat you. I do not give to you, but to our Blessed Lady." His purse was ever open to Mother St. Euphrasia, and when she spoke to him of her desire to have at Angers a Convent of Magdalens, similar to the one already existing at Tours, he at once purchased a house close to Tournemine, which happened to be in the market, and placed it at her disposal. It was soon altered and arranged so as to serve its intended purpose, and was opened on the 28th of August, the feast of St. Augustine, the Patron Saint, as the reader may remember, of M. de Neuville.

He died a peaceful and holy death, on the 3rd of December, 1843. Those who were permitted to see his room, with its bare walls, uncarpeted floor, and scant fittings, together with the extremely simple furniture of the small house in which he lived, could not but have imagined that he was a poor man. And such indeed he was, in spite of the lordly Château de la Fresnais at St. Aubin de Luigné, which he had inherited, together with its superb appointments and retinue of well-trained servants. He had, as we have seen, disposed of his patrimony in order to devote himself more entirely to good works, as well as to a life of penance, fasting, and mortification of every kind. The following is the last letter he wrote to Mother St. Euphrasia. It is dated March 12th, 1843:

" Dear Madam,—To-day is the eve of the feast of St. Euphrasia, the track of whose footsteps you have discerned in the desert, and have followed them faithfully. If she had this advantage over you, that it was in her power to offer a vast fortune in sacrifice to her Celestial Spouse, you on the other hand enjoy a privilege which does not appear to have fallen to her lot. For the space of thirty days, she carried from place to place a pile of large stones, whilst you for the last seven years have been occupied in carrying living stones to build up on every side spiritual temples wherein our Lord takes delight. How great must be the affection wherewith your kind patron, who is now the companion of angels, regards you. You are beloved by God and by men; I rely on you to obtain my salvation. And if some day, thanks to the potency of your prayers, I find myself standing upon the holy mount where faith is changed to sight, the respect and gratitude I feel for you will find freer, fuller expression. This being the day on which you dispense your favours with more than your usual liberality, I venture very humbly to beg that you will give the habit to Philomena.

" Your unworthy servant,

" NEUVILLE."

M. de Neuville was not deceived in his confidence that Mother St. Euphrasia would assist him with her prayers after his death. As an acknowledgment of the debt of gratitude she owed him, she had a solemn

Requiem Mass sung, *coram episcopo*, in the church of the convent; while to all the houses under her jurisdiction she sent a circular letter, bidding each community to have Mass said for the soul of their benefactor, and to devote to the same object their Communions on several days, besides reciting the *De profundis* daily during three months. Nor did Mother St. Euphrasia ever cease to hold the pious M. de Neuville in affectionate remembrance. It was as a monument of his memory, and in fulfilment of a wish he had often been heard to express, that she set about enlarging the house, and erecting a Novitiate which in respect of size had no equal in Europe. Whenever she met with a gentleman who manifested a deep interest in her work, she was wont to say: "I really think Providence has sent us a second M. de Neuville!"

CHAPTER VI

FOUNDATION AT ANGERS.

THE little colony which had emigrated from Tours set to work without loss of time, in order to arrange and render their future abode habitable. Mother St. Euphrasia was the life and soul of all that was done. Her first care was to prepare a room which might be used as a chapel, and in which our Lord might come to dwell. She selected the best apartment she could find, caused it to be cleaned and repaired, and placed an altar there. The friends of the new foundation deemed it an honour and a pleasure to supply all that was necessary. Mgr. Montault gave a pair of silver cruets; Mdme. d'Andigné, a monstrance and a censer; M. Breton and M. de Neuville provided everything else that was needful for the sacristy. The first Mass was said on the feast of Corpus Christi, to the great joy of the saintly foundress, who from that day forward began to see, in no very distant future, the realization of her fondest hopes.

But if the chapel was the most important, it was by no means the only thing which claimed her time and attention. The various houses and outbuildings were many of them literally falling to pieces, while the wall which enclosed the entire property was not only cracked in many places, and tottering to its fall, but here and there fissures were seen, and it was entirely

broken down. An amusing proof of this is afforded by
the fact that, some time after the Religious were settled
in their house, two of them discovered in a hay-loft a
drunken man fast asleep among the trusses of hay. He
had entered through a breach in the wall, and had
sought this place of shelter in order to sleep off the
effects of his carouse. During the early days of their
life at Angers, Mother St. Euphrasia and her associates
were extremely poor. Their sole means of lighting the
room in which they sat of an evening was a single
tallow candle, a broken glass serving as a candlestick.
They gained a scanty living by needlework, but sometimes even this resource failed, and Mother St. Euphrasia
was obliged to go to the vegetable garden, and tie up
bunches of carrots, &c., which she sent to be sold in the
market by a young girl she had brought with her from
Tours. Upon the sale of these depended the dinner of
the Community. This young girl was devoted to the
Sisters, and later on became one of the Magdalens.
She was remarkable for her cleverness in doing
embroidery, and it not unseldom happened that the
little colony had to wait until some piece of work which
she had in hand was finished and paid for before they
could even purchase a loaf of bread. But poverty
never daunted the subject of this biography. Unpro-
vided with money she came to Angers, and made her
first foundation, and we shall have occasion to see, in
the sequel, how frequently she sent forth her daughters,
with an empty purse, to found new convents.

Yet in spite of their poverty and hard work, as well
as their simplicity and charity, Mother St. Euphrasia
and her associates had much to suffer from the tongue
of ignorant and groundless calumny. She was herself,
as a matter of course, the principal object of attack.

It was said that she aimed at achieving personal aggrandizement for herself, that her object was to bear a crozier in her hand, and be styled "the Right Reverend the Lady Abbess." It is needless to add how far such vain ambitions were from the mind of the humble and modest servant of God. Her serenity was not ruffled by all this meaningless gossip, but what really distressed her, during the early part of her sojourn at Angers, was the absence of penitents. The delight, therefore, with which the first arrivals were welcomed by her may be better imagined than described. They had, with few exceptions, been formerly employed in a lucifer-match factory in the town, and some of them were very wild spirits indeed. It was all the more difficult to get them into shape, because the nuns, being so poor, could only offer them indifferent fare. But Providence watched over them. One day the present of a mattress was sent to Mother St. Euphrasia by Mdme. de Boylesve, sister of Mdme. d'Andigné. It appeared unusually heavy, and on opening one of the corners, the sum of three hundred francs ($£12$) was discovered, which the donor had placed there in order to help the house, on which, from the very first day, the foundress had bestowed the name of the Convent of the Good Shepherd.

She had been, as we have seen, re-elected Superior of the Sisters of the Refuge at Tours in 1828. Her term of office had not yet expired, hence she was recalled by the Council of the house. Three of the parish priests of Angers, M. Vincent, curé of St. James', being of the number, went to Tours, in order to obtain permission to keep her. But their attempt proved fruitless. M. Fustier, the Vicar-General, and the Council of the Refuge, were equally inexorable, as was also the Refuge at Caen, to which an appeal was made. Hence Mother St. Euphrasia had no choice, but was compelled to quit Angers. Her grief was very great, because God had already shown her how much was to be accomplished in that city for His glory. Yet she was consoled by the conviction that if the path by which He was leading her was a *mirabilis via*, as Holy Church expresses it, it was none the less the path appointed for her.

Before returning to Tours, she established the enclosure. On the 31st of July, 1829, the feast of St. Ignatius, and her own thirty-third birthday, M. Prieur was delegated by the Bishop to bless the new house, in the presence of all its friends. The next morning she set out for Tours, her place at Angers being taken by Mother Mary of St. Paul, who had arrived the day before, accompanied by a *sœur tourière*.

It is not necessary to enlarge upon the delight with which their beloved Superior was welcomed home by the Sisters of the Refuge at Tours. In order to give expression to their feelings, some of them had composed little poems in her honour, which were duly recited, to her no small amusement.

During the thirteen months she was absent from Angers, she never ceased to dwell there in spirit, and to feel an almost irresistible longing to return. " I shall never change my mind," we find her writing to Sister Stanislaus, the Sister Assistant at Angers, " I cannot do so, for I believe it is the will of God that I should not be anywhere except at Angers. Help me, dear Sister, with your prayers, in order that my unworthiness and many sins may not place an obstacle in the way."

Before long it became plain to every intelligent observer that her presence was indispensable, if the Convent at Angers was to realize the expectations of its friends. Scarcely (if we may so speak) had the sound of her carriage-wheels died away in the distance, when the whole face of things became changed, and a sort of dulness and stagnation settled down over the place. The work of reparation stopped at once, the relations between the Religious and the penitents became strained and unsatisfactory, the zeal of even the most generous benefactors suddenly grew cold. M. de Neuville himself held aloof, although he had spoken of undertaking to build a new chapel, when he was under the influence of the courageous foundress. Now, however, his projects were received with coldness, and fears were expressed as to their prudence. In fact, dread of the future paralyzed, as it so often does, exertion in the present. The little Community grew poorer and more destitute. Everything seemed to aggravate their difficulties, the very elements were hostile to them. For the winter of 1829–30 proved to be an exceptionally severe one, hunger and cold tried all poor families, and the inhabitants of the Good Shepherd Convent more particularly. They not unfrequently found themselves destitute of the common necessaries of life.

It was only natural that these trials should intensify the desire which those among the penitents who had known their foundress felt for her reappearance in their midst. She furnished them with a constant subject of conversation ; they told their companions about her, and were never tired of repeating instances of the wonderful way in which she extricated them from difficulties, found some resource in every emergency,

H

and, in short, spread cheerfulness and contentment all around her.

At this juncture, when the very existence of the house seemed imperilled, one of those strange coincidences happened which the children of this world call by the name of chance, but in which the children of God delight to recognize the gracious hand of their loving Father. M. Dufêtre, the Superior of the Refuge at Tours, was appointed to preach the Lent at Angers. As a matter of course, he paid a visit to the Good Shepherd Convent. He delivered an address to the penitents, and saw something of them. Their piety and good dispositions so delighted him, especially when he remembered the hardships they had endured during the winter, that he promised as a reward, to grant any reasonable request they might address to him. One and the same exclamation broke forth from every mouth. " Send our dearest Mother back to us ! " they cried ; " let Mother St. Euphrasia return to Angers." As the result of this visit, M. Dufêtre wrote to Mother St. Euphrasia as follows, on the 3rd of March, 1831 : " The house at Angers stands greatly in need of you. It is capable of a wide development, if only it could have the benefit of your spirit, of your zeal and power of organization."

On the feast of the Ascension in this same year, the second triennium of Mother St. Euphrasia expired. The Sisters of the Refuge at Tours elected Mother Mary of St. Paul to be their Superior, and Mother St. Euphrasia was appointed to rule over the house at Angers. The sceptre thus placed in her hands she was destined to wield as long as life should last, while she was destined also to extend the limits of her kingdom to the very ends of the earth.

Mgr. de Montblanc signed her *Exeat* without any restriction, or any conditions as to the length of her absence from Tours. No sooner was this document placed in her hands, than she prepared to depart. But when the last moments approached, her affectionate heart was deeply pained by the thought of quitting the dear Sisters whom she had known and loved ever since her entrance into the Refuge. She felt that any formal leave-taking would only bring about a distressing scene, which could do no one any good. Therefore she slipped out unperceived by the Religious, and was then driven to the Ursuline Convent, of which, as we have already said, her friend and former teacher, Mlle., now Mother de Lignac, was Superior. But as the evening drew on, and she found herself alone in the cell set apart for her use, her courage failed, and a feeling of deep depression came over her. She had a strong presentiment that she should never revisit the Refuge, and she could not bear the thought of leaving her Sisters without one final farewell. Then occurred one of those direct interpositions of Providence which are so frequently to be met with in the course of her life. Quite unexpectedly some one came to tell her that M. Pasquier, a holy priest who was one of the Canons of Tours, and confessor to Mgr. de Montblanc, wished to see her in the parlour. When she entered the room, he said to her: " Take care that you do not return to the house you have just left. God has made known to me that your present state of mind is a temptation. The very idea of retracing your steps is displeasing to Him ; He has commissioned me to announce to you His will and His designs in regard to your future. Set out for Angers as soon as possible. God intends that a great work should be accomplished there through your instrumentality for the promotion of His glory." These words restored tranquillity to the troubled soul of the listener; imparting to her, moreover, courage and the confidence of success. Early next morning she started for Angers, with two companions. They reached their destination on the 21st of May, 1831. Within the enclosure of the Good Shepherd many a heart was throbbing with impatience. As soon as their carriage was heard to be approaching, the bell, which was the only one the house possessed at that time, was set ringing in their honour. The joy with which the entire Community welcomed back into their midst their beloved Mother St. Euphrasia, can only be compared to the demonstrations of delight which mark the return of a dear and valued parent to his family circle, after a protracted period of absence. She brought with her fresh life, new vigour and activity. Her first visit to the penitents gave her grave cause for anxiety. She discovered a feeling of restlessness and impatience which might have led to serious results. By her prompt action, and the exercise of her powers of persuasion, a better state of things soon prevailed. On the 25th of October in the same year, three of the penitents took the habit of the Magdalens, in order to dedicate themselves to the religious life.

But for a considerable length of time the penitents were a constant call upon the zeal, energy, and patience of Mother St. Euphrasia. Indeed, she did not hesitate to say that they were one of her crosses. The first-comers were, of course, under no small disadvantage, since they had not the traditions of order and submission which those who came later on inherited. They had been accustomed to a life of reckless gaiety and undisciplined self-will. It cannot, therefore, be a cause

sermon preached by Father Gloriot, of the Society of
Jesus. He came to say Mass in their temporary chapel,
and took as the text of the address he subsequently
delivered to them, " And thou, Bethlehem Ephrata, art
a little one among the thousands of Juda : out of thee
shall He come forth unto me that is to be the ruler in
Israel."[1]   Then, animated by a prophetic spirit, he
continued : " Little flock of the Good Shepherd, poor,
despised, and unknown as thou now art, the day will
come when thou shalt be one of the glories of the
Church."

It is scarcely necessary to say that immediately
upon her return to Angers, Mother St. Euphrasia had
renewed the relations with M. de Neuville which had
unfortunately been interrupted during her absence. Her
enemies had never relaxed their efforts to prejudice
him against her, and they had met with a certain
amount of success. She had been represented as rash,
hasty, and possessed of an insatiable desire for novelty.
But these walls of prejudice fell down in a moment
before the charm of her presence and of her sanctity.
M. de Neuville, who was himself versed in the science
of the saints, and had that discernment of spirits
which is the privilege of those souls who abandon
themselves implicitly to Divine guidance, from that
day forward devoted himself, as we have said in a
preceding chapter, to second her projects and further
her designs, so that he merited to be called the founder
of the house. Nor did he content himself with doing
good on a large scale. Once a week he visited the
Community, who gave him the name of *Bon Père*. Every
day, while their poverty lasted, he sent something
towards their dinner. He had a servant named Louis,

[1] Micheas v. 2.

who entered into his master's ideas, and carried them out with marvellous tact and discretion. If, during his daily visit, he chanced to hear that some fresh postulants were expected on the morrow, a suitable supply of beds and bedding was sure to make its appearance. If he was told that some of the Sisters were sick, he brought next day some light and delicate dishes, in the hope of tempting their appetite. Was some special recreation or little festivity to be held? he never forgot to inform M. le Comte, who devised some pleasant surprise for the occasion.

In 1832, Mother St. Euphrasia owed to her generous benefactor the accomplishment of her dearest wish. Through his liberality a new chapel was commenced, to the great joy of the whole Community. M. de Neuville laid the first stone, which was blessed by Mgr. Montault. Mother St. Euphrasia, whose practical sense in regard of the affairs of this life was as remarkable as her higher gifts, was singularly fortunate in her choice of an architect, M. Desnoyers by name. Not only were his talents greatly above the average, as far as his profession was concerned, but he was a good and practical Catholic. He took a deep interest in the work of the Good Shepherd, and when the chapel was finished, he declined to accept the *honorarium* due to the architect. To the great joy of Mother St. Euphrasia, no workman employed met with any accident while the building was in process of construction, everything, on the contrary, went forward happily, swiftly, and well. She wished, in the first instance, that the choir should be constructed so as to contain forty persons at the most. M. de Neuville, however, did not fall in with the idea. "Yours is no ordinary work," he said to her; "it will grow and extend, so that you will have here more than three hundred Religious." These words were literally fulfilled. The choir of the nuns was seventy-six feet long and twenty-eight wide, forming the upper part of the cross in the shape of which the church was built. The right arm was for the Magdalens, the left for the Penitents, while spacious tribunes were appropriated to the different classes of children. In the sanctuary a handsome marble altar was so placed that the officiating priest could be seen by all classes of the Community. On the 11th of April, 1833, the bell of the new chapel was blessed, and on the 14th of the following May, Mgr. Montault, accompanied by a numerous body of the clergy, blessed the building, to which was given the title of the Assumption. The friends of the house vied with one another in the rich gifts they offered on this joyful occasion. M. de Neuville gave a silver monstrance, a splendid missal, and a set of altar-cards beautifully framed. A few months later he added a ciborium and a veil for the Blessed Sacrament. Madame d'Andigné presented handsome candlesticks, a crucifix, a carpet for the sanctuary, and an altar-lamp. Mother Chantal of Jesus contributed two extremely valuable dalmatics. The feelings of Mother St. Euphrasia may be better imagined than described.

From the very beginning of the time when she found herself appointed Superior of the house at Angers, she devoted the utmost care and attention to the Novitiate, for she knew that upon this depended the future of her Community. She desired to have as many subjects as possible, hence she received postulants who had no dowry to offer, if, after carefully testing their vocation, she discerned in them real good-will and an earnest wish to promote the salvation of souls. Above all things she strove to inculcate a spirit of humility and a love of the hidden life. "Our sole ambition," she frequently said to her novices, "is to be known to God alone. Hide yourselves from the eyes of your fellow-creatures, for a Religious who loves to make herself known, deserves nothing but contempt." Noticing on one occasion that a novice, to whom she had seen fit to administer a reproof, showed a certain amount of ill-temper afterwards, she wrote her the following note:

"My dear Sister,—You must be very weak and very imperfect, if you do not know how to receive a reproof which you have really deserved. Your self-love is wounded, and revolts against the correction, while you are foolish enough to listen to the voice of the tempter. O my child, how long will you resist the influence of grace? Meditate in secret, enter into yourself in the presence of God, and all will yet be well with you."

This prediction was soon fulfilled. The novice acknowledged her faults, asked pardon for them, and regained her peace of mind.

Mother St. Euphrasia attached immense importance to religious silence in the Novitiate. She appointed certain penances for those who were found wanting in this respect. Yet no one was ever more careful to prevent this silence and recollection from producing melancholy or depression. It deeply grieved her to see any of her children suffering from gloom and sadness of spirits. She always did her utmost to make the novices merry and cheerful at their recreations, and she invariably succeeded. No one could feel dull where she was. Her vivacious tongue, her inexhaustible store of amusing and edifying anecdotes, brought smiles and animation to every face, while her own countenance beamed with joy on seeing those around her so happy.

The first extension of her work at Angers was the reception of the *Enfants de la Providence.* It came about as follows. An association of charitable ladies had entrusted the care of these children to a person who had devoted herself to them with praiseworthy attention for sixteen years. She was no longer capable of prosecuting her work, and the President of the association requested Mother St. Euphrasia to take the poor children under her wing, £12 10s. being the sum to be paid annually for each of them. The proposal was willingly acceded to, and on the 10th of June, 1832, the first children, twenty in number, were received within the walls of the Good Shepherd. Thanks to the unflagging zeal of the foundress, rooms had been prepared for them, quite apart from the portion of the house appropriated to the penitents, and apart also from that used by the nuns. The very day after their installation, the Bishop paid a visit to Mother St. Euphrasia, for the express purpose of telling her how much pleasure it gave him to know that these children were placed under her charge.

In the course of the next year (1833) she established, with the full approval of M. Montalant, Vicar-General, and also Superior of the house, a third class of " Preservation children," as they are called. They were the lambs of her flock, consisting of young children, innocent as yet of evil, but whom the wretched and degraded atmosphere of their poverty-stricken homes exposed to an early initiation into every kind of vice and immorality. For them also a separate abode was provided, in which they dwelt under the watchful care of some of the Sisters, who made them their especial charge. Even the parlour, where they were allowed at stated times to see their relatives, was distinct from the other parlours. It was in this isolation of the various classes, that Mother St. Euphrasia gave such unmistakable proof of her talent for organization.

Yet many trials, crosses, and vexations, of a more or less serious kind, constantly happened to temper the joy with which the consolidation and development of the Angers foundation inspired her. One day we find her writing as follows: " Everything seems to go wrong just now. I never have a quiet moment, while every hour brings me some unwelcome piece of news. I hear that the building has come to a standstill, or that the cost of some portion of it will be enormous. Every post brings me a disagreeable letter, frictions occur with regard to the doctor or the confessor. Then, again, temptations are rife among the penitents, one of whom ran away and had to be brought back. As to the poor, imperfect Superior, she has a slight attack of fever, and is, moreover, suffering from a disgust of her vocation. O my God, how dark and thick are the clouds which have gathered over this house! "

Those only who have borne the heavy burden which the government and management of such a house must necessarily entail upon its head, can fully understand how difficult and trying, nay more, how exceedingly painful is such a post, more particularly in certain crises of its existence. To stand beside the sick-bed, or even the death-bed, of the inmates of the house, without being able to assuage their sufferings, or retain even the best-beloved and most useful a little longer upon earth; to listen to the complaints of the discontented and dry the tears of the depressed; to struggle with material difficulties of every kind, more especially want of money, difficulties which appear as if they formed a rampart of brass, which no effort of will could over-throw. And besides all this, to be strong and courageous when every one around is weak and mistrustful, is the task of every Superior. Such was the task of Mother St. Euphrasia, and she was always found equal to the occasion. Although she was naturally extremely sensitive, so that, in the outset of her career, annoy-ances and contradictions had a great effect upon her, she so completely conquered herself that, as far at least as her exterior bearing was concerned, they produced upon her no possible impression. Interior serenity and secret joy became the invariable expres-sion of her countenance, even in the midst of the gravest preoccupations and most severe trials. What is still more surprising, her habitual cheerfulness of manner never deserted her, and the more she suffered, the brighter and more charming did she seem at recreation. Indeed, those among her daughters who were privileged to know her intimately, used sometimes to say among themselves, when she had displayed greater animation than usual: "Our Mother has some serious anxiety weighing upon her, or has had some very bad news!"

CHAPTER VII.

WE have seen how, under the blessing of God, the work of the Good Shepherd grew and was developed by the zeal and energy of Mother St. Euphrasia. We have seen how the difficulties which beset the foundation at Angers, far from daunting her resolution, inspired her with fresh courage, stimulated her to more and greater exertion. We have seen how valiantly she encountered the obstacles in her path, and how successfully she surmounted them. The many and severe trials connected with that foundation served to detach her from creatures, and to bring her nearer to God, the only source of strength and consolation. There is no fuel, St. Ignatius says, which makes the fire of the love of God burn more brightly than the wood of the Cross. We shall now see how Mother St. Euphrasia was being prepared for a work far more important than the government of a single house, the care of a single flock ; how the experiences she passed through at Angers served to strengthen her in the virtues necessary for the accomplishment of the enterprise she was destined to carry out.

"The foundation at Angers," she writes to a fellow-Religious, "has been watered with my tears. But faith teaches us that the more we suffer, the more God is glorified, and this thought will avail to soothe the keenest sorrow. You wish, my dear Sister, that in writing to you I should let my heart speak; but silence is the language best befitting a heart so poor and so suffering as mine. However, since you too desire to find solace on Calvary, let it be the subject of our conversation. The trials that come upon you ought to bring you near to God, and to Him alone. The knowledge of this is very necessary, but it cannot be acquired by meditation; the Cross is indispensable to render us acquainted with it. What is man, and what is his favour? What are human consolations? What are human delights? Have they any permanence? When the soul has learnt by experience the true answer to these questions, her one great desire will be to detach herself from all that is not God; to separate herself from creatures, from whom too often she only meets with censure, neglect, and even treachery. In this, again, we see the infinite mercy of God, Who is so jealous of our affections, that in order to draw our hearts to Himself, He will make use of means the most painful to nature."

Hitherto each of the Houses of Refuge had been entirely independent of the others, and the sphere of action of each had been confined to the limits of the town in which it was situated. This state of things did not satisfy the all-embracing charity of Mother St. Euphrasia; her apostolic zeal longed for a wider range, a more extended field of exertion. She desired to spread the work of the Good Shepherd to all the ends of the earth, to carry the beneficent influence of her Order wherever there were lost and scattered sheep to be sought for, to be delivered from the beasts of prey in watch for their destruction. The idea of establishing a Generalate, with the sanction of the Holy See, suggested itself to her as the best, the only means of accomplishing this design. The more she thought over it, the more certain she felt that it was inspired by God, that it was His will, and that He had chosen her to be instrumental in fulfilling it. Times without number, when she was kneeling in the chapel before the Blessed Sacrament, or in the hours of meditation, it was given her to see what great results might be obtained for the glory of God and the good of souls by the extension of the Order in the manner she proposed. Her project was the formation of a Mother House, with a large Novitiate, which would be the centre of life and authority, whence offshoots could be planted in other lands, branch communities founded, all remaining under the jurisdiction of a Superior General. She felt convinced that if she succeeded in the realization of this project, many important advantages would accrue to the Order. The life of a Religious Community, she was wont to say, does not consist in what goes on in one particular house, but in all the houses which form a whole, and which ought to resemble the members of a body animated by one and the self-same spirit; or the branches of a tree springing from a single trunk, and nourished by the same vivifying sap. The edifying example of one house where great fervour prevails, is a stimulus to others to attain a like degree of perfection; each vies with the other in the endeavour to observe the Rule as exactly as possible, to realize to the utmost the ideal proposed in their Constitutions. On the other hand, if in one Community discipline is relaxed and tepidity creeps in, the visit of the Mother General will serve to revive the flagging ardour, to rekindle the charity that has grown cold. If one house succeeds, all the others share in the joy of a success which is also their own; and the blows of adversity are less keenly felt by those who are not called upon to suffer alone.   Misfortunes which might overwhelm a Community standing by itself, are but a slight shock to the strength of the whole body; and the sorrow of the afflicted members will be soothed by the ready assistance and sympathy of their brethren in Religion.

But it is principally in the interchange and distribution of subjects that the benefit of the Generalate is felt. A Superior who has a number of houses under her command, can dispose of her subjects in accordance with their different abilities, their different tastes and attractions. One will be found who aspires to a missionary life; if she possesses the qualifications for it, her Superior will allow her to follow her bent. The character of another leads her to desire a life of retirement and seclusion; a post will be assigned to her out of sight of the world. Moreover, the range of choice will be far less circumscribed, when the Superior has occasion to select individuals to be placed at the head of the various houses.

Each day that went by strengthened Mother St. Euphrasia's determination to establish a Generalate in her Order. At length she took into her counsels a priest in whose judgment she had confidence, and confided her design to him. He approved of it most heartily, and promised to mention it to Mgr. Montault, the Bishop of the diocese. This holy prelate, whose immense zeal for the glory of God was only equalled by the prudence that guided all his actions, witnessing the rapid growth of the Good Shepherd, and the marvellous manner in which generous benefactors were raised up on all sides for its support, expressed his opinion that the appointment of a Mother General would be of great benefit to the Order, and that it was already sufficiently developed to bear the extension which the change would involve. He announced his intention of writing to Rome on the subject.

Meanwhile, Mother St. Euphrasia, who always loved to make her Sisters one with herself, and keep back no secrets from them, told the Community over which she presided of the project she had been led to form, and whereby alone her thirst for the salvation of souls could be satisfied. All the nuns entered thoroughly into her feelings, and were quite enthusiastic in their approval and their delight. Nothing else was talked of at recreation; the newly professed Sisters and the young novices drew their seats as close as they could to that of their Superior, and eager voices joined in discussing the possible extension of the Order to all imaginable parts of the world. With the happy hopefulness of youth, which can see no difficulties in the future, they already pictured to themselves flourishing communities on the distant shores of America, or beneath the burning skies of India. Little did the older Sisters, who sat by listening to their merry chatter, dream how soon these sanguine anticipations were to be fulfilled.

Encouraged by the reception her project met with when she announced it to the Community, Mother St. Euphrasia invited them to unite their prayers to hers that she might obtain light and guidance from on high. With the consent of the Sisters, she appointed the *Inviolata*[1] to be chanted daily during two years, in order (1) that it might be made known to her whether the idea of the Generalate truly came from God; (2) that they might get good subjects who would be of real

[1] This antiphon will be found at the end of the present chapter.

I

service to the house. For the same intentions the Sisters also promised to go to Holy Communion on fifteen consecutive Saturdays, and some of them asked permission to practise some corporal austerities to assist the same object.

For the furtherance of this great scheme, Mgr. Montault, whilst awaiting the approbation of the Holy See, authorized the Good Shepherd to make any fresh foundations that might be asked for, and added to the Constitutions of the Order the following clauses, which he thought the increase of the Community rendered necessary:

1. As union is strength, in order to labour more fervently and more successfully for the glory of God, all the houses that are founded from the house at Angers, will always preserve union with it, and will render one another mutual assistance.

2. The novices will be trained in this house, in order to acquire the spirit of the Order.

3. If any Religious who has been sent to another foundation wishes to return to the Mother House, she will be free to do so, provided her wish arises from a reasonable cause.

The Bishop of Angers was the only direct Superior of the Institute, and Mother St. Euphrasia felt that she had every reason to be thankful to Almighty God for having given her, in the person of Mgr. Montault, a wise and kind friend, to whom she could look for counsel and support when she had to make foundations in other dioceses. Nor was it long before the house of Angers was called upon to send out colonies. The first appeal came from the Bishop of Mans, who wrote to request that a foundation of the Good Shepherd might be made in that town. The journey from Angers to

Mans is a long one, and, as the reader is aware, the facilities for travelling were, sixty years ago, very different from what they are at present. The time of year, too, was most unfavourable, for it was still the depth of the winter. But no distance was too great, no enterprise too arduous for the courageous Superior, where the welfare of her Order was concerned. On February 9, 1833, she set out for Mans, accompanied by the chaplain of the convent, with the purpose of inspecting the house which was offered to her and arranging matters with the Bishop. Everything appeared to augur well for the success of the new foundation, and towards the end of April Mother St. Euphrasia once more journeyed thither, in order to instal the Superior and the Religious who accompanied her.

It must not be imagined that the proposal for the several convents to remain united with the Mother House, under the government of one Superior, instead of their being separate, was everywhere well received. When it became known in other houses of the Order, it encountered great opposition. The projected change was stigmatized as an unwarrantable innovation, an uncalled for departure from the primitive Constitutions of the Institute. Motives of ambition and vanity were imputed to Mother St. Euphrasia ; and the Superior of the house at Tours addressed to her a letter of respectful but firm expostulation and protest. She thought herself justified in doing this, because a somewhat similar attempt at combination had been made in 1807, when the Paris house was to have been constituted the central house of the Order. That attempt had proved a failure, and it was feared that the present one would be equally unsuccessful, and only bring discredit on the house at Angers. The resistance she met with from her Sisters in Religion, the outcry that was raised, was a painful surprise to Mother St. Euphrasia, and caused her poignant sorrow. Even in the Community under her own immediate control, a note of discord made itself heard. Of the six Sisters who had come from Tours, three disapproved so strongly of the change that they returned to the convent whence they had come. The defection of these Sisters was a wound to Mother St. Euphrasia's heart which the fidelity of the others could not avail to heal.

The return of the Sisters to Tours strengthened the Superior there in her determination to resist the establishment of the Generalate. In junction with one or two other houses, she appealed to the Archbishop, and he, who had never viewed the house at Angers with much favour, fully coincided with her. In order to arrest at the fountain-head the evils which he predicted would ensue from the attempt to effect a change in the administration of the Order, he announced his intention of recalling Mother St. Euphrasia to Tours. It will readily be imagined that the Community at Angers were thunderstruck at these tidings. Their consternation and alarm were however allayed by the production of the letter of obedience (*Exeat*) given by the Archbishop to Mother St. Euphrasia on her departure from Tours, transferring her unconditionally and with no limitation of time from his archiepiscopal jurisdiction to that of the Bishop of Angers, to whose authority they were now exclusively subject. Mgr. de Montblanc, however, saw things in another light: about the middle of July he arrived at Angers, to demand *in propriâ personâ* the return of the Religious who had formerly been under his sway. Accompanied by the Bishop of the diocese, he proceeded to the convent, where several of the clergy were assembled, and he was received with every mark of the respect due to his rank. He at once stated the object of his visit, and requested a private interview with the Superior. Mother St. Euphrasia, however, declined to see him except in the presence of the Bishop and of the Chapter of the Community. Unable to conceal his annoyance, the Archbishop spoke most severely to Mother St. Euphrasia, repeating to her all the charges that the tongue of calumny had brought against her. She listened in silence, without uttering a word. Then, asking permission to speak, she briefly and simply stated the facts that justified her conduct, refuting every one of the accusations brought against her. The Archbishop again expressed his wish to confer with her alone. " Monseigneur," she replied, casting herself at his feet, " I am ready to listen with humble submission to everything your Grace may think fit to say to me. But, with your permission, my Bishop must be present; if I have done anything blame-worthy, I should wish him to know of it." Touched by the affection and trust these words displayed, Mgr. Montault spoke out in defence of her who had always been to him an obedient and devoted daughter; he also reminded his metropolitan of the *Exeat* which he had himself given to her, and which was carefully pre-served in the archives of his palace. The Archbishop, unable otherwise to escape the difficulty, adopted the expedient of saying that he remembered nothing about the document, and that it had been given without his consent. He continued to insist on the return of the Religious to Tours, alleging that his suffragan had exceeded the powers conceded to him for the disposal of his subjects. To put an end to this painful discussion, Mgr. Montault, on his knees, humbly asked the Archbishop's forgiveness for any offence he might unintentionally have committed. This generous apology fully appeased the irritated prelate, the cloud passed from his brow; he voluntarily renounced any and every right to the religious obedience of Mother St. Euphrasia and the other nuns who came from Tours, and thus the threatened storm passed over.

Firmly convinced as the subject of this memoir was of the purity of her intention, that it was not her own aggrandizement she was seeking, but the good of souls; and that her desire to see the Good Shepherd combined into one united Congregation arose from the belief that thereby a more vigorous life and greater stability would be infused into it, she yet wished to satisfy herself thoroughly that the idea of the Generalate was inspired by God. She mistrusted her own judgment, fearing to be misled by those fantastic dreams which occasionally trouble the imagination even of Christians who are sincerely desirous of doing right. To remove all doubt, she consulted men of prudence and enlightenment; above all, she earnestly entreated our Lord to make His will plainly manifest. With holy boldness, she ventured to ask a sign, saying that if it pleased Him to send her a large increase of good and useful subjects, she should take it as an indication that He approved her design. The answer to this petition was not long delayed. Vocations were multiplied; postulants, admirably suited for the work, presented themselves in the most unexpected manner, many of them being led to the Order by circumstances so singular as to appear little short of miraculous. Moreover, about this time tidings came from Rome that the project was favourably regarded by the Holy

Father, and was to be laid before the next meeting of
Cardinals.

Thus encouraged, Mgr. Montault, who watched with
paternal care over the interests of the Good Shepherd,
and was most desirous for the Generalate, knowing
how slowly Rome moves, and that a considerable time
would elapse before the formal decision was known,
gave his sanction to the additions to the Constitutions
which had been provisionally drawn up, the principal
points of which have already been mentioned. Besides
these, there were several fresh regulations concerning
the Council of the Congregation, and the election of the
Superior, which was to be for a period of six years.
These new rules were accepted and subscribed by all
the Professed Sisters in the houses of Angers and of
Mans.

Shortly after the publication of this new Constitution, Mother St. Euphrasia was invited to extend
the sphere of her activity in three different directions.
The first proposal for the foundation of a house as an
offshoot of Angers came from Poitiers. It was promptly
responded to; the conditions offered by the Bishop
were accepted, and in November, 1833, the Sisters
chosen for the work were sent to make selection of a
suitable house. This proved no easy task. The nuns
were kindly received and entertained by the Sisters of
the Sacred Heart; they remained with them three
weeks, but were quite unable to fix upon a domicile.
At the end of that time, Mother St. Euphrasia, who
expressed herself in the most grateful terms for the
hospitality extended to her daughters, would allow
them to avail themselves of it no longer. Still less
would she allow them, as was suggested in a moment
of discouragement, to return to Angers. She bade

them at once take up their abode in the building placed at their disposal by the Bishop, small though it was, and ill-adapted for their requirements; she entreated them not to shrink from the Cross, and sought to inspire them with a courage as indomitable as her own. " I should indeed be grieved," she wrote to them, " if the work at Poitiers was given up. Believe me, dear and much esteemed Sisters, we consider your sorrows are our own. How much I regret that you did not go straight to the house the Bishop offered you. The great secret of a foundation, St. Teresa says, is to take possession first of all. We will do all we can for you ; our prayers, our Communions, shall be offered for your success. Begin at once; do not abandon the work of God."

Six months later, when Mother St. Euphrasia visited Poitiers, she found a well-organized and flourishing Community established there. The nuns stood well with the clergy, and were so much esteemed by the inhabitants of the town, that their principal benefactors had formed themselves into an association, to watch over the interests of the convent, and help it in case of need. They had moreover a good friend in the Bishop, an old man whose stately appearance and gentle courtesy of manner inspired universal respect. A member of the ancient aristocracy of France, he was chaplain to Queen Marie Antoinette before the Revolution, and to the Duchess d'Angoulême subsequently to 1815. When the foundress of the Good Shepherd made his acquaintance, he had already ruled the diocese for fifteen years, and had effected a complete revival of religion and of ecclesiastical discipline. She was much struck with his dignified bearing, the distinction of his manner towards all who approached

him, from the highest to the lowest. Moreover, she
recognized in him a prelate of eminent sanctity and
virtue, to whose care she gladly confided her spiritual
children. "Poitiers," she wrote, "is a source of
abundant consolations to me. No one could have
acted more wisely than the Superior; every one loves
her. She proclaims the Generalate; but she does so
with such tact and judgment that, far from offending,
she wins all hearts. Our Institute owes her a great
deal." The Superior who had earned so high an
enconium was one of those who had accompanied
Mother St. Euphrasia from Tours, Mother Stanislaus
Bedouet, her friend and fellow-worker, for several years
Assistant at Angers.

If the Good Shepherd at Poitiers was commenced
in trials and poverty, much more so the next one
which was founded at Grenoble. Of this it may
truly be said, that it was planted in the shadow of the
Cross. For some time past there had been a Refuge
in the town for the reception of penitents; but of late
years it had been almost given up, on account of the
lack of funds for its maintenance. The Bishop, desirous
to restore it to a state of efficiency, wrote to the
Superior at Angers, begging her to send a few Religious
qualified to manage the house. This request could not
be otherwise than welcome to one whose heart glowed
with ardour for souls. She could not, besides, fail
to remark the similarity of the circumstances which
prompted the appeal, with those that occasioned the
establishment of her own beloved house at Angers,
whereon so abundant a blessing had rested. Accordingly, with ready compliance, five Sisters were
appointed for the work; they were still to remain
subject to the same Superior, in spite of the distance

to which they were about to be moved. Till then, the little colonies sent out from Angers had been settled on what may be called the outskirts of the diocese; but now they were to carry on their apostolate in a more remote locality. The separation was therefore keenly felt on both sides, although the travellers little knew the hardships that awaited them at the end of their journey. They reached their destination on the 23rd of December; until the day after Christmas they remained with the Ursulines, who opened to them the doors of their convent, that they might recover from their fatigue before installing themselves in their future habitation.

The history of this foundation was at the outset an unbroken series of sufferings and humiliations. The house given by the Bishop was all but empty; it contained neither beds, blankets, nor wood to make a fire. The Sisters were completely destitute of the necessaries of life; they had to work till midnight in order to procure bread to eat; more than once they did not break their fast for twenty-four hours. This state of starvation lasted for six months. It may be imagined how the sad tale of their woes afflicted the loving heart of their Mother. She was most anxious that the foundation should succeed, as it would give the Order a footing in the south of France, into which it had not yet penetrated. On this account she was doubly grieved to hear of the difficulties encountered by the Sisters. Each post brought a more distressing account of their struggles and privations. At last Mother St. Euphrasia felt she could expose them to such a state of things no longer. Sorely as it went against her to do so, she would have recalled them but for the determined opposition of Mgr. Montault. "The tempest will pass over," he assured her, "and it will be followed by a great calm." She therefore waited in hope and prayer, only sending from time to time such sums as she could economize from the daily expenditure, for the relief of her necessitous children. She knew how true an interest the Bishop took in all the sorrows and joys of the Community, for on many occasions he had proved this by little acts of thoughtful kindness; for instance, he had come to the convent to bid the Sisters God-speed on their departure for Grenoble, and soften by a few words of cheering encouragement the pain that he was aware the separation would cost them.

His prediction was erelong fulfilled; the patience of the Sisters, the prayers of their fellow-Religious, obtained its reward. Alms began to flow into the coffers of the house at Grenoble; plenty and prosperity took the place of poverty and want; the work was established on a firm basis, with the full approval and co-operation of the Bishop of the diocese. But although they had fought a good fight, the Sisters at Grenoble were not yet to be crowned with peace and tranquillity. A year after their arrival in the city, they had to pass through a worse trial than that of poverty. Some individuals who preferred the Refuge as it formerly existed, contrived to prejudice the mind of influential persons against the new Institute. They prevailed so far with the Bishop, Mgr. de Bruillard, as completely to change the opinion he entertained of it, and to induce him to give orders to his Vicar-General to write and tell Mother St. Euphrasia that her subjects would shortly be sent back to her. The letter was placed in her hands before Matins on Christmas Eve. Deeply distressed by the tidings, she wrote immediately to expostulate with Mgr. de Bruillard. During the

Midnight Mass she laid her sorrows before the Infant Jesus, beseeching Him to protect the foundation at Grenoble. She learnt later on that during the same night, just as the Bishop was finishing his Mass, a secret inspiration urged him to destroy the letters of dismissal which were drawn up ready for his signature. Thus the Sisters were allowed to remain at Grenoble. From that day forth the growth and development of their work was so astonishingly rapid, that before many months had elapsed the house they occupied proved far too small for the numbers who sought admission, and they were compelled to remove to one of larger dimensions.

The following is the antiphon referred to on p. 113:

Inviolata, integra et casta es Maria,
Quæ es effecta fulgida cœli porta,
O Mater alma Christi carissima!
Suscipe pia laudum præconia
Nostra, ut pura pectora sint et corpora,
Te nunc flagitant devota corda et ora.
Tua per precata dulcisona,
Nobis concedas veniam per sæcula.
O benigna, O Regina, O Maria,
Quæ sola inviolata permansisti.

[*Translation.*]

Spotless and pure, Mary Immaculate,
Now high exalted, Heaven's shining gate,
Christ's own beloved Mother, deign to take
Our hymnal praise for thy dear Son's sweet sake.
See, loving tongues and hearts entreat that we
In mind and body may be chaste like thee.
O gracious Queen, preserved alone from sin,
By thy sweet prayers forgiveness for us win.

CHAPTER VIII

ESTABLISHMENT OF THE GENERALATE.

THE period of Mother St. Euphrasia's Superiorate terminated at Pentecost, 1834. She was immediately re-elected, in accordance with the new Constitutions, for a term of six years by the unanimous votes of the four houses of Angers, Mans, Grenoble, and Poitiers. Placed thus once more at the head of the Order, the energetic foundress received her re-election as a definite sign that it was God's will that she should promote with redoubled ardour the scheme she had so much at heart. She met with warm encouragement from Mgr. Montault, whose determination rose in proportion to the difficulties that presented themselves. The Bishops in whose dioceses the new foundations had been made, also appeared to favour the project.

The time of trial and conflict was however soon to come, as it must come to every good work which is to achieve a lasting success. It pleased God to make known to His servant that the design of the Generalate was in accordance with His holy will, and enlighten her supernaturally as to the future of the Institute. At the same time it was revealed to her that before her desire could be accomplished, a period of contra-diction and suffering must be passed through. One day when, after receiving Holy Communion, she entreated our Divine Lord to fulfil His gracious promise, and expedite the progress of affairs, she distinctly heard an interior voice which said to her: "Wait; be silent and prayerful; suffer and hope." From that moment she never wavered in her firm conviction of the ultimate success of her endeavours, or doubted that Providence would give her the means of accomplishing an enterprise which He had declared to be in conformity with His good pleasure.

We have seen what a storm of opposition was aroused in the older Refuges on the first suggestion of the Generalate, this modification of the form of government being considered wholly incompatible with the designs of the founder, the Ven. Father Eudes. The storm now burst out afresh, in a quarter whence it was least expected. M. Moreau, the Superior of the house at Mans, at first an enthusiastic advocate of the Generalate, suddenly changed sides, on discovering that there was no thought of fixing it, as he desired, at Mans, in which case he would have been given authority over the whole Order. He not only en-couraged the Refuges of Tours and Caen in their opposition, but brought strong pressure to bear upon the Religious under his jurisdiction in order to gain them over to take part against their foundress. Further-more, he employed his influence with the Bishop of Mans, Mgr. Bouvier, who, seeing no objection to the erection of the Generalate, had been content to await the decision of the Holy See upon the matter. Unable to resist M. Moreau's persuasions, in the month of June, the prelate went in person to Angers, and asking to see each of the ten novices who had gone thither from his diocese separately, he strongly urged them to return to Mans. Not one of them could be prevailed upon to do so. On taking leave of Mother St. Euphrasia, the Bishop was compelled to admit that his mission had been fruitless. " But," he added, " this will not prevent our breaking off with you." " I can assure your lordship that our esteem for you will thereby in no wise be diminished," was the foundress's courteous rejoinder.

Not many months later the severance took place. It was a terrible blow for Mother St. Euphrasia. Fondly as she cherished all her foundations, anxiously as she watched over each individually, Mans was dearer to her than any other. It was the first offshoot from the parent stem, one which she had planted with her own hand, tended with loving care and attention. Human affection, we are told, is the fuel of human suffering; and the greater the love, the greater the sorrow in which it eventuates. The servant of God had now to experience the truth of these words; this was the first wound her maternal heart had sustained, and she felt it acutely. Not only was her first-born, her favourite child, torn from her arms, but she feared besides that the defection of this her eldest daughter, coming as it did at a critical juncture, might lead to other secessions, and thus the cause of the Generalate might be seriously imperilled. Keenly as she suffered, not a word of expostulation or recrimination passed her lips; she acted throughout in the most conciliatory spirit. Mgr. Montault did the same, leaving the nuns full liberty to remain at Mans or return to Angers, as they judged right. Five of the number, who would not give up their connection with the Mother House, decided to return thither; the remainder, amongst whom was the Superior, gave way to the unremitting and urgent persuasions of M. Moreau, who never rested until he had gained his point. The Bishop afterwards much regretted the rupture, as he frankly acknowledged, when, in the early part of the following year, he again paid a visit to the Mother House; it was then, however, too late to draw back.

The loss of Mans was not the only, though it was perhaps the severest trial that Mother St. Euphrasia had to pass through at this period. Her opponents at Tours did not remain inactive. The older Refuges formed a league, offensive and defensive, among themselves; and by their representations the Archbishop was stirred up to take measures against the new system of government. He wrote to Mgr. Montault, urging him to exert his authority to put down what he was pleased to designate as " the unfortunate schism," to call his Religious to order, and re-establish the unity and charity which ought never to have been disturbed. And upon Mgr. Montault replying that no departure had been made from the Rule drawn up by Father Eudes, and that his subjects by its modification desired greater, not less, union to exist between the different houses of the Order, the Archbishop announced that he had already written to Rome to protest against the innovations introduced by the new Constitutions, and to entreat the Holy Father himself to take in hand the cause of the Refuges. In this appeal he was supported by no less than twelve prelates, in whose dioceses Refuges existed, and whose opinions coincided with his own.

At the outset Mother St. Euphrasia's sensitive nature rendered her keenly alive to the contradictions and calumnies of men. After a time she learnt to rise superior to them, and though they caused her poignant anguish, they failed to disturb her interior serenity. " My daughter," she wrote one day to Mother St.

Stanislaus, "I know full well how many pens are employed to my disadvantage, but this, I own, does not trouble me. Oh, how infinitely rather I would be the accused than the accuser! Without, it is true, Hell seems to be let loose against me; but within, peace, like a river, inundates my soul." And yet the devil, seeing how much good her work was effecting and would effect, often assaulted her terribly. Sometimes he sought to terrify her by strange noises in her cell. To defend herself against these she had recourse to holy water and to prayer. One evening when she was more than ordinarily tormented, she sent for one of the Magdalens, and asked her to pray with her for an hour. The unearthly tumult soon broke out afresh; struck with horror at the sounds, her companion exclaimed: "Reverend Mother, this is the doing of the Evil One; he is enraged on account of all you have done to save souls, and rescue them from eternal damnation."

But as Mother St. Euphrasia remarked, the disturbances were all external. Not only did she possess her own soul in peace, but the interior of the convent over which she ruled afforded her abundant consolation. It had been greatly embellished and enlarged by the liberality of their generous benefactors, Mdme. d'Andigné and M. de Neuville, who seemed as if they could not do enough to render the house beautiful and complete in every way. An atmosphere of repose and quiet pervaded the monastery. No one, witnessing the unanimity and concord that prevailed among the nuns, the exemplary and edifying behaviour of the Magdalens, .and the excellent dispositions of the Penitents, which surpassed all that their venerated foundress had dared to hope, would have suspected the force of the adverse

J

blasts which shook to its foundations and threatened to overthrow the fabric she had reared with so much care. The blessing of God rested also upon the house at Poitiers, it was flourishing beyond all expectations; while Grenoble had entered upon a new phase of existence, days of plenty and prosperity having succeeded to the first sad period of destitution and friendlessness.

For some time past, Mother St. Euphrasia had felt strongly moved to apply to the Holy See for the official recognition of the Generalate. "One day," she tells one of her daughters, "during Vespers, at the *Magnificat*, the impulse to do so became so irresistible that I could not repress my emotion. I begged one of the Sisters to take my place, for tears choked my utterance; leaving the choir, I took refuge in my cell, and there, with a trembling hand, I began to write to the Cardinal Vicar at Rome, beginning with the words: 'Behold the handmaid of the Lord; be it done unto me according to thy word.' I felt such alarm at the step I was taking, that, hardly knowing what terms to use to express my submission, I ended thus: 'I prostrate myself in the dust at your feet (I wrote upon my knees) and I desire only the greater glory of God. If the Sovereign Pontiff and your Eminence see obstacles to the appointment of a General Superior, I submit most humbly to your decision.'" Not knowing to whom to address her petition, she asked a priest who came to the convent to instruct the novices, which of the Cardinals was nearest to the person of His Holiness. He mentioned to her the name of Cardinal Odescalchi, who had lately been given the post of Vicar-General to the Sovereign Pontiff. In this he was guided by the special providence of God, Who deigned, not long afterwards, to encourage His servant by a vision, which dispelled the doubts she entertained as to the prudence of the step she had taken. "A short time after I had written to the Cardinal," we again quote her words, "a very extraordinary thing happened to me. One night, when I had fallen into a calmer sleep than I usually enjoyed, I seemed to see a prelate who was unknown to me. He was dressed in the robes of a Cardinal; his countenance bore the stamp of gentleness and sanctity; his whole appearance inspired me with respect. He said to me: 'Fear not, my daughter, your work will be approved. I am chosen by God to be its protector.' After uttering these words he disappeared, leaving me filled with comfort and consolation. My astonishment was indeed great," she continues, "some years later, on my first visit to Rome, when I recognized in his Eminence Cardinal Odescalchi, the very prelate who had appeared to me. I related my dream to him; he appeared much struck by it, and said: 'This is a very remarkable thing, let me tell you what happened to me also about the matter. For some time I had been anxiously looking for a Congregation of Religious who devoted themselves to the work of raising fallen women. I had not met with any who took the charge of young girls, and I constantly asked God to vouchsafe to grant my prayer. One day, whilst I was celebrating Mass in St. Peter's, I earnestly entreated that through our Blessed Lady's intercession I might discover the Order of which I was in quest. On that very day your letter reached me.'"

Under circumstances such as these there is no wonder that Mother St. Euphrasia found an advocate and protector in Cardinal Odescalchi.

We must now return to Angers, where, on the feast

of the Assumption, the convent gates were again opened to give egress to a little band of Religious. A little band indeed, for they were only three; but if their number was small, their courage was great; they had sat at the feet of their beloved Mother, and learnt of her the faith and courage that is born of supernatural charity. The mission of the three Sisters was to found a fresh house; their destination was Metz, within the fortified walls of which, on the sunny banks of the smiling Moselle, they were to tend the wandering sheep of the Good Shepherd. On the occasion of her visit to Poitiers, not long after the foundation had been made there, Mother St. Euphrasia became acquainted with a young Jesuit, Father Barthès, who happened to be giving a retreat in the Convent of the Sacred Heart. He entered very fully into her projects and encouraged her to prosecute them. On her return to Angers, she asked for him to give a retreat to the Community; he went there, and was much pleased and edified by all that he saw. The unruffled cheerfulness which Mother St. Euphrasia displayed under the trials that were then thickening around her, impressed him most favourably in respect of the Institute. He felt convinced that the Good Shepherd was destined to exercise an influence as widespread as it was salutary; and when, shortly after, he was removed to Metz, he gave so glowing an account to the Bishop of the work going on at Angers, that the good prelate, who was most solicitous for the welfare of the flock committed to his charge, desired much to see a similar institution in his own episcopal city. The request which he made to this effect was promptly responded to; although there were at that time eighty nuns in the Community at Angers, yet, so extensive was the work, and so many the different classes it comprised, that only three Sisters of capacity and experience could be spared to go elsewhere.[1]

The journey to Metz was a long one; the Sisters were four days in accomplishing it. On their arrival they were received in the Convent of the Sacred Heart, while the Vicar-General, M. l'Abbé Chalandon, busied himself in finding several charitable ladies who would interest themselves in the new foundation and take the new-comers under their protection. A house was provided for them, one of the rooms being fitted up as a chapel, and a priest who acted as tutor in a gentleman's family undertook to say Mass for them daily, until a regular chaplain could be appointed. A preservation class, consisting of fifteen young girls, was already formed, and a work-room opened under the good ladies' auspices.

Although the Sisters met with so kind a reception at Metz, and everything appeared to promise well for the work they were sent to inaugurate, the bright picture was not without its shadows. The committee of ladies were inclined to be dictatorial and lay down the law as to what the Religious were to do and leave undone. The Sister Superior felt that this interference would hamper her sadly in observing the Rules and carrying out the designs of the Institute, and in preserving the uniformity which it was the desire of their foundress to establish in all the Communities under her rule. She was much vexed to find that it was the charge of orphans, not penitents, that the Sisters were required to assume, since, as we know, Nuns of the

---

[1] The reader will remember that the foundation at Metz was the fourth offshoot from the Mother House at Angers, the first three having been made within the space of ten months.

Good Shepherd cannot consider their vocation is being fulfilled, so long as they do not seek after the lost and wandering sheep. Mother St. Euphrasia fully shared in her daughter's feeling of regret and disappointment, yet she was conscious that much tact was needed in dealing with their benefactors, and that if any umbrage was given to them the success of the foundation would be rendered more than doubtful. She had formed great expectations in regard of this colony at Metz; not only did she hope to obtain many recruits from Lorraine, but she trusted that, after having made good their footing there, her daughters would penetrate thence into Germany, and thus enter upon a fresh sphere for the exercise of their ministry. Consequently she deemed it of the utmost importance that a favourable impression should be made upon the inhabitants of Metz, and, above all, that no offence should be given to the lady patronesses. A brisk interchange of letters went on between Angers and Metz in the early days of the foundation, those of the Mother to her children containing wise and sagacious counsels.

" We all hope," she wrote, " that you will act in a prudent and conciliatory manner towards M. Chalandon and the ladies of the committee. Acquaint them with our plans gently and deliberately, as opportunity offers. With regard to your means of support, leave all arrangements to M. Chalandon; Providence will reward you for your submission, you will not be allowed to want. Only be very discreet, and ready to yield; whatever it may cost you, do your utmost to ensure the success of the foundation. If the ladies wish it so much, begin with the dear little orphans. But talk about the penitents continually, and you will gain your point before long."

A few days later she wrote again in the same strain:
" We think, with regard to the penitents, it will be
best to wait until you can get another house. Beware
of appearing rash and over-eager ; defer to the ladies
of the committee, and consult their wishes with all
courtesy, but without pledging yourself to anything.
Do not resent their assumption of authority, it will only
be for a time. When you have once got the enclosure,
you will be exempt from all interference. Do not be
discouraged, I have the fullest confidence in you. As
far as I can judge, it seems advisable for you to take
the house formerly occupied by the Visitation ; wait
until you can have it, even at the price of much dis-
comfort. The chapel and choir will be of immense
importance to you."

The event proved the wisdom of these counsels ;
they were strictly followed, and the result was that in a
short time the little Community, having surmounted its
first difficulties, was enabled to form a class of penitents, open a school for girls, and lay the foundation of
a thoroughly prosperous house.

Meanwhile, Mother St. Euphrasia, having despatched
her letter to Cardinal Odescalchi, awaited the result in
prayer and in patience. She solemnly confided the
cause she had so much at heart to the Blessed Virgin,
addressing her in accents of tender love and filial
piety. " My dearest Mother, if this work will promote
the glory of your Divine Son, and the salvation of the
souls which He shed His Precious Blood to redeem, I
beseech you to take it under your protection ; hide it in
your sacred heart, bring it to a happy conclusion."
Novenas were made, processions organized, litanies
chanted, mortifications practised by the Community at
Angers, as well as in the other houses who remained

faithful to them, in order to obtain the fulfilment of their hopes. On hearing that the chapel of Our Lady of Fourvière had been desecrated on the occasion of an insurrection at Lyons, Mother St. Euphrasia suggested to the Superior at Poitiers that it would be well to erect an altar to the Mother of God under that title in her convent, as a work of reparation.

Another celebrated patron was added to the inter-cessors of the Order at that time, St. Philomena, whose remains were discovered in 1802, in the ceme-tery of St. Priscilla, in Rome. The small phial of blood, and other tokens usually employed by the early Christians to mark the tombs of martyrs, indi-cated that she had shed her blood for the faith. M. de Neuville, than whom no one was more keenly interested in the welfare of the Order, who participated in the sorrows, the joys, the trials of each nascent Community, and who, in his humility, esteemed it a privilege, a special grace for which he devoutly gave thanks to God, to associate himself with the Religious and co-operate in their good works, was the first to introduce this *cultus* at Angers. A beautiful statue of the Saint was by his orders placed in the chapel of the Good Shepherd, and the devotion was warmly espoused by Mother St. Euphrasia. She applied at Rome for some of the relics, which had already become an object of veneration to the faithful, and been the means of effecting numerous miracles. By ordering special prayers to the Saint in all the convents under her rule, she did much to propagate the devotion, and the martyred virgin did not fail to repay her by soliciting on her behalf many favours from on high.

More than two months had elapsed without a reply to her letter having reached the Mother Foundress,

when one evening, after the Community had, in accordance with their daily practice, gone in procession to the
chapel of our Lady, to plead for the erection of the
Generalate, one of the younger nuns, stepping up to
Mother St. Euphrasia, told her that she had heard
from the lips of the Blessed Virgin a distinct promise
that their prayer would be granted. " In proof that
this is not an illusion on my part, dear Mother," she
said, " you will to-morrow receive a letter from Rome."

In fact, the very next morning a letter from Cardinal
Odescalchi was placed in Mother St. Euphrasia's
hands. With trembling fingers she broke the seal, and
great was her delight to find it full of encouragement
and kindness; the course she was to pursue being
plainly pointed out to her. " The greatest impediment
to the success of your scheme," he wrote, " is the
opposition offered by the clergy. This will have weight
with the Holy See, but it can be overcome if your
Bishop, who, you tell me, strongly upholds you, will at
once write to the Holy Father in your behalf. On
the receipt of his letter, I will lay your request before
the proper tribunal, and erelong the matter will be
decided."

From that time the matter in hand made rapid
progress. There were at that moment in Rome two
Religious, both of whom were in a position enabling
them to render material services to the cause of the
Generalate, and who exerted themselves most actively
and effectually to obtain a decision in its favour. One
was a Franciscan, Father Vaures, French Penitentiary
at the Vatican. During a visit to Angers, he had made
himself acquainted with the work of the Good Shepherd,
and ever since had been one of the firm friends of the
Order. The other was a Jesuit, Père Kohlmann, who

filled the post of Consultor to the Congregation to whose judgment the question was referred, and he prepared the papers to be laid before the prelates that composed it.   To secure the good word of one in so influential a position was consequently of no small importance to the petitioners, and this happily had been done.   When writing to Rome, Mother St. Euphrasia had confined herself to a simple statement of facts, without any mention of her opponents, or any attempt to refute their arguments and accusations.   Her letter was carefully read through by Father Kohlmann at the last sitting of the Council, after all the objections had been fully considered.   When he reached the last page, he laid it down on the table before him, and placing his hand upon it, said in a tone of decision : "That is where the truth lies."   This dictum was unanimously approved and accepted by the Sacred Congregation.   The letter written by Mgr. Montault finally removed all hesitation.   In it he stated his reasons for advocating the proposed change of government with a precision, a lucidity, a force, surprising in one who had passed through eighty years of toil and struggle.   He was, moreover, supported by the concurrent testimony of the Bishops of Poitiers, Grenoble, and Metz.   On the 8th of January, 1835, a decree was passed establishing the convent at Angers as the Mother House of the Institute, the Superior of that convent being declared Superior General of all the others that had been, or might be founded from it. The distinctive name of the Congregation under the government of the Superior General was thenceforth to be that of Our Lady of Charity of the Good Shepherd ; to this, *of Angers* was added, to remind the new foundations whence they came, and where their obedience was due. This decree was approved and confirmed by the Sovereign Pontiff on the 16th of January. It is satisfactory to know that not a single dissentient voice was raised against the Generalate, although no less than thirteen letters of a nature antagonistic to it had been received.

We are told that when the draft of the decree was read aloud, Father Kohlmann remarked that the clause empowering the Superior General to found refuges and exercise jurisdiction over them, referred only to France. Thereupon he rose, and requested that for the word *France*, the *whole world* might be substituted. " It seems you want to make a second Society of Jesus of this Congregation," Cardinal Odescalchi observed, with a smile. " Exactly so, your Eminence," replied the Father, resuming his seat. " It shall be so," the Cardinal answered, " for indeed this work deserves to be universal." Thus it came to pass that no geographical limit was placed to the jurisdiction exercised by the Superior of Angers.

Mother St. Euphrasia had, as we have seen, received a supernatural intimation of the success which would finally crown her efforts. God was now pleased to reveal to her that the moment of granting her petition had come. One day, when kneeling before the crib, and imploring the Infant Saviour to make known His will respecting the Generalate, she distinctly heard a voice issuing from the lips of the *bambino*, which said three times : " I have given the law." The same day witnessed the approval of the cause. Another singular fact is recorded in the annals of the Order. On the very day, at the very hour in which the decree was signed, the Religious at Angers, while at their evening recreation, were startled to hear the great bell of the convent peal forth three loud strokes, without any hand having touched the rope.

It will readily be imagined with what rejoicing and delight the tidings of the settlement of this important matter was received at Angers. Mgr. Montault had no sooner heard the good news than he despatched the Vicar-General, Mgr. Régnier, to impart them to the Community. He found the Sisters assembled in the community-room. " I have come to announce a great favour to you," he said on entering; "you must take care that it does not make you proud." " No fear of that, Father," one of the nuns instantly answered, "the Mother who has taught us not to be cast down by adversity, has also taught us not to be lifted up by prosperity." M. Régnier, who had formerly been hostile to Mother St. Euphrasia's projects, was now fain to acknowledge the wisdom of her proceedings. From that time forth he was one of her firmest allies; when raised to the see of Angoulême, his first act was to call the Nuns of the Good Shepherd to his episcopal capital, and whenever he was at Angers, he invariably made a point of going to say Mass in the convent.

One of the senior Sisters at Angers, writing to communicate the joyful intelligence to the Superior at Metz, tells her: " We were all assembled in Chapter, when our dear Mother came, and bade us go in silence, two and two, to the choir, where a letter from Rome would be read to us. Kneeling there in the presence of our Divine Lord, we listened to the happy news with glad hearts. It was impossible to restrain our tears now that the consummation of our cherished hopes had really come. Our venerated Superior General began to intone a psalm of thanksgiving; then we recited the *Sub tuum*, and made a vow to have a procession in honour of our Blessed Lady daily for nine days, and to recite the Office of the Immaculate Conception for three years."

But although the decree was approved, it was not yet promulgated, and the adversaries of the Generalate would not lay down their arms. They made a fresh attack, alleging that gross misrepresentations had been made to the Council. So far did they prevail, that the Holy Father ordered the postponement of the Brief confirmatory of the decree, until further inquiries had been made. He even spoke to Cardinal Gregorio of a revocation of the decree. The Cardinal had no difficulty in showing that the objections had been overruled, but Gregory XVI. still hesitated. "How many are the letters that Bishops have written against Mother St. Euphrasia?" he asked. "There are thirteen letters, your Holiness." "And what has she said in her own defence?" rejoined the Holy Father. "Not a single word." "Then," said the Pope, "she is in the right. I will at once confirm the decree by an Apostolic Brief." This was accordingly done; the Brief, dated April 3, 1835, was forwarded to Mother St. Euphrasia. She had it framed, and hung up in the choir of the chapel. Once more her antagonists returned to the charge. If the Generalate was to be established, they said, Tours ought to be its seat. It was from Tours that Angers was founded; besides, the Archbishop of Tours, being metropolitan, had a prior right to have the Mother House under his sway. But the grievances of the older Refuges found little hearing at the Vatican. *Roma locuta, causa finita est.*

Mother St. Euphrasia was desirous to retain for her nuns the habit as she had originally received it at Tours. She wished for no alteration; but the other

Refuges insisted on the adoption of another dress by what they considered as the new Order. The matter was referred to the Holy See; it was determined that the habit should remain the same, except that a blue cord was to replace the white girdle, and that the figure of our Lord as the Good Shepherd was to be engraven on the silver heart suspended from the neck.

The Religious of Angers were extremely anxious that the Bishop of the diocese should be the Superior General of their Congregation.   P. Kohlmann, who was a man of great prudence, experience, and foresight, strongly dissuaded them from urging this point, and took great pains to convince them that the proposal was unwise.   "The Bishop whom you now have," he argued, "is of one mind with yourselves, but who knows whether the views and opinions of his successor will coincide and harmonize with your own?   In what an unenviable position your Mother General would be placed, should she find herself compelled to engage in a contest with her Bishop and your Superior.   The Mother General ought to be absolutely free to govern the Order and dispose of her subjects as she thinks fit. Believe me, by the arrangement you propose, you would be preparing a scourge for your own shoulders. To facilitate the extension of any Order, nothing is better than that it should be under the sole and imme- diate jurisdiction of the Holy See."   Future events, as we shall see later on, proved how sound was this judgment, and Mother St. Euphrasia had reason to congratulate herself on having followed his guidance. She requested the Holy Father to appoint a Cardinal Protector, who should also be Superior of the Order of the Good Shepherd, and in compliance with her wish, Cardinal Odescalchi accepted the post.

We will conclude this somewhat lengthy chapter with a short extract from a letter of congratulation written by Father Kohlmann to the Mother General, on the happy occasion of which we have been speaking.

" This work appears to be essentially the work of the Most High. Everything about it is miraculous. The Apostolic spirit, which inspires so many chosen souls with the purpose of consecrating their lives to this glorious vocation, is miraculous; the generous spirit which prompts your pious foundress,[1] as well as many other benefactors, to devote their fortunes to this good cause is miraculous; the rapidity wherewith the Order has spread is miraculous; and no less miraculous is the extraordinary speed with which this business has been conducted at Rome. What in the ordinary course of affairs would have taken three or four years to accomplish, has been brought to a termination within the space of as many months, in spite of the opposition of powerful enemies. All this should teach us to go forward with open-hearted confidence, trusting entirely in Him Who has seen fit to bless thus abundantly a work which is exclusively Divine."

[1] Sister Chantal of Jesus, formerly Mdme. Cesbron de la Roche, to whom the Mother Superior gave this title, which belonged by right to herself.

CHAPTER IX

THE wide and rapid diffusion of the Order of the Good Shepherd has abundantly proved the wisdom of uniting the various convents under one ruler. To give universality to her Institute was the primary result that Mother St. Euphrasia desired to gain from the erection of the Generalate. She set to work to show herself not unworthy to bear the title of Superior General, to receive the favours bestowed upon her by the Holy See. Before her death she was the means of founding one hundred and ten convents in different parts of the world, all bound together in the unity of a vigorous life under one common head. The blessing of God, which had been remarkably accorded to the enterprise at the outset, has continued visibly with it ever since. Though only formally recognized, as we have seen, by the Sovereign Pontiff, Gregory XVI., in the year 1835, it possesses now as many as one hundred and eighty-five convents, of which thirteen are in Great Britain and Ireland, and thirty-six in the United States of America. The Order of Our Lady of Charity of the Refuge, on the other hand, has, during the years between 1820 and the present time, only increased the number of its houses to thirty-one. Of these eighteen are in France, two in England, two in Ireland, and six in America. The two English houses are at Bartestree, in Herefordshire, and at Waterlooville, near Portsmouth. All the houses are entirely independent. The only bond of union between them is, that all are engaged in the same charitable work for souls, and all follow the same Rule and Constitutions. But they have no common centre of unity, no General Superior, and therefore no unity of government. This independence of the various houses has doubtless been the impediment to the development of the work.

In order to infuse her own cosmopolitan spirit into the Sisters, we find Mother St. Euphrasia addressing them thus :

" Now that we have been privileged to see the Generalate erected in our Order, with the full benediction of the Head of the Church, the Successor of St. Peter, whose desire it is to see our houses multiplied throughout the whole world, you will go forth and pitch your tents from one end of the earth to the other. Your zeal must not be contented with one town, one foundation ; it must comprise all lands and all peoples. St. Paul said : ' I am neither Greek nor Roman ; I am a citizen of every land.' St. Francis Xavier too used to say : ' I am not only a Spaniard, I am besides an Indian, a Chinaman, a Japanese ; in fact, that is my country wherever I go to preach the Gospel.' Here, my beloved daughters, are examples for your imitation. These should be the dispositions of every soul truly imbued with the spirit of our Institute. We must bestir ourselves, we must no longer sit still. Since we are all of us pastors, or if you will, shepherd-esses, we must not confine ourselves to one narrow spot. As for me, I do not wish any longer to be called French : I am Italian, English, German, Spanish ; I am American, African, Indian ; I con-

K

sider every country my own where there are souls to be saved. Let us not fear to make our home on distant shores, when we see that there too there are lost sheep to be brought back to the fold. From Italy, from Bavaria, from all parts of Europe; from America, Africa, Asia, Oceanica, these wandering sheep must be sought out. The greater the promptitude wherewith you respond to the call, the greater will be the triumph you achieve."

The real nature of the work, which was to receive such widespread extension, is well set forth in a circular letter addressed by her to the Catholics of Provence, with the sanction of the Archbishop of Aix. It may be called at once the *apologia* and the programme of her work :

" Religion comes from Heaven bearing with her a panacea for all the ills of suffering humanity. She is essentially the benefactress of mankind, and can adopt as her own the words of her Divine Author, and say, ' Come unto me, all you that are weary and heavy laden, and I will refresh you.' The orphan, the aged, the infirm, the sick ; the unfortunate beings who are deprived of the light of reason, all, in a word, whose lot is to suffer, draw near, in answer to her call, to take shelter beneath the shadow of her wings. She alone possesses the infallible secret of alleviating every human woe.

" But there are evils of another nature, there is a deep and ever-widening wound, the sight of which fills every Christian, every right-minded person, with feelings of horror and compassion. I mean immorality. Is it possible for religion to regard this with indifference, for supernatural charity to be repelled at the sight of this contagious leprosy? By no means ; her mission is pre-eminently to restore health to the soul, to save it from perdition. There is no moral malady, how hopeless soever it may appear, to which she cannot apply a remedy. To the cure of this evil, therefore, her attention ought to be, and is, more especially directed.

" Saints and apostolic men, in all ages, have deplored the existence of this evil, and have endeavoured by every means in their power to arrest its progress. At length Father Eudes founded a Community of Religious with this object. Immense were the services rendered by it until the end of last century, when it was suppressed. The necessity of reviving so valuable an institution has ever since been felt. Isolated houses were established in several towns ; and last year, in order to facilitate its diffusion throughout the whole world under the government of a Mother General, Gregory XVI. gave to the house at Angers the title of the Mother House, and to the Congregation of which it was the centre, the name of the Good Shepherd. The blessing bestowed by the Father of the faithful upon this Institute, and the prayers he offers to Heaven on its behalf, will not be unproductive of results. The house of Angers has been founded for only six years, and already offshoots from it exist at Grenoble, at Poitiers, at Saumur, at Metz, at Nancy, and at Puy.

" The object of our Order is twofold; that of offering a shelter to the tempted and of giving refuge to the fallen. If there is one Order which deserves to meet with universal sympathy, which appeals to the heart of every unprejudiced person, of every one who values religion, morality, and the welfare of humanity, it is undeniably the Institute of the Good Shepherd.

" We have asylums for the treatment of mental maladies, hospitals for the cure of corporal diseases.

Does not ordinary justice require us to provide, in these days, when license is unchecked, a refuge for the weak, a home where the evil effects of unbridled passion may be cured ? It is only when removed from dangerous occasions, most of all in complete seclusion, that conversions take place; whereas the best resolutions melt into thin air when brought face to face with the temptations that led to the first fall. Where is the zealous priest, the father of a family, the Christian mother, the chaste and pious woman, who would not consider it a privilege to share in the foundation and maintenance of a house which has so strong a claim on the public interest. Whoever contributes to the preservation of innocence, the reform of manners, the extirpation of a vice which corrodes society, helps to promote the peace and happiness of families, the salvation of a vast number of souls, and finally, his own sanctification, without depreciating any other charitable work. We may venture to remark, that never was there an institution whose aim was more exalted, or one more deserving of generous patronage and support.

"There may be perhaps some prejudiced persons who, regarding the sores we would strive to heal as altogether beyond cure, consider this praiseworthy enterprise as a forlorn hope. God forbid that Christian people should take so despairing a view of the case. Faith and experience concur in leading us to anticipate a happier result. The Saviour calls to repentance all sinners, without exception ; He, the Good Shepherd, tires not in His pursuit of the erring sheep, and every day He brings fresh wanderers back to the fold. Innumerable are the sinners, from Magdalen down to our own day, who have become glorious trophies of Divine grace, and have edified the Church by the fervour of their repentance.

" If we confine ourselves to the present, we shall still find just ground for the indulgence of hope. The successes achieved by the older foundations warrant us in expecting that much good will be done by that which has just sprung into existence. During the six years that Angers has been established, the numbers who have sought admission to that house alone may be counted by hundreds. They are there now, seeking to expiate the sins of their past life by the voluntary practice of penance. Of institutions of a similar kind in other parts of France a like tale could be told. We commend these encouraging facts, which no one can gainsay, to the consideration of all who desire to form a right judgment in the matter. It will be acknowledged that they are of a nature to stimulate charity to fresh and resolute action."

When exhorting her nuns, Mother St. Euphrasia was wont to place before them the work of reclaiming the fallen as the chief, the main object of their vocation. " We are told in the Gospel," she said to them on one occasion, " that the Good Shepherd leaves ninety and nine sheep to hasten after one that has gone astray; in like manner, let us leave ninety and nine good works for the purpose of bringing back the lost sheep of the house of Israel. By this I mean, if you are unable to undertake the care of several different classes, let the penitents and the Magdalens take precedence of any other. I have noticed that those houses invariably prosper where the work is confined to those two classes. Above all, my dear daughters, whatever you do, do not found a Community of Magdalens unless they can be suitably domiciled. They must have plenty of air, and perfect seclusion; it would only be exposing them to danger and to temptation were we to place them where there is not a garden, nor a suite of rooms in which complete isolation can be secured for them. Here at Angers, the centre of our Institute, we have a variety of institutions, because we have to form the novices for work among different classes; then we have various buildings, each detached from the others, and we have abundance of space, so that we can provide for the needs of all. The several communities see nothing of one another; we have a sufficient staff of mistresses, and the grounds are spacious enough to admit of a separate portion being allotted to each."

Subsequently to the reception of the decree from Rome, which, as we have seen, placed the Generalate on a firm basis, the first foundation made by Mother St. Euphrasia was that of Saumur. When travelling backwards and forwards between Tours and Angers, she had greatly admired the beauty of this rich and fertile province of France, and she knew only too well how great were the spiritual necessities of the city which bears its name. Several attempts, made by private individuals on behalf of erring women, had completely failed. In 1832, however, M. Bernier, head priest of the parish of St. Peter at Saumur, turned his zealous efforts on behalf of his parishioners in this direction. His first idea was to confide the care of the poor young girls over whom he had gained some influence, to the Augustinian Sisters. But various legal difficulties placed insurmountable obstacles in his path. While he was completely at a loss in what direction he should turn his steps, he received a letter from Mother St. Euphrasia, who was a complete stranger to him, expressing her ardent desire to found a house of her

Order in Saumur, and at the same time begging him to come to Angers in order that she might explain her wishes to him. Struck by the coincidence, he lost no time in setting out for Angers. What he saw and heard there caused him to come to a speedy decision, and no sooner had he returned home than he set about carrying his plan into action. A man of great energy, he exercised a remarkable ascendency over all who surrounded him, and seldom failed to gain them over to his way of thinking. He did this all the more readily because his iron hand was covered by a velvet glove, and he counted all his endeavours for nothing if only he was not baulked of his purpose. He possessed great gifts as an orator, and his sermons were frequently compared to the flash of burnished steel. He was an immense favourite with the officers of the cavalry school at Saumur, who used to go in a body to hear Mass at St. Peter's whenever they could find out that M. Bernier was to be the preacher.

He went from house to house in order to obtain funds for the new foundation; and the glowing terms in which he depicted the attractiveness of the Order, decided several persons to seek admission into it as novices. He also persuaded a lady, who devoted herself to the charge of some orphan girls, to promise to give them over to the care of the Sisters of the Good Shepherd as soon as they should arrive. He sought and found a suitable abode, personally superintended the needful alterations, and then proposed to the Mother General that she should purchase what the Revolution had left of an ancient abbey, in order that it, with the surrounding grounds, might form part of the new foundation. This abbey had formerly been so splendid as to be called the *Belle de l'Anjou*. It consisted of three magnificent piles of buildings, and within its walls were woven during the middle ages the artistic tapestries which in our day afford a study to archæologists.

Mother St. Euphrasia was delighted at the prospect thus held out to her of restoring the once beautiful chapel, and rekindling the sanctuary lamp, which wicked hands had extinguished. After visiting Saumur, and consulting Mgr. Montault, she decided to purchase the abbey with its grounds, and on the 31st of July, 1835, sent five Religious to take possession. The foundation prospered exceedingly, and in the course of some years the ancient chapel was restored to almost its pristine beauty.

Meanwhile, several of the houses greatly desired a visit from their Mother General. Feeling her presence to be really needed, she left Angers towards the end of August in this same year (1835), and went first of all to Metz and Grenoble, passing through Nancy, where she had long wished to make a foundation. She also stayed a few days at Poitiers, and returned to Angers before the end of September. She had in reality been absent scarcely a month, but it seemed to her Community that they had been deprived for a year at least of the light and joy which her presence afforded them.

Nor did she reach home any too soon. In October an epidemic, the nature of which we are not told, broke out in the house. It was of a highly contagious as well as dangerous description, and it carried off many victims. Deeply as the affectionate heart of their Mother felt the loss of those whom she so dearly loved, she was consoled by their holy deaths, and by the perfect resignation with which they submitted to the will of God. Her belief in the Communion of Saints was, moreover, one of the most marked features of her piety, and it helped her to bear up under her losses. She entreated the Sisters to pray for one another, to offer up their merits and penances for the relief of the suffering. Gladly would she have adopted as her own the beautiful words of a modern writer, who after telling us the touching story of a holy abbot in the middle ages, who led a bereaved and weeping mother into the choir that she might listen to the voice of her departed son, goes on to say: " We know not what may be possible. We know so very little. But we believe in the Communion of Saints, and we may hope so very much."

Another stay and support to her was her trust in the intercession of the Saints. She was deeply grateful to the Sisters at Poitiers, who sent her a relic of St. Radegunda, to whose protection she attributed the cessation of the epidemic.

A great joy was, however, in store for Mother St. Euphrasia after this season of affliction had passed. In 1835, she was able to carry out her long-cherished project of founding a house in Nancy. The three Sisters whom she sent thither, on the 30th of November, found everything at first smiling and prosperous. But clouds soon darkened the sky. The ecclesiastical authorities, having been prejudiced against the Generalate, declined at first to allow the house to be opened as a dependency of Angers, wishing it to be regarded as independent and self-sufficing. But Mother St. John of the Cross, whom Mother St. Euphrasia had brought with her from Tours, and whom she had appointed Superior, stood firm. Gradually all difficulties were removed, and four years after its foundation, the house at Nancy was securely established and surrounded by friends. Doubtless the wise and loving counsels which the Superioress constantly received from the Mother General, did much to strengthen her hands and enable her to persevere. We cannot do better than lay before our readers two of these epistles, written during the early days of trial.

"22nd November, 1835.

"Your letter is before me. What crosses you have to bear, my beloved daughter! I have foreseen them for the last three days; whilst making my meditation, I had a presentiment that they were coming. You do well to tell me all. Do not be afraid, my dearest daughter. We beg and entreat you, my beloved children, for the love of God and of the good work in which we are engaged, to say, in all obedience, to Mgr. de Nancy, that nothing will ever induce you to break with the Mother House, and that you will have neither novitiate nor professions; and after all, if the work does not meet with his approval, you would be extremely sorry to make a foundation. Do not distress yourself about this, my daughter; you know we have been asked for both at Rome and in Belgium. You need not mention that, but preserve your liberty of action. You might go and found a house abroad, taking with you Sisters St. Margaret and St. Benedict. Oh, my dear daughter, be firm; the powers of darkness will do their worst. O Blessed Cross, let us hold fast to thee! Yes, grief and suffering are our lot; but let us rather die than give way; how many souls are reaching out their arms to us for help! My poor children, you are indeed on Calvary, as I am; my soul, too, is crucified. Do not purchase the house of

Turique, if you perceive that you are not wanted there.

"You are the eldest daughter of this undertaking, and we have entire confidence in you; we wish you to be at the head of all that is set on foot. Be not concerned about Metz; I am sending away two subjects, and I intend, with the help of God, quietly to put down various little abuses; I am also going to write to Grenoble and Saumur. The essential thing is devotion to our cause. By that you console me for all else; then the great kindness of the Mother General of Christian Doctrine touches me deeply. Tell her how much I feel it, and how greatly I respect her for it. What I should most regret about Nancy is Mgr. de Janson, he is so good! Then think of all the souls! On the other hand, I think of you as friendless and alone, in the bitter cold and snow, and worst of all, as the victims of calumny. We are truly grieved on your account, but we will have recourse to prayer, we will pour out our sorrows to the Sacred Hearts of Jesus and Mary. I enclose a copy of the Brief; show it to Mgr. Donnet, and tell him very respectfully that you are irrevocably pledged to abide by it; and that if his Grace feels disinclined to receive you in accordance with the spirit of the Generalate, you are prepared to take your departure. The Chapter desires me to assure you that as far as you are personally concerned you have nothing to fear. We shall certainly support you throughout. Farewell, dearest daughter, farewell! My station is at the foot of the Cross. I shall look eagerly for news of you. Mind you do not buy the house without having first told the truth. Jesus Christ will be your strength; let me beg you to speak out without losing your dignity, or giving way to fear."

"From our Monastery at Angers,

"25th November, 1835.

"The Lord hath done great things unto us, and holy is His Name."

"What graces Mary has obtained for you, my beloved daughter! Your letter, written on the Presentation, gave us all fresh life. My God, what afflictions we have passed through! Knowing what trouble you were in, we could only send up our sighs to Heaven on your behalf; prayers, processions, Communions, Masses, none of these means have been neglected. Our Sisters were deeply grieved by the expressions which the Bishop Coadjutor employed; M. de Neuville was so hurt, that he wanted you recalled forthwith to this our foretaste of Paradise, where tranquillity reigns. At last the Star of the Sea has appeared, and the shades of night have fled before her! Now you are safely domiciled, my dearest daughters, you seem to be at peace. At last I feel reassured concerning you; for two nights I could obtain no rest. Your promise to write all particulars to me is an additional consolation; how we shall long for the post to come in! We should have written sooner, only I did not know where to find you. Now you will have had two letters, and they shall not fail in future. Shall you soon be settled at Turique, and do you meet with kindness? Tell us everything, my dear daughter, write frequently and at full length. You know my affection for you.

"After all, do not fear, little flock, for the Divine Pastor is with you. Yes, this foundation of Nancy, so dear to all of us, will prosper for the glory of God and of our holy Institute. Already they are writing from Amiens about the foundations to be made there.

Truly God's designs are inscrutable, who can fathom them? We see this little cloud, so small at first, about to cover the whole of France. Let us be imitators of St. Francis Xavier, for the most exalted mission is ours. Endeavour to establish a model house of penitents, that is our chief aim."

The year 1835 was fertile in good works for the Order of the Good Shepherd. We have seen the care and watchfulness with which Mother St. Euphrasia devoted herself to the class of penitents. She was now to be rewarded by the formation of a new and most edifying class, formed from among her children. Some of the penitents, who were conscious that they had no vocation for the Magdalens, yet dreaded to return to a world whose dangers and temptations they knew only too well, mentioned of their own accord to their directress their desire to remain always within the walls of the Good Shepherd, and consecrate their lives to help and serve those who had been their companions. No sooner was this wish told to the Mother General, than she gladly fell in with it, seeing in it a Divine inspiration, and feeling how greatly these consecrated souls would aid the Religious in the management of the penitents. To distinguish them from these, she chose for them a special dress of plain black. She drew up a Rule for them, and this first class proved eminently successful in furthering the conversion of the poor girls who had arrived but recently. A retreat preached to them by a Jesuit Father incited the greater number of them to extraordinary fervour. Some begged to be allowed to wear hair-shirts, chains of iron, and to fast on bread and water. In the beds of others were discovered bundles of nettles, branches of thorns, and pillows filled with stones.   It is hardly necessary to add that the prudence of their Mother put a check on this ill-regulated, though well-meant zeal.   She strove to make her children understand that nothing is so pleasing to God as the mortification of our self-will through obedience to the will of another.   She spared no pains in doing everything that might promote their sanctification.   A formula which she composed, and which consists of wishes, supposed to be addressed by the entire Congregation to the consecrated penitents, is too touching, beautiful, and characteristic to be omitted here.

" Penitent souls, who dwell in solitude and in forgetfulness of the world, fortunate sheep whom the Good Shepherd has sought after with the utmost solicitude, and who have responded faithfully to His call, may you never wander from the safe and tranquil path into which Providence has directed your steps! Continue, by your constant observance of the Rule laid down for you, to walk in the way that leads to the heavenly country, which is the object of your hopes. This is what we desire above all things, for your perseverance is the greatest consolation that can be given to us as the fruit of our labours.   By your virtues you will be the glory of the whole Community; and after having enjoyed here below the peace and happiness that are to be found in the practice of humility, obedience, and charity, you will go to receive from the hands of an infinitely merciful and infinitely generous Father that Eternal Kingdom which He has promised to the penitent no less than to the innocent."

Yet another class was to be formed before the year 1835 drew to its close.   The Prefect of Maine-et-Loire having paid a visit to the Good Shepherd, was so pleased with the perfect order and discipline which prevailed throughout the establishment, that he asked the Mother General to receive young girls over fifteen who had been condemned to various terms of imprisonment. She never refused any proposal in which she saw a means of doing good to souls, and answered in the affirmative. Shortly afterwards, the first detachment of youthful criminals arrived at the Good Shepherd. This was a fresh interest for Mother St. Euphrasia, and we shall have more to say of her new charges in another place. Suffice it for the present to say that the experiment proved a most successful one, and that many of the girls implored to be allowed to remain in the house which had sheltered them, long after the term of their sentence had expired.

In the early part of December, Mgr. Montault, in whose palace the Bishop of Bardstown, in America, was staying for a short time, took his visitor to see the Good Shepherd. The latter, Mgr. Flaget, was a man of more than ordinary sanctity, and had a considerable reputation as a thaumaturgist. He was delighted with Mother St. Euphrasia, and she felt for the holy prelate the deepest admiration and respect. His advice and encouragement greatly cheered her as to the future of her work. He was, moreover, able to render her substantial service during the sojourn he made in the Eternal City after quitting Angers. He defended her against those who calumniated her, he related to His Holiness all the good she was doing, and prepared the way for the foundation of a house in Rome. Later on, we shall find him summoning to America the first daughters of Mother St. Euphrasia who ventured to cross the Atlantic.

Blessings continued to pour down upon the Mother House at Angers, to the grateful surprise of its humble Superior. Vocations were numerous and suitable. Among those we may mention that of Mdme. de Couëspel, who had long been a benefactress of the convent. Her husband, to whom she had been married for eight years, commanded the 44th regiment of the line, and was an officer of much distinction. In the midst of his brilliant career he was struck down by a fatal malady. His devoted wife brought him to Angers, and nursed him with the utmost care and tenderness during a painful and tedious illness. He died a holy and edifying death, thanks to the pious efforts and unceasing exhortations of his admirable wife. During her residence at Angers, she became intimately acquainted with Mother St. Euphrasia, and shortly after the decease of M. de Couëspel, she entered the Good Shepherd as a postulant. She was received with joy, and took the habit on the 10th of March, 1836, together with the name of Sister Mary Teresa of Jesus, which Mother St. Euphrasia had expressly chosen for her.

Yet all was not sunshine. In regard to pecuniary matters, many difficulties arose, although they were borne with such cheerful courage that Mdme. Andigné used playfully to term the Mother General: *Madame de l'Espérance.*

In those early days of foundations, however, she found her post an arduous and difficult one. Not even by practising the strictest economy could she contrive to meet the multifarious expenses the house entailed on her. Many a time she had recourse to the Blessed Virgin for assistance, and many a time did her gracious Patroness intervene in the most unmistakable manner to enable her to pay the debts incurred by the Community. She was, however, most disinterested in regard to financial arrangements. In receiving postulants, she never considered the amount of their dowry; she was always ready to take in destitute children; she gave liberally to all the new foundations. The donations of benefactors were applied to the purchase of land, or the erection of fresh buildings. Hence holy poverty prevailed in the convent, but it was borne cheerfully, nay, gladly, by the Sisters. One of the professed, Sister Mary of the Angels, told her brother, who was the head of the College of Combrée, that she must deny herself the pleasure of writing to him often, in order to spare the cost of postage. She was a true daughter of Mother St. Euphrasia, and the joy wherewith she accepted these privations for the love of God reminds one of St. Francis of Assisi. The hardships of the Novitiate may be gathered from a letter written by a novice, in no spirit of complaint, but rather of rejoicing, not long after she had received the habit. " In the refectory the only dish provided for us was cabbage, moistened with a little vinegar, and at midday some very indifferent soup. We never had a fire in the Novitiate; we used to go out in the snow, and stamp our feet to get a little warmth into them." The spirit of abandonment to Divine Providence which Mother St. Euphrasia possessed to so great an extent, sustained her daughters under circumstances repugnant to the natural man.

CHAPTER X.

EARLY in 1836, a house was founded at Amiens. This was effected mainly through the instrumentality of the Jesuit Fathers, two of whom obtained from their Superiors leave to make over to the Good Shepherd an edifice which the Society was about to vacate. The property was called Blamont, and was situated not far from Amiens. Mother St. Euphrasia accepted the offer with joy, and the purchase was soon completed. Her grateful heart never forgot the kind attentions she received from the Jesuit Fathers on this occasion. Later on, when in their turn they came to make a foundation at Angers, she showed them every kindness in her power. She sent them wine, and linen for the sacristy; and three times a week "Bijou," the horse belonging to the convent, wended its way to the house of the Fathers, loaded with fruit, vegetables, and other provisions. At a later period, in 1855, one of the Fathers recalled to the memory of the Sisters at Poitiers the generosity of Mother St. Euphrasia. "We were so very poor on our first arrival at Angers," he said, "and really your Mother General sent us almost everything we needed. Besides," he added, "the provisions were all cooked." This fact evidently enhanced in no small degree the value of the gifts from the good Father's point of view.

The foundation of Lille followed quickly upon that of Amiens. Mother St. Euphrasia appointed Sister St. Basil, a Religious for whom she had the highest esteem, to fill the post of Superior. Before the period fixed for her to leave Angers and enter upon her new duties, she was suddenly carried off by a choleraic attack, at the early age of twenty-six. Her death was no small grief to Mother St. Euphrasia, who was herself absent just then in Paris on necessary business. Sister St. Basil had greatly dreaded the post she was to fill at Lille. It was a pious belief among her Sisters, that as soon as she learned the intention of her Superiors in regard to her, she had offered herself to God as a living holocaust, in order to promote the prosperity of the Order, which was very dear to her heart. Her agony was long and terrible, her sufferings being greatly aggravated by the absence of her beloved Mother General.

The foundation at Puy was the next that was made. While the negotiations were proceeding, an epidemic again broke out at Angers, and raged with great severity. The care of the sick engrossed Mother St. Euphrasia, who spent all the time she could spare in the infirmary. One morning she told the Sisters, that God had inspired her with the thought that the visitation from which they were suffering was the result of a lack of promptness on their part in making the foundation at Puy. The idea grew stronger within her day by day, until she could resist its influence no longer. Gathering together the Sisters who were destined to found the new house, she thus addressed them: "My children, you must set out at once. There is no time for delay. I know that I am asking a sacrifice at your hands, but the disease which is raging in our midst will not cease

its ravages, as long as you postpone your journey."
Those to whom she spoke these words showed themselves worthy of their vocation.   They made their
preparations with all speed, and left Angers as soon
as they could, in spite of the rigour of an abnormally
severe winter.   Their road led them across a moun-
tainous country, half buried in snow and ice.   Yet
these generous souls rejoiced in the hardships they
were called upon to endure, animated as they were,
not only by zeal for souls, but by a desire to help and
relieve the suffering Sisters they had left at Angers.
Truly they showed themselves worthy pupils of the
servant of God who had trained them in His service.

Meanwhile her heart was wrung with anguish as
she beheld her children sick, dying, and dead around
her.   Azrael, the Angel of Death, was busy indeed
amid the Community of Angers.   The Mother General
wrote to all her friends and protectors, telling them her
sorrows, and entreating their prayers.   Among the
numerous letters which she received in reply, one
written by M. Alleron, the Superior of the Carmelite
Convent at Tours, is so simple and beautiful, that we
cannot refrain from giving it a place in these pages,
especially as it was warmly appreciated by Mother
St. Euphrasia.   It refers to three young novices of rare
piety and promise, who all expired within a week, after
acute sufferings.   It is dated January 6th, 1837, and
runs thus :

"Were I to attempt to tell you how intensely I
sympathize in the grief which is afflicting your maternal
heart, I should be merely expressing feelings that
you, I trust, already know quite well.   *Dominus dedit,
Dominus abstulit.*   Our Lord is taking away what He
had given you ; believe His words, put your whole

trust in Him, and He will restore to you a hundred-fold. He Who was able 'out of stones to raise up children to Abraham,'[1] will know how to replace the beloved children, whom He has been pleased to summon already to their eternal reward, because, 'being made perfect in a short space, they fulfilled a long time.'[2] They have been taken up to Heaven, clothed in white robes of unspotted purity, and thus adorned, they shall for ever and ever 'follow the Lamb whithersoever He goeth.'[3] Do I pity you, sorrowing Mother? Certainly not, for even through your tears you are able to see all things by the light of faith. Do I pity the dear children whom you mourn? Oh, no! Full well do I know that, however happy they may have been with you on earth, they are a thousand times happier amid the joys of Paradise. Strive, therefore, to rejoice in the Lord at the thought that they have gone before you to His immediate presence, and strive also to train those whom He has left you with more vigilance and zeal than ever, in the steep and difficult path which leads to Heaven. It is evident that the devil hates you with a peculiarly bitter hatred. He desires to have you, that he may sift you as wheat. But our Lord will pray for you that your faith may not fail, and that following His example you may confirm your Sisters."[4]

At length the dread Angel spread his wings for flight, and hovered no longer over the convent at Angers. Meanwhile blessings of every kind had been showered upon the house at Puy. The Sisters had been most kindly received, and had met with liberal and warm-hearted benefactors. His lordship the Bishop

---

[1] St. Luke viii. 3. [2] Wisdom iv. 13. [3] Apoc. xiv. 14.
[4] St. Luke xxii. 31.

was exceedingly gracious, and showed in every possible way how deep was the interest he took in their welfare. He paid them many kind attentions, he visited them frequently, said Mass for them, sent them presents of household linen, of coverlets and furniture.   Not content with this, he established a charitable association for their especial benefit. Nay more, the priests who lived in the episcopal palace told the Sisters that they had never known him to be so zealous on behalf of any other good work.

As the number of foundations increased, so did the labours of the venerated foundress increase. Her days, and often a portion of her nights, were filled to overflowing.   She laid the greatest stress on keeping up a constant and frequent correspondence between the Mother House and its dependencies.   When she received a letter from her children at a distance, containing interesting and edifying accounts of their proceedings, their benefactors, their penitents, she used to gather together her Community, and read the epistle aloud.   Her greatest pleasure was to share her joys with others, and bestow upon them a portion of her own happiness.   She desired that circular letters should be sent round annually by the various houses, in order to serve as a sort of conversation on a large scale between the Sisters.   But let us quote her own views on the subject :

" Do you know, my dear daughter, the name that in the language of my heart I give to the Community letters ?   Well, I will tell you : I call them *Christmas flowers*.   December and January are the spring-time of our year in the Good Shepherd.   During these two months we are privileged to walk up and down in the meadows of the Order, and there gather flowers whose

fragrance will revive and stimulate our zeal. I assure
you, my children, that what I read in one of these
letters often suggests thoughts for my meditation for
more than a week. I love to contemplate the little
acorn which the Blessed Virgin has commissioned her
unworthy handmaid to plant. I have witnessed its
development, watched its growth year by year; now
I see it become a stalwart oak, extending its branches,
spreading its verdant foliage, affording shelter beneath
its shade to thousands of torn and bleeding sheep.

" If these letters are to be Christmas flowers, they
must not be kept back until April or June; if they
are to be flowers at all, they must be written in an
unaffected, straightforward manner.

" Let there be a mutual exchange of good wishes,
of kind messages; and let facts be narrated in dignified
but simple language. By the recital of edifying inci-
dents, by the expression of pious and holy feelings, you
may make the work of the Good Shepherd known and
esteemed, and besides procure for us the consolation of
enjoying some moments of real happiness."

We have spoken of the Mother General's extensive
correspondence. We cannot omit to mention the claim
which the duties of hospitality also made upon her
valuable time. Yet she never counted the hours lost
which were spent in entertaining the numerous visitors
who presented themselves at the door of the convent.
Her great natural tact, and keen insight into character,
enabled her to suit herself to persons of the most
opposite nationalities, dispositions, and states of life.
It is no exaggeration to say that every one who came,
went away delighted, and strongly attracted towards
the beloved Superioress. She was most anxious to
inculcate upon her children the necessity for hospitality,

not only as a means of gaining friends and benefactors
for the various convents, but as being, in itself, a
Christian duty. We will again allow her to speak for
herself, by giving an extract from one of her meditations on the subject.

"Above all things, show great kindness to our
Sisters when they are on a journey; receive them
with the utmost cordiality. Hear how the Apostle
St. Paul urged upon the early Christians the practice
of fraternal charity: 'I commend to you Phebe our
sister, who is in the ministry of the Church; that you
receive her in the Lord, as becometh saints, and that
you assist her in whatsoever business she shall have
need of you. For she also hath assisted many, and
myself also.'[1] The same Apostle, writing to the
Corinthians, beseeches them to show deference to those
who have dedicated themselves to the ministry of the
saints, 'and to every one that worketh with us, and
laboureth.' And again he says: 'They have refreshed
both my spirit and yours.'[2] Indeed, my dear daughters,
you in like manner afford me the greatest consolation,
when I see you give our Sisters a hearty welcome.

"'Use hospitality one towards another.' These are
words which may well be applied to us, since charity
is, as it were, the very essence of our vocation. Our
Mother House ought to be like the house of a kind and
affectionate grandmother, whose children and grand-
children, when they go to visit her, are sure to be
received with fond caresses. On the arrival of any of
our Sisters, we ought to pay attention to their comfort
in the minutest particulars; we ought to make them
rest, see that they take refreshment, wash their things
for them, do all one can to render them cheerful and

[1] Romans xvi. 1, 2.   [2] 1 Cor. xvi. 16, 18.

happy, by treating them with the greatest kindness, in all humility and charity.

"Talk quite familiarly to the Sisters who come here; if they appear glad to come, do you show by your manner the pleasure that it gives you to have them with you. Let us conduct ourselves in such a way that it may be said of us, in the words of the Sacred Scriptures: 'The multitude had but one heart and one soul: neither did any one say that aught of the things which he possessed was his own; but all things were common to them.'[1] The inhabitants of the Libanus are said to have the spirit of the ancient patriarchs: when they entertain travellers, they hold them in such honour, especially if they are priests or religious, that words fail to describe the respect they show them, the attentions they lavish on them. Amongst other things, they present their guests with a variety of perfumes, with the freshest milk, the choicest fruits, the sweetest cream, the most delicious cheese, the most appetizing dishes; they kiss their hands, they summon all the members of the family, all their children, to make an obeisance to the strangers and humbly entreat their blessing. They think it an honour to assist them to mount their horses, they touch their garments with veneration; and when the moment of departure comes, they stand and look after them, following them with parting salutations, with good wishes for their journey. Do not let it be said of us, my dear daughters, that we are less courteous than the people of the Libanus, that we do not equal them in practising the duties of fraternal charity.

"The Superior of several convents of the Thebaid, was accustomed frequently to exhort his monks to treat

[1] Acts iv. 32.

with the greatest respect any Brothers who might come to visit them. I always like to read what is said in the Life of St. Anthony on this subject. That great Saint, finding that his disciples often came to him, took pains to grow some vegetables and cultivate fruits, that he might have something to set before them. It was always a gala-day when the Saint received his spiritual sons. He invariably sent them away pleased and contented, and he himself was quite happy at having been able to encourage and console them. Thus it is that all the Saints have acted. Let us learn of them to do likewise."

But it was not only strangers and friends whom she received in this graceful and winning fashion. She spared no pains to gain over those who, if they cannot be termed personal enemies, had at least hindered and opposed her work. Hearing that M. Dufêtre, who was Vicar-General at Tours, and whose name the reader will doubtless remember, since he was one of the most strenuous opponents of the Generalate, was coming to preach a course of sermons in one of the churches of Angers, she gladly availed herself of the opportunity thus afforded her of attempting to effect a reconciliation which she had long desired to bring about. As soon as she heard of M. Dufêtre's arrival, she sent one of the out-Sisters to inquire after him. When he came to pay her a visit, as courtesy compelled him to do, she gathered together all the Sisters, and begged him to deliver a short address to them. He was so deeply touched by the manner in which the venerated foundress treated him that he openly acknowledged himself to have been mistaken, and declared that he was fully convinced that what he witnessed was indeed the work of God. Mother St. Euphrasia asked him to bless a little chapel dedicated to St. Joseph, which had just been erected in a part of the grounds, and showed him so much frank cordiality and thoughtful kindness that she gained a signal victory. We cannot do better than quote a brief extract from a letter he addressed to her about a month after his return home: "Your frank and simple explanations, my dear child, have been an immense relief to me. From henceforth I trust there will not exist between us even the shadow of a cloud. Never again shall I stand aloof from your work, but rather I shall entreat our Lord to make me worthy to take some share in it, and so gain a portion, if only a very small one, of the vast store of merits which your Congregation cannot but gain."

On the 11th of May, 1837, Mother St. Euphrasia was re-elected Superior by her Sisters for the second time, under the presidency of Mgr. Montault, who addressed her thus: " May the graces which have been granted you hitherto, be showered down upon you afresh, and in ever-increasing measure, proportioned to your continually increasing needs, for your work grows with every new day. This house was founded in a manner nothing short of miraculous, nor is its growth less surprising. It is the glory of my episcopate, and the good works there carried on will never come to an end."

The foundations of Strasbourg, Rheims, and Sens, followed very quickly upon the re-election of the Mother General. An attempt made at Bordeaux was somewhat premature, and on this account proved abortive. The fields were not ripe for the harvest, the conditions imposed upon the Sisters rendered it impossible for them to carry out their Rule, and keep close to their Constitutions. The very atmosphere they breathed was full of enmity. Persecution, prejudice, misrepresentation, surrounded them on all sides. "I have just received," writes Mother St. Euphrasia, "a letter six pages long, containing nothing but reproaches and hostile expressions. I mean to recall the Sisters in about a week."

Her patience and resignation were soon rewarded by the success and prosperity which attended the foundation made at Arles. At the end of a very few months, the Religious who had been sent there were able to announce that they had already forty persons in their house. Later on, when their position was more assured, they built a new convent, outside the city, and quite in the country. It was situated on the road which leads to Crau, close to a chapel which is both very ancient, and highly celebrated in the religious history of Arles. It is called by the common people the chapel *de l'Agenouillade.* In the middle ages, some highway robbers who had pillaged the Cathedral, made a halt on the spot where it stands, in order to divide their booty while yet they were protected by the darkness of night. A single Host fell from the ciborium on to the road. In the early morning, a knight whose dwelling was at Crau, was riding home, and passed the same way. All at once his horse refused to proceed: neither spur nor caress could induce the animal to move. His master alighted, and perceived the Sacred Host. Instantly remounting, he rode back to Arles, in order to inform the clergy of what had occurred. They went in solemn procession to fetch the Blessed Sacrament. The knight, who was a man of ample means, built at his own expense a chapel on the scene of the miracle. Until very recent times, Mass was said annually in this chapel on the first Sunday of May.

The close of the year 1837 brought a great joy to the Mother General. Her devotion to Our Lady of Dolours had long caused her to be desirous of erecting a Calvary at the end of the convent garden. The generosity of Mdme. d'Andigné now enabled her to carry out her wish, and to place on either side a statue of our Blessed Lady and of St. John. It was altogether completed by the beginning of November. On the 6th, Mgr. Montault came and blessed it, with much pomp and ceremonial.

Mother St. Euphrasia suffered much about this period from attacks of intermittent fever, which caused great anxiety to those around her. But, unless unusually severe, she did not allow them to interrupt her labours. Early in the following year she had sufficiently regained her strength to be able to undertake the journey to Rome, respecting which we shall have much to say in our next chapter.

CHAPTER XI

EVER since the erection of the Generalate, the desire to found a house in Rome, near the Protector of the Congregation and under the eye of the Sovereign Pontiff, had been among the dearest wishes of Mother St. Euphrasia's heart. She felt that she would in this way give a fresh proof of her loyal devotion to the Holy See, and obtain a larger share of the blessings which the martyrs who laid down their lives within the walls of the capital of the Christian world, are wont to bestow with so liberal a hand. Father Vaures, who had shown himself so staunch a friend to the Good Shepherd, fell in with the wish of the Mother General. He addressed a petition to Pope Gregory XVI., in which he put forward, in a forcible manner, the great advantage which the unhappy female prisoners would experience if they could be confided to the care and teaching of the children of Mother St. Euphrasia. He also explained to His Holiness that it would be no difficult matter to summon some of these Religious to Rome, since the Generalate was producing such abundant fruit, by the confession even of those who, in the outset, had most firmly opposed it. Cardinal Odescalchi also did his very utmost to plead the same cause. The result was, that the Holy Father empowered

His Eminence to make every arrangement for the foundation of a convent in Rome.

But an outbreak of cholera, which occurred at this period, caused the plan to remain in abeyance for some months. It was not until the spring of 1838 that Cardinal Odescalchi was able to write to Mother St. Euphrasia and tell her that she might at any time send some of the Sisters to take up their abode in the Eternal City. He added that they would find suitable accommodation for themselves and their penitents, and that he should make a point of seeing that their needs were all supplied. His Eminence concluded by expressing a wish that the Mother General should, if possible, accompany her little caravan, and by assuring her that he should make a point of being at the convent, ready to receive her. No words could express the joy this kind letter gave her. It furnished a new incentive to her zeal. She urged the Religious who were to go to Rome to fresh diligence in the study of Italian. A Chapter more solemn than usual had been held, with a view to their nomination. Although she had attained the advanced age of seventy-five, Mdme. d'Andigné entreated permission to make one of the party, promising on this condition to defray the whole expenses of the journey.

At length, all arrangements being concluded, the Mother General left Angers on Easter Tuesday, April 18, 1838, accompanied by five Religious as well as by Mdme. d'Andigné. They spent the first night at Saumur, and the next at Tours, where they were most kindly received and hospitably entertained by Mlle. de Lignac, whose name is already familiar to the reader. It was a great pleasure to Mother St. Euphrasia to relate to her faithful friend of former days all that God had been pleased to effect through her instrumentality, and the wonderful manner in which the Order of the Good Shepherd had prospered and been developed. In the course of her journey she spent five days at Puy, and was rejoiced to find in the convent seventy-five penitents under the care of the Sisters. She paid a visit to Mgr. de Bonald, in order to thank him for the kindness he had shown her children on their first arrival. Her reputation had preceded her to Puy. Whenever she appeared in the streets or in the churches, a crowd of the poorer classes would gather round her, in order, as they phrased it, "to see the Saint who did so much good everywhere." We cannot enter into every detail of the journey, which offers, moreover, no very striking features. Mother St. Euphrasia never lost sight, for a single moment, of her sole aim and object, the extension of her Order with a view to the conversion of sinners. We have seen how she insisted on the duty of hospitality and courtesy to strangers, and wherever she alighted on her way to Rome she met with a warm reception. On the 1st of June the party embarked at Marseilles on board a steamboat bound for the Levant. It touched at Leghorn on the eve of Pentecost, so that they were able to hear Mass.

Thus far everything had smiled upon them, but a great disappointment awaited them when they reached Civita Vecchia. Father Vaures had said that he hoped to be able to meet them there, and serve as their guide. He was, however, nowhere to be seen. The newly arrived travellers had great difficulty in finding a conveyance to transport them to Rome. The most extortionate prices were demanded of them. It was only after a wearisome delay that they succeeded in obtaining a suitable carriage, so that they were able

to start at eleven o'clock in the morning.   As soon
as she could obtain a glimpse of Rome, Mother
St. Euphrasia ordered a halt to be made.   She alighted
and respectfully kissed the soil which had been watered
with the blood of countless martyrs.   At ten o'clock
in the evening of Whit Monday, June the 4th, the
travellers, proceeding on foot from a feeling of humility,
reached their goal at last.   But the soldiers on guard
were about to close the city gates for the night,
and, seeing Religious arriving so late, imagined them
to be spies, and began to abuse them.   In order to
silence these evil tongues, Mother St. Euphrasia produced her passport, which, however, failed to allay
their doubts, and, in spite of all she could urge, the
soldiers insisted that some of their number should be
allowed to take their place in the carriage.   The Custom
House was happily passed through, but the annoyances
of the Religious were not at an end.   They asked for
the address of some convent where they could spend
the night.   Having been directed to the Convent of
St. Martha, they ordered their driver to proceed thither.
The portress, however, not understanding their imperfect Italian, and astonished to find Religious wandering
in the streets at so advanced an hour, refused them
admittance, and literally shut the door in their faces.
Whither could the weary travellers turn their steps?
To put the crowning touch to their misfortunes, the
coachman, tired of driving them about in the now
deserted streets, stopped in a quiet square, desired
them all to alight, then, after receiving the payment
which had been agreed upon, remounted the box
with alacrity, and drove off as fast as he could.   At
that moment the hour of midnight sounded forth from
all the clocks of the city.   The situation was a painful

M

and perplexing one. But Mother St. Euphrasia's readiness of mind and fertility of resource never deserted her. She asked a passing stranger to direct her to the house of the Jesuit Fathers. Having ascertained where they lived, she sent two of her Sisters to ring at their door. They stood outside for a quarter of an hour, which seemed an hour at least to them. At last the porter opened the door, and as soon as he understood the state of affairs, he awoke one of the Fathers, who came to the help of the weary and belated travellers, and took them to an hotel, kept by some kind-hearted French people. Here they finally found food and shelter.

The beginning was not very encouraging, but the next morning brought consolation in the shape of a visit from Father Vaures, who was most apologetic for having failed to meet them at Civita Vecchia, and said that he was to blame for all the disagreeables they had encountered on reaching the gates of Rome. He informed Cardinal Odescalchi, who sent two of his own carriages to the hotel, in order to convey the Mother General and her companions to St. Peter's, where they were to receive the blessing of His Holiness. When Gregory XVI. approached, Father Vaures pointed out Mother St. Euphrasia to him, and he raised his hand and blessed her. The next visit which the strangers paid was to Cardinal Odescalchi, Father Vaures acting as their interpreter. His Eminence received them in his study with the high-bred courtesy and charming simplicity that characterized him. He expressed his deep regret for all the annoyance they had undergone, and went on to say that he regarded them as sent by God to relieve his own conscience and aid him in his ministrations. It being his office to judge the penitents who were brought to him by their parents and guardians, he explained how deeply it had grieved him to consign these poor girls to prison, since he feared the atmosphere which they must there inhale could never be anything but prejudicial to their souls. "Now," he concluded, "the Sisters of the Good Shepherd will relieve me from a weighty responsibility."

Shortly afterwards, several of the parish priests of Rome came to visit the Sisters, in order to show them the house destined for them. It stood in the Via Longara, and was called the Convent of La Scalette. In former days it had been a place of refuge for penitent women. The exterior of the building was repulsive in the extreme, reminding the beholder of a prison. The interior, however, was so cheerful and pleasant as entirely to remove the first painful impressions. There was a chapel with a tribune, a choir with a grating, about thirty cells opening into a wide corridor, a very large refectory, a good-sized garden with several running fountains of excellent water. The Mother General saw at a glance how easily the house might be so arranged as to suit the requirements of the Rule. The twelve girls, however, who were living in it, furnished her with a far more difficult task. Their only Superior had hitherto been an aged penitent, whom, unfortunately, it was not possible for them to respect. They were extremely idle and ignorant, spending the greater part of their time in sleeping, or in strolling about the garden. They had not energy enough to do the ordinary house-work, so that dirt and disorder reigned everywhere. Their religion consisted solely in a few external practices, the true meaning of which they could not in the least comprehend. The reader will believe what efforts Mother

St. Euphrasia made to win over these poor creatures
and to gain their confidence. She showed them every
kindness she could think of, and on the day when the
Religious came to take formal possession of the house,
she provided them with a much better dinner than
usual.   It may readily be imagined how thoroughly
they appreciated this attention ! Many of them were
not destitute of excellent qualities, both of head and
heart, which only wanted to be called out by good
influence and judicious training.   For instance, a
penitent who had behaved in a disrespectful manner
to one of the Sisters, afterwards came and literally
threw herself at her feet, in order to implore her pardon.
By little and little, the Religious taught their unhappy
charges to do needlework, and attend to household
matters.   Thus cleanliness and order gradually came
to reign where dirt and disorder had too long prevailed,
and when these latter finally fled, the spirit of evil,
which had too long pervaded La Scalette, took its
departure in their train.

Some days after her arrival in Rome, Father Vaures
called upon Mother St. Euphrasia in order to inform
her that the Holy Father intended to grant an audience to herself and her daughters. Her heart beat
very fast as she ascended the wide staircase of the
Vatican. Upon reaching the Pope's ante-chamber, she
mentally rehearsed the ceremonial to be observed, so
anxious was she not to fail in any particular. When
Cardinal Odescalchi presented the little group to His
Holiness: "Here is my Good Shepherd," Gregory XVI.
said, kindly. " Come nearer, Reverend Mother, come
nearer also, my dear children." When they had all
respectfully kissed the Pope's slipper, he desired them
to be seated, and proceeded to converse with them in

a tone of truly paternal kindness, speaking at some length of their Institute, of the difficulties they had surmounted, of the great good they had done, and of the still greater benefits they would confer upon society by multiplying their foundations. His Holiness promised that they should always find in him a protector, and recommended them to the care of Cardinal Odescalchi, who was greatly pleased to see what a favourable impression Mother St. Euphrasia was making. Her frankness and simplicity, her pious and reverent bearing, her folded hands, touched the benevolent heart of Gregory XVI., who when the audience had come to an end, remarked with a smile to Cardinal Odescalchi: " I really believe this good Mother General mistook me for Almighty God Himself!" She, on her part, was charmed with the kindness and condescension shown her by the Sovereign Pontiff. As she descended the staircase of the Vatican, she remarked to her companions: " My dear children, how fortunate you are in thus coming to live at Rome, in the immediate vicinity of the Vicar of Jesus Christ!"

She made a point of paying a visit to several communities who had shown her special courtesy, and particularly to the Sacré-Cœur, where her reputation had preceded her, and she was welcomed with affectionate respect. The Superior of the school begged her to address the pupils. She excused herself on account of her ignorance and inexperience, alleging that she was only accustomed to speak to poor orphans and persons who had grievously offended God. " Therefore," she said, " I am quite unfit to exhort these young ladies, who belong for the most part to distinguished families, members of the Roman aristocracy." When at last she gave way to the repeated urgencies of the Superior, and went into the class-room where the young girls were assembled, she fascinated them all. They hung upon her lips while she related, in the eloquent and forcible manner which was peculiarly her own, several of the remarkable conversions and edifying death-beds it had been her privilege to witness.

She also received visits from many great ladies, who were deeply interested in her work. Among them we may mention Princess Borghese, Princess Piombino, sister of Cardinal Odescalchi, Princess Gabrielli, niece of Napoleon I., the Duchess of Bracciano, and many others.

It is needless to tell how deeply the first sight of St. Peter's impressed Mother St. Euphrasia, nor with what profound interest she visited the shrines and sanctuaries of Rome. Following the injunction of Gregory XVI., she took her Religious with her, before the enclosure was established. The little band was fortunate enough to be present, on the 29th of June, the feast of the holy Apostles, at Pontifical High Mass in St. Peter's. Mother St. Euphrasia never forgot that day. The majestic pomp of the ceremonial lifted her, as it were, out of herself. She could have imagined nothing so splendid and glorious outside the Heavenly Jerusalem. And indeed, when the Vicar of Jesus Christ, borne upon the *sedia*, preceded by a long procession of Religious, Prelates, and Cardinals, made his appearance, carrying the Sacred Host in a magnificent monstrance of the purest gold, it appeared to her that she was already privileged to gaze, as in a·vision, upon the beauties of the Celestial City.

At length her visit, so fortunate and prosperous, so rich in benefits and blessings for both herself and others, drew to a close. It had the happiest termination. The day before her departure, His Holiness again received her, and gave her a parting benediction. Thus cheered and fortified, she left Rome on the 4th of July, embarking at Civita Vecchia with Mdme. d'Andigné. On the 17th she reached Angers, and presented herself at the convent gate. She had kept the date of her arrival a secret, and was therefore received with a burst of enthusiastic delight. " Here is our Mother! Here is our dearest Mother!" was the universal cry. A solemn *Te Deum* was chanted after Mass, and subsequently a set of verses, which one of the nuns had composed in her honour, was sung in the largest of the community-rooms. There was much to hear and much to tell on either side. Mother St. Euphrasia was never weary of relating all the wonders she had beheld, and of telling the joy it had afforded her to visit the holy places which are to be found everywhere in the Eternal City. Let us, however, not forget that Rome, in 1838, differed widely from the Rome of our own unhappy days. The capital of Christendom, it can, indeed, never cease to be, but it was not then the capital of Italy. Wicked and sacrilegious hands had not been stretched forth to despoil of his possessions the earthly representative of the Great Head of the Church. Peace and piety reigned, where anarchy and godlessness now hold sway.

We will give to the reader a discourse delivered to the Community by Mother St. Euphrasia, shortly after her return from Rome. Dating from this period, her children began to write her words down as they fell from her lips.

" I would have you ever bear in mind that, since the house of Angers rightfully bears the title of Mother

House, it alone is in possession of the special graces
necessary for the government of the other houses; it
alone has received the benediction of the Holy Apostolic
See conferring those powers upon it. When, in virtue
of holy obedience, you, my dear daughters, go to one
of our foundations, set before you the Mother House
as the model for your imitation; do not give the
preference to any other, even although you may consider it as very perfect in every respect.

"You all know the ivy, how feeble a plant it is.
Left without support, it cannot rise from the ground;
but plant it by an oak, and it will cling to it tenaciously,
climb upwards, grow quickly, and remain always fresh
and green. Rome is our oak, with which we will ever
be closely united; thus we shall have the strength and
support we need in moments of difficulty and danger.
I do not mean to say that we must appeal to Rome
to decide every little question that may present itself;
nor do I flatter myself that no occasion will ever occur
on which Rome may not see fit to administer to us
reproofs and correction. Rome, we know, is a mother,
and we also know that mothers very often have good
reason to chastise their children. 'What son is
there,' St. Paul says, 'whom the father doth not
correct ? ' [1]

"Or it may happen that misrepresentations are
made at Rome, that a proud and discontented subject
deceives the authorities. This should not discourage
you; the truth invariably triumphs at Rome. Our
work is God's work, and He will surely watch over it.
Let your heart and mind be ever fixed upon our Lord,
upon Rome, upon our Congregation, like the sunflower,
which is so called because it always turns towards the

_____
[1] Hebrews xii. 7.

sun; or the needle of the compass, which always points towards the north.

"I cannot describe to you, my dear daughters, the emotions that I, together with your Sisters, experienced when we entered Rome. As soon as we caught sight of the Eternal City, we fell upon our knees, and kissed the hallowed ground with profound veneration. While in the Basilica of the Vatican, standing at the foot of the altar where rest the remains of the holy Apostles Peter and Paul, I was interiorly urged to promise Almighty God that I would be ready to give my life, if need be, for each one of our foundations. At the same moment our dear Sister Mary Teresa of Jesus was inspired to make the same vow. The Holy Father and the Cardinals gave us the most kindly and paternal assurances of the interest they took in our work.

"His Holiness told us that he considered the Institute of Our Lady of Charity of the Good Shepherd as one of the choicest jewels in his crown. Let us strive not to fall short of what the venerated Head of the Church expects of us, by strict fidelity to all the observances of our Rule, and of our holy Constitutions.

"Do not swerve to the right or to the left, my dear daughters, as do unstable souls. Preserve the sacred trust of your vocation inviolate. Do not allow yourselves to be swayed hither and thither by every blast, after the manner of pusillanimous souls. It is not impossible that some one may advise you to introduce novel practices into our Institute, with the best of intentions perhaps. It behoves you to stand firm, to keep closely to what is prescribed, and not listen to the persuasions of any one who has not the spirit of our Order, or be induced to do anything not in accordance with our holy Rule. Keep your religious observances in all their pristine purity.

"Acquaint yourselves thoroughly with everything that concerns our Institute, even to the smallest details. Be very recollected, gathering up the spiritual sustenance that is imparted to you, like little birds picking up grain by grain the seeds which form their food. If any one of you is thoughtless, giddy, inattentive, all instruction will be lost on her. One might as well scatter corn into a running stream.

"Remember, my dear daughters, that nothing can be changed in our Rule or our Constitutions, without the sanction of the Sovereign Pontiff. By his Brief establishing the Generalate, he confirmed them as a whole and in every particular. Therefore, if any difficulty arises, we must have recourse to the Cardinal Protector of our holy Congregation; we must appeal to Rome, whence come light and guidance. You are placed once and for ever under the protection of the Church; and since it is impossible that Holy Church should ever fail, it is impossible that a Religious Congregation which continues loyally submissive to her supreme authority can ever be destroyed. Should it meet with persecution, the Church will watch over it, as a mother watches over the child whom she sees exposed to danger. And if in any particular spot this sacred tree can produce no fruit, the Church in her wise providence will transplant it to a more favourable clime.

"Never cease to give thanks to God for the immense benefit you have received from His hands, in being born within the fold of the Catholic Church—the Holy Roman and Apostolic Church, whereof you are now doubly the daughters. You are, as it were, in the

ante-chamber of Heaven; one step more and you will
be there. And if the foot of any one should unfortunately slip, let her not lose heart, but trust in God and
rise up quickly. Our task is to people the Church with
holy souls. The Vicegerent of Jesus Christ rejoices
every time that we ask of him permission to establish
another house. Priests who are labouring with apostolic
zeal for the conversion of souls would often be at a loss
how to provide for the safety of the prey they snatch
from the jaws of Hell, were it not for the ready shelter
offered to them in our houses.

"A burning zeal consumes me when I meditate upon
our sacred vocation, for I see that it resembles that
of the missioners more than any other. Sometimes
I seem to hear plaintive voices, the voices of young
children, of little heathen girls, crying out to me: ' My
Mother, my Mother, come and rescue us!' We must
have constant recourse to prayer. Our Lord bids us
ask with persistence, if we would obtain our petitions;
He desires us to be the children of prayer, of toil, of
sacrifice. It is not for us to remain quiescent, like
stagnant water. We must be prepared to bear with
patience, crosses, humiliations, contradictions, if we
would draw down upon our Institute and ourselves the
benedictions of Heaven.

"I used at one time to be very sensitive to the
contradictions that we met with, especially from certain
quarters: I felt them acutely. Now no outward circumstances disturb the peace of my soul. At Rome when
I beheld the Catacombs where the remains of the holy
martyrs are interred; the terrible cavern, through the
narrow mouth of which the Apostles were let down;
the Coliseum, that amphitheatre where so many heroic
souls were put to the cruellest tortures, I said to myself:

What are our sufferings, what are the trials we have to bear, compared with torments such as those? Let us then be willing to suffer, to suffer in union with the Church, which in every age has had her share of calumnies, afflictions, persecutions.

" By your sufferings, your fervour, your prayers, in intimate union with the Church militant, you will alleviate the pains of the Church suffering, and you will render your own way easier finally to reach (even though this should be through the gate of martyrdom) the Church triumphant, of which you will become members. But it is rather by bravely carrying the Cross, by steadfast and exact observance of all that our sacred Constitutions, our Directory, our spiritual exercises prescribe for your guidance, that you may attain the honour of being regarded as little short of martyrs. Endeavour, then, to be very fervent. God has great designs for each one of you. Beseech Him to grant you His love, the love of souls, and you will see what marvels this Divine charity will effect in and for you.

" I shall often talk to you about Rome, and tell you of all the wondrous things I saw there."

During her visits to the Catacombs, the Mother General had been inspired with an ardent wish to transport to her convent at Angers the sacred remains of one of the virgin martyrs who sleep in that quiet resting-place. Pope Gregory XVI. gave her leave to take home with her the body of St. Acapes, which had been discovered in the Catacomb of St. Callistus. Her name was engraved upon her tomb, on one side of which was placed a phial containing her blood; on the marble was the brief but touching inscription: *Acapes*

in pace. Mdme. d'Andigné at once ordered, at her own
expense, a reliquary to contain the venerated remains.
But unluckily, the tradesman from whom it was ordered
failed to keep his promise and complete it in time.
To the great disappointment of the travellers, they
were thus compelled to depart without it. Later on
it was sent off, but instead of being addressed to the
Mother General, it was addressed to the Bishop of
Angers. The authentications had all been overlooked,
and it was necessary to write to Rome in order to
obtain them. No sooner were they received, than
various difficulties arose regarding the removal of the
relics from the Cathedral, where they had been placed,
to the Good Shepherd. Mother St. Euphrasia was
sorely grieved. She feared that her Community would
be deprived of the possession of the reliquary, which
belonged, however, entirely to them. By the advice
of M. de Neuville, she at once wrote to Rome, requesting that a formal declaration might be drawn up and
sent to her, declaring that the relics, and the case
which contained them, were her exclusive property.
In course of time this was duly arranged, so that on
the 12th of January, 1839, Mgr. Montault caused the
relics to be translated to the convent. This was done
in the evening, and at that time of the year the daylight
had long vanished. All the Religious, each bearing a
taper in her hand, awaited the relics at the entrance
to the enclosure. They bore them in procession to
their own chapel, where an altar had been prepared
for their reception. A *Te Deum* was sung, after which
every member of the Community in turn venerated the
relics. The next morning, the body of the Saint was
removed into the outer chapel, where it was to remain.
Year by year, as January 12th came round, Mother

St. Euphrasia celebrated the anniversary of an event which she regarded as so happy an omen for her whole Community. Nor was she deceived in her expectations. St. Acapes showed herself the protectress of the Good Shepherd in many remarkable ways, by means of favours granted at the termination of novenas made in her honour. Besides this, two of the nuns obtained, through her intercession, cures which were regarded as miraculous.

Mother St. Euphrasia cherished a very special affection for her Roman convent. She wished it to be a model house, presenting, in the capital of Christendom, an ideal type to all those who wished to judge her work by its results. In spite of all the need entailed by numerous foundations made elsewhere, she constantly sent gifts of money to Rome. So thoroughly had she imbued the Community at Angers with her spirit in this regard, that all its members took a deep interest in the progress and prosperity of the foundation. It was mentioned prominently in some verses which were composed for the feast of St. Euphrasia. The beloved Mother General kept the feast this year with more than usual display. God had showered down blessings upon her: she desired to show her gratitude by bestowing gifts on her dear children. Her greatest delight was to give, and the numerous alms she had received enabled her to indulge her liberal spirit. She sent off a package containing the linen necessary for each class, and for every Sister a newly-bound copy of the Little Hours.

She was much gratified when, a few months after her visit, Gregory XVI. expressed his wish that a second convent should be established in Rome, in order that a larger number of prisoners might be received.

The house of La Lauretana, thus named because the church attached to it was dedicated to Our Lady of Loretto, had been given by Leo XII., in 1818, to the Society of Roman Ladies of the Confraternity of La Lauretana, in order that they might receive penitents. These ladies ruled over the young women they received until 1840, in which year they addressed a petition to Gregory XVI., praying that their establishment might be handed over to the Good Shepherd of Angers. The Sovereign Pontiff at once summoned to Rome, for the second time, some members of this Congregation. Mother St. Euphrasia promptly sent three of her Religious to make a new foundation. When they entered La Lauretana, they found the altar and the picture of Our Lady of Loretto, which had been placed there by the venerable Father Angelo Paolo, of the Discalced Carmelites. At first they had much to contend with in the shape of poverty and other trials, but erelong the house became very prosperous, and, as it was better known, it had many distinguished visitors among the great ones of the earth and the Princes of the Church.

But of all the visitors, the most welcome was the saintly foundress, who revisited Rome in 1843. She gave permission to the nuns of La Lauretana to enlarge their house, in order to receive some children whom the Princess Doria supported in a separate house. His Holiness was delighted at the idea, and contributed £100 towards the new buildings, which were commenced without delay. The Mother General left there, as a remembrance of her visit, a silver ciborium, which is still preserved with the utmost care.

CHAPTER XII.

TIME OF TRIAL.

We have seen how great a success was the visit which the Mother General paid to Rome in 1838. Everywhere she was welcomed, everywhere she was well received. From the highest to the lowest, all combined to do her honour, and to show the pleasure that her presence among them was the means of affording. Peace and joy attended upon her footsteps, and the delightful impression made upon herself remained with her until her latest breath.

Such seasons of refreshment are to be found here and there in the lives of the servants of God, but they are usually the preparation for a time of trial which is not far off. The shade of the tall palm-trees, and the cool water from the pure, sweet springs, are intended solely to enable the traveller to resume his journey across the scorching sands of the desert with renewed energy and fresh courage. Mother St. Euphrasia returned to Angers in July. In the following November she sustained a heavy loss, through the entrance into the Jesuit Novitiate of Cardinal Odescalchi, the Protector of the Good Shepherd. His counsels had been her support in the past, and to him she looked for guidance and direction in the future. He was a man of eminent sanctity, and gifted, moreover, with an acute

intelligence and sound practical judgment. Vicar of
Rome, Bishop of Sabina, Grand Prior of the Knights
of Malta, he laid all his honours and titles at the feet
of the Supreme Pontiff, and withdrew to Verona, in
order to enrol himself among the sons of St. Ignatius.
His departure created a great sensation in Rome. But
his numerous friends among the aristocracy did not
weep for his loss so bitterly as did the poor. To them
his charity had been absolutely inexhaustible. When
he found a distressing case of sickness and want, he
not unfrequently bestowed his own household linen
upon the sufferers. When he finally quitted Rome, he
left a sealed letter, not to be opened until after his
departure. In this letter, he left the whole of his
fortune to charitable institutions, with the exception
of certain annuities to his servants. Out of the money
thus placed at his disposal, Gregory XVI. sent a considerable sum to the Convent of the Good Shepherd.
The Religious were inconsolable for the loss of their
Protector and friend. But no one grieved so deeply
as Mother St. Euphrasia, and no one had so much
cause for sorrow. She regarded his Eminence as the
real founder of her work, and felt that God had spoken
to her through his lips. When she quitted Rome in
order to return to Angers, she considered that she was
leaving there the true Superior of her Order, who was
to resolve all her difficulties and clear up all her doubts.
The news of his entrance into the Jesuit Novitiate
came upon her like thunder out of a cloudless sky.
But the intense and most real belief in the Communion
of Saints, of which we have spoken in a former chapter,
sustained and fortified her. She knew how much the
prayers of our absent friends can do for us, even while
they are yet prisoners in the flesh. She loved to think

N

that our dear Guardian Angels can carry messages for us to and fro, so that we may pray and labour in union with those from whom distance separates us, as far as personal intercourse is concerned.

> Thus do we walk with them, and keep unbroken
>   The bond which love doth give,
> Hoping that our remembrance, though unspoken,
>   May reach them where they live.

In the course of his journey to Verona, the Cardinal wrote from Florence a touching letter to the Nuns of the Good Shepherd, then residing in Rome. He bade them an affectionate farewell, and told them that he had recommended them to the Pope in a special manner, and that His Holiness had promised them absolute independence in the government of their house, and had further declared that he would appoint over them a suitable Protector. Cardinal Joseph della Porta, Cardinal Vicar, was appointed shortly afterwards to this office.

The constant interest which Mgr. Montault took in her work was no small comfort and support to Mother St. Euphrasia. He considered the Good Shepherd to be one of the chief glories of his diocese, he loved the humble and the poor, and took a fatherly pleasure in watching over the penitents. He had seen the early struggles of the convent, he had helped it to tide over its difficulties, he had stood by it in its trials. Now he beheld it in all its force and ample extension. The Novitiate, which contained a hundred and thirty novices, gave the happiest promise for the future. The Mother General kept in her own hands, as far as possible, the direction and instruction of this important branch of her subjects. She was aided in her task by six of the most experienced among the professed nuns. But she always explained the Rule herself, and strove to infuse into the young Religious the real spirit of the Order, together with her own zeal for the conversion of souls. She was fully aware that the surest way of building up a Community is to diffuse throughout it the spirit of its foundress, which is the atmosphere in which all its members ought to live and breathe. This object she kept constantly before her, and she left no means untried in order to form her children in their vocation. With this aim she frequently addressed them at some length, and in this place we cannot do better than give our readers an opportunity of perusing for themselves one of these discourses.

"The excellent Religious whom it has lately been our privilege to entertain for a few days, said, on taking leave: 'Oh! what are we in comparison to the Nuns of the Good Shepherd?' Do you suppose that it was the pleasant manners, the attentions of a few novices, that prompted those words? Certainly not. It was the order, the regularity with which all our duties were fulfilled, that they admired so much; the assiduity each one of us displayed in seeking the welfare of our poor children; the spirit of sacrifice, the devotedness that they remarked in the mistresses of the classes; it was that, and nothing else, which delighted them. People look upon you as so many saints, my dear daughters; it is on this account that you are wanted in every direction, that missioners and others who are zealous for souls claim your services. Take heed lest these persons should find themselves deceived in the opinion they have formed of you; I mean you must prove yourselves to be saints in reality.   Redouble your efforts, strive to advance more and more rapidly in the path of perfection.

"It is said that St. Chantal's novices became in the space of a few months such perfect Religious, that she could make any use of them that she pleased.   Would that I could have, for one year at least, her spirit of sanctity to enable me to form in the Novitiate, in a short time, mistresses for the different classes, Religious fitted to be superiors and foundresses!   They would be the greatest acquisition to us, for more than one of our undertakings are in an unsatisfactory condition, and stand in sore need of reinforcements.

"A Religious of the Good Shepherd ought to take equal pleasure in her work, whether she is sent to a new foundation, or whether the care of the classes is given her.   She ought not to say: 'I had very much rather be at Angers, I do not know how I shall ever make myself feel at home here;' or, 'Some other employment would suit me far better.'   Would this be showing herself a good Religious?   It would not even be acting as a Christian, for does not every good Christian feel the obligation of bearing with vexations and making sacrifices?   How many persons living in the world have their will thwarted from morning till night, without uttering a word of complaint as to their lot!   Can it be right then for Religious to complain of what they do not like, they who ought to be proficient in the love of the Cross, so necessary as this is to the attainment of perfection?   Believe me, when the love of the Cross, the desire for suffering and abnegation of self, disappears from amongst us, the hour of dissolution for our Order is near at hand.

"Let us suppose that, yielding to your importunity, I allow myself to be persuaded to leave you the choice of the place whither you would like to go, and to assign to you the employment best suited to your tastes. Depend upon it, you would all be as miserable as you could be. You would be miserable in this life because of the remorse that would torment you, and you would be miserable in the next life because there the judgments of God would fall upon you in all their severity and overwhelm you.

"When the time comes for you to leave the Mother House you are quite distressed, you shed many tears, feeling as you do most acutely the separation from all you love best in the world. This feeling is natural, it is the offspring of a grateful heart; I do not blame you for it, quite the contrary. I like to see in you this fond religious attachment, and I am convinced as long as it is a grief to you to leave the Mother House, the life and prosperity of our Order are secure.

"Always bear in mind that the love for souls is the only foundation upon which our Order rests, and only by this love can it be maintained. Do you know what I call the love we ought to have for souls? I call it *appreciative love*. The Saints loved souls, because they had been purchased at the cost of the Saviour's Blood. They appreciate at its true value the soul of a poor, ragged gutter-child, full of faults; the soul of a great sinner, of an erring woman, because these souls are the objects of God's love, and our Lord has shed His Blood for their redemption. St. Francis Xavier was stirred by thoughts such as these when he devoted himself to win souls. A Religious who shrinks from difficulties and dislikes, or one who says, I should like this or that, without regard to anything but her own satisfaction; alas for her! because there can be no true love for souls in her heart.

"What are we doing in the world, and for what purpose are we here, if not to work for the salvation of our fellow-men? Let us unite ourselves to our Lord in the Blessed Sacrament. There He continually anni- hilates Himself, presenting Himself to the Eternal Father as a sacrifice in reparation for the insults offered to His Divine Majesty, for the transgressions of those who wander from the right way, of those who shut their eyes to the fact that they are by their iniquities heaping up to themselves wrath. But Jesus loves these erring souls, and evermore He shows to His Father the wounds wherewith He has suffered Himself to be wounded for their salvation. These souls belong to him; He has acquired the right to them by so many titles, He desires that all should be saved, and should be united to Him for all eternity. Was it not to rescue them, to ransom them, that He came down from Heaven? Behold and see how infinite is the Divine charity!

"And we, on our part, are we never to do anything for Him? Shall we make Him no return for all that He has done for us? Ah, yes, we will bring back to Him some of the souls that are so precious in His sight. If we do this, then at the hour of death, in the supreme moment when we must appear before Him Who ought to be the one only object of our love, at that moment, I say, those souls, the souls whom it has been our privilege to help on their way to Heaven, and who have arrived before us at their goal, will come and lay their palms and their crowns at our feet, recognizing in us the instruments of which it pleased God to make use to lead them to Himself. How great will then be our joy! What gladness, what rejoicing will fill the courts of Heaven when the

Nuns of the Good Shepherd make their entry there in triumph!

"I will say no more, my dear daughters, for this is a subject so vast that, were I to enlarge upon it, I should never have done speaking. I will only bid you love our dear penitents more and more, and learn to appreciate more highly your vocation, that precious gift which God in His goodness has bestowed on you, and for which you can never be sufficiently grateful to Him.

"Remember, too, that whatever may be the occupation assigned to you, whether your fingers ply the needle or hold the pen, whether you are employed in the kitchen or any other kind of work, the salvation of souls must be ever before your mind as the end and object of your labours. You know what was the mission which the Son of God came to fulfil upon earth; remind yourselves that to a certain extent you are privileged to call your vocation a similar one. You may well deem this to be an honour; you may well be proud of the noble enterprise which is entrusted to you. Let us present to our Lord the souls that He has ransomed with His Precious Blood, with His Life; let us offer them to Him as a pledge of our love, as our claim to the eternal recompense which He has in store for each one of us."

Mother St. Euphrasia frequently varied her discourses with anecdotes of some penitent, whose story she thought would interest the novices and give them an idea of what their future work was to be, and of the class of persons with whom they would have to deal. We will again allow her to speak for herself:

"This very morning we received a poor young

woman, twenty-five years of age, who was in a state of such extreme misery and destitution, that she was reduced to despair. It was truly distressing to see her. Among other things I asked her whether she had made her first Communion. 'Perhaps I have, and perhaps I have not,' she answered, 'for, to tell the truth, I really do not know what the expression, "to make my first Communion," means. I remember that once, when I was dangerously ill, what is called the Viaticum was brought to me, but indeed I am ignorant what It is. All that I know about is sin, and its eternal punishment!' I asked her whether she would like to partake of some refreshment, for, seeing her tattered and soiled clothing, I thought she might be hungry, as she was so wretchedly poor. 'O Mother,' she exclaimed, 'as soon as I come here, you offer me food! Yesterday I was positively starving, and I could find no one to give me a crust of bread! I am dreadfully ashamed of appearing before you in the state in which I am, and I would gladly have begged from door to door, if I could thus have procured a more decent gown.' Then she burst into tears, and cried so bitterly, that the sight of her emotion moved me deeply. 'My dear child,' I said, 'have you remembered to pray sometimes to our Blessed Lady?' 'Oh, yes,' she replied, 'even when I was leading a sinful life, I do not think I ever forgot to say daily at least one *Ave Maria.*' A charitable lady chanced to meet this poor girl in the street, and seeing her pitiable condition, she had compassion on her, and brought her here. This was evidently the work of Our Lady Immaculate, whose loving-kindness is so marvellous, and who extends her care and protection even to sinners who scarcely remember her."

We have seen how the wonderful prosperity and rapid extension of the Good Shepherd cheered the latter years of Mgr. Montault. And when extreme old age prevented him from paying his accustomed frequent visits to his beloved daughters, M. Mainguy, the chaplain of the convent, used to communicate to his lordship all the joys and sorrows of the Community. One day he found the venerable prelate in his drawing-room, trying to walk up and down the apartment. "Tell Mother St. Euphrasia," he said, "that I am endeavouring to get up my strength, in order that I may come and pay her a visit." About a week later, the announcement was received that he was actually on his way to the convent. The Religious received him at the entrance of the enclosure. In spite of his zeal, he appeared greatly fatigued, and was compelled to remain seated in an arm-chair, while he delivered a touching address to the nuns, concluding in the following words : " I feel that my course is nearly run, I am approaching the portals of the unseen world. My dear children, when the passing-bell is rung, to announce that I am in my agony, I entreat you to pray for the poor Bishop of Angers, in order that the Supreme Judge of all men may deign to show him mercy." His voice died away in his throat, he gave the blessing to the Community, and then dismissed them in silence.

He detained the Mother General for some time longer, in order that she might give him full details about her various foundations. When she had finished, he said : " Truly this work is of God ; I perceive it more clearly than I have ever done before. I consider myself most fortunate in having been selected by God to aid in establishing it." Mother St. Euphrasia was profoundly moved. Her grateful heart fully appreciated all the kindness she had received from Mgr. Montault, and she was much touched by the effort he had made to pay her this visit, which she felt certain would be his last.

Nor was she wrong. Only a few days later, the good old man, who had attained the advanced age of eighty-five years, was stretched upon his death-bed. The evening before he expired, he signed his name for the last time to a form of Rules which had been drawn up for the penitents. Then he said to M. Mainguy, who was standing beside his bed: "Do not forget to remind the Community of the Good Shepherd of the request I addressed to them on the occasion of my last visit. I also wish that when I am in my agony, the Blessed Sacrament should be exposed in their chapel." His decease took place on the 29th of July, 1839, and only a short time before he breathed his last, he recommended to M. Régnier, his Vicar-General, the Convent of the Good Shepherd. Thus almost his last words were uttered on its behalf, as his last signature was made in its favour.

His loss was a new and a real sorrow for Mother St. Euphrasia. She bitterly mourned for him, and caused a Solemn Requiem to be celebrated for him in the chapel, requesting at the same time all the members of her Order to offer for him their prayers and Holy Communions.

In the beginning of 1840, the Mother General felt it to be her duty to make a visitation of her various houses. M. Régnier, whom we have just had occasion to mention, and who was then Vicar-Capitular, gave her permission to leave the convent for a time, accompanied by two of the Sisters. The three Religious set out accordingly. They had only reached Auxerre, how-

ever, before Mother St. Euphrasia became so seriously
ill, that all idea of pursuing the journey became manifestly out of the question, and the little party was
obliged to return to Angers. Yet in this short space of
time she had been able to have an interview with the
Archbishop of Sens and the Bishop designate of Puy,
and also while passing through Paris had learnt that
the Queen was favourably inclined towards the Institute,
and was about to recommend it to the Archbishop in
order that a foundation might be made in the capital.
A letter which she wrote from Sens to the Sister
Assistant at Angers, shows in how resigned and
Christian a spirit she accepted the vexations and contradictions which Divine Providence ordained for her.
"The will of God has compelled me to pause on my
way. We can do nothing but adore it, and submit in
silence. My soul is in perfect peace, because I am
conscious of having done all that I possibly can. Do
not be cast down, dear children; though we were unable
to prosecute our journey, we fulfilled the will of God
none the less by attempting it."

Just at the time when the Mother General was
returning, wearied and out of health, to Angers, the
new Bishop, Mgr. Paysant, made his entry into his
episcopal city. As he had been the Superior of the
Refuge at Caen, it was natural that Mother St.
Euphrasia should feel somewhat apprehensive in what
manner he might regard her work, and should fear
that he would be decidedly opposed to the Generalate.
This dread was, however, happily soon dispelled.
On his first visit to the Good Shepherd, he evinced the
kindest interest in the whole Community, appointed
M. Régnier to be its Superior, and assured the
Religious that in his opinion the Generalate was an

institution absolutely necessary to supply the needs of the time. In order to prove that his professions of friendship and paternal kindness were not mere empty phrases, he consented to preside at several clothings and professions which were shortly to take place.

In 1838, Mother St. Euphrasia had lost the wise Protector of her Order, Cardinal Odescalchi; in 1839, the death of her long-tried and faithful friend, Mgr. Montault, had deeply grieved her. And now, in 1840, her affectionate heart was to receive a still deeper wound. In March of that year, our Lord saw fit to summon to His immediate presence Sister Mary of St. Anselm Dobrais, who died at the age of twenty-six years. She came originally from Mans, and since her profession she had acquired in the Community such a reputation for sanctity, that on her death, her Sisters in Religion wished to preserve her heart; they placed it, surrounded with lilies and violets, in the cloisters, near an altar of St. Radegunda.

Mother St. Euphrasia sorrowed deeply for the loss of this beloved daughter. " Alas !" she wrote to the Superior at Poitiers, " I cannot see what I write, my eyes are blinded with tears, my paper is blotted with them. I have just come from the death-bed of a nun of pre-eminent sanctity. Our dear St. Anselm is gone from us. She is in the blissful presence of God. That sweet, saintly child, who loved you so fondly, is now no more. Oh, my daughter, I believe, I feel certain that she is in Heaven. I must leave it to our Sisters to tell you the rest. I cannot write for crying, but if my pen is silent, my heart speaks to you." The writer of the above words, whose strong faith made it easy for her to realize the unseen world, was so thoroughly convinced of the sanctity of this admirable Religious, that when the doctor, who was about to take out her heart before her interment, experienced some difficulty in straightening the arms which were crossed upon her breast, she spoke to the rigid corpse as she would have spoken to a living sentient being, " My dear daughter, in virtue of the obedience you always practised so promptly, do not prevent us from carrying out our purpose." True to the habit of obedience, even in death, the nun, at the sound of her Superior's voice, allowed her stiffened arms to fall by her side immediately, so that the surgeon was enabled to proceed with the operation without hindrance. This incident, inscribed in the annals of the Order by the spiritual daughters of the beloved foundress, has been handed down from generation to generation.

It may perhaps appear almost incredible that a temperament so intensely sensitive as that of Mother St. Euphrasia should be able to bear up against the succession of painful emotions through which she had to pass. A nature less finely strung, a character less well-balanced, might have broken down under the stress; as for her, she sought relief in action, she regained strength in undertaking fresh labours for the cause she served. The departed Sisters were not forgotten by her; far from it, their memory was enshrined within her heart; she loved to think of them as still forming part of her Community, as fellow-workers aiding and assisting her in Heaven. From the example of their virtues she drew support and encouragement for herself and those around her; witness the edifying discourse addressed to her Community on March 29, 1840, in which she sketched the religious career of Sister St. Anselm, and pointed out the spiritual profit that her Sisters in Religion

might derive from the contemplation of her admirable
example.

" Do you not all feel with me, my beloved daughters,"
she said, " that it is impossible to realize the fact that
our dear Sister Mary of St. Anselm is no longer amongst
us ? We cannot, indeed, at all accustom ourselves to
the void her departure has made in our midst.   Let us
think of her in Heaven, where she is praying for the
Community, for each one of us ; and the consciousness
that she is happy will go far to alleviate our grief.

" Our Lady herself called her to her service, for she
was an earthly reflection of her virtues.   She was full
of the Spirit of God.   What judgment was hers, and
what wisdom !   How vast was the store of spiritual
treasures that chosen soul contained !   Every one compared her to St. Aloysius Gonzaga ; she had his angelic
purity, his total abandonment to the will of God.

" This Sister, whose loss we all mourn so bitterly,
was throughout her whole life a model to others.   In
the bosom of her family she was the joy and consolation
of her parents, on account of the excellent qualities
with which she was so richly endowed.   Her brothers
and sisters idolized her.   Severe with herself, indulgent
towards others, she never lost an occasion of making
herself useful or giving pleasure to those with whom
she was brought into contact.   When it was a question
of paying visits, or accepting invitations for the evening,
it was her constant habit to let her sisters go instead of
herself, alleging that she was of too dull a nature to
go into society.   Then in a cheerful tone she would
add : 'Now, while you are away, I will finish your
embroidery for you ; I shall enjoy doing that far more.'
By means of these little self-imposed sacrifices, which

young people do not find easy, she prepared herself for that vocation, the thought of which was so dear to her.

"A short time before she went into Religion, whilst she was talking one day to her director, M. Régnier, about the attraction she felt for our holy Order, she said to him with truly admirable humility: 'I am afraid lest, being so great a sinner, I may only pollute the sanctuary by my presence.' Little did you imagine, sweet Sister, how you were destined to embellish it!

"'That is not what I am thinking of,' M. Régnier replied; 'I am thinking of your mother's grief, and how necessary you are to her.' 'God will give me the grace to conquer those obstacles,' she answered. When M. Régnier brought her to us, he said: 'Here is a saintly soul, a character of sterling worth. Receive her as a gift from the hands of God.'

"As a Religious she was an embodiment of the Rule. Those who wanted to know what was enjoined at any particular time had only to look what Sister Mary of St. Anselm was doing. She was very well educated; she understood Latin and could draw well; English was as familiar to her as French. And yet when her mother asked her how she was employed at the Good Shepherd, she answered with the gentle manner habitual to her: 'I am a burden to the Community, but our Sisters are so kind, that they never allow me to feel it.' 'But you were so useful at home, so necessary to us all!' 'Dearest mother,' she replied, 'it was your affection for me that made you think so.' Humility and obedience seemed to be the life of her soul; her habit of constantly looking to God enabled her to detect her slightest imperfections; all she did was done in the right way and at the right time. When the time came to appear before God, we cannot doubt that she had kept all her vows in their integrity. She was not one of those plants which are withered by the scorching blast of pride; she was a flower whose chalice received the morning dews, and daily increased in freshness and beauty. Her soul was stored with the richest virtues, like the ships that come from distant isles, laden with costly treasures. Her pure, disinterested charity excluded no one from its embrace. She sought out the simple, that she might instruct and amuse them; she did not shrink from the sad, for she saw she could enter into their feelings; she liked the company of the young novices, because they cheered and enlivened her. In spite of her chronic sufferings, and the interior trials through which it pleased God that she should pass, she never lost her habitual serenity. So beautiful a life could not fail to be crowned by a no less beautiful death.

"Our dear Sister St. Anselm saw her end approach not only with calmness, but with joy. During her last illness her virtue shone more brightly than ever; always cheerful, always patient, she longed for the moment that would end her earthly career. When in her agony, she hesitated to break the long silence of night in order to ask for some trifling relief. She even reproached herself with having said that she was thirsty. At the point of death, she still offered her sufferings on behalf of the good works of our Institute, which she loved dearly. She offered them for our intentions. And when we urged her to pray for her recovery, feeling that her only desire was to depart, and yet fearing to disobey, she rejoined: 'If you wish it, dear Mother, if our Sisters wish it; but oh, how hard it is to me to do so!' Then in faint accents she was heard to murmur: 'How sweet it is to die!' A few moments later, going up to her bedside, I said to her: 'My child, we will go up to the house of the Lord.' 'Oh, yes, my Mother,' she replied with a look of intense happiness, and immediately expired.

"The memory of this humble Religious will abide with us for ever. In accordance with your wish, my dear daughters, we have had her heart taken out. Placed in a transparent urn, it will stand in a niche in the cloisters, and above it these words will be inscribed: 'He that humbleth himself shall be exalted.' The sight of it will be an incentive to you to imitate so fair an example. Above all, you will say to yourselves: Our dear Sister, Sister Mary of St. Anselm, whose loss we regret so deeply, never spoke a word whilst going about the monastery.

"Thus the fragrance of her virtues will continue to pervade the quiet cloisters that are so dear to us, and future generations will learn what fair flowers bloom in the garden of the Celestial Spouse."

During this period of trial, the Order had been spreading rapidly. Houses had been founded at Chambéry, Perpignan, Mons, Namur, Nice, Bourges, Lille, and Avignon. To enter into a detailed account of each of these would be manifestly impossible, and would, moreover, present an aspect of sameness as a whole, though differing more or less in minor particulars. We will relate at greater length the history of the foundation of Avignon, both because it possesses more individuality of character, and also because it was attended with manifold trials and cares.

The Archbishop of Avignon, impressed by the accounts he had heard on all sides of the admirable work the Good Shepherd was doing, wrote as early as

o

1838 to the Mother General to request her to send some
of her Religious to make a foundation. As we have
frequently had occasion to observe, she could never
refuse a proposal of this kind. Accordingly, she shortly
afterwards despatched a little colony of Sisters, who
placed themselves at the disposal of the Archbishop,
Mgr. du Pont, in order to found a convent of their
Order. He received them most graciously, and gave
them much valuable advice as to their relations
with the authorities of the city and the benefactors
of their house. He warned them that much prudence
and tact would be required if success was to be ensured,
but encouraged them by adding that quiet perseverance
would overcome all obstacles. The Sisters listened all
the more attentively to these counsels, because their
beloved Mother General had impressed them with the
necessity of practising docile submission in regard to
Mgr. du Pont, whom she wished them to regard as
their father, and the chief of all the benefactors they
might meet with at Avignon.

Yet, notwithstanding these happy auspices, the sky
soon clouded over, and manifold trials and annoyances
became her portion. She received letters which informed her that means sufficient for the foundation
were not forthcoming, and that it would, moreover,
prove absolutely superfluous, as the Sisters of St. Thomas
of Villanova, who were already settled in the city, were
accomplishing all that the Good Shepherd could possibly
do. The enemy of all good, in order to wound her in
the most sensitive part, stirred up some unprincipled
persons to strive to inspire her with distrust of the
Archbishop. These calumniators represented his Grace
as being hostile at heart to the work she was carrying
on. They said that, far from taking a genuine interest

in it, he discouraged those who were desirous of becoming its benefactors. Knowing that frankness and candour are the surest means of putting an end to painful situations of this nature, she wrote quite plainly to the Archbishop, informing his Grace of these malevolent rumours. He thanked her for her straightforward conduct, and, when answering her letter, assured her that his kindly feelings had undergone no change, but that he counted himself most fortunate in seeing a Convent of the Good Shepherd established in his archdiocese. He did more than this. In an *Imprimatur*, which explained to the faithful the object of the Order, he recommended the house at Avignon to the charity of all over whom he ruled. In conclusion, he stated that the Institute was held in high esteem by the Sovereign Pontiff, and by all the members of the Sacred College.

Yet the foundation of which we are speaking was destined to cause much grief to the Mother General. A year after its commencement, it was well-nigh swept away by an inundation of the Rhone. The whole Community was compelled to beg temporary shelter from the Sisters who managed the public hospital of the city. When at last the Religious were able to reenter their convent, ruin and desolation met them everywhere. Their own resources were inadequate to cope with the emergency, and they turned for help to their beloved foundress. The funds at her disposal happened to be just then running somewhat low, but in all her financial difficulties she was accustomed to appeal to our Lady and the Saints. Far from allowing herself to be discouraged or cast down, she promised her heavenly protectors she would make some fresh foundations if they would deliver her from her present straits. And now, as she had scarcely the means of carrying on her work, she gathered together the members of the Council of the house at Angers, and solemnly declared that, if she were freed from the difficulties which were pressing upon her, she would found a house at Bourges. Her prayer was heard and answered, nor was she found wanting as far as her part of the engagement was concerned.

An anecdote, which shows how anxious she was to give external proof of the deep gratitude she ever cherished towards her benefactors, may suitably close this chapter. In order to express these feelings, she sent to the Holy Father, about the end of 1839, a basket of artificial flowers, made in the convent at Angers. So skilfully had these flowers been fashioned by the deft fingers of the nuns, that lack of perfume alone distinguished them from blossoms wrought by the hand of nature. His Holiness was much gratified by this graceful attention, and caused the pleasure he felt to be signified to Mother St. Euphrasia in terms which inspired her with fresh devotion to the See of Peter.

CHAPTER XIII

MUNICH.

THE first foundation made on German soil was indirectly originated by a young novice, Mlle. de Baligand, who came to Angers from Treves. During the time she spent in the Novitiate, one of her uncles, who occupied a distinguished position in the city of Ratisbon, wrote to ask her for some information concerning the Order of the Good Shepherd. He was so delighted with all he heard, that he went straight to the Bishop, in order to obtain his permission to found a house in the city. His lordship listened in the kindest manner to the account given him, but he said that an authorization must be obtained from the King before it could be possible for him to invite a foreign Community to settle in his diocese.

King Louis I. of Bavaria had, ever since his accession to the throne in 1825, done much for the cause of the faith. He had gladly witnessed the establishment in his dominions of a large number of Religious Communities, and it was highly improbable that he would close the door against an Order like the Good Shepherd, which would so manifestly promote the welfare of his people, especially as he had a great affection for the French nation. The Constitutions of the Order were accordingly laid before him, and he was so much delighted with them, that he commanded the Court chaplain, M. Eberhard, to obtain further details. He lost no time in paying a visit to the convent at Strasburg. All that he saw and heard so entirely satisfied him, that the report which he gave to His Majesty on his return, induced the King to request that two of the Sisters might be sent to Munich, in order that he might have an interview with them. The Mother General sent the Superior of the house at Nancy, Sister Mary of St. John of the Cross, accompanied by another Sister. The Monarch received them with marked kindness, and arranged with them about the foundation of a house, not indeed at Ratisbon, but in the capital, where the work to be done would be on a more extensive scale.

When Sister St. John of the Cross arrived at Angers, in order to give Mother St. Euphrasia an account of her mission, she brought back with her a novice, Mlle. von Müller by name. She belonged to a Bavarian family of great distinction, and had long cherished a strong desire to enter the religious life, although no Order with which she had as yet become acquainted corresponded to the desires of her soul. Her father happened one day to give her an account of the work carried on by the Good Shepherd. She immediately became conscious of a strong attraction to join it, and requested him to permit her to enter the Novitiate at Angers. He granted her desire on the condition that, if she remained in the convent, she should return in due course to the house which was to be founded at Munich. The Mother General considered this petition to be a very reasonable one, and consented accordingly. Mlle. von Müller took the name of Sister Mary of the Sacred Heart, and her virtues, together with her large fortune, contributed not a little to the prosperity of the house.

Some months later, King Louis sent M. Eberhard to Angers, in order that he might escort to Munich the Sisters selected to make the foundation. Mother St. Euphrasia sent in the first place Sister Mary of St. John of the Cross, and Sister Mary of St. Helena. When they reached their destination, their own house was not ready for them, and they were therefore received under the roof of a charitable lady, Mdme. de Schoso. She welcomed them most warmly, and hospitably entertained them until they could be installed in their convent, on the 9th of November, 1840. The King agreed with Mgr. de Gebsattel, the Archbishop of Munich, to bestow upon them a property which went by the name of Freising, and comprised not only a mansion, but very extensive grounds. It was situated in a suburb of Munich, called Haidhausen.

The solemn installation was conducted on a scale of almost regal magnificence, to the surprise of the two humble Sisters, who had never witnessed anything of the kind in their French houses. After a Solemn High Mass, sung in the parish church of Haidhausen by his Grace the Archbishop, and a sermon preached by M. Eberhard, before an audience composed of several princesses of royal blood, and all that was most distinguished among the aristocracy, the Religious were conducted in triumphal procession to their new home. A band of musicians began the march; they were followed by several hundred little girls, beautifully dressed in white. The streets were garlanded with flowers, and the same fragrant ornaments strewed the roadway. No sooner had they entered the most spacious apartment of their convent, than the Dean of the

Cathedral, in the name of the Archbishop, delivered a brief, but beautiful address, in which he painted, in vivid colours, the abundant harvest to be expected from the grain of mustard-seed now sown in the rich and fertile soil of Bavaria. The Count of Seinsheim, Minister of Finance, then approached in his turn, and presented an offering of 10,000 florins, given by His Majesty from his private purse, with a view to aiding in the erection of a chapel. Finally, the venerable Archbishop, in spite of his eighty-three years, blessed the house and grounds. From that day until his lamented death, he took the most lively interest in the Community.

It is not difficult to imagine the joy with which the account of all we have just related was received at Angers. Mother St. Euphrasia set, of course, a more than usual value on the house at Munich, because she knew that upon it depended the future of the Good Shepherd in Germany. In December she sent three more Sisters; among them was Sister Mary of the Sacred Heart (Mlle. von Müller), who was appointed Sister Assistant. But the bright sunshine of these early days did not make the saintly foundress forget that clouds must gather and storms descend upon her children. She had learnt by personal experience the truth of the German proverb, which tells that the promise of a fine day is not always fulfilled.[1] Sorrow and suffering were not far off. The house, which was a large villa, erected with a view to summer occupation alone, afforded them but scant shelter from the cold of a bitter winter. M. Eberhard, who had been appointed their Superior, and who superintended the new buildings in course of construction, was compelled to quit

[1] "Man soll den Tag nicht vor dem Abend loben."

Munich, to such a degree was he pursued by the calumnies of Protestants, who did all they possibly could to drive the Sisters out of the city, and circulated many false and depreciatory reports concerning them. Indeed, so serious a pass did matters reach, that the friends of the Good Shepherd became utterly discouraged, and sometimes advised the Sisters to abandon their post and return to France. It was on occasions similar to this that Mother St. Euphrasia wrote to her children letters which, like the following, were calculated to reanimate their courage and cheer their drooping spirits.

" ' They that sow in tears, shall reap in joy.'

" My poor dear afflicted St. John of the Cross,— You are indeed pierced with a sword of sorrow ! How pleasing your soul must be in the sight of God ! We have received both your welcome letters ; humanly speaking, I am deeply distressed, but, viewing it in the light of faith, I feel persuaded that the work will ultimately succeed. Let me entreat you, my beloved daughter, not to abandon your post ; be firm in your refusal to admit of interference on the part of the civil authorities, with their enslaving stipulations, their delusive promises. Yes, do your utmost to stay at Munich ; preserve your liberty, and be content to be poor, if such be God's will ; do not bind yourself in any way, and, above all, do not forsake this mission, unless you are actually compelled to do so. God be thanked a thousand times for the kindly dispositions, the generous devotion of our excellent Father Eberhard, whom we deeply venerate and love. Beg him to stand by us, to support this work, for which he was so desirous, and to which he has been so helpful. An opening has presented itself for us in London, of a most advantageous nature. What a rich harvest of souls awaits us there! Nothing could have been better than the behaviour of our Sisters; yet as his lordship obliged them to return here, the fate of that undertaking is very uncertain. A large house, ready furnished, has been given to us. The Sisters promised to go back erelong, but the Catholics say their arrival produced a great sensation. They brought back with them six young ladies, such charming girls! How I wish that you could send us a similar number, for our consolation and your own. Pray earnestly, and we will do the same; the tears you shed will bear fruit for the good of the whole Order. You will conquer by means of the Cross; we have always met with severe trials, and they have always resulted in the glory of God and the triumph of His cause. The greater our sufferings, the greater the benefits that have accrued to our work. There is promise of a plentiful harvest at Munich, that is why the enemy of all good has sown his cockle. But the Master of this harvest slumbers not nor sleeps; let us therefore take courage. . . . St. Jerome learnt Greek when he was thirty years old. Do you, then, my dear daughter, learn German; you have abundance of time at your disposal. Rely upon the Divine help, and apply yourself to the task."

The King never withdrew his support and protection. On the contrary, he continued to show them marked signs of his royal favour. For instance, he caused a garden to be definitely made over to them, when certain members of the municipality desired to take it from them in order to build a hospital on the site. One morning he paid an early visit to the convent

in order to make a personal inspection of the whole
house. He was greatly delighted with all he saw, and
openly expressed his admiration of the Order. Later
on the Queen came several times. It seemed as if
our Lord and our Blessed Lady were desirous of showing the Sisters definite and visible encouragement in
the midst of their trials. The same providential
features which marked the Angers foundation were
repeated at Munich, and the Mother General was
glad to see her children walking in the road she had
herself traversed. One day a priest belonging to the
Cathedral of Augsburg called at the convent, and asked
to see the Mother Superior. He brought an offering of
9,500 florins, the gift of a benefactress. Another day,
a pious peasant woman brought them 5,000 florins, the
savings of a lifetime. The name of this truly generous
soul is not known to the world, but none can doubt
that the recording angel has inscribed it in letters of
gold in the pages of the Book of Life. Thus watered
from fountains of the purest charity, the foundation
could not but grow and prosper, in spite of evil tongues.
In 1844 it numbered twenty-six Religious, eighty penitents, seventy members of the so-called " preservation
class," besides fifty children in the school.

The letters of Mother St. Euphrasia to Mother
St. John of the Cross, who was, as we have said, the
first Superior of the Munich Convent, are full of affectionate counsel and advice. The foundress, seeing the
spiritual as well as temporal gifts showered down upon
her children, could not allow doubts or fears to enter,
even for one instant, into her courageous soul. We
have inserted a letter written in a minor key, we shall
now introduce another written in a more jubilant
strain.

" From our Monastery of Angers,
        " July 23, 1840.
" ' The Lord hath broken my bonds ! '

" Like David, you too, my most devoted daughter, have sung a canticle of praise to our merciful God ; and I with all your Sisters, unite our voices to yours in the same joyous strain. Your welcome letter brought fresh life to us ; we exult in God, Who has broken the chains wherewith you were held captive. My beloved Bavaria, we shall not lose you after all ! What you tell me about the church and the convent is delightful. How good God is ! We have now established ourselves on firm ground, though in a somewhat inhospitable region. You know how fond I am of the Germans, and of you above all, my daughter, who are of the greatest assistance to me. Many will be the prayers we shall offer, many the vows we shall make on your behalf, that our Lord Himself may be the corner-stone of the noble edifice you are raising ; that you may abide in His Spirit, and live by His grace ! . . . I have much that I might tell you of our various foundations, but I have no more light, no more strength ; I am over-whelmed with labours, with graces, with crosses. God, and God alone, sustains me : He is our greatest treasure."

In order to complete our account of this foundation, one of the most interesting and remarkable among those made by Mother St. Euphrasia, we must antici-pate somewhat, in order to give, in her own words, an account of the visit she paid to Munich during the autumn of 1851. She had just been re-elected Mother General, and on this important occasion the Superior of Munich had come to Angers. She was most anxious to take

Mother St. Euphrasia back with her, and show her the Munich House. The Bishop graciously gave her leave to do so, but although the election took place in July, she had to wait until the beginning of September before setting out, so many and manifold were the business matters which claimed the time and attention of the foundress.

The little party finally set out on the 8th of September, the feast of our Blessed Lady's Nativity. Besides the Munich Superior, there were two Sisters and M. Benoist, head Chaplain of the Good Shepherd. Mother St. Euphrasia, desirous of sparing the Angers Sisters the pain of leave-taking, heard Mass, received Holy Communion, and was well on her way before the appointed hour for the Community to rise. Her travelling companions rejoined her at Tours. She spent three days in Paris, during which she stayed, of course, at the house she had established there. But she found time to visit her beloved Carmelites, and thus records the pleasure she had experienced in a letter written to Angers: "The Carmelite Nuns were so good as to show me a dress which their holy Mother St. Teresa had cut out and made with her own hands for the Infant Jesus. I kissed it on my knees on behalf of you all, my dearest children. I also venerated a bone from the right arm of the saintly Mother, and I saw an old cloak which once belonged to dear Mother Anne of St. Bartholomew, with which she used to cover St. Teresa when they were travelling together in cold weather."

After quitting Paris, the journey proved a very trying one for Mother St. Euphrasia. The railway at that time went no further than Bar-le-Duc, and the diligence was therefore the sole means of conveyance. One of her fellow-travellers warned her to beware of persons who might try to procure for themselves the places reserved in the diligence for travellers coming from Paris. Two such persons made their appearance as soon as the train reached Bar-le-Duc, and by their plausible pretences, succeeded in persuading Mother St. Euphrasia to give up the places reserved for herself and her party. She had to pay dearly for her courtesy and kindness. The carriage promised in exchange was a miserably shabby, half broken-down conveyance, the door would not shut properly, the springs were out of order, the horses matched the rest. All through the night she jolted along over a barren part of the country, until at two o'clock the next morning, they drew up before an unattractive looking inn. After alighting, they had a long while to wait, and when at last the landlady made her appearance, the reception she accorded them was the reverse of gracious. Annoyed at having been disturbed in the midst of her slumbers, she showed no compassion for the exhausted travellers. She even refused to make a cup of coffee for Mother St. Euphrasia, who was in a very suffering state. So the dear Mother had to go to bed without partaking of even the slightest refreshment.

The next morning saw her again on her way. She visited in turn Nancy and Strasburg, finding much to occupy her time and attention at both places. The journey from Strasburg to Munich was full of minor inconveniences and annoyances. Before they started, a lay-sister lost all their railway tickets, which involved a considerable outlay. One bright feature cheered their toilsome path. At Augsburg, the family of one of the Angers Sisters received the little party with the utmost respect and cordiality, and entertained them

with every hospitable attention. When at last the goal
was attained, all the hardships of the journey were
speedily forgotten. We will give the impression made
upon the Mother General, in her own touching and
expressive words. The subjoined letter was written to
the Sisters at Angers :

" Munich, October 26, 1851.
" 'How beautiful are thy tents, O Jacob!'
" My dearly-loved daughters,—At length, after
encountering endless impediments, difficulties, and
fatigues, we last night reached this incomparably
delightful spot; I found some of your welcome letters
awaiting me here. Their brevity disappointed me;
I felt a little sad at receiving no news of interest from
our own country. I confided my sorrow to our Divine
Mother, and in commending you all to her sacred heart,
I regained my peace of mind.

" What shall I say to you about Munich? I can say
that as a Community it is undeniably without an equal
in Christendom. Mother St. John of the Cross ought
to have told me what to expect.

" Let me go back to the beginning, and describe our
reception, which was assuredly intended to do honour
to the Blessed Virgin and this her Institute, in the
person of her insignificant little servant. Let no one say
a word to me of the coldness and indifference of the
Germans! Never did I witness so grand a *fête*. First
of all, when the train stopped, several ladies in their
carriages were awaiting us. A little boy of six years
old came up to me, and taking my hand, said to me :
'Come with me, Madam, I have a carriage here for
you; I know all about it, I do. Come, I will show you
the way.' He led me to a carriage and made me get

in. He was a lovely child, like a little angel. He told the coachman not to drive quickly, and himself got into a carriage in which his mother was seated; a third carriage was provided for the lay-sisters, who, by-the-bye, behave admirably. This sweet child had announced our arrival not only to the Community, but to all the neighbourhood. Some thousand persons had assembled at the opening of the magnificent avenue leading to the church. The young ladies of the school were all dressed in white, crowned with wreaths, and carrying baskets of flowers in their hands. The chaplain conducted us with great politeness into the splendid church. Never in my life have I beheld such a festal scene. The bandmaster of the Chapel Royal struck the first chords of a grand *Te Deum*, which was taken up by our young Sisters with their sweet voices, reminding one of the heavenly choirs. The keys of the enclosure, in silver gilt, were handed to me by the Superior; then, a procession having been formed, our good chaplains were escorted with due solemnity to the community-room. There we gave vent to our emotions; we wept for joy. The Reverend Mother displayed the most charming tact and deep feeling; she embraced us warmly, and all the Sisters did the same. When the evening came, they vied with one another in serving us, and in anticipating our every want."

In fact, the visit of the venerated foundress to her convent at Munich was celebrated as the advent of a person of no small importance. All the bells of the convent rang out a merry peal. A crowd had collected before the door composed mainly of the parents and friends of the children who belonged to the school, and who had gathered together, to see, as they expressed it, "the Mother of the white Religious." Mother St. Euphrasia went straight to the chapel, where she placed in the hands of our Lady the key of the house, which had been presented to her on her arrival. She ordered that the wreaths and flowers, which the children had carried, should be laid at the foot of the altar. Unfortunately she soon began to feel the effects of what she had undergone during her journey. A violent attack of influenza, accompanied by constant sickness, weakened her greatly. But with her habitual unselfishness, and constant thought for others, she set to work again as soon as the severer symptoms were subdued, paying and receiving numerous visits. The Archbishop, Mgr. Raisach, who had recently been elevated to the Cardinalate, came on two occasions to the convent, and had prolonged interviews with her. The Count von Seinsheim, whom we have already had occasion to mention, called one day in order to escort her to the palace, as His Majesty wished to see her. He received her with marked kindness and evident pleasure, and asked many questions as to the development of the Order, inquiring particularly whether she was satisfied with the house at Munich.

Before bringing this chapter to an end, we will relate one of the most remarkable instances on record in which the venerated foundress exercised the gift she possessed of discernment of spirits, and of insight into the future. It occurred in connection with the vocation of the present revered Mother General, to whom she foretold the career destined for her in the Divine counsels.

Towards the close of November in the year 1845, a young lady, Mlle. Verger, a native of Pin-en-Mauges, the birthplace of the heroic leader of the Vendean

P

armies, came to the Good Shepherd at Angers, with a friend who was desirous of entering the convent. After arranging matters with the intending postulant, Mother St. Euphrasia turned to her companion, and bent on her one of those scrutinizing looks which seemed to penetrate beyond the limits of human vision, and read the secrets of the soul. "My child," she said to her, "you too will come to this house." Mlle. Verger was taken by surprise at these words; she had, it is true, a decided inclination toward the religious life, but nothing was further from her thoughts than any idea of asking admission into the Good Shepherd. She said this to the Mother General, adding that she knew nothing at all about the Order. "It is God's will that you should serve Him in this convent," was the reply, "of that I can assure you, my child. Our Congregation, and the works in which we engage, are exactly suited to one of your character; you will come to us on the 8th of December, in the company of your friend." "That would be quite impossible, Reverend Mother," the young girl protested; "I am utterly unprepared to take such a step, and there are only a few days from now till then. Besides, my father, to whom I am almost indispensable, would not allow me to go." "You will come to us in spite of all," the Mother General confidentially replied, as she took leave of her visitor. When the latter returned home, she could not shake off the impression that the Divine will in her regard had been made known to her. All the obstacles which she thought insuperable, vanished in the most marvellous manner; the way was unexpectedly made plain for her. She had not time, when her decision was taken, to acquaint the nuns with it; but the Mother General was so firmly convinced of the truth of her own prediction, that she sent to meet her, as well as her friend, at the boat. On her reaching the convent she greeted her with the words: "I knew quite well that you would come."

The new postulant passed through the novitiate without distinguishing herself in any way from her fellow-novices. About a year after her Profession, she received orders to go to another house as second Mistress of Penitents. She was astonished at this appointment, for, in her humility, she considered herself unfitted to fill that or any other post. Her astonishment was increased when, on going to take leave of the Mother General, the latter fixed her eyes upon her with a peculiarly tender expression, and said: "My child, a special blessing from on high will rest on all you undertake. You will build a beautiful convent for us at Perpignan, you will found a house at Barcelona, and you will one day be the Provincial." The young Religious felt somewhat embarrassed; she could not believe that these predictions, of which she could hardly comprehend the meaning, regarded her own future. "You forget, dear Mother," she rejoined, "to whom you are speaking; you are mistaking me for some one else." "No, my child, it is indeed you whom I mean," answered the Mother General. Yet, in spite of this assurance, Sister Ste. Marine (such was her name in Religion), felt convinced that her Superior, in absence of mind, had addressed to her words intended for another. She repeated to no one what had been said to her until the eve of her departure, when she confided her secret to the Mistress of Novices. "Do not doubt the accuracy of what our Mother said, but lay up her words in your heart," was the advice given to her; and upon this she acted.

Seven years later, Sister Ste. Marine was appointed Superior of the house at Perpignan. This foundation, which was made in 1839, had never prospered. With the arrival of the new Superior a fresh era set in. Not only did she entirely rebuild the convent, from designs which the Bishop of the diocese had approved, but she also bought a country house, to serve as a second convent, appropriated to the orphans and Magdalens. The estimate for rebuilding the convent exceeded 150,000 francs (£6,000), and necessary as she deemed the work, Mother Ste. Marine hesitated to commence operations, for she had no funds in hand. But the Mother General urged her to begin at once. "Do not be afraid," she said; "Providence will come to your succour." And so indeed it was. No sooner was the work taken in hand, than the sum of 20,000 francs (£800) was sent her by a generous benefactress, and before the end of five years all the expenses were paid by means of donations from various persons. The same thing occurred with regard to the country house. The price asked for it was 100,000 francs (£4,000); whence would this sum be forthcoming? Again the Superior listened to what appeared to be the dictates of prudence; again the Mother General, inspired by a supernatural confidence, would hear of no delay. "Purchase it at once, my daughter," she wrote. "Can you doubt how to act when it is a question of raising another temple to the glory of God?" This undertaking proved as successful as the other, thus exemplifying the words of Mother St. Euphrasia, "The greater the zeal we display in the service of God, the more abundant are the blessings with which our exertions will be crowned."

Twice during her lifetime, the servant of God sent Mother Ste. Marine to Barcelona, for the purpose of making arrangements for opening a house there. On both these occasions she met with no encouragement, and it was not until 1880, twelve years after Mother St. Euphrasia's death, that the Order obtained a footing there. Mother Ste. Marine being sent once more into Spain by order of the then Mother General, encountered no opposition, and her perseverance was rewarded by the foundation of a large and flourishing house.

It may be imagined that she felt half alarmed at seeing the predictions concerning herself fulfilling themselves one after another in so remarkable a manner. She could not help fearing that the burden of the Provincialate would also be laid upon her; and therefore avoided everything which might possibly bring her into notice. She even refrained from going to Angers, lest she should thereby attract attention to herself. But her efforts to efface herself were of no avail. In 1889, she was recalled to the Mother House, to fill the post of Provincial of France. Thus the third prophecy was duly accomplished, improbable as this appeared at the moment it was uttered, for at that time the establishment of Provinces had not been so much as suggested, and Mother St. Euphrasia was then by no means desirous that it should be effected, as in 1855 it ultimately was.

These predictions relating to her own future, which, after the death of the Sister to whom alone she communicated them, were known to no living being besides herself, were disclosed by Mother Ste. Marine, in proof of the sanctity of the venerated foundress, and for the greater glory of God, on her elevation to the Generalate in 1892. Are we not justified in supposing that this final step in her career was also revealed to Mother St. Euphrasia; and that, although she did not divulge all that in the light of the Divine foreknowledge she was permitted to see, it was given her to recognize in the stranger from La Vendée, who accompanied her friend to Angers, a future ruler of the Order, destined one day to succeed her as its third Superior General?

In our next chapter we shall have to cross the Channel, in order to see how gladly the Nuns of the Good Shepherd were welcomed, and how thoroughly they were appreciated, even on the shores of Protestant England.

CHAPTER XIV.

LONDON.

No one who follows the history of the Order of the Good Shepherd, can fail to be struck with the marvellous manner in which the finger of Providence is manifest throughout. *Hic digitus Dei.* The Mother General, like the saintly M. Olier, took a deep interest in the conversion of England, and had long entertained, as may be gathered from her letters, an ardent desire to found a house in London. This foundation actually came about in the following manner.

M. Eberhard, whose name is already familiar to us in connection with Munich, when passing through Paris upon a certain occasion on his way to Angers, profited by his comparative nearness to the coast, to cross the Channel and visit a friend of his, M. Jauch, a priest attached to the German Church in London. From him M. Eberhard learnt that there were in his parish several young girls, who were desirous of embracing the religious life in some Order where they could devote themselves to the salvation of souls, and strive to bring back to God those who had been so unhappy as to wander from the paths of virtue. It was only natural that M. Eberhard should speak at length of the Good Shepherd as established at Angers, and M. Jauch was delighted with all he heard. But what were his postulants to do? They had no fortune at their disposal. His friend, however, well knowing the generous spirit of the Mother General, undertook to lay the case before her, since M. Jauch expressed a definite desire to see a convent of the Order founded in London. Those who have followed Mother St. Euphrasia thus far in the story of her life, will not be surprised to find that she gladly consented to receive the English postulants, in whom she beheld, with prophetic eye, the first-fruits of a rich and splendid harvest. Thus it came to pass that in May, 1840, she sent to London Mother Mary of the Angels, the Superioress of the house at Lille, and another Religious. M. Dehée, their Superior, accompanied them. M. Jauch, who did not know how great was the zeal of the foundress, was altogether taken by surprise when the Religious made their appearance, and declared that, as yet, he had no house to offer them. M. Dehée returned to France at the end of a fortnight. But the daughters of Mother St. Euphrasia were not to be so easily discouraged. She had infused into them her own courage, and absolute dependence upon Providence. Besides, she did not recall them, and so they remained, in virtue of holy obedience, ready to endure poverty and humiliation. But gradually the clouds lightened. The six young Englishwomen, whom the Mother General had consented to receive as postulants, began to make the work of the Good Shepherd known in their respective circles, and several persons of rank and distinction took an interest in the two lonely Sisters. Among these we may mention the Marchioness of Wellesley, Mgr. Griffiths, Vicar Apostolic for London, and M. Voyaux de Franoux, priest in charge of the Chelsea mission. Mgr. Griffiths asked to see the Constitutions of the Good Shepherd. When he had read them, he gave his unqualified permission for the foundation of a house, but he added, that the many calls upon the limited resources at his command, forbade him to defray the costs, which must therefore be undertaken by the Order. The Marchioness of Wellesley promised a handsome annuity, and Mother St. Euphrasia would have begun the work at once, had not Mgr. Paysant, Bishop of Angers, whose permission she asked, forbidden her to do so, on account of the large outlay which must inevitably be made. She promptly obeyed, and, much as it grieved her, recalled Sister Mary of the Angels, whose disappointment was softened by the fact that she could present to her beloved Mother six English postulants, and that the way was smoothed for a foundation in the future, since Mgr. Griffiths was anxious for it. We can imagine how affectionate was the welcome afforded to the strangers, and how soon they were made to feel quite at home amid their new surroundings.

An unlooked-for difficulty, however, presented itself. The English girls did not know French sufficiently to make their confessions in that language, and there was no priest in Angers well enough versed in their mother-tongue to hear them in it. Mother St. Euphrasia, while showing a priest, who came from Nantes, over the convent, happened to speak of the embarrassing position in which she was placed in regard to her new charges. This priest, who knew the zeal and con-descension of his Bishop, whose confessional in the Cathedral of Nantes was literally besieged by the poor, assured the Mother General that if she would address herself to his lordship, she would not be dis-appointed. Thus emboldened, she wrote the following letter to Mgr. de Hercé. We insert it, not only because it displays so much tact, and so admirably tells its own tale, but because it proves how versatile was Mother St. Euphrasia's pen. She could write touching addresses, affectionate and familiar letters to her own children, while not the less did she know how to approach a dignitary of the Church in a manner which could not but win any heart, unless that heart were made of stone.

"My Lord Bishop,—One of the priests of your Lordship's diocese recently obtained from our ecclesiastical Superiors the permission to inspect our convent: we had much pleasure in showing him over it, in compliance with his wish. During the course of his visit, we happened to mention to this good priest the difficulties we were in with regard to providing a confessor for some young English ladies whom we have lately received into our Novitiate, since there is not a single priest here who understands English. He informed us that your Lordship was thoroughly conversant with that language, and that he knew your fatherly kindness too well not to feel sure that you would be willing to assist us. It is in virtue of this assurance that we now venture to take the liberty of addressing your Lordship, and while offering you our most humble respect, to beg you to let us know whether it is within your power to render some spiritual aid to this little band of foreigners.

"If your Lordship were perchance coming anywhere in the vicinity of Angers, even within a distance of thirty or forty miles, we would gladly, provided you would allow us to do so, send the dear children there, in order that they might have the consolation of confiding all their little woes to your sympathizing heart. And if Heaven were to grant us so great a favour as that your Lordship should yourself honour us with a visit, we should entreat you to put the climax to our happiness, by condescending to preside at the ceremony of their clothing, and receive their vows in their own language. Should we be so fortunate as to obtain the favour we now venture to solicit, might I further request that we may be acquainted with your purpose a short time beforehand, so as to be able to translate the ceremonial and make due preparation for the auspicious day.

" I am really ashamed, my Lord, of asking so much ; perhaps you will think me too bold. I must trust to your great charity to excuse me ; I will also trust to your tender love and zeal for souls to succour those for whom I now plead, and who unite with me in the expression of deep gratitude and profound respect wherewith I remain, your Lordship's most humble and most obedient servant and daughter in Jesus Christ."

Nothing could be more courteous and kind than the reply of this admirable and saintly Bishop. He thanked Mother St. Euphrasia for applying to him, as if she had conferred upon himself some personal favour. As soon as his engagements allowed him to do so, he came to Angers, and stayed two days at the convent. From that time forward, he never ceased to take the liveliest interest in the little English colony, and in the house which was before long founded in London. He had spent some years of his childhood and early youth in England, where he had received a great deal of kindness, and his grateful heart had ever felt a sincere affection for the hospitable shores which had sheltered him.

The first group of English novices were thus the means of bringing together Mgr. de Hercé and Mother St. Euphrasia. On the 27th of September, 1840, a fresh band of postulants arrived from England. They were sent by M. Jauch, and brought letters from various persons, begging the Mother General to lose no time in founding a house in London. M. Voyaux de Franoux, whom we have already mentioned, offered them a house at St. Leonard's, and promised to do his very utmost for them. Mother St. Euphrasia felt that the time for action had arrived. She obtained the authority of the Bishop, and on the 11th of November, 1840, she sent forth two Sisters, together with an English postulant, who was to act as interpreter, and M. Mainguy, who had kindly volunteered to be their escort.

The day of their departure for London was a great event for the whole Community at Angers. Before setting out, the two Sisters were obliged to divest themselves of their white habits and put on an ordinary black dress, suited for travelling. Perceiving the pain this cost them, Mother St. Euphrasia, whose ready tongue never failed her, consoled them by saying: *Nigra sum, sed formosa*—" I am black, but beautiful." [1]

Of the two Sisters she sent, one was Mother Mary of St. Joseph (Regaudiat). She had joined the Angers Community as long ago as 1831, and had been thoroughly trained by Mother St. Euphrasia. She was no ordinary Religious, and it must be apparent to all that no common courage and determination were required to start for England with only one other Sister, both being absolutely ignorant of the language. She had, moreover, only £40 as the sum-total of her resources. Nor must we forget, that more than half

[1] Cant. i. 4.

a century has elapsed since the time of which we are writing, and that a journey from Angers to London, which is now, owing to the endless multiplication of railroads and steamboats, scarcely to be called a journey, in the modern sense of the term, was then a really formidable undertaking. The natural apprehensions of the Sisters were increased by the total wreck, on the rocks off the coast of Jersey, of the steamboat in which they had intended to embark. We can imagine how miserable were their experiences on board a small coasting vessel laden with hides, which conveyed them from St. Malo to Southampton. On arriving in London, they found a dense November fog hanging like a pall over the city. This did not tend to raise their spirits, but the morrow brought them a far severer trial. The little party went to Chelsea, in order to obtain advice and help from their kind friend, M. Voyaux. M. Mainguy had no idea of any clerical dress, except his cassock, and he had arrayed himself in a green coat over a crimson waistcoat, to the infinite amusement doubtless of every one who saw him. When the travellers reached Chelsea, they were ushered into a room where M. Voyaux lay stiff and cold, prepared for burial. He had expired only the evening before. The shock was a terrible one, but faith and fortitude enabled them to bear it. In a few moments they knelt down to pray for the soul of their departed friend, and rose, sustained by the hope that they would, to quote their own words, "experience his intercession in Heaven, whose help had been denied them on earth."

The position of the two nuns was a most painful and trying one, especially after M. Mainguy had left them in order to return to Angers. Vexations and annoyances of every kind were their portion. Mgr. Griffiths showed them much kindness, and procured for them a temporary shelter in the Benedictine Convent at Hammersmith. After a long and harassing search, they at last succeeded in obtaining a house in which to receive penitents. All the possessions they brought to furnish their new abode consisted of two beds, a table, a chest of drawers, two chairs, a coffee-pot, some plates, and a frying-pan. Their trust in God's fatherly providence was rewarded, for the Benedictines, with the assistance of a Spanish lady resident in the neighbourhood, undertook to provide them with breakfast and dinner until they could support themselves.

Mother St. Euphrasia was kept fully informed of all the tribulations which made the lot of her daughters in London no easy one. In spite of all difficulties she was extremely desirous to see them established in the land which once bore the title of the Isle of Saints, and was known as the Dowry of Mary. She had therefore recourse to the intercession of the Blessed Virgin. After having had a Mass said on behalf of the new foundation, in presence of the whole Community, she made a promise to recite the *Memorare* daily during a whole year for the success of the house in London.

" I regard the London convent as our daughter," she wrote to the Superior, " it may be a great expense to us to provide for her, but we must not abandon her, even though we may have to work hard night and day, and make great pecuniary sacrifices." She often talked to her own Community about the trials of their Sisters in England, at the same time expressing her firm belief that the protection of our Blessed Lady would not be wanting to that house. Speaking to them upon this

subject on the 24th of March, the eve of the Annunciation, she said :

"To-morrow, my dear daughters, our Sisters in
England will be installed in a permanent domicile,
where they can take in penitents and homeless children.
We may say that on that day, this long-wished-for
foundation will fairly come into existence, but it will
need our continued support and assistance ; it is a long
time before a new-born infant can stand alone. I am
really delighted to think that this happy event should
take place on so auspicious a day. Our kind St. Joseph
has, one may be sure, had his share in helping on the
good work ; but he wishes his holy Spouse to have all
the credit of it, and he will present it to her as his
bouquet de fête. I believe St. Euphrasia has had something to do with it too ; perhaps she has pleaded with
Almighty God on behalf of the foundation. In order
to place ourselves more completely under the protection
of Mary and Joseph, we will include Our Lady of
Dolours amongst the intercessors we invoke, in the
processions of the month of March."

The necessary documents with regard to the acquisition of their house, were signed by the Sisters on the
feast of our Lady's Compassion, but it was not until the
month of May, 1841, that they were able to take actual
possession of it. Gradually it was suitably arranged
and furnished. Mgr. Griffiths blessed the apartment
which served as a chapel, and subsequently paid the
nuns a second visit, in order to give their First Communion to the penitents who had been received, and also to
confirm them. In spite of their extreme poverty, Mother
Mary of St. Joseph was resolved to begin the work of
the Order. On the 21st of June, she received two
penitents into the house. The joy she and her com-

panion felt on that memorable day repaid them for all the trials and disappointments they had endured since leaving Angers. But they had many difficulties still to overcome. Needlework was in these early days one of the chief resources of the house. For this important branch of their undertaking the nuns were obliged to rely almost entirely on the exertions of a generous and devoted girl of sixteen, who afterwards joined the Community as a lay-sister. For hours she would traverse the London streets, asking for orders at various business houses, and often having to return home without any promise of work, weary and footsore, yet willing and eager to renew the next day the same arduous labour. She was, indeed, one of the principal supporters of the work at this critical period of its existence, and, as such, deserve to be mentioned in these pages.

One remarkable case of conversion in those early days merits also to be recorded. A London magistrate asked the Sisters to receive a woman who was constantly brought before him, and to whom repeated terms of imprisonment had done no good. Nothing could control her violence. In the paroxysms of her rage she was more like a wild animal than a human being, and used to break everything within her reach. Though not a Catholic in name even, the nuns consented to receive her. The poor creature proved to be an absolute heathen, never having been baptized. After suitable instruction, the Sacrament of Baptism was administered to her. Her stormy nature became completely changed through the gentle government of the Sisters, and the influence of prayer and the sacraments. About five years subsequent to her reception into the convent, the magistrate who had interested himself in her case, called in order to inquire whether any reformation had taken place. Great was his astonishment at the account he heard, but when he saw for himself the face, once wild and hardened, now calm and smiling, with a bright look of peaceful happiness, words failed him, and his eyes grew dim with tears. Most cordially did he acknowledge, before taking leave, the marvellous change which had resulted from religious training. As the number of penitents increased, it became necessary to procure a larger house. A property called Beauchamp Lodge was secured, a chapel erected, and a laundry built; and two hundred penitents now form the usual number resident. Thus was the courage of Mother Mary of St. Joseph crowned with complete success.

The second foundation in the United Kingdom was made in 1851 at Dalbeith, near Glasgow, and the third about the same time at Arno's Court, near Bristol, a house generously given to the nuns by Mr. William Gillow, who was then practising as a doctor in Torquay. In 1858 a foundation was commenced near Liverpool, at the request of the Bishop, Dr. Goss. Four Sisters were sent from London. The way for their coming had been prepared by the Redemptorist Fathers, who had been preaching a Mission in the city, and were anxious that the Sisters of the Good Shepherd should come to the aid of penitent sinners. Very soon one remarkable conversion rewarded their pious exertions. An unhappy woman, thirty years of age, was brought to the convent. Her stature was almost gigantic, and her strength was as abnormal as her height. Passionate and extremely irascible by nature, she did not hesitate, if anything chanced to annoy her, to indulge in blasphemous language, and she even went so far as to strike a child

Q

who was seated at work beside her. With the help of God, the patience and gentleness of the Sisters overcame her passionate outbursts : the lioness was changed into a lamb, and the Superioress was able to write to Mother St. Euphrasia as follows : " We are now abundantly rewarded for all our sacrifices." Eight years later Manchester had a Convent of the Good Shepherd. For the house at Pen-y-lan, near Cardiff, in Wales, the nuns are indebted to the generosity of the Marquess of Bute. The next foundation was at Newcastle-on-Tyne, and there is one also at East Finchley, near London, appointed for the training of the novices' for all the English Province. The permission for this foundation was given with the greatest readiness by Cardinal Wiseman, to whom all English Catholics owe so heavy a debt of gratitude. His Eminence appended to his permission the flattering condition, that the Provincialate and the Novitiate should always remain in his diocese. We have thus given some details regarding the commencement of the work of the Good Shepherd on English soil, and the rapid progress it made. We shall now relate a few particulars in connection with the visit paid by Mother St. Euphrasia, in the early part of 1844, to the convent at Hammersmith. But before giving an account of her journey, we will introduce an incident which occurred just before her departure, and which shows the marvellous power she exercised over those who were brought under her influence.

A young penitent, who had not long been received into the Good Shepherd, and whose more than ordinarily perverse and unruly character caused the greatest trouble and anxiety to Mother Mary of St. Vincent of Paul, mistress of the largest class, finally persisted in her resolution to leave the convent, and resume the sinful life she had been leading in the world. The excellent Mother employed every means that charity and love for souls could possibly suggest in order to shake this fatal determination. But all her exertions availed nothing. At length she went to Mother St. Euphrasia, told her the state of the case, and begged for advice. "Fear nothing, my dear child," was the unhesitating answer; "our Lord will change this wolf into a lamb. I will go to the chapel and pray with this intention, and then I will make an unlooked-for appearance in the class-room." An hour afterwards she entered the room, but found the poor young girl more resolved than ever to leave the Good Shepherd. The foundress called her to come close to her chair, then she made the sign of the Cross on her forehead, and said: "Go, my dear child, go at once where the devil is calling you, if you have the courage to do so." These words, and still more the manner in which they were uttered, had an instantaneous effect on the girl to whom they were addressed. She fell on her knees at the feet of Mother St. Euphrasia, begged her pardon, and entreated as a favour that she might be allowed to remain where she was. From that day forward her conduct was most exemplary, and when her time came to die, she expired in the peace of the Lord.

But to resume our narrative. Mother St. Euphrasia had already received at Angers visits from Mgr. Griffiths and the Rev. Mr. Robson, who was Superior of the London house. Her children, however, ardently desired a visit from their beloved Mother. In the beginning of June, 1844, she at length found an opportunity of gratifying their wish. She could not make up her mind to put off the habit she had worn for thirty years.

Protestant prejudice was diminishing year by year in England, and she appears to have had no reason to regret travelling in her religious dress. On the contrary, when she landed at Dover, some poor Catholic women, gladdened by the sight of her habit, brought their children to her that she might bless them. We can readily understand the pleasure this afforded her affectionate heart, and she considered it a good omen regarding her first footsteps in the country which she loved to call "the Isle of Saints." The first sight of London greatly impressed her. Unluckily the travellers found no one to meet them at the station, as they arrived a day earlier than they were expected. Fortunately a kind-hearted gentleman, who had been their companion ever since they left Calais, stepped forward, and asked if he could be of any service to them. On hearing the state of affairs, he took them to a French hotel. By a strange coincidence, the master of this hotel, M. Payliano, turned out to be one of the chief benefactors of the Hammersmith Convent. The next morning he declined to accept any remuneration from his guests, and his wife was delighted to escort them to their journey's end, where it is needless to say that they were received with unfeigned joy and the most cordial of welcomes. Her first visit was, as usual, to the chapel, the second to Mgr. Griffiths.

She also visited many of the Catholic churches and chapels in London and its immediate vicinity. In several of them she was deeply grieved not to find the Blessed Sacrament, which, from motives of prudence, had to be kept in the sacristy. She thus related one of these occurrences to her Community at a later date:

"During our sojourn in England, we entered a church in London, when it pained me not a little to

miss the sanctuary lamp from its accustomed place
before the altar. 'Where art Thou hidden, O my
Divine Lord and Master?' I inquired, in the depths of
my soul. The priest who was showing me over the
church, seemed to guess what was passing in my mind,
for he said : 'The Blessed Sacrament is not here. We
are compelled to keep It in hiding like an outlaw.'
'And yet, Father,' I answered, 'who but our Lord
can be King in the Isle of Saints?' Then he took us
into the sacristy, where a solitary lamp, burning before
an oaken chest, revealed the humble abode of the King
of kings. I fell on my knees, and during the time I
spent in adoration, I promised Him that I would cause
chapels to be raised to His honour in the land I was
now visiting."

It struck a chill to the warm and loving heart of
Mother St. Euphrasia whenever she beheld ancient and
beautiful churches, which Protestant hands had pro-
fanely wrested from those who built and endowed them,
and which were cold and bare, given up to a meaningless worship. We have narrated the above incident,
not only to illustrate the love and reverence of Mother
St. Euphrasia for the Adorable Sacrament of the Altar,
but also to mark the immense change which, through
the goodness of God and the prayers of our glorious
Martyrs, has been effected in England during the half-
century which has elapsed since 1844, the date of the
episode we have just related.

The visit of the venerated foundress was the source
of manifold blessings to the convent at Hammersmith.
The ladies who had helped the house, hearing of her
presence, begged to be allowed to call upon her. Some
of them were Protestants. Among these latter we may
mention Lady Robert Peel, wife of the Prime Minister.

Canon O'Neil and the Rev. Mr. Long, confessor to the convent, also desired to make her acquaintance. Her presence served not only to excite the fervour of her children, but to stir up a spirit of liberality in regard of them. Large sums of money were given them by Protestants. The house was freed from taxation as being a charitable institution. Two of the penitents desired to go to Angers, in order to enrol themselves among the Magdalens, and they were able to carry out their wish. Yet, much as Mother St. Euphrasia enjoyed her visit to Hammersmith, and great as was the brightness and happiness she was the means of shedding around her, the climate of London soon began to tell upon her health. Business matters, moreover, required her presence in France. She was obliged to take her departure, but before returning to the Mother House she visited several of her foundations. It was not until the 26th of July that she again found herself at Angers.

The subjoined address is too long to be given *in extenso*, although it is too admirable to be passed over altogether. It thoroughly illustrates the spirit of the foundress, her courage, her zeal, and the degree in which she possessed what has been so aptly termed " the common sense of sanctity." It does not appear to have been written on her return from the particular journey upon which we have been dwelling, but it may suitably draw to a close our account of her London experiences.

At the close of a long absence from Angers, during which she had visited no less than fourteen of the houses under her sway, Mother St. Euphrasia addressed to her Community a lengthy discourse, in order to inspire them with the same ardent zeal and love for their Order, ever burning within her own breast, which her tour of inspection had had the effect of rousing to a livelier, more vivid flame. We give some extracts from this address.

"Wherever I went," she said, "I reminded our beloved Sisters of these words of our Venerable Father Eudes: 'The employment of their heart and mind, their whole object and endeavour, ought to be to render themselves worthy coadjutors and co-operators with our Lord Jesus Christ in the work of saving the souls He has ransomed at the price of His Blood.' Let us reflect upon the import of these words, my dear daughters, and put them into practice.

"I can never be grateful enough to Almighty God for having granted me the privilege that it has been to me to assist our houses in the south of Europe. The favour I now ask of Him is that I may be enabled to start afresh, when the winter is over, on a visitation to our foundations in the north. On my return, if such be His will, I will gladly sing my *Nunc dimittis*. I found a spirit of the most perfect docility prevailing in all our convents. There were, of course, many things needing reform; but wherever there was any irregularity, it arose from inexperience. It was said to me sometimes: 'We were sent here so young! But we are prepared to do everything you wish, to fall in with all you say.' Thus, as you may well imagine, all was soon set right.

"Religious perfection does not consist in having no defects, in never doing anything wrong; it consists in this, that having once been told of a fault, we should correct it at once.

"One of the things against which we must be on

our guard, is entertaining prejudices, taking up ideas against some one of our houses, or even some country in particular.

" Wherever you may be placed, do not fail to do your utmost to keep up the customs and practices of the Mother House. Yet you must exercise judgment, and bear in mind that in certain matters it is incumbent upon you to know how to adapt yourself to circumstances, doing the best you can, remembering that the spirit of our vocation requires us to make ourselves all things to all men. I will give you an instance, which will show you how indispensable it is to carry out this principle. In one of our Roman houses the table was French, and several customs were adhered to which were entirely alien to Italian usage. What was the result ? The penitents could not accustom themselves to it, and but few conversions were made. Now in the other house I found the meals served in Italian fashion, and it was evident that the penitents were contented and attached to the house. Thus there was less difficulty experienced in gaining them for God.

" In all the rest, your Rule ought to be, above all and before all, your guide, your leading star ; and with regard to the practices to which you are habituated here, let it be your great delight to keep to them as closely as you are able.

" It is my wish that all our convents should have the same stamp for their letters as that in use at the Mother House. I also like to see the refectories all on the same plan, the table utensils, as far as possible, being of pewter. One of our good Mothers used to say : ' Silver plate belongs to great people ; pewter is fitting for Religious. Let us leave these modern inventions to those who live in the world.' St. Augustine, however, allows nuns to have silver spoons because of their greater cleanliness.

" I am determined henceforth to make it my endeavour more than ever to support and encourage our Sisters in the new foundations. They are so admirable ! Take the greatest care never to say a single word that could cause them the slightest annoyance. No letter calculated to hurt the feelings of any one in any way whatsoever must be sent from this house ; and if unfortunately this should ever be the case, I declare before you all, that letter will not have come under my sight. The Mother House cannot do too much to please those virtuous Sisters. We must assist them by sending them zealous fellow-workers, good mistresses of penitents, for this is one of the most essential requisites in a house of the Good Shepherd.

" Mark my words, my dear daughters, that house is sure to go on well where there is a good Superior ; an Assistant who is devoted to her work, and who helps the Superior in everything; and a capable Mistress of Penitents, with another under her, well skilled in needle-work. And in order that you may render yourselves really useful in the monasteries whither you may be sent, each one ought to strive to perfect herself in her own department ; for instance, let the one who has no aptitude for intellectual occupation turn her attention to sewing, embroidery, mending, or ironing ; let her learn how to prepare the work and direct the workers. Let each one do her work well, whatever it is. Our Lord intends every one of you to be instrumental in doing a great deal of good. Rejoice, therefore, give thanks to Him, and be of good courage.

" Without zeal on your part, my dear daughters, without your self-denial and self-sacrifice, our houses could not be maintained. I feel assured that they will never want the necessaries of life, nor do I fear that the Divine protection will ever be withdrawn from them; but of one thing I am quite certain, that without a staff of Religious entirely devoted to their work, they cannot be kept up, they cannot go on; it is an impossible thing. And who, I ask, can be perfectly devoted, who has not the spirit of the Cross, who has not the love of the Cross? I would have you, therefore, continually remember, my dear daughters, that it is on Mount Calvary that we are founded."

CHAPTER XV

THE year 1841 opened happily for the Good Shepherd, since it witnessed the establishment of a house in Paris. It began in poverty, and, after struggling on for about a year, contending with difficulties of every kind, received in January, 1842, a visit from the foundress. She was deeply impressed with the necessity which existed for the carrying on of her work in the metropolis of France, and felt that to ensure the success of the undertaking, her presence for a time was required there. As we have seen before, in so many instances, she poured oil upon the troubled waters, conciliated every one, hiring a larger and more suitable house, so that soon after her return prosperity reigned in Paris and joy at Angers.

Mgr. Bourget, Bishop of Montreal, having journeyed to Rome in order to arrange some business matters connected with his diocese, was advised by the Propaganda to pay a visit to Mother St. Euphrasia in order to induce her to found a house in America. Accordingly he went to Angers, where the impression he made was a most favourable one. His sanctity, his simplicity, the interesting accounts he gave of the American missions, won all hearts. Nor was the pleasure he received less than that he gave ; so that he accepted with gratitude the offer made him, that he should be accompanied on his return journey by a little colony of Sisters. But all efforts to overcome the determined opposition of Mgr. Paysant, Bishop of Angers, to a foundation on the distant shores of the New World, proved fruitless. The project had therefore to be abandoned, to the grievous disappointment of Mgr. Bourget and also of Mother St. Euphrasia. She, however, never ceased to hope that our Blessed Lady would some day open to the Sisters of the Good Shepherd the vast field of labour which lay waiting for them.

A few months afterwards the Bishop died very suddenly, during the course of a pastoral visitation. Only a few weeks later, Mgr. Flaget, the Bishop of Bardstown, whose name is already familiar to our readers, quite unexpectedly addressed a letter to Mother St. Euphrasia, imploring her to send some of her children to America, and dwelling in detail on all the good they would effect there. She could not regard this coincidence as other than providential, and she wrote at once to ask advice from Cardinal della Porta, Protector of the Good Shepherd. He was almost immediately removed by death from the scene of his labours, Cardinal Patrizi being appointed in his stead. This latter proved a faithful and unfailing stay and support to Mother St. Euphrasia in the midst of the varied tribulations she was destined to encounter. Besides the loss of Cardinal della Porta, the year 1842 was marked, in the convent at Angers, by two occurrences which greatly distressed her.

In February, one of the penitents, feigning illness, obtained permission to retire to the dormitory before her companions. She then fashioned a rope out of the sheets of her bed, and let herself down into the street.

The out-Sisters hastened after her, and speedily brought her back to the house. She was extremely sorry for what she had done in a fit of temper, and humbly begged the Mother General to forgive her. It may be imagined how readily this was granted, but the evil did not end here. The bad newspapers of Angers unfortunately got wind of the affair, and invented all sorts of fabulous stories, prejudicial to the house and its inmates. The house was represented as a prison, furnished with secret dungeons, where tortures were inflicted, while the runaway was depicted as an interesting victim, who had, in a paroxysm of despair, thrown herself from the garden wall, and thus effected her escape. At last a democratic paper went to such lengths, that Mother St. Euphrasia felt herself compelled to follow the advice of M. Régnier, the Superior of the Community, and prosecute the editor of the newspaper in question. The result was that the writer of the articles had to tender to her his humble apologies.

All this, as we have said, happened during the month of February, but a heavier sorrow was soon to reach the maternal heart of the foundress. On the 29th of March, while she was celebrating her feast, which had been transferred on account of Holy Week and the Easter solemnities, and was happy in the midst of her beloved religious family, a messenger suddenly appeared in her presence, bearing the terrible news that several of the younger girls who were living in the convent had fallen into a piece of water situated in the grounds. They had amused themselves with the punt which was moored on the side of the lake, and used for the purpose of fishing. Three were drowned. The consternation of the Community may be imagined, and

the bitter grief of Mother St. Euphrasia. Her sole
consolation in these distressing circumstances was to
know that the poor girls had been to confession and
received Holy Communion on the morning of the day
which witnessed their tragic end. She experienced
more than ever, on this sad occasion, the difficulties
that beset the post of a Superior. To console others
while one's own heart is breaking, requires an almost
superhuman effort, while the burden of responsibility
which rests perpetually on the shoulders, is felt at such
times of mourning to be more than usually heavy. Two
soldiers, attracted by the cries of the girls, had hastened
to their aid, and plunged at once into the water, with
the hope of saving them. To each of these brave men
Mother St. Euphrasia presented a gold watch, on which
was engraved their name and the date of their heroic
action. About five months after the death of Mgr.
Paysant, a new Bishop was appointed to the see of
Angers, in the person of a priest from the diocese
of Nantes. This nomination gave much satisfaction
to the Community of the Good Shepherd, as the
future Bishop, M. Angebault, was already well known
to them, through his having been Vicar-General of
their kind and faithful friend, Mgr. de Hercé. The
consecration of Mgr. Angebault drew, as a matter of
course, several Bishops to Angers. At this conjuncture,
happily for Mother St. Euphrasia, a letter was received
by her from Mgr. Flaget, who, having removed the seat
of his bishopric to Louisville, renewed his request that
a colony of her Sisters might be sent out to him. He
wrote also to M. Régnier, who had just been appointed
to the bishopric of Angoulême, and who forwarded the
epistle to Mgr. Angebault, now seated on the episcopal
throne of Angers. He gladly and promptly acceded to

the petition of his American brother, so that all difficulties in the way of the project were removed, to the
unutterable joy of Mother St. Euphrasia.

Universal enthusiasm prevailed throughout the Community. Each Sister desired to be among those who
were to make the conquest of souls in the New World.
Five were chosen, the nationality of each being different.
Mdme. d'Andigné volunteered to defray the expenses of
their outfit, to supply them with bedding and to provide
them with a chalice, to be used in their first chapel.
Many kind people, inhabitants of Angers, also sent
them various useful gifts. The moment of parting was
a bitter one. Mother St. Euphrasia felt as if she could
not tear herself from her beloved Sisters, whom she
would probably never behold again in this life. At
length, summoning up all her energy: "Go, my
children," she exclaimed, "in the name of holy obedience!" Then the gates of the convent were closed
behind the five missioners, whose places thenceforth
knew them no more. They had a rough passage across
the Atlantic, but were most kindly received on landing
by several of the American Bishops, each of whom on
beholding the little band, felt a wish spring up in his
heart that he, too, could possess in his diocese, some of
these devoted Sisters, who had dedicated their lives to
the reclaiming of Christ's wandering sheep and lambs.
It may be imagined how constantly the affectionate
Mother whom they had left, followed them with her
thoughts and prayers. Moreover, she wrote to them
before she heard of their arrival; and they, in their
turn, communicated to her every little detail of their
journey. When at last she received the glad news that
they had reached Louisville in safety, and had been
cordially welcomed by Mgr. Flaget, and his coadjutor,

Mgr. Chabrat, her heart overflowed with grateful joy. She shall express her feelings in her own words, as contained in the following letter :

" ' I will send My Angel before you.'

" My dear, good devoted daughters,—The Angel of the Lord will watch continually over you; He has already preserved you from great dangers, through the gracious protection of our Lady. How much I thank you, my beloved daughters, for having written from New York. With what delight we welcomed your dear and interesting letter, pressed it to our lips, carried it to the crib. There, kneeling at the feet of the Infant Jesus, I placed it in His sacred hands, after we had all kissed it affectionately. My poor children, I was deeply touched by all you told me. How much you have suffered! You have been crucified both in soul and in body. Dear Mary of the Angels, I shed tears over the account of your struggles ; and yet, my child, I confess that I envy you. You are happy to be engaged on the most important of our missions. My beloved St. Aloysius, you give us details more precious to us than gold ; and all the time you were feeling so ill, so exhausted! How dearly I love you in our Lord, my best of daughters! Sister St. Joseph, too, whom we all love fondly, you are none the less charitable and thoughtful for others amid all your sufferings. You have the blessing of the Holy Child Jesus, and that of the Bishop of Angoulême besides. That excellent prelate looks upon you as his daughter ; write him a long letter in English, and let our good Sister Mary of St. Aloysius write in French, in the name of your little Community. Tell him about your saintly Bishop, for whom he has so high an esteem. Above all, mind you write to our worthy Bishop of

Angers, who has been so very kind; and also send a letter six pages long to our good parish priest of St. Jacques, enclosing a few lines for his curate. They will read those letters everywhere.

"I must now send a message to our dear Sisters St. Reparata and St. Marcella, to whom we are fondly attached in Jesus Christ, and whom we embrace most lovingly, together with our three American Mothers. Keep up your courage, faithful little band. Fight the good fight, gain victory after victory, rejoice the Church, be the joy of our hearts and the glory of our Congregation. You would give me great pleasure, my dearest daughters, if when you can spare time you would write to our foundations. You would edify them immensely, but suit your own convenience as to when you write. Will you also tell us all about the first two American penitents whom you expect to receive; tell me what are their names, what is their appearance, what are their dispositions, and what is the place whence they come? And talk to the two dear children about us as well. I am going to tell you a great secret, my dearest daughters; no one in France knows it but myself alone. I want you to pray earnestly for this intention. Yesterday evening we received a letter from the Bishop of Algiers, begging us for the sake of the Precious Blood of Christ to spare him twelve Religious to found a house at Hippo, not far from the resting-place of the great St. Augustine. What a glorious mission this will be, if it is really confided to us! But you are ahead of us all, my brave missioners. You five have been the earliest to cross the frontiers of Europe; the love of God and of our holy Institute has borne you to the shores of the New World. I suppose that you are now at Louisville. We long

R

for another letter from you as ardently as the thirsty hart pants after the fountains of water. The sight of it will delight our benefactors, and our chaplains, all of whom beg to be most kindly remembered to you.

" Farewell, faithful little flock ! Grow and multiply ; sanctify the continent of America and people it with saints."

Not long afterwards, at the earnest request of Mgr. Bourget, a foundation was made at Montreal. The work grew and spread. Houses of the Order were begun at New Orleans, at Chicago, at Cincinnati, at Baltimore. To give a detailed account of each of these would be manifestly impossible ; we will therefore select for more special mention the house which was raised at Chicago, on account of the peculiar interest which attaches to its story.

The little band of Mother St. Euphrasia's daughters who settled on the shores of Lake Michigan, threw themselves heart and soul into their work. Twelve years later a large and extremely flourishing convent bore ample testimony to the success that had attended their exertions. But alas ! a vast conflagration broke out in Chicago ; fanned by a high wind, the flames laid a great part of the city in ashes, and made a complete wreck of the Convent of the Good Shepherd.

The letter in which the Sisters communicated the tidings of the disaster that had befallen them to the Mother House, does not contain a word of sterile lamentation or of unavailing complaint. On the contrary, it breathes an elevation of spirit which shows how thoroughly the writers had inbibed the sentiments of their venerated foundress.

" The Good Shepherd at Chicago has been destroyed in an incredibly short space of time, like a little scrap of paper used to set light to a candle. It had been founded twelve years. Some persons, hearing of its total destruction, might deem it a great pity that so much trouble should have been expended on the erection of a house which was to disappear from the face of the earth just as it was beginning to do some real good. Do not, dearest Sisters, distress yourselves on this account. Your Sisters who have carried on this work for God in Chicago are not discouraged; far from it, they believe all the more firmly in the promise of the future; the star of hope lights up the ruins they behold around them. When the day again dawns, it will be all the brighter because of the dark night by which it was preceded. During the twelve years that are past, we were not inactive; we received under our roof more than a thousand children (penitents). Baptism was administered to forty-four of these, who, enslaved as they were to Satan, would, but for this Refuge, never have been emancipated from his bondage, nor entitled to claim their heavenly inheritance. A great many children made their First Communion and were confirmed. A considerable number of our beloved penitents consecrated the remainder of their life to Our Lady of Dolours, and ended their days in this tranquil asylum of penance. Had the sole result of all our labours and toils been to snatch one single soul from the jaws of Hell, we should consider ourselves greatly privileged by having been chosen (unworthy as we are) to be instrumental in the conversion of that soul."

The good Religious went on to narrate one of those striking conversions which alone would have been

sufficient compensation for all their exertions; a Nun
of the Good Shepherd has indeed learnt to estimate at
its true value the worth of a soul ransomed by the
Precious Blood of a God made Man.

A poor girl, named Agnes, had been brought against
her will, by her mother, to the Good Shepherd at
Chicago. She could not resign herself to the loss of
her liberty. Through the influence of the Sisters she
was however induced to dedicate herself for three years
to Our Lady of Dolours, and assume the habit of the
"consecrated" penitents, firmly purposing at the end
of that period to return to the world. When the day
came her mother, distrusting the girl's resolution,
refused to take her home. Agnes gave way to an
outburst of anger and indignation. It seemed as if all
the good she had gained during her long period of
penance, was to be swept away at a single blow.
Dreading lest this should indeed be the case, the
Superior of the Good Shepherd persuaded the mother
that her wisest course would be to accede to her
daughter's wish. The woman accordingly went to the
convent, and in the kindest manner offered to restore to
Agnes the liberty for which she longed. For a few
moments the girl was silent; then she exclaimed: "Do
not think about me any more. Since I am now free to
do as I choose, I mean to spend my days in this holy
retreat, and never see anything of the world again."
Thereupon she immediately went to the chapel, and
remained on her knees before the Blessed Sacrament,
absorbed in devotion, until she was called away by the
Sisters. Who can tell what she asked of God in those
moments of recollection? Only a few days after, she
asked to see a priest, as she was wishing to make a
general confession, "because," she added, "I shall die

soon." From the time that her confession was made, her life was one of uninterrupted spiritual delight. She frequently expressed her conviction that her end was near at hand, and so indeed it was. One day the infirmarian thought she appeared to be seriously ill, and the doctor who was summoned pronounced her condition to be extremely critical. It was deemed advisable to administer the last sacraments to her. Two days later, she inquired what festival it was that the nuns were preparing to celebrate on the morrow. She was told that it was Our Lady of Mount Carmel. A look of rapture lit up her countenance. "Oh!" she exclaimed, "that is the day on which I am to be in Heaven! Be quick, help me to dress, that I may go at once on my way." The infirmarian was obliged to raise her up and seat her on the edge of her bed. Nothing would content her, short of being completely dressed; her veil which she wore as a consecrated penitent had to be brought her, and shoes put on her feet; upon this she particularly insisted. Every preparation was made as if a long journey was in contemplation. The bystanders looked on in silence, in bewildered amazement. Agnes would not tolerate any delay: "I must make haste," she said, "or I shall be too' late for the festival." When all was at length done according to her wishes, she sank back exhausted, and asked what the time was. On being told, she rejoined: "That is well, now it is time for me to go." The infirmarian gently raised her head from her pillow; devoutly she uttered the holy names of Jesus, Mary, and Joseph; then her spirit took flight to its home on high, there to keep glad festival to all eternity.

The Religious, on consigning the mortal remains of this favoured child of Mary to the grave, felt that it would have been well worth founding the convent of Chicago, if merely for the sake of saving that one soul by its means.

A new and more commodious convent soon arose on the ruins of the former building, and the work of the Good Shepherd grew so greatly in public favour, that during the Chicago Exhibition, one of the leading journals of the United States devoted several columns to an article in which the Order was praised in a manner which, considering that the newspaper was a Protestant one, is gratifying in no small degree.

The sentiments displayed by the nuns of Chicago, in presence of their great calamity, shows how completely they had learnt, as we have said, to walk in the steps of their foundress, and this was indeed none other than the spirit of the saints. We are forcibly reminded, in connection with the pathetic story of Agnes, of a remark made by St. Francis di Geronimo, who laboured long and earnestly in order to reclaim erring women. Some priest who happened to be visiting him, ventured to remark that he considered the efforts of the Saint to be, to a large extent at least, vain and wasted toil. " How many of your so-called penitents persevere ? " he asked; " is it not well known that the greater number of them return to the paths of sin ? " The Saint immediately replied: " If all my labour had resulted in the conversion of but one poor soul, I should not for a moment deem it to be thrown away."

But it is time to return to Mother St. Euphrasia. In October, 1842, Mgr. Régnier, who had recently been appointed to the see of Angoulème, wrote to request her to come thither, in order to make arrangements for founding a House of the Good Shepherd in his episcopal city. She set out on the 28th of October,.

accompanied by one of her Religious. Scarcely had
the travellers taken their places in the *coupé* of the
diligence, the upper part of which was heavily loaded,
than the cumbrous vehicle, starting off suddenly, gave
a violent lurch, and turned completely over on the side
where Mother St. Euphrasia was sitting, so that the
weight of her companions fell upon her. She remained
as calm and self-possessed as if she had been in her
own room at home, and immediately repeated aloud an
act of contrition and the *Memorare*. At least half an
hour elapsed before the captives could be released, and
her first thought, on finding herself once more in safety,
was to hand over the purse which contained the money
for the journey to the Sister who was with her, in order
that it might be distributed among those who had come
forward to free them. Very few, however, among
the crowd which had collected accepted the proffered
gratuity. The greater number esteemed themselves
only too happy, in having been able to render assistance to the Mother General of the Good Shepherd.
One very poor man, in particular, was emphatic in his
refusal. " I am the person obliged," he said. " My
daughter gave me the greatest anxiety, and you,
Reverend Mother, have made an angel of her." In
order not to disquiet the Community, Mother St.
Euphrasia re-entered the convent by a small back
door. The doctor, who was summoned, could discover
nothing serious in her condition, and pronounced her
to be suffering merely from shock to the system. She
had, however, received a very severe bruise in her side,
the effects of which grew more and more distressing
with every passing year, impeding the action of both
liver and stomach. In fact, it became at last a
cancerous tumour, which, after a period of sixteen

years, resulted ultimately, as we shall see, in her death, which took place in 1868.

Every inquiry was made as to the cause of the accident, but nothing could be discovered. The spot on which the diligence had been standing when it was overturned, was perfectly level, and though somewhat overloaded, the vehicle was quite sound and in good repair. The driver was taken before the magistrates, but Mother St. Euphrasia pleaded his cause with so much charity and ability, that he was completely acquitted. After resting for a few days, she resumed her interrupted journey. When she reached Angoulême, Mgr. Régnier did not hesitate to assure her that the devil had caused the accident, since he could foresee all the good which her children were destined to accomplish there.

CHAPTER XVI.

THE DARK CONTINENT.

IN the early part of 1843, a pressing appeal reached the Mother General from Mgr. Dupuch, Bishop of Algiers. He wrote to beg her " on his knees " to send some of her Religious to his diocese. And here we must pause for an instant to remark that one secret of the surprising success which attended the venerated foundress was that she had the wisdom never to go where she was not invited. This fact strikes us more and more, as we proceed with the history of her life. Instead of importuning this Bishop to admit her Sisters into his diocese, and that priest to receive them into his parish, she waited to be herself importuned, invited, entreated.

Her joy was great at seeing another continent thus opened to her zeal. Nor had she any difficulty in finding among her subjects those who were ready and even eager to go forth as missioners and fulfil her behest. Africa, they remembered, was the land of their holy Father, St. Augustine, and every house of the Order sent a contribution towards the expenses of the new foundation. As the time for the departure of the little colony drew near, Mother St. Euphrasia one day addressed to her Community the following exhortation, which is too admirable and too much to the point to be omitted in these pages.

" More than fourteen hundred years ago, my dear daughters, our holy Father, St. Augustine, composed the Rule which we observe, and which is the admiration of the whole Church. For many centuries no cloistered Order has found its way into Africa, the Divine Office has not been chanted there; now it is for us to cause the long-forgotten strain to be heard again in that once famous land.

" The exemplary Daughters of St. Vincent and the Sisters of Christian Doctrine have, it is true, preceded you on those distant shores, but these Communities, admirable as they are, are not cloistered, and do not recite the Sacred Office. This latter part is reserved for you, my beloved daughters. Your departure for Africa, therefore, causes the heart of every one amongst us to thrill with joy.

" Four Doctors have enriched the Latin Church with their writings : amongst these, the works of St. Augustine are the most numerous and the best. What sweetness, what force is in his words. Nothing can compare with the beauty of his writings. Read our holy Rule, and you will perceive every line to be replete with unction. Only look at the first chapter : ' Love God above all things, and after God your neighbour.' This great Saint loved God so fervently ! How much he would now rejoice in the mission we are undertaking ! I have not the least doubt that this important enterprise has been greatly aided by his powerful prayers. The inhabitants of the land whither you are going, barbarians as they may be, yet cherish to this day the memory of the Saint, and notably the remembrance of his love for souls. We read in his Life, that being desirous to establish a Community at Hippo, he communicated his designs to his flock, adding:

'What do my people say to this?' And when all present clapped their hands in token of approval, he said: 'I am well pleased, for the voice of the people is the voice of God.' Hippo is now destroyed, but the spot where his tomb was raised is still held in veneration, and quite recently Mgr. Dupuch has had a small chapel erected on the site. This has now become a place of pilgrimage, not only for Catholics, but also for the Arabs. You will see those hallowed places, my beloved daughters, and also the one where that most inestimable book, *The Confessions of St. Augustine*, were written. You will then recall to mind the fourth century, when a great number of Religious adopted the Rule of this holy Bishop. The thought occurred to me last night, and again this morning still more forcibly, that the present century will witness the revival of primitive fervour in the Church of Africa.

"We are assured, my beloved daughters, that in general you will be well received in Algeria. The Arabs and Bedouins have a predilection for white garments, and your habit will command their respect. You will have many penitents there, and many souls whom you may be instrumental in saving.

"This foundation has been attended by several very remarkable circumstances. Mgr. Dupuch, the Bishop of Algiers, in obedience to whose call we are going thither, told me that while he was saying Mass in our chapel at the altar of St. Philomena, the Saint intimated to him that in our Congregation he would find the Religious suited to carry on the charitable works he desired to establish in his diocese. He never forgot that suggestion; and it is owing to the protection of St. Philomena that we have been enabled to carry out our undertaking, in spite of all efforts on the part of our hellish foes to hinder it.   Then again our own Bishop of Angers felt himself strongly urged, almost against his own will, to accelerate all arrangements for their foundation.   Yesterday morning, when a confidential messenger went to the palace for the reply to an inquiry which we had made to his lordship, 'Tell the Reverend Mother,' he said, 'that I really have not time to write a line to her; but let her proceed with the nominations, and in the evening I will go round and give my sanction to what she has done.'

" Nor is this all; only yesterday evening we wanted five hundred francs (£20) to make up our Sister's travelling expenses.   We did not know where they were to come from, and now, most unexpectedly, some one has given us the exact sum.   But shall I tell you, my dear daughters, what you must do if you wish to obtain such signal favours in yet greater profusion? Observe the holy Rule with exactitude; recite the Office according to the rules laid down in the Directory, and remember the words of St. Augustine: 'Do not mar the harmony of your chants by the discord of your life.'   Be humble as he was.   When, before his conversion, he went to ask an interview with St. Ambrose, he was sometimes kept waiting; but far from taking umbrage, he was reluctant that the venerable prelate should be disturbed on behalf of one so unworthy.   It was this humility which made St. Ambrose predict that Augustine would become a great Saint.   Later on, these two great luminaries of the Church blended their light in a single flame.

" At a subsequent period St. Augustine received some letters from St. Jerome, who, in his desert solitude, had allowed himself to be prejudiced against him, and wrote to him thus: 'Because you are a priest, because you are talented, because you are a Bishop, you think that you can do better than your seniors; but let me tell you that it is the old oxen who step most firmly.' What was St. Augustine's reply? 'Would that I had the wings of a dove! I should fly to your feet, you who are my father in the faith.' Such is the humility of the Saints, my dear daughters; they strive who shall abase himself most profoundly. St. Peter greeted St. Paul with these words: 'I salute thee, who art the Apostle of the nations.' And St. Paul said in reply: 'I salute thee, the corner-stone of the Church and the Father of all the faithful.'

"Cultivate obedience also, my dear daughters; bear ever in mind that when you were appointed to this mission it was said to you: 'Daughters of obedience, you are chosen to go to Africa; you will go thither in the spirit of obedience, and in the spirit of obedience you will remain there.' Oh, I entreat you, do not weary of this mission, whatever the difficulties you may encounter; be assured, besides, that you will win the respect of Africa, the blessings of Heaven. But let me repeat once more, be humble and be obedient, like your great example, St. Augustine."

The Religious set out for their journey to Africa on the 30th of March, 1843, under the direction of a young German lady, who had recently been professed, and who belonged to a family of no small distinction. Their departure was attended with as much solemnity as that of the American Sisters had been. Mgr. Angebault came to the convent in order to give them his blessing, Mdme. Andigné presented to them the sacred vessels needed for their chapel, and, what is far more touching, because it shows how thoroughly the admirable foundress had imbued her children with her own spirit of union and charity, every class of the Angers Community wished to offer their departing Sisters some gift, either fashioned by their own hands, or purchased by the money they had earned by their labours. Thus, the novices gave what was necessary for the sacristy, also a communion-cloth, a cotta, an alb, a chasuble. The children belonging to the school gave cruets; the penitents, an altar-cloth. Every one was eager to do something, however little, to aid in an undertaking which was dear to the hearts of all. In order that the sleep of the travellers might not be rest-less or disturbed during their last night at Angers, Mother St. Euphrasia did not announce beforehand to her children the day on which they were to leave her. They only learnt the fact when, after Mass, they heard the sound of the organ, and found that the verses which had been composed in view of such circum-stances, were already sounding in their astonished ears.

Scarcely were they established on the shores of the "Dark Continent," in a shabby dwelling at Mustafa, outside the gates of Algiers, than sickness and death, poverty and want, came to visit them, and sanctify by sorrow and trial the beginning of their enterprise. The owner of the house which had been let to them, profiting by the absence of the Bishop, gave them a summary notice to quit. The most robust of the Sisters died erelong of malignant fever. The Superior was attacked by the same disease, and became so seriously ill, that her life was well-nigh despaired of. The Mother General, deeply distressed, wrote to tell her that she *forbade* her to die. Out of a spirit of obedience, the sick Religious asked of God that her life might be prolonged, and she speedily recovered in a manner that was little short of miraculous.

It became necessary to seek a new abode. Thanks to the kindness of the parish priest of Mustafa, a suitable property was secured for them. The house was named El-Biar, and was a short distance from Algiers. Under the rule of its able Superior, it grew and flourished so that in course of time it gave shelter to upwards of three hundred young girls. Our mention of El-Biar furnishes us with another opportunity of illustrating the prudence of Mother St. Euphrasia, even where mere worldly matters were concerned.

The Bishop, Mgr. Dupuch, was desirous that the Sisters should give up this house, and move into one for which he had just paid a high price, and which would, he thought, provide greater safety for them, as it stood within the gates of Algiers. But Mother St. Euphrasia steadily and firmly refused to affix her signature to the deed of purchase. Time soon justified her caution. The next year Mgr. Dupuch, who had no genius for finance, was obliged to leave Algiers on account of the grievous amount of debts which had accumulated upon his diocese. If Mother St. Euphrasia had bought the house above referred to, she would, under these circumstances, have been obliged to pay down a sum which would have severely taxed the resources of the Community.

We will now ask our readers to look forward with us to the year 1865, when the house at Algiers sustained a great loss in the death of the Superior. This exemplary Religious may, in her own sphere, have been termed a second Mother St. Euphrasia, for she excelled in all the virtues for which the Mother General was most remarkable. The same spirit of devotion and self-abnegation was to be seen in her, the same intrepid courage in overcoming the difficulties that presented themselves in founding a house, the same exactitude in observing every detail of the Rule.

The high esteem in which Mother St. Euphrasia held her appears from the eulogium she pronounced upon her in speaking of her, after her death, to the Community of Angers. " I consider," she said, " that Mother St. Philomena was perfect as a Religious. From the outset she chose for herself everything that was most humiliating and distasteful to nature; and she went on continually ascending higher and higher, until she reached the summit of perfection. Her obedience was unalterable, her humility, above all, most deeply rooted. In founding the house at Algiers, she had a hard struggle with poverty and hardship. Not long after she landed on the coast of Africa, she had to be taken to the hospital by the Sisters of Charity, for she was prostrated by a fever, contracted on her arrival in the country, from the stifling atmosphere of the dirty, ill-ventilated apartment in which she was lodged From that time forth she liked to talk of the days spent in the hospital as amongst the happiest of her life."

Again, at another time, the Mother General spoke to her Community of the virtues of this apostolic woman, dwelling upon the lessons which her Sisters in Religion ought to learn from the example of one so well-fitted to be their model. " We delight in reading the Lives of the Saints, my dear daughters," she said, " because in them we find an example of every virtue. But how much the more have we reason to rejoice when we are privileged to find in our own Order, in our very midst, individuals of eminent sanctity whom we shall do well to imitate. Now our dear, our ever-to-be-regretted Mother Prioress of Algiers was a woman of extraordinary sanctity. Endowed with special grace from her childhood, we may safely assume that she never lost her baptismal innocence. At the early age of five years, it pleased God to give her so clear an insight into His designs in her regard, that she resolved to consecrate herself to the salvation of souls. I leave you to judge whether she acted up to this vocation. In her life we behold and admire zeal, self-abnegation, the spirit of self-sacrifice, in their highest degree. Well might she say with the Apostle: 'I live, now not I, but Christ liveth in me.'[1] Her life was one long act of immolation; again the words of St. Paul may be applied to her: 'I die daily.' Let us then, my dear daughters, pray for the eternal repose of one who on earth never allowed herself to repose. The death of this deeply deplored Mother is to me indeed one of the greatest sorrows that have befallen me since I have been at the head of this Congregation. Since yesterday I have been thinking how I could make you understand what in reality a life is that is dedicated to the salvation of souls, a life such as hers was for whom we now mourn (I cannot speak of her by name), a life of labour and mortification. I am firmly convinced that our dear Sister was a martyr to her self-devotion. I believe her to be a great saint, and a victim no less than a saint. Yes, the Community of Algiers had for their Superior one of the finest fruits that the tree of the Good Shepherd has produced. If we cannot aspire to equal her in sanctity, we can find many things in her which we may imitate. We belong to the same stock, we grow in the same soil; we profess the same faith, we

---

[1] Galat. ii. 20.

S

have taken the same vows, we serve the same God as she did."

The heart of Mother St. Philomena (who in the world bore the title of Baroness de Stransky) was, at the Mother General's desire, brought to Angers, and deposited in the cloisters of the convent, in the niche where the heart of Mother St. Anselm Debrais had already been placed, a quarter of a century earlier.

Towards the close of the year 1845, at the request of Mgr. Guasco, Bishop of Cairo, Sister Mary of St. Teresa went thither at the head of a little colony of Religious. Mother St. Euphrasia wished that Mgr. Hercé should give them his blessing in person before their departure. He was unable to comply with their request, but he wrote a very kind letter, in order to take leave of them, and wish them a prosperous voyage. His desires were fulfilled, and the fellahs saw the boat which was bearing the travellers to their destination glide down the hill amidst rich crops of corn and luxuriant flowers. One poor ignorant negro imagined them to be angels come down from Heaven. The King of Sardinia, Charles Albert, defrayed the expenses of their journey from Genoa to Alexandria, and continued to help them after they were settled in their house. The Sardinian consul, M. Vernani, treated them with extreme kindness, while Mgr. Guasco not only welcomed them, but before long requested that a second company of Sisters might be sent out. So signally did their work prosper, so widely did it extend, thanks to the liberal support afforded by the Viceroys of Egypt, that a second house, situated just outside the city, had to be added to the first, which occupied a central position in Cairo. The Sisters opened a school for poor children of every religion and every nation, and it was soon thronged with scholars : Turks, Jews, Syrians, Arabs, Ethiopians, Copts, Armenians, Greeks. In a few years' time these houses contained, beside the penitents and Magdalens, no less than six hundred children, fifteen different nationalities being represented in their number.

It had for a long time been one of Mother St. Euphrasia's most cherished projects to found a mission for the rescue of African slaves. She longed to extend the work of the Good Shepherd so that it should reach the oppressed and degraded inhabitants of the Dark Continent. In her childish days, when accounts of the atrocities connected with the slave-trade reached her island home of Noirmoutier, she had listened with horror and deep compassion to the recital of the woes of the unhappy captives, left to perish on the sands of the desert, or exposed in the market-place to be sold to the highest bidder. The impression then made upon her had never been effaced; her heart still beat in sympathy with the suffering negroes, and she earnestly desired to do something to alleviate their cruel lot. This feeling was strengthened when she received into the convent at Angers some young African girls who had been ransomed at Cairo by the charity of a priest. In reference to these children she addressed her Community as follows :

"One day while we were on our journey to Rome, we were obliged to alight from the diligence at the bottom of a steep hill, and proceed on foot, in order to relieve the horses. As we toiled slowly up the ascent, we met a little shepherd-boy, in charge of a flock of sheep, some of which were white, and others black. 'O happy little shepherd!' I said to myself; 'you have got both white and black sheep in your flock. Now, I have plenty of white ones, but, alas! as yet I have not a single black one.' These black sheep, my dear daughters, whom I have for many years desired to count amongst my flock, are the unhappy negresses, ruthlessly carried off from their parents' side, or, it may be, even sold by these parents into slavery for a few pieces of silver. The story of what these poor creatures have to suffer is heartrending. How delighted we all ought to be to help in releasing them from their two-fold bondage. Let us at least hope that we shall have the happiness of rescuing some of them.

" What care we will take of our little black children when they arrive! How patiently we will instruct them! My heart beats high at the thought that Ethiopians, Nubians, Abyssinians, all will here receive the white robe of baptismal regeneration. Who can tell whether the Sisters of the Good Shepherd may not, at some future day, pitch their tent amid these uncivilized tribes on the banks of the Nile ? "

Little more than two years had elapsed since this prediction was uttered, when Mgr. Guasco's invitation was received. It will be understood how gladly the Mother General welcomed it, since it afforded her the opportunity of gratifying her cherished wish. No means that her ingenuity could devise—we have seen how fertile she was in resources—was left unemployed to promote the success of this enterprise. In order to enlist public sympathy on behalf of the African races, she issued a circular asking all charitable persons who might wish to have a child rescued from slavery in their name, to contribute the sum of twenty-five or thirty francs with this object. An appeal such as this is never made in vain in France : donations flowed in, and, as we have just said, the house at Cairo was started under most favourable auspices, and prospered in a manner that surpassed all expectation.

Until these foundations were made in Africa, Mother St. Euphrasia's efforts had been directed almost exclusively to the conversion of those who were already Christians in name. For these souls she wrestled more or less successfully with the enemy of mankind; victory was not always on her side. But in the convents of Algeria her aim was to liberate and bring into the Church those who were groaning under the yoke of paganism; to cleanse them in the laver of Baptism, to teach them the knowledge of God and bring them to Christ. She had the soul of a true missionary; nothing gave her greater joy than to hear that her daughters had employed the benefactions bestowed on them in rescuing some child from a life of slavery, if not from a miserable death, and thus giving a new member to the family of the Good Shepherd.

At the close of the year 1855, eight young negresses, thus ransomed, were sent from Egypt to the convent at Angers. The Mother General warmly welcomed this addition to the flock under her charge, and placed them at St. Nicholas. This house, in the immediate vicinity of the convent of Angers, was formerly a Benedictine Abbey of great architectural beauty. Founded in 1020, by Foulques, Count of Anjou, on his return from the Holy Land, in fulfilment of a vow made to St. Nicholas, the buildings had, since the Revolution, been abandoned and had fallen into complete disrepair. Mother St. Euphrasia's attention had often been attracted to them, on account of their perfect situation, besides the historical associations and religious interest attaching to them. When opportunity offered, she purchased the half-ruined edifice, and restored it, establishing there a colony of *détenues*, the juvenile prisoners committed to her charge by Government. In this fold she placed the "black lambs," over whom, owing to their close proximity to her own convent, she watched with maternal care. The frail appearance and extreme attenuation of one of the little Africans caused her considerable anxiety. Soon it became apparent that this child of the desert could not bear the cold of our northern climes; her increasing debility added to a hacking cough, made it desirable to baptize her as soon as possible. But how was she to be instructed, seeing that she understood not a word of any language but Arabic? Mother St. Euphrasia was never at a loss for expedients when anything of real importance was at stake. She sent for the Superior of "Nazareth" House, who, having been at Tripoli, was to some extent conversant with the tongue of the little stranger. For hours at a time this good Religious knelt by her bedside, patiently endeavouring to instil into her mind the truths of our holy religion. Her efforts were not unsuccessful; erelong the child expressed a wish to be baptized. The Mother General, who had been untiring in prayer on her behalf, desired to be her godmother; the ceremony was performed by the chaplain in presence of the whole Community, the neophyte answering by means of her interpreter. Transformed by the waters of regeneration, the little African became indeed a new creature; her countenance beamed with happiness and celestial joy. Three days later, her baptismal robe being yet unsoiled, she was removed from the kingdom of grace, into which she had but just been admitted, to the kingdom of glory.

where there is neither bond nor free, but all are one in Christ Jesus.

A second foundation was made at Oran, in accordance with the request of Mgr. Pavy, the new Bishop of Algiers. The Government granted the Sisters a house at Miserghin, at a short distance from Oran. Thither Mother Mary of St. Teresa, the Superior of El-Biar, conducted two of her Religious. The Mother General sent as Superior one of her most valued daughters, Mother Mary of the Sacred Heart of Mary. She herself took a special interest in this foundation, because there were in the neighbourhood of Oran so many poor wandering sheep to be reclaimed, so many Mussulman girls to be converted.

A third Algerian foundation was made in the province of Constantine, not far from the capital. Three Sisters came from Algiers to make the necessary arrangements, until the arrival of additional subjects from Angers. The Bishop, Mgr. Pavy, purchased a splendid property for them. Their temporary abode was a small mosque, but erelong suitable buildings were erected. The Vicar-General, who was the Bishop's brother, became the Superior of the convent, and the firm friend of its inmates, who were also greatly indebted to the Jesuit Fathers for much kindness received from them.

M. Ferdinand de Lesseps, whose name is so well known in connection with the Suez Canal, felt that religious influence, of one kind or another, must be brought to bear upon the moral condition of Port Said, the town having been at that period but recently erected. Being acquainted with the Convent of the Good Shepherd at Cairo, he earnestly desired that a house of the Order should be established at Port Said, where the necessity for it was growing daily more urgent. He expressed his wish to Mgr. Vuicic, Bishop of Alexandria. His lordship lost no time in writing to Mother St. Euphrasia, begging her to send him some of her Sisters. He added that, in compliance with a wish of M. de Lesseps, they would be required, in addition to their usual duties, to take charge of a small hospital outside the convent walls. This condition was so entirely at variance with the fourth vow taken by members of the Institute, that to comply with it might have brought failure on the foundation. But the talented foundress was never at fault. Her ingenious mind found a way out of this difficulty, as she had done out of so many before. She consented to establish the hospital at some distance from the house, insisting at the same time that it should be managed by out-Sisters.

It seemed as if Providence had prepared, expressly for this foundation, a Sister whose prudence and mental gifts made up for her lack of experience, for she was still quite young when called to undertake what proved to be a task of no ordinary difficulty. Sister Mary of St. Elizabeth was residing at Malta, when called to preside over the house at Port Said. She had spent the greater part of her life in the East, and was highly educated, speaking several languages, especially Greek, with fluency and ease. Possessed of high courage, she did not shrink from facing the difficulties and privations which awaited her in a town, lately built in the desert, and far from human aid and support. Many were the hardships and sufferings she had to endure, together with her brave companions. At first they found it absolutely impossible to establish the enclosure, or to build a chapel. Although those who had desired their coming remained as well disposed as ever towards them, the action taken in regard to many matters was far from being as prompt as the circumstances required. At length, owing mainly to the kindness of M. de Lesseps, President of the Suez Canal Company, all obstacles were smoothed away, and the first church erected in Port Said was the chapel attached to the Convent of the Good Shepherd.

CHAPTER XVII

WHEN the year 1847 dawned upon the world, the horizon was seen to be hung with heavy and portentous clouds. Terrible inundations had ravaged a great part of France, the harvest of the preceding autumn had proved a complete failure, so that the price of wheat had risen to an almost incredible extent. In ordinary times, the supply of flour required for the Mother House at Angers cost £120 a month; this sum was now more than trebled. " Should the price of flour continue to go up," wrote one of the Sisters to the house at Munich, " we shall literally not know which way to turn, in order to keep our poor dear penitents. The quantity required to feed eight hundred mouths is not small, so that we are at present spending £400 on flour alone." In addition to these calamities, work, which had hitherto come in so abundantly, now ceased to offer itself. Sometimes there was literally none to be had. In her deep distress, the foundress lifted her eyes to the Queen of Heaven. She felt herself interiorly impelled to place the Institute under her special protection and to proclaim her its foundress and Superior General. She further bound herself by vow, to have a solemn procession of the Blessed Virgin every Saturday for a whole year, and to arrange certain pious exercises to be punctually performed by the various classes, in the name of the entire Community, and in the honour of the Most Blessed Trinity, the Five Wounds of our Lord, and the Seven Dolours of His august Mother. Mother St. Euphrasia solemnly pronounced her vow, kneeling before an altar of Mary, decorated for the occasion. It was ratified by the whole Community on their knees. "We have had to make very great sacrifices," wrote Sister Teresa of Jesus to the Superior at Arles; "our dear Mother preferred to go into debt to the amount of £500, rather than to send away one of her children. On the contrary, our classes have increased in number."

On account of the misery and want which were almost universally prevalent and the thunder which, muttering as it did in the distance from time to time, heralded the fearful storms which were to mark the next year (1848), no fresh foundation was made in 1847. This fact is worthy of record, because it was the only year, since the erection of the Generalate, in which no fresh offshoot had been put forth by the vigorous and flourishing Institute.

Yet consolations were not wanting. In the midst of the unusually severe winter of 1846—1847, a miraculous multiplication of bread took place at the convent of Bourges, which had always been remarkable for its spirit of fervour and faithful observance of the Rule. Work became scarce, the supply of flour ran low, and one hundred and sixteen persons had to be fed. These facts, taken together, could mean nothing but a threat of famine. At this conjuncture, the process for the beatification of the Venerable Germaine Cousin was being carried on at Rome. The Superior of the Bourges convent, Mother Mary of the Heart of Jesus, who had been a novice at Angers in the early days

of the Order, felt herself irresistibly impelled to invoke
Germaine. She ordered that a novena of prayers
should be made to her, and some pages of her Life read
daily in the refectory. She further distributed medals
among the Community, and hung one up in the granary
where the flour was kept. It was the business of two
of the lay-sisters to make, every five days, the bread
necessary for the Community. They were accustomed
to use, on each occasion, twelve bushels of flour, which
made twenty large loaves. The Mother Superior told
them to use thenceforward only eight bushels, hoping
that Germaine Cousin would make up the rest.
This attempt, however, was entirely without result,
the bread only lasted three days. A second and third
experiment proved equally fruitless. The Superior
then decided to order the Sisters to use, in future, the
ordinary quantity, but the thought only struck her in
the evening after Matins, when the time for strict
silence had begun. Addressing herself to the saintly
shepherdess, " Dear Germaine Cousin," she said, " you
really must work a miracle for us, and supply the flour
which is wanting. The time for silence has begun, do
not compel me to commit an infraction of the Rule
by giving fresh orders at this hour." On the morrow,
twenty loaves, each weighing from twenty to twenty-two
pounds, were produced from the eight bushels. At the
second baking, still greater wonders were witnessed, for
the dough itself swelled to an almost incredible extent.
This was only the beginning of the favours showered
down upon the convent by the Venerable Germaine.
The store of flour in the attic was used quite freely,
yet for two months it never diminished. These wonders
were at first kept secret, but in August, 1847, a com-
mission was sent from Rome, in order to examine into

them. While it was sitting, a fresh miraculous increase of dough took place. After a prolonged and critical examination, the judges pronounced the miracles to be authentic. If we have drawn special attention to them, it is because, taken together, they form the fourth miracle necessary for the beatification of Germaine Cousin, which took place in 1854. Mother St. Euphrasia, in whose character gratitude formed one of the most prominent traits, commemorated these favours every autumn, by placing before the statue of the Saint, which had been erected in the cloister, a miniature sheaf of corn, gathered from the fields belonging to her own farm of Nazareth.

To trials of an external nature, more painful associations were soon added. Although at the outset Mgr. Angebault showed himself kind and complaisant in his intercourse with the Mother General, he had not long filled the see of Angers before he began to exercise his authority over the Convent of the Good Shepherd in a somewhat unjustifiable manner. He had, it appears, conceived the idea that he was Superior General of the whole Order, by virtue of his position as Bishop of Angers, where the Mother House was situated. The real Superior was, as we have already pointed out, the Cardinal Protector at Rome. This mistake on the part of his lordship gave rise, as will readily be understood, to certain differences and disagreements of a very unpleasant nature, and when, not content with exercising his spiritual jurisdiction, the prelate claimed the right of regulating matters appertaining to the interior government of the Order, a struggle ensued, painful in the highest degree to Mother St. Euphrasia. She was accustomed to be on the best of terms with her diocesan, and had proved herself invariably an obedient daughter

to the Bishops of Angers and Nantes, Mgr. Montault
and Mgr. de Hercé, from whom in her turn she had
received ready assistance and kind encouragement.
Her extreme sensitiveness, her natural desire to please,
her profound respect for authority, and her habit of
submission to her ecclesiastical Superiors, combined to
make it most difficult to her to resist the Bishop's
demands, and caused her to feel keenly the coldness
and displeasure he manifested in consequence of her
resistance. Nothing was omitted on her part to pro-
pitiate and conciliate him; his wishes were complied
with in every particular when they did not entrench on
the prerogatives of the Mother General, or clash with
the Constitutions of the Order. At length it was
necessary to appeal to Cardinal Patrizi, the Protector
of the Order, to persuade Mgr. Angebault that he was
under a misapprehension as to the extent of his powers,
both in regard to the Mother General and the Cardinal
Protector himself. After the interchange of several
letters on the subject, he finally yielded the point;
silenced, but not convinced, as his subsequent negotiations with other Bishops testified.

Mother St. Euphrasia made every advance towards
complete reconciliation with the offended prelate. She
referred every question to him for decision, and asked
his permission in cases where no obligation existed for
her to do so. She made a point of showing him every
attention in her power, every mark of deference and
respect. On the occasion of his visits to the convent,
the apartment in which he was to be received was
decorated with garlands, and the most distinguished
ecclesiastics of her acquaintance were invited to meet
him. Whenever presents of a suitable nature were sent
from the foreign houses to Angers, they were offered

at the Bishop's house for his lordship's acceptance.
But all these overtures of friendship were in vain.
Mgr. Angebault had unfortunately been prejudiced
against Mother St. Euphrasia during his residence at
Nantes, by a religious community in that city, and she
had the mortification of seeing her intentions misinter-
preted, her actions misconstrued, her protestations of
submission regarded as deceit and duplicity. To the
end of her days this was one of her severest trials, that
she found it impossible to establish cordial relations
between herself and her Bishop, or convince him that
the claims she resisted were at variance with the
statutes of the Order and the decisions of Rome.

With the advent of 1848, came the outbreak of the
long-dreaded storm. One could easily have imagined
that the Good Shepherd, founded as the Order was
with a special view to the benefit of the lower classes,
would have enjoyed immunity and peace, even in days
of ferment and revolution. Mother St. Euphrasia was,
moreover, everywhere known for her charity and indulgence in regard of the poor. Let us quote her own
words, taken from an address to her Community:

" Be careful to treat working men with the greatest
civility. Do not keep them waiting in the parlour
when they ask to see you, lest they should become
impatient or even abusive. Sometimes a poor working
man will go without his dinner in order to visit his
daughter who is under our care. If you keep him
waiting, he may lose his day's wages. Then what is
to become of his children at home? You must be
extremely kind and thoughtful with regard to the poor."

Yet hatred of God, and of His servants, overrides
and thrusts into the background every better and more
humane feeling, in the case of the avowed enemies of

religion. One day a band of miscreants assembled beneath the windows of the convent, making an alarming uproar, and shouting, " Away with the nuns! Down with the nuns!" With great difficulty the Marquess of Colbert, who was in the house at the time, induced the ruffians to disperse. They were overawed by the absolute fearlessness with which he stepped out from the doorway and stood in their midst. His dignified demeanour, and air of high breeding, impressed them even more than his well-chosen words. One by one they slunk away, silent and ashamed. Yet the sky did not clear. Several times, in the course of this sad year, Mother St. Euphrasia had cause to fear that her convent would be pillaged and burnt to the ground. Fortunately she found protection in an unlooked-for quarter. The Prefect of Angers, who, since he had lost the lawsuit which he had brought against the house in 1842, had never ceased to try and injure it by every underhand means he could devise, now veered completely round. He went to call on the Mother General, assured her of his good-will, and sent twenty policemen and as many soldiers to guard the premises against any possible attack.

Meanwhile, every post brought most distressing news from other houses. On the 26th of February the convent of Bourg was wrecked, the entire Community being driven out. We may here remark, that it was never found possible to reopen this house, so high did the tide of popular hatred run. Mother St. Euphrasia was eventually compelled to sell it. Mâcon and Dôle scarcely fared any better; Lyons only escaped after terrible threats and alarms. When the news of these evil doings reached Italy, the disgraceful example of the French was only too readily followed by the Italians.

The inmates of the convent at Genoa were forced to leave their house, and obtain shelter as best they could. It was afterwards completely sacked, and taken possession of by strangers, so that when, in 1857, the nuns desired to re-establish themselves in the city, they were obliged to buy another habitation.

Meanwhile, the Mother General, deeply distressed at the troubles which had befallen so many of her houses, endeavoured to find means of lessening the evil effect of the calamities she was impotent to avert. After consulting her Council, and invoking the enlightening aid of the Holy Spirit, she proceeded to write a circular letter to the Superiors of her convents, containing practical advice suited to the time of trial through which they were passing. She admonished her daughters above all things to aim at retaining possession of the houses; to adopt without scruple a secular dress, if the religious habit was obnoxious to the populace; to conduct themselves, whilst remaining within their enclosure, as much as possible like ordinary persons living in the world, and to earn their bread by the labour of their hands, if they could no longer fulfil their vocation as Religious entrusted with the training of young persons of their own sex. She also exhorted them to follow most closely the counsels of their ecclesiastical Superiors, and whatever the cost, not to give up their houses. And if, in spite of all their precautions, they were forcibly expelled from their convent, with maternal tenderness she bade them remember that they always had a home at Angers; that in the Mother House they would find a fond Mother and affectionate Sisters ready to welcome them, willing to share with them to the last all that they had for the supply of their own wants.

T

As a postscript to the copy of this letter which was sent to the Superior at Namur, Mother St. Euphrasia added the following words in her own hand: " Is there any sorrow like unto my sorrow? I beg you to pray fervently for our beloved Institute, for your attached, your unhappy Mother!"

And to the Superior of the house at Munich she wrote thus:

" ' Lord, save us, we perish.'

" Our Divine Master sleeps in our storm-tossed vessel. Words fail to tell you the extent of our misfortunes, they beggar description. Alas, my dearest child, I have hardly a moment's breathing-time. This is what has prevented me from writing to you, to you who are more loving and devoted than ever, who write with a frankness greater even than your wont. The whole Church is now in a state of affliction. If as yet your tranquillity is undisturbed, may it only remain so! We pray constantly for you, my beloved daughters. Angers is Mary's favoured city, our Sion is at peace, honoured and loved by all, whatever their creed. But her tribes are dispersed, her virgins are wanderers and exiles, their temples, their dwellings, are sacked, pillaged, destroyed by fire. Our unhappy Sisters come to us here; they have not bread to eat. How deeply they are to be commiserated!

" We are, to the number of several hundred here, without work, without alms, without benefactors; yet peace reigns amongst us, and perfect concord. Some four hundred penitents have already been turned out of different houses; the property which has been lost, stolen, or burnt may be estimated at 500,000 francs (£20,000); sixty of our professed nuns have been

banished, they come to us at all hours of the day and
night.

"You would be quite touched were you to see the
obedience, the humility of our Sisters who are with us.
Their tears flow freely, but they are tears of resignation. I have not a word of reproof to utter, but oh!
the burden of care that weighs upon me. My God,
come to my aid! Thanks be to God, the regularity
and order of our house is perfect. This is due to our
Lady's wise government. Our choir and the singing
are beautiful. Our buildings and the farms annexed
are unequalled anywhere."

During a period of trial such as this of which we
are now speaking, Mother St. Euphrasia's courage rose,
and her character showed itself in all its supernatural
strength. She viewed all these calamities in the light
of faith; she accepted them as from the hand of
Providence; she bade her daughters look to the source
whence they came, and to the object for which they
were sent. The following address, delivered to the
Community towards the end of the year 1848, will show
how she taught them to love the Cross and to sanctify
suffering.

"The year which has just closed has been for us,
my dear daughters, a year of suffering, and at the same
time of improvement. Like the cedars of Lebanon, we
have been struck with the axe; we have been subjected
to trial, in order that afterwards we may throw out
fresh shoots and acquire a more vigorous growth. It
is well for a Religious Order to be thus tried from time
to time, to impart a fresh stimulus to it, and prevent it
from declining in fervour.

" St. Vincent of Paul esteemed it a great misfortune for any individual or any Congregation to be without suffering.   St. Ignatius thought the same.   One day this eminent Saint was observed to be extremely down-cast.   On being asked what made him so sorrowful, he replied : 'I am sorely afraid lest in one of our Provinces the Fathers should have, by some infidelity to grace, rendered themselves unworthy to participate in the Passion of Jesus Christ, because hitherto they have met with no crosses.'

" You will observe, my dear daughters, that our holy Order has from the very outset encountered a thousand adversities.   For the first ten years, our Mothers were joined by no novices.   During that time they certainly were not fed on milk and butter and honey;   they already had to bear very grievous crosses.   You see how now and again the Father of the family comes to plant these crosses in our midst.   Nor is this all.   He is not satisfied with scattering here and there the seed of those sufferings which are His gift to the children He loves, He transports us into His own plantation, where we are exposed to the blast of persecution and calumny, in order that the root of our humility may strike more deeply into the soil, that we may rise higher, extend our branches, and bring forth more abundantly the fruits of our holy vocation.   God has great designs for our Institute ;   it is only by the way of the Cross that we shall find the means of accomplishing them.

" Hence it is clear that we must live in God and for God, we must be entirely dedicated to Him ; this is for us both easy and necessary.   That it is an easy matter will be readily understood, if it be borne in mind that all our actions, even the very least, tend, in virtue of our sacred Rule, and in accordance with its intention, to bring us near to God ; and how necessary a matter it is, you know better than I can tell you, for many amongst you have learnt its necessity from their own experience. See how these good works, which we perform with countless sighs and arduous toil, which require from us a daily, a life-long sacrifice, meet with adverse criticism, are crippled by opposition, if not blackened by slander. Unless they appear to prosper, the accusation of imprudence is almost certain to be laid to our charge ; our rashness is blamed, our enemies raise a laugh at our expense. Who can fail to see that we should be foolish indeed if we were actuated by any other motive than the desire to please God. Let us endeavour so to live that we may be entitled to say with all boldness : ' My life is in God, all my actions are for Him.' A young Religious whose heart was full of these sentiments, in the fervour of her love wrote twenty-four couplets, expressive of the holy joy that inundated her soul. Of each of these couplets, this was the refrain :

> In God I live, for God I live ;
> The greatest bliss that Heaven can give
> I find it everywhere.

" You have taken your stand on Mount Calvary, my dear daughters ; see that you learn, upon this high ground, to plant your feet so firmly that the wrongs which men may do you will have no power to make you swerve. Human injustice is indeed very hard to bear, and not unfrequently it has proved a cause of stumbling even to just persons."

The subsequent spread of the Order proved how true were the words of the foundress, that the free use

of the knife causes a tree to put forth fresh branches.
Later on petitions for fresh foundations poured in from
all sides. From Italy, Prussia, Austria, England,
Scotland, Ireland, China, Hindustan, the West Indies,
North and South America, Australia, and Oceanica.

Before we conclude the story of a year so rich in
trials, we will relate an occurrence which, although it
occurred some few years earlier in this history, was
occasioned by the same spirit of evil which reigned in
1848. It caused Mother St. Euphrasia no little grief.
Out of a cloudless sky, a thunderbolt fell upon the
convent at Poitiers. One of the penitents, whose conversion had for three months appeared hopeless, insisted
in a fit of anger that she should be allowed to leave
the house. The Sisters, hoping that when her passionate
temper had worn itself out, she would see things in a
different light, refused to permit her to go until the next
morning, especially as winter had set in, and it was
already dark. Urged on by an enemy of the Good
Shepherd, she not only left, but went before a magistrate, and accused the Sisters of having detained her
by force, and her companions of having beaten her.
She showed some bruises, which she had inflicted upon
herself, but which she declared to be the result of blows
received in the convent. Without waiting to examine
into the affair, two of the Religious and nine of the
penitents were arrested and taken to prison. At the
first news of this sad occurrence, Mother St. Euphrasia
set out for Poitiers. But she came too late. She could
only comfort her afflicted children, and impress upon
them the necessity of submission to the will of God.
The Sisters spent a week in prison. During this time
they had the privilege of daily Mass, and when brought
before the Court of Assizes they were completely

acquitted. It may readily be imagined with what gratitude the Community fulfilled the promises they had made in their hour of need, both to Almighty God and to St. Philomena.

The two houses founded at Rome, of which mention has been made on a previous page, did not long remain the only ones in Italy. The work carried on by the Religious of the Good Shepherd was so highly appreciated that in a short time houses were opened at Turin and Genoa. One of the most important Italian foundations was that of Imola; an additional interest attaches to it because it was from Cardinal Mastai, afterwards Pope Pius IX., but at that time Bishop of Imola, that the invitation came. His letter reached Angers shortly before Mother St. Euphrasia was re-elected as General in 1845, and she hastened to accept it, although every time that a fresh detachment left the Mother House it was a fresh grief to her to part with her daughters. When the four Sisters chosen for the mission arrived at Imola, they were conducted to the episcopal palace, where the Cardinal was waiting to receive them. "Here are my children of the Good Shepherd at last. Welcome, welcome!" he exclaimed. Then, with his own peculiar charm of manner and winning smile, he inquired whether the convent was ready for them. On hearing that it was not, he insisted that they should remain at the palace as his guests, and ordered that a suite of apartments should be placed at their disposal until all arrangements should be completely finished. Every day for more than a month the Sisters heard Mass in the chapel of the palace, and dined with the Cardinal at his table; not unfrequently he even joined them at their recreation, and sat chatting with them with the utmost kindness and familiarity about the work of the Institute and the convent at Angers. The profound affection the Sisters manifested for their Mother General, and their joy at her re-election, struck the Cardinal forcibly. "It is evident," he remarked, "that perfect harmony exists between the Superior and her subjects. As long as this union exists, the Congregation will prosper, and will accomplish great things, for union is strength." His Eminence was also much amused at a proof which the Sisters gave of their attachment to the Mother House. He had observed that they had brought with them a small box, carefully sealed up, which they evidently regarded as very precious. On it were inscribed the words: "If I forget thee, O Jerusalem, let my tongue cleave to my jaws."[1] Imagining that this box contained relics, the Cardinal one day asked that its contents might be shown to him. His surprise was great when, on the lid being removed, it was found to contain nothing but common earth. "Whatever is that for?" he inquired. "This is earth taken from the garden of our convent at Angers, your Eminence," they replied. "We shall put it in the middle of our garden here, and plant a rose-tree in it; then we shall know that the roses have grown on the same soil on which our dear Mother House stands."

All that he gathered from the conversation of the Sisters led the Cardinal to form a high opinion of Mother St. Euphrasia. He admired her eagerness in the service of God, her generous devotion, her love of the Cross, her confidence in Divine Providence. Perceiving that there was nothing the good Sisters loved to talk about as well as their home at Angers, he kindly indulged them in this, and asked about the

[1] Psalm cxxxvi. 5, 6.

employments of each hour. One evening, when he had been with them at recreation, he suddenly inquired: " What is done at Angers at the close of recreation ? " " The Mother General calls the Community around her, gives them the orders for the next day, exhorts them to the practice of mutual charity, and dismisses them with her blessing." " Well, then, we will do the same," the Cardinal rejoined, on hearing this reply. He then addressed to them a few eloquent words of encouragement and admonition, told them the intention with which they were to approach Holy Communion on the following morning, and departed after giving them his episcopal benediction.

It may be imagined how happy the Religious thought themselves in finding so kind a friend. His fatherly interest in them did not cease when they removed to the convent; all the decorations of the chapel were made at his expense: the tabernacle, candlesticks, the sacred vessels, being all provided by the same liberal benefactor. After presiding in person at the blessing of the house, and the ceremony of installing the Superior in her post, he promised to send them some penitents on the morrow. Accordingly, the next day three unhappy girls were brought to the door. As they came by compulsion, not of their own free-will, they could scarcely be induced to cross the threshold, and created quite a scene by their loud voices and angry words. But no sooner did they perceive the Sisters, who gently invited them to enter, than they calmed down, and became docile as lambs. The persons who had conducted them thither could not refrain from asking the reason of so sudden a change of demeanour. " Do you not see," one of them replied, " these white nuns have a power over us which you

have not. They need not fear we shall give them any
trouble." When this incident was told to Cardinal
Mastai, he was quite delighted.

A year later, on the death of Pope Gregory XVI.,
he was called away to attend the Conclave. Mother
St. Euphrasia, writing on this occasion to the Community at Imola, expressed the certitude that she felt
that he would be elected to fill the Chair of Peter, and
her prediction, for which there was no apparent reason,
was, as we know, fulfilled. Pope Pius IX. was ever a
good friend to the Order of the Good Shepherd, nor did
he forget, amid the cares of his exalted station, the
convent he founded during his episcopate at Imola.
After the lapse of twelve years he visited it again, and
went over all the house, expressing the utmost satisfaction at all he witnessed there. As he passed through
the refectory, where the penitents were at supper, he
stopped for a moment, and, to their great delight, asked
to taste their bread. It was long before the visit of the
Holy Father ceased to be a topic of conversation in
the convent, and, it need hardly be added, the penitents
were never heard to complain of the bread set before
them. Whilst Cardinal Mastai was still Bishop of
Imola, he often employed one of the Sisters who first
went thither, as his secretary. She was remarkably
skilful in making pens, and habitually used to cut the
quills with which his Eminence wrote. In remembrance
of these little services, and the kind manner in which
he had accepted them, she ventured to send a pen,
which she had fashioned and ornamented with great
care, to the Vatican at the time that Council was
sitting, with the humble request that His Holiness
would do her the honour of using it to sign the dogma
of the Immaculate Conception. The Holy Father,

with his accustomed courtesy and affability, willingly granted her this favour.

One very successful foundation, amongst others subsequently made in Italy, was that of Modena. It is noteworthy as having been the one entrusted to Mother M. de Coudenhove, who succeeded Mother St. Euphrasia in the office of Mother General. This Religious, the gifted and accomplished daughter of a noble Austrian family (of Dutch origin), led a retired life, devoting herself to the care of an aged relative, after whose death she gave herself to other good works, until she attained the age of forty. At that time she happened to read a little book by the Countess Hahn-Hahn, entitled *Le bon Pasteur d'Angers.* Strongly attracted by the description given of the vocation and work of a Nun of the Good Shepherd, she was hesitating whether to ask admission into the Order, when the arrival of the Sisters in Vienna in 1853 decided her. She had not been long in the Novitiate before Mother St. Euphrasia's practised eye discerned in her the qualities which would make her a valuable auxiliary. It was only the lack of any subject equally well fitted for the task that induced her to appoint her as Superior at Modena. She parted from her with the greatest reluctance, and embraced the first opportunity of recalling her to her side as first Assistant General. In this capacity Mother de Coudenhove's intellectual culture, excellent judgment, and rare tact had full room for their exercise.

The foundation of a house of the Order in Vienna, which was the means of bringing Mlle. de Coudenhove into contact with the Religious over whom she was subsequently to rule, was suggested by the Emperor Francis Joseph I., who, acting in concert with his

mother, the Archduchess Sophia, instructed the Minister
of State to represent to Mother St. Euphrasia their
wish to have a house, with a Refuge and Reformatory
School, in his capital. At the same time, Cardinal
Rauscher wrote from Vienna that the desire expressed
by the Emperor was shared by the clergy and leading
Catholics of that city. This new summons was no less
welcome to the Mother General than earlier ones had
been, nay, it was even more so than some others, since
it gave her the entry of the Austrian Empire. She
acquainted the Community with it one day at recreation, with unfeigned delight, predicting for this fresh
undertaking great success in the future. The event
verified her words; it did, in fact, prosper marvellously.
An old episcopal residence, occupying a most advantageous situation in the open country, a few miles from
Vienna, surrounded by verdant hills and shady woods,
was utilized for the convent. In a few years' time it
contained four hundred and fifty inmates, and was constituted the central house of a new Province, all the
subsequent foundations in Austria being dependent on it.

The following year (1856) witnessed the departure
of a second band of Sisters, to found a house at Suben,
in Upper Austria. They, too, went thither by the
special request of the Emperor, who was desirous of
placing them over a reformatory for juvenile delinquents. Some monastic buildings, formerly inhabited
by Augustinian Fathers, but vacated by them in 1787,
and now somewhat dilapidated, were set in order for
their accommodation, one hundred and ten female
prisoners being committed to their charge. The
influence of the Sisters over these girls was most
beneficial, and resulted in the conversion of a great
number.

As we peruse the record of one successful foundation after another, and of the numerous and varied enterprises undertaken by the Sisters, all of which were brought to a happy result, we are apt to forget at how great a cost all this was accomplished. Unremitting was the labour, unceasing the self-abnegation needed for the task. Mother St. Euphrasia constantly reminded her children of this, even when all was, comparatively speaking at least, going well with them. The following brief address may be fitly introduced here, as an exemplification of what has just been said :

" All Israel is now at peace; and if this tranquillity should unhappily be disturbed, it will be the doing of those amongst us who are not dead to themselves. This spirit of self-love is capable of one day working the ruin of our Congregation, or at any rate of proving an effectual bar to its advancement. It is very certain, my dear daughters, that persons who live a life of ease, flattering to the senses, have not the work of God at heart, and that, far from contributing to its furtherance, they leave it to languish and die out. As we know it to be impossible, says St. John Climacus, to keep one's eyes raised to the heavens and at the same time to fix them upon the earth, so we can readily understand that it is equally impossible for any one who is too much attached to the things of this world to have a real affection for heavenly things. In like manner, it is impossible that any one should labour zealously for the glory of God and the salvation of souls, whose thoughts are set upon the gratification of self. We must get quit of this love of self and of earthly things, if we are to raise our hearts to God and to the things of God. Great enterprises require perfect detachment. We ought to apply ourselves right bravely to acquire this virtue, than which none is more necessary for the conquest of our natural inclinations and aversions. We must love all that is humble, everything that humiliates, that mortifies and extirpates self-love within us. A very bitter sacrifice is this, and one which costs our poor human nature a hard struggle.

" It would be a sure sign that the world had not lost its hold upon you, if you were to manifest a preference for one employment rather than another, for one house, for one individual in particular; if you were to attach great importance to those paltry trifles which harass a soul that is entangled in miseries of that kind, and impede her free ascent to God. The Saints knew what it was to die to themselves, they were never heard to say: This or that sacrifice is beyond my strength, that office is too arduous for me to undertake, I cannot possibly leave this house, or go to that other. In our Congregation we must not have any Religious so imperfect as to retain such a miserable attachment to their own likes and dislikes.

" Remember, my dear daughters, the sweet interior joys that God gives for their consolation to the generous souls who seek after Him alone."

CHAPTER XVIII

GLIMPSES OF MANY LANDS.

WE have seen how full of trial for the Order of the Good Shepherd was the year 1848. Yet it was not destined to close without a measure of consolation, since it was to witness the first foundation which was made on the soil of Ireland. Like so many others, it came about in a manner which was evidently providential.

For more than twenty years a pious and energetic Catholic lady, Miss Reddan by name, had directed in the city of Limerick, which was her native place, a House of Refuge for penitent women. She had carried on her charitable labours with zeal and prudence, and her efforts had been crowned with no small success. But the idea that it was her duty to become a Sister of Mercy took possession of her mind. She consulted the Bishop, who did all he could to dissuade her from quitting Limerick, as her departure must of necessity deal a death-blow to the important work under her direction. However, his representations had no effect, and she went to London. Happening to pay a visit to a friend living at Hammersmith, she saw the Convent of the Good Shepherd, and was so greatly edified by all she witnessed there, that she at once formed the wish to obtain some of the Sisters for the charge of her own house in Ireland. The Bishop approved the proposal, and a formal request was forwarded to Mother

St. Euphrasia, who, we need hardly say, gladly complied with it. Erelong Miss Reddan had the joy of installing some of the Nuns of the Good Shepherd in the house she made over to them. She wished to enter the Order, but, contrary to general expectation, she proved to have no vocation for it. God was, in truth, calling her to be a Sister of Mercy. As such she went out to California some years later, with a band of missioners, and died there in the odour of sanctity.

The Limerick Convent grew and prospered. Mother St. Euphrasia had to send numerous groups of Sisters from Angers, in order to satisfy its increasing needs. Besides the penitents, there was an industrial school, carried on with the sanction of Government. The Mother General took a special interest in this convent, on account of its rapid growth and the ardent spirit of piety which prevailed within its walls.

A second foundation was made, ten years later, at Waterford. A zealous and earnest priest had for many years superintended a House of Refuge, within whose walls he had gathered thirty-four penitents. At his death, he had entreated Father Crotty, who was an intimate friend of his, to carry on the good work. This Father Crotty had promised to do, and he had faithfully kept his word. Various difficulties, however, arose in his path, and when he heard of the Limerick Convent of the Good Shepherd, he felt that the best thing he could do was to transfer the charge of the penitents to the children of Mother St. Euphrasia. The Bishop fully concurred in his project, and the result was that five Religious soon afterwards arrived from Angers. They were installed in the house occupied by the penitents, who gained their living by washing. But the Sisters had much to contend with. The young girls had been accustomed to fetch the linen, take it home, purchase whatever they deemed necessary for the household, and, in short, dispose as they pleased of their earnings. It will readily be imagined how all but impossible it appeared to put an end to this state of things, and establish the order and regularity necessary in a duly organized convent. The penitents possessed, however, a strong spirit of faith and a love of work, so that, by sparing neither time nor patience, the Sisters succeeded at last. Indeed, it was at Waterford that the first Community of Magdalens was founded upon Irish territory.

A third foundation was made shortly afterwards at New Ross, and, after a lapse of several years, a fourth house was opened at Belfast, by request of the Bishop, Dr. Dorian. This house was the source of great consolation to the Mother General, as were the other convents founded in Ireland. The last, which was at Cork, was begun by a charitable gentleman in that city. We are not told the name of the town in which the following incident occurred, but it is too striking to be omitted from these pages. The conduct of the zealous priest, whose name is also left without any mention, closely resembles the method pursued by St. Francis Jerome, the Apostle of Naples. Indeed, we might almost imagine that the son of Erin had read the Life of the Saint and resolved to imitate his virtue. A Convent of the Good Shepherd having been founded in the town referred to, a holy priest was much distressed at not being able to induce any of the poor sinners, who were, alas! only too numerous in his parish, to enter its sheltering walls. He pondered upon the subject long and anxiously, until at last a bold idea one day struck him while he was in his confessional.

U

He resolved to carry it into execution without delay. As soon, therefore, as the time for hearing confessions came to an end, he took his rosary and his Breviary in his hand, and still wearing over his cassock a surplice and stole, he went straight to a street which had a very bad reputation, knelt down on the pavement, and began to say his beads aloud. Some of the passers-by fell on their knees beside him and joined in his petitions. In this manner he spent the whole night, moving from one street to another throughout the worst quarters of the town. At first his pious efforts were absolutely unsuccessful. The poor sinners whom he was striving to save, closed their windows and hardened their hearts. But, as the day began to dawn, signs of relenting commenced to manifest themselves. Several young women stole softly out of their houses, and recited the Rosary with tears of repentance. One, more hardened than the rest, openly mocked at them. She leant out of window, and taking a bottle of wine, said she would drink to their health. The bottle broke between her fingers and seriously injured her hand. She regarded the accident as a judgment from God, and at once joined her companions in prayer and in expressions of earnest repentance. A procession of penitents was thus formed. They all declared that they could not leave the priest, to whom they owed so much, until he had placed them in safety within the walls of the Good Shepherd. He hired several close carriages, and took twenty to the Mother Superior of the Convent, saying to her, "Rejoice with me, on account of the lost sheep which I have found." Then he added: "And other sheep I have that are not of this fold; them also I must bring."[1] Day after day fresh penitents presented

[1] St. John x. 16.

themselves, begging for admission. When four days had elapsed, their number amounted to fifty. The older penitents gladly gave up their own beds and their best clothes to them. The Superior was puzzled as to how room could be found for the new-comers, but she called to remembrance the words of the Mother General: "The angels will come down from Heaven to extend the walls of your houses in order that sufficient space may be found for our dear penitents. And the angels, who waited upon our Lord, will come and help you to find them food." The occurrence made quite a stir in the town, as it found its way into the newspapers, and was alluded to in the most flattering terms. The parish priests presented their indefatigable fellow-labourer with a handsome chalice, as an expression of their admiration for his heroic devotion.

To conduct reformatories for juvenile delinquents forms part of the work of the Good Shepherd. Even Protestant Governments were glad to commit young female prisoners to the care of the Sisters, as was the case at Bristol and at Waterford. This had for some time been the case in France, and formed an important branch of their apostolate. The house near Angers bore the name of Nazareth, and we shall now proceed to give the history of it.

For several years Mother St. Euphrasia had entertained the idea of having a farm in the immediate vicinity of Angers, with the produce of which the convent could be supplied. She had been unable to carry out this plan until 1846, when she succeeded in purchasing a small estate on the outskirts of the town. It was situated on the road leading to the Champ des Martyrs, a hallowed spot, the resting-place of innumerable victims of the Revolution. The house, which was much dilapidated, had served during the Reign of Terror as a place of concealment for one or two priests; and it was from the windows of the room chosen to form the chapel, that M. Gruget, the *curé* of the Holy Trinity, had frequently, disguised as a labourer, given the absolution to groups of condemned persons who passed by, being led out to execution. The first business was to put the buildings into thorough repair; for the Mother General did not intend merely to derive material advantage from the acquisition of this property, she wished to make it an industrial farm, where the young prisoners confided to her by the Government could be employed in open-air work, the cultivation of vegetables, the care of poultry, &c., at the same time that they received a moral and religious training, which would by God's grace fit them, when their term of detention was expired, to return to their homes as respectable and useful members of society. She, therefore, took active steps to obtain the official recognition of this institution (which was called Nazareth) by the Government. Her efforts were successful; on the 13th September, 1852, she had the satisfaction of receiving an Imperial document formally approving this Reformatory. Already in March of the same year, thirty-eight young girls had been transferred thither from the House of Correction at Rennes; and at the request of the Mother General, a second and larger detachment had followed only two months later. Great preparations were necessary for the reception of so large a number; Religious had to be chosen to undertake the care of the prisoners, and to superintend the alterations in the house; rooms had to be arranged, beds had to be purchased, clothing had to be made. To this last part of the business the novices and professed nuns of the

Mother House devoted themselves for some weeks, plying their needle and scissors with the greatest zeal and energy.

Mother St. Euphrasia desired to be present herself when the last detachment, consisting of seventy-five youthful prisoners, arrived from the prison at Rennes. As the diligence was very late, it was nearly 10 p.m. when they got there, so she was obliged to spend the night at Nazareth. On her return to the Good Shepherd the next morning, she gave a description of what had passed to the Community. "I wish I could have had you all there to receive them," she said. "At first they appeared shy and downcast; but no sooner did they find themselves in front of a good fire, blazing and crackling in the wide kitchen chimney, than our little birds began to warble. We gave them all a plate of hot soup, with meat and wine. That unlocked their hearts! Poor things, it was so long since such a feast had been set before them!

"On the morrow a fresh surprise awaited them. The prison uniform was to be exchanged for the frocks which you have so kindly busied yourselves of late in making for them. They looked at one another in silence, unable to divine what this metamorphosis might mean. It was otherwise when they were allowed to walk in a part of the grounds. 'Then we are not in prison any longer?' one of them asked. 'No, dear children, you are at the Good Shepherd, where you must learn to love and serve God, and learn to work too, that later on you may be useful to your families.' 'Thank you, Sister.' 'That is not the way to speak,' one of the bigger girls broke in, 'they are *Mothers* here,' and she accompanied her rebuke with something more emphatic than words. Let us, my dear daughters, show ourselves to be truly Mothers; let us be watchful guardians of this flock which is committed to our charge. The work will be arduous, but how glorious will be the reward." Her words were no less effective than her example. Few indeed are those who know, as she did, how to infuse into those who surrounded her, her own spirit of unfailing patience and charity, of unflagging zeal, of untiring and dauntless courage. The best illustration of what has just been said, will be found in her own eloquent words, as contained in the address which we subjoin.

" 'Take this child and nurse him for me; I will give thee thy wages.' [1]

" May it not be said, my dear daughters, that these words, addressed by the daughter of a great King to the mother of Moses, are now addressed to you by a great Queen, by Holy Church herself? To you she confides the charge of her children, those children on whom the world turns its back, and whom she therefore clasps with all the more tenderness to her maternal bosom. What an honour is shown you when you are chosen to be associated to the work of our Lord Jesus Christ Himself.

" What became of Moses, the little child apparently destined to perish in the waters of the Nile? He became the deliverer of God's people. What can become of this poor penitent who is committed to your care? She may perhaps become a true Magdalen, a Thais, a Pelagia. How glorious is the work to which you are called, my beloved daughters! But how great the need for prayer if you are to accomplish it well. For this intention each one amongst us ought to offer

1 Exodus ii. 9.

all her sacrifices, all her sufferings, all her mortifications, all her good works; thus every moment of our lives will be dedicated to the salvation of these precious souls. When reciting the Office, when singing, when at work, the only object you have in view ought to be to promote the glory of God, the good of souls. How I rejoice to hear all your voices join in chanting the Sacred Office, especially on festivals. It fills me with such sentiments of devotion that I weep for joy. I have no doubt that your piety and fervour contribute greatly towards the salvation of souls.

"You see how much God loves these poor souls. He seems to work miracles in the Congregation only on their behalf. It is for their sake that we are wanted on all sides. Whithersoever we turn, these words sound in our ears: 'Take this child and nurse him for me.' It must be acknowledged that it is to the lost sheep that we owe our vocation, since, but for them, our Congregation would never have come into existence; and all the benefits conferred upon us are in consideration of what we do for them.

"May you be enabled, my dear daughters, to understand more and more fully all that it is incumbent upon you to do on behalf of these precious souls. This I desire above all things for you. Endeavour to fulfil your fourth vow in its greatest perfection. This vow may be summarized in two words: charity and zeal. You will do well to make this the subject of reflection, of frequent reflection. Only by charity and zeal will you enter into the Kingdom of Heaven. The Apostles had charity and zeal, and what wonders they worked. Our Ven. Father Eudes had charity and zeal, and he founded, not our Order alone, but several other Congregations besides. M. de Neuville had charity and zeal, and he was successful in founding this house at Angers, the cradle of our Institute, from whence many other foundations have been made, all of which become in their turn refuges where countless erring souls find safety and salvation. The venerated Bishops who ask for our services, the founders and benefactors of our convents, are all actuated by charity and zeal. What shall I say of our chief benefactress, Mdme. d'Andigné, whose only thought and object is to do good? Many other persons I might also mention who are continually giving proof of their charity and zeal.

"If it should happen sometimes that you perceive the poor children who come to us to be covered with dust from the world's highway, to speak of nothing worse, follow the example of the holy woman who with her veil wiped the Sacred Face of her Divine Master; and upon their countenances you will be able to discern the Blood of the Saviour, by Whom they have been cleansed.

"It may with justice be said that our fourth vow is the mainspring of our vocation. This vow it is which gives you the impetus to soar, which bears you across the ocean to distant climes where there are souls to be sought and won for God. Why do our novices learn English, Italian, German? Why do the English, the Italians, learn French, 'everybody's mother-tongue,' as one of our dear American Sisters called it? Not merely for the sake of adding to their knowledge, but in order that they may make use of that knowledge for the conversion of a greater number of penitents.

"Let all your penitents be very dear to you, whatever their nationality. Devote yourself vigorously to making them happy, and you will rejoice the Heart of Jesus, the Heart of the Blessed Virgin; you will, moreover, rejoice the Church, to whom Jesus and Mary have bequeathed their love for souls. 'Nurse these children for me,' she says to us, 'I will give you your wages.'"

We must not omit to mention another branch of Mother St. Euphrasia's work, but acquaint our readers with what are termed the "consecrated penitents." In order to understand their position, it must be remembered that by a wise and indispensable rule no penitent, to however high a degree of sanctity she may have attained, can ever be received into the Order of the Good Shepherd. Yet many penitents, after remaining some years in the house, desire earnestly to devote themselves permanently to the service of God. They are allowed, after due probation, to consecrate themselves by a simple vow, promising to remain in the house for the space of one year. This promise is renewed annually. These *consacrées*, as they are termed in French, do not wear the ordinary uniform of the penitents, but have a black dress with a distinctive badge, and if they persevere in their good purpose, a silver cross as a mark of their perpetual consecration. The influence of these consecrated penitents over those who have recently entered the house is no small help to the nuns in their efforts to keep up a high tone among the ordinary penitents. When all are gathered together, the black-robed figures of the *consacrées* are seen among the others, like officers in a regiment of soldiers.

It has already been related, in the course of this history, how Mother St. Euphrasia purchased the deserted abbey, dedicated to St. Nicholas, with a view to receiving there the overflow from the house at Nazareth, whose inmates already numbered three hundred. As soon as possible, thirty of their number were drafted to St. Nicholas. The practised eye of the Mother General soon perceived the desirability of uniting St. Nicholas and the convent at Angers by means of a tunnel. But this was no easy task. The tunnel had to pass under the high-road leading from Angers to Nantes, and the permission of the authorities might very probably be refused. Mother St. Euphrasia brought all her tact and influence to bear upon the prefect and the mayor of the city, and won them over to her side. Yet the obstacles which nature placed in the way of the undertaking were even more difficult to overcome, since the greater part of the subterranean passage would have to be bored through the solid rock. Although fully aware of these and various other obstacles, Mother St. Euphrasia no sooner obtained the authorization from the civic authorities, than she set a gang of work-men to commence the task. This was in May, 1854, and by means of a series of blasting operations, seconded and aided by the strokes of the pickaxe, the subway was, on the 26th of August, so far completed as to permit Mother St. Euphrasia with all her Com-munity to pass through it. On the 28th, M. Joubert, the Superior of the convent, solemnly blessed the little chapel which had been arranged at St. Nicholas in what had formerly been the refectory of the monks. He also blessed the tunnel, walking through it preceded by two acolytes bearing lighted candles. By the end of September it was completed, having cost upwards of £800.

As the year was drawing to its close, a still greater joy was in store for the devoted Servant of God.

A fresh sphere of activity was unexpectedly opened to the Sisters of the Good Shepherd in a distant clime. The Mother General was asked to found a house at Bangalore, in the Eastern provinces of India. The invitation came from Mgr. Charbonneau, who had for many years been engaged in missionary labours among the Orientals. On being appointed Bishop of Jassen, he desired to obtain for the district under his charge the aid of the Good Shepherd. Mother St. Euphrasia was ready to respond to his appeal. She laid the proposal before her counsellors; they approved it without a dissentient voice. The Community received the announcement with enthusiasm: every one was anxious to be chosen for the Indian mission. The selection of a suitable Superior to undertake the new foundation was an important matter; the Mother General, according to her habitual custom, sought counsel from the source of all wisdom. After spending an hour in prayer before the Blessed Sacrament, she made choice of a German Sister, Frl. von Schorlemer, a member of one of the oldest Westphalian families, noted for its staunch adherence to the Catholic cause.[1] At the age of twenty-six years, she had given up the bright prospects offered by the world, to embrace poverty and humility in the convent at Angers under the name of Mother St. Teresa. A sound judgment, and a force of character almost virile, united to strong affections, fitted her to be the leader of the little band who, under the escort of Mgr. Charbonneau, were to start without delay for India.

---

[1] The brother of this lady, Count Schorlemer d'Alst, afterwards distinguished himself in the Prussian Parliament as one of the orators of the "centre," who supported Windhorst in the opposition to the *Kulturkampf.*

When the day of their departure came, Mother St. Euphrasia could not bear to bid farewell to her beloved daughters. She determined to accompany them as far as Paimbœuf, where they were to go on board the boat, in order to postpone as long as possible the painful separation. The travellers broke the journey at Nantes, where they were entertained by the Sœurs de la Sagesse, who had the care of the Hospital of St. Jacques in that city. Before Mother St. Euphrasia retired to rest, she visited all the wards of the hospital, addressing to each of the patients a word of sympathy or encouragement, delighting them all with her gentleness and charity.

During the night that followed, Mother St. Teresa could not sleep. In the silent hours of darkness the thought that she was about to bid adieu for ever to the beloved house at Angers, and to the Mother General, to whom she was deeply attached, rent her soul with anguish; while the responsibilities and difficulties she would encounter on the unknown shores of India rose up before her in the most vivid colours, the most alarming proportions. Her fortitude gave way, she cried and sobbed like a child. She was overheard by Mother St. Euphrasia, who occupied the adjoining chamber. Filled with compassionate sympathy for her daughter's grief, of which she guessed the cause, this good Mother hastened the next morning to tell her she would find a substitute for her; nay more, she pressed her to accept the post she offered her in Germany, representing to her the good it would be in her power to do in her own country, and the pleasure it would give to her relatives to have her near them again. But her arguments were in vain: Mother St. Teresa was resolute. She had heard Mass and been to Communion, and grace had triumphed over nature. The terrors of the night had passed away, no trace remained of the conflict that had taken place: her countenance was pale, but calm and tranquil. " Since I received Holy Communion," she said to the Mother General, " I feel that I have the courage to cross the seas, to go through fire and water, to overcome all obstacles, if only for the sake of saving one single soul. I am aware that crosses await me; but I can say from my heart with St. Francis Xavier, 'More, Lord, more!' I assure you that it is with joy and gladness that I go."

At Paimbœuf the final leave-taking took place. Never did Mother St. Euphrasia feel more keenly than on this occasion the parting from her daughters; she embraced them again and again, ever adding some fresh words of endearment, some fresh counsels and admonitions. She accompanied them on board the vessel, inspected their cabins, commended them to the care of the sailors, to each of whom she gave a trifling gratuity to secure their good offices. At length she was obliged to set out on the return journey to Angers, before the vessel that was to carry them to India set sail, as it was detained in port by contrary winds. Several persons who had witnessed the touching farewells on board were much struck with the mutual, unfeigned affection and grief that was displayed. " We should not have imagined it possible," they said, "that a Religious Superior should be so fond of her subjects. Judging by the love that exists among its members, this Community must be just like a family."

Six months elapsed and no news of the travellers had reached Angers. The Mother General began to be uneasy; each day, when the post came in, she glanced eagerly at her letters in the hope that the one she longed to see might be amongst them. At last it came, on the eve of the Assumption; and Mother St. Euphrasia communicated its contents to the anxious Sisters when they met in Chapter. The missioners wrote from the Mauritius; they had been becalmed at sea, and had suffered greatly from the heat of the equatorial regions.

On the same day that the letter in question reached Angers, the five travellers arrived at Bangalore, after a fatiguing and tedious journey from the coast in one of the bullock-carts of the country. They were kindly received; an Indian Prince, whose ancestors were converted to the faith by St. Francis Xavier, came with his wife and daughter to pay them a visit, bringing with him some very acceptable gifts. The Sisters at once opened a school for native children of the poorer class (to teach whom one of the Sisters learnt Malabar), besides another for European girls, in which English was the language spoken. The school was well attended; in the course of a few months the White Sisters, as they were called, had as many as sixty scholars. But the joy felt at the successful inauguration of this new mission was soon clouded by the tidings of the loss of one of the Sisters, who was summoned to receive her eternal reward almost before her labours had begun. The account of her death and her funeral, contained in a letter written to the Mother General by a Bangalore missioner, M. l'Abbé Clemot, was so touching, that it was published in one of the Angers papers, and sent to every house of the Order. The obsequies of this humble Religious had resembled a triumphal procession. More than fifteen hundred persons, of every mode of belief, followed her to the grave, so great was the respect felt for one who came to that heathen land to teach and train a few poor children. When the coffin, which had been borne through the streets on the shoulders of six stalwart Catholic soldiers, was lowered into its last resting-place, all present, whether worshippers of idols or servants of the true God, pressed forward reverently to cast a handful of consecrated earth into the grave. It was found necessary to close the cemetery, in order to prevent the natives from bringing the heathen offerings of incense, fruit, and flowers.

Deeply as the little band deplored the loss of one of their number, they could not close their eyes to the fact that their departed Sister had done more by her death to help forward the mission, than she could have hoped to do by long years of unremitting toil. The funeral ceremonies, at which the Bishop officiated, deeply impressed the receptive mind of the thoughtful Orientals. When they entered the crowded church, listened to the solemn chant of the Requiem, and beheld the lofty catafalque on which lay the body of the deceased on an open bier, young girls standing around bearing tapers and scattering flowers, their native refinement caught the meaning; they felt the spirit of hope and victory wherewith the Christian regards the death of the just. Their attitude throughout was one of respectful sympathy, not of curiosity. A few days after the funeral, a poor old woman, whose daughter, baptized by one of the Bangalore missioners, had been among the earliest pupils of the departed Sister, presented herself at the door of the convent, bringing some wax tapers, flowers, and incense. "They are for the venerated *raniastri* (maiden) who is dead," she said, timidly, her eyes meanwhile brimming over with tears.

Mother St. Teresa did not end her days in the mission she had been instrumental in founding, and of which she was the Superior. Her health broke down utterly, and to recruit it she was compelled to return to Europe. As soon as she had regained her strength, her apostolic zeal gave her no rest; she went as Superior to New Orleans. The voyage thither was most disastrous; the vessel was boarded by privateers, and the passengers taken captive. When set free, Mother St. Teresa made it her endeavour to revive in the Convent of New Orleans the spirit that prevailed in the house at Angers. She died in 1865. So far was she from having any presentiment of her approaching end, that in the last letter she wrote to the Mother General she said, referring to the recent decease of the Superior of the house in Chili: "As for me, it appears that I am not good enough to die yet; my health is as good as it was before I went to Bangalore."

The year 1855 brought with it special joys and blessings which truly rejoiced the apostolic heart of the venerated foundress. It opened to her zeal the continent of South America, where a large number of houses were destined to be founded. The Chilians had not forgotten in the New World the faith and piety they had learned in their far-away Spanish homes. They thoroughly admired and appreciated the work of the Good Shepherd, although it was only by report they had become acquainted with it. In December, 1854, there arrived at Angers an envoy from the Archbishop of Santiago, the capital of Chili. He was empowered to request that some nuns might be sent out to his country, where a convent of ample dimensions was already awaiting them. He brought with him the funds which were needed both to defray the expense of the voyage, and also to purchase the *trousseaux* of the Sisters. Mother St. Euphrasia lost no time. She chose seven Religious, who left the Mother House on the 3rd of January, and reached their destination on the 13th of March. During the voyage, they had experienced the greatest kindness from the captain and the whole of the crew. The first mate was specially attentive to them, making over to them a little store of preserved fruits and other dainties which his mother had given him before he left home.

After a brief halt at Valparaiso, they went to San Felipe, near Santiago. In this latter city they stayed under the roof of the Poor Clares until they could remove to their convent at San Felipe. They were conducted thither in great pomp, by a rejoicing multitude, as had already been the case at Munich. But when the ceremonial was over and the crowd of visitors had departed, the Sisters, being left to themselves, perceived that the rose-coloured glow faded away, and looking quietly round, they found themselves face to face with some unpleasant realities. The Religious who had occupied the house before them, had not only been very careless in the observance of their Rule, but had allowed many parts of the building to become utterly dilapidated. But the daughters of Mother St. Euphrasia knew better than to sit down and indulge in vain regrets. With the utmost energy they pushed on the necessary repairs, and their convent was soon in perfect order. The foundation proved so successful, that before the end of the year a second was made at Santiago.

The saintly foundress, like almost all the Saints and eminent Servants of God, suffered severely from the. assaults of the evil one, who at times succeeded in filling her courageous soul with fear and dread. He

v

hated her, he hated the work she was carrying on with signal and brilliant success. The sight of souls she had snatched from his clutches, stirred up his malignant rage. He therefore did all he could to depress and discourage her. Not unfrequently did she describe, in vivid tints, when speaking to her Religious, these terrible attacks of the devil. They generally took place when she was on the eve of making a fresh foundation. On March 31, 1860, we find her speaking as follows: "It is a long time since we have made three foundations at the same time, as we are now doing. The devil puts forth all his power when he sees that we are going to make new efforts to wrest from him those souls which he regards as his property and his prey. I assure you that I feel the full force of these storms and tempests, stirred up by Satan and his emissaries, for at such times my nights are dreadful. In the midst of a feverish excitement which I can describe as nothing short of infernal, I see everything in so gloomy a light, that if I were to utter my thoughts aloud, they would discourage the whole of the Council of the house. I say to myself, 'No, this foundation cannot possibly be made.' But when the morning comes, I view everything in a different light, and I am very careful not to communicate to my Sisters these distressing experiences."

On the 8th of September, 1867, the Feast of our Blessed Lady's Nativity, the Community of Angers celebrated the fiftieth anniversary of the religious procession of Mother St. Euphrasia. The affectionate devotion of her children rendered this day worthy of being termed her "golden wedding." The convent was everywhere decorated with wreaths of fresh foliage, and garlands of sweet-smelling flowers. Skilful hands had done their utmost, and the result was graceful and elegant beyond all power of words to describe. After a Clothing and Profession, the Community, in all its various branches, congratulated their beloved Mother. Always desirous of promoting the glory of God, rather than her own, she had in readiness for this day of rejoicing, a statue of Our Lady of La Salette. The Superior of the Convent of Santiago also presented to the Mother House at Angers a statue of the Sacred Heart, as a *souvenir* of this auspicious day, during the whole of which these two statues were surrounded with choice flowers and lighted candles. The different classes of the Community passed in turn before them, blessing and thanking the Immaculate Mother who watched over them from her throne in Heaven, and also the dear thoughtful Mother who, while still on earth, cared for them with such tenderness and truly maternal devotion.

After this happy day, Mother St. Euphrasia experienced a series of trials which ended only with her death. The attacks made upon the Papal territories placed several of her convents in Italy in great danger. She deeply felt the sorrows of the Church, and of the Sovereign Pontiff, to whose august person she had always been devoted, and whose commands she had ever regarded as if proceeding from the lips of the Divine Head of the Church.

Her enemies could not rest. Seeing fresh foundations arising on all sides, they united in making one final effort to destroy her prestige, and undermine her power and authority. A lengthy memorial was drawn up and sent to Pope Pius IX., in which she was accused of tyranny, pride, and hypocrisy. The appointment of an Apostolic Visitor was demanded, who should have full powers to examine the Community at Angers, as Mother St. Euphrasia had, it was stated, refused to tolerate any ecclesiastical Superior. In order that this examination should be properly made, it was requested that Mother St. Euphrasia should be compelled to quit the house for a period of four months at least.

Every one knows that pride and hypocrisy are faults which cannot be hidden either in the world or in the cloister, and Pius IX. was not duped by these false and malignant representations. His Holiness commanded the Cardinal Protector to forward a reply, and to say that no complaint had ever been preferred against Mother St. Euphrasia, but that she was, on the contrary, beloved and revered by all her Religious, and by all the inhabitants of the houses she had founded. The Holy Father refused absolutely to send her away from Angers during a period of four months. This, he declared, would be an act of unjustifiable severity and cruel harshness. Many more details might be added concerning this painful affair, which constituted one of the last, and certainly one of the severest trials which God laid upon His faithful servant. But she was always ready to forgive her enemies, and why should her biographer dwell upon their unkindness and animosity. Our Lord, in His love for this elect and favoured soul, permitted her to be misjudged, misrepresented, and hardly used, in order to purge away any last remains of earthly dross, and fit her to enjoy for ever the ineffable delight of beholding His face in Heaven. Meanwhile she, on her part, acted out the beautiful words of the poet:

And, through that last and direst storm,
Descried by faith her Saviour's form.

She was deeply wounded, but she bore her sorrows in silence, with an heroic patience which makes her a model to all Christians. The effect upon her physical forces was disastrous in the extreme, as mental suffering must inevitably be. On the 15th of May, 1867, she was suddenly seized by a violent attack of pneumonia, with which her enfeebled condition rendered her less able to cope. Within a very few days, she was in imminent danger of death. All human means proved ineffectual to stay the ravages of the disease. On the 19th of May, the invalid, of her own accord, suggested that she should take, during nine days, a small portion of the water which comes from the miraculous spring of La Salette, at the same time repeating daily the litany which invokes our Lady under that title. Almost immediately after she had partaken of the water, her breathing became easier. She was evidently relieved, and sank into a gentle sleep. On awaking, she said to the Sister who was watching beside her: "As my mind is constantly preoccupied with the afflictions we have to suffer from without, I dreamt that I saw our Congregation surrounded by a huge net, in which many stitches were dropped. I was extremely vexed on perceiving this, but the Blessed Virgin said to me: 'If you attempt to mend this net, I shall leave you to complete the task alone and unaided. I desire to complete the whole work with my own hands.'"

From this time a gradual, but most satisfactory convalescence set in. The beloved Mother General bore her weakness and suffering with the most admirable patience and resignation, never ceasing to occupy herself with the affairs of the house. She even took her usual interest in the commissariat department, and would ask how the various vegetables were growing, and whether the store of flour was properly kept up.

On May 29th, the eve of the Ascension, she was able once more to partake of Holy Communion. It was brought to her in her room at five o'clock in the morning. She arose from her bed in order to receive our Divine Lord on her knees: she had also persisted in keeping her fast unbroken. The next day, and the next, the same consolation was vouchsafed her, but on Saturday she dragged her feeble frame down to the chapel of the Novitiate, where she received the Bread of Angels. The next day being Sunday, she not only went to Communion in the same way, but heard Mass also. She paid a brief visit to the Community after dinner, and the joyful surprise of her children may be well imagined. "I could not restrain my ardent desire to come and see you all again once more, my dearest children," she said. "The doctor has given me leave to say these words to you, and so I will tell you how grateful I am to you for all the prayers you have said for me, and all the care you have lavished upon me. I want also to assure you I love you with all my heart."

From this time Mother St. Euphrasia resumed, little by little, her ordinary manner of life. She was aided by the soft, sweet summer weather which prevailed. All traces of weakness of the chest disappeared, and she was able to attend, as formerly, to the business of the Order. Her children rejoiced at a restoration which appeared complete. But alas! their hopes were doomed to disappointment. Before the end of the year her strength began to fail, though as yet she refused to allow herself any rest, or any special indulgences.

Ere we proceed to relate the history of her last painful illness and holy death, we shall give a more detailed account than we have hitherto done of the spiritual gifts and graces granted to her by God, and of the manner in which she corresponded to those gifts and graces, as well as of her personal virtues.

CHAPTER XIX.

DEVOTION TO GOD AND THE SAINTS.

HITHERTO the greater part of this history has been occupied with an account of the labours, trials, and fatigues undergone by the Servant of God with a view to the salvation and sanctification of others. The time has now come for us to consider her in the light of one who aimed at her own perfection before God. It is all the more necessary to do this, because the eminent degree of virtue to which she attained was the real secret of her marvellous success.

Her power proceeded from her constant union with God. In the midst of her numerous and pressing occupations she never lost her sense of His presence, and her days may be described as one long act of mental prayer. It was the foundation-stone, so to speak, of her spiritual life. In order fully to comprehend the value she attached to it, and the importance with which she regarded it in respect of the Nuns of the Good Shepherd, we have only to read the addresses she from time to time gave them. We will here quote one devoted to this subject. It is too long to be given *in extenso*, but its excellence must be obvious to all who read the subjoined extracts from its wise, clear, and judicious pages :

" See, my dear daughters, that you abound in fervour, in zeal for the salvation of souls; and as a

means to this end, cultivate a love of mental prayer, of
Holy Communion. Where, indeed, can you hope to
obtain the strength you need to perform your work well,
if not in the presence of the Author of all grace ? The
more completely a Religious is animated by the spirit
of her vocation, the more will she delight in meditation
and prayer, for from that salutary exercise she will
derive power to labour efficaciously in the work of
bringing erring souls back to God.

" Let us remember that mental prayer ought to be
our preparation for Holy Communion, and that in this
Sacrament of Love our hearts ought to be kindled with
the sacred fire of the spirit of prayer, whence come all
the graces we need for our own sanctification, and for
that of the souls confided to our care. It would indeed
be deeply to be deplored were we, who beyond all
others ought to be assiduous in mental prayer, we,
whose need of drawing from the fount of grace is so
great, to stand aloof from it because of our temptations, or our spiritual trials. These trials are rather
an additional motive for drawing near to God, Who
is the God of peace and of consolation.

" When you are about to commence your mental
prayer, consider that the Lord your God invites you to
it, and that He is ready to bestow upon you the light
and the grace which are necessary to pray well. If in
your prayer you experience dryness, aridity, if you find
difficulty in bringing your intellectual faculties into
play, this may perhaps be a trial sent to you by God.
In that case bear it patiently, remain humbly at His
feet, assuring Him in all simplicity of heart that you
have no other wish but to do what pleases Him. At
other times, this oppression that you feel, this difficulty
that you experience in your prayer, may proceed from

want of preparation on your part, from carelessness, from habitual dissipation of mind, from want of mortification, or from a certain attachment to creatures which separates you from God. If so, I counsel you to apply a prompt remedy to the evil, entreating our Lord to give you the resolution to remove every obstacle which may hinder your perfect union with Him in prayer. Above all, remember that to shrink from encountering humiliations, crosses, sufferings, is tantamount to giving up mental prayer.

" Have recourse, under these circumstances, to the Physician of souls; beseech Him to make your spiritual infirmities known to you, to grant you the grace to cure yourself of them. Trust implicitly in His power and in His mercy; and thus you will be able to hold at bay carelessness and tepidity, and to unite yourself closely to God in the fervour and recollection of your meditations. The soul that is a prey to constant anxiety, and which allows herself to be impeded by a thousand fears, will make no progress in the spirit of prayer. Little by little darkness will enshroud her mind, grace will not find free entrance there, and she will remain in a state of torpor, impotent to rouse herself for active usefulness.

" Bear also in mind, that without humility there cannot be the spirit of prayer. Pride, the Holy Spirit tells us, places us at a distance from God. ' The prayer of him that humbleth himself shall pierce the clouds,'[1] but the Lord rejected the prayer of the proud. If, therefore, you desire to pray well, cultivate humility, and avoid distractions. These are the two things most indispensable for you and for every one. Recollection and humility are the foundation on which

[1] Ecclus. xxxv. 21.

mental prayer rests, just as mental prayer is the support whereby recollection and humility are sustained.

" St. Teresa says that our Lord does not bestow His graces upon a soul unless that soul is humble and recollected, conscious of her own nothingness. The humility of the great Saint whose words we have just quoted, exalted as she was to the highest stage of contemplation, was proportioned to the greatness of the favours she received from God. The lights vouchsafed to her in mental prayer enabled her to discern her slightest defects, so that she believed herself to be heaping up ingratitude and sins, and she used lovingly to complain to God that He only chastised her for her infidelities by the bestowal of fresh graces. Nevertheless she too, as a matter of fact, as the punishment of some trifling faults, experienced for the space of more than fifteen years such aridity that she used to say she would rather suffer martyrdom than endeavour to recollect herself for meditation. The worst of all was that the enemy of mankind had the cunning to give her to understand that she was too great a sinner to engage in mental prayer, and that it sufficed well enough for her to say the Office and recite vocal prayers ; so that when the bell sounded for the hour's meditation, she would sometimes go and hide herself in the garden, as if to escape from the presence of our Lord, while at the same time she felt the keenest pain at being separated from the Beloved of her soul. Her confessor, to whom at length she mentioned this temptation, told her at once that it was a snare of the evil one, who sought in this manner to lead her to perdition. Convinced that he was right in this opinion, she resolved never again to be deterred from the practice of mental prayer, but to persevere in it faithfully unto death, whatever it might cost her to do so. Often at times of dryness, she would say to God : ' The more, Lord, you hide your-self from me, the more will I seek after you ; the more you fly from me, the more I will run after you.' Some-times she would take up a book, and find relief in reading for a space.

" It is thus that you must act, my dear daughters. The more our Lord appears to withdraw Himself from you, the more earnestly you must seek after Him with loving perseverance, not letting yourselves be overcome by languor or somnolence, but keeping your heart awake with holy aspirations, according to the impulse and inspiration of the Holy Spirit, and making use of the excellent books you have within your reach, the excellent methods which have been pointed out to you. After all, experience will teach you that it is only by prayer that you learn how to pray well. That is why, when the disciples of St. John of the Cross went to him begging that he would instruct them in the practice of mental prayer, his usual reply was this : ' Practise it, practise it.' This is the answer I feel inclined to give to those who come to me with the same question.

" Mental prayer is a private audience granted us by God, in which He manifests Himself to us in order to lavish His graces upon us. Believe me, my dear daughters, no one can initiate you into this close communication between the soul and her God ; no one can disclose to you the secret of this intercourse of the creature with the Creator. What you must do is earnestly to entreat God to instruct you in the method of converse with Him, and strive to render yourselves worthy to have this favour bestowed on you. Prepare yourselves constantly for prayer by great fidelity in the

performance of all your duties, and then present yourselves before your Divine Lord in all simplicity of soul.
Listen to His voice when He speaks to your heart,
when He bids you correct this or that fault, when He
suggests that you should make this or that sacrifice.
Ask of Him pardon for your faults; give thanks to
Him for His numberless benefits, implore from Him
fresh favours for yourselves, for others, for our Sisters
who labour in distant lands. As far as you can, exercise your understanding, your memory, your will;
above all, awaken within your heart sentiments of love,
of gratitude, of devotion. In a word, your prayer
should be characterized by zeal, self-denial, sacrifice;
and it should be no less fervent and persevering when
God leaves you desolate, than when He consoles you
with ineffable spiritual delights. In fact, let it deserve
to be called an apostolic prayer, because its motive is
not merely the wish to please God and glorify Him by
your service, but also the ardent desire to lead all the
world to love and serve Him, even at the cost of your
own life.

"Mental prayer is the source whence we derive
courage to endure the humiliations, the contempt, the
pain, the anguish which meet us in the discharge of
our duties. If there is any good in us, we must
acknowledge it to be the fruit of our prayer, for every
spiritual grace comes to us by that channel. Without
an interior spirit, without mental prayer, how futile is
our toil; one sees eventually that no good comes of it.
Never, my dear daughters, can you expect to labour
successfully for the salvation of souls, unless you have
previously sought in silence and in prayer the light
which is indispensable for your guidance. The Religious
who are actuated by the Spirit of God convert many

more souls than those who are endowed with great talents, and have the gift of easy and fluent speech.

"Let nothing be dearer to you than this holy exercise, and you will then be like the tree spoken of in Scripture, 'whose leaf shall not fall off; which shall bring forth its fruit in due season.'[1] Watered constantly with the dew of grace, the little garden of your soul will be ever verdant, ever rich in flowers; the seeds of good desires will spring up and bear abundantly the fruits of virtue. Observe that the only soil which produces these fruits is that of mental prayer, of prayer made aright. And this you may hope that yours is, if you are sincerely desirous of what is good, if you strive after your own perfection. But if you make no progress in virtue, if you are indolent and careless in the discharge of your duties, there is surely some serious defect in your prayer, since the fruits which it ought to produce are lacking. If this be so, awake as soon as possible to a new life, lest you become withered and dry plants, incapable of absorbing the dews of Heaven. The heart of the Religious who neglects meditation, or who is careless about it, is, as Holy Scripture says, like an empty cistern, which allows the water of grace to escape and be lost."

Next to Mother St. Euphrasia's appreciation of mental prayer, we may place her intense and fervent devotion to the Blessed Sacrament. It was indeed the Life of her life. Her instructions abound with earnest exhortations, intended to excite her hearers to a constant love and devotion to our Lord in the Blessed Sacrament of the Altar. Nor did her practice fall short of her teaching. Rare indeed were the occasions on

[1] Psalm i. 3, 4.

which she allowed weariness or suffering of body to deprive her of Holy Communion. Over and over again did the Religious see her painfully drag herself down to the chapel, in order that she might there receive the Bread of Angels, for so great was her respect for the King of kings, that she would not permit the Sacred Host to be brought to her cell, if by any possibility she could betake herself to her place in the choir. When on a journey, she did not hesitate to prolong her fast until a very late hour, if by so doing she could gain the privilege of receiving Holy Communion.

It was a privilege indeed to behold her, whilst she was engaged in making her thanksgiving. Her perfect recollection was reflected upon her countenance, and imparted to it something truly angelic, as many of her Religious have testified. During these sacred colloquies with her God, she often formed her most important decisions with regard to her foundations. " After I had received Holy Communion, our Lord commanded me to do this," she would not unfrequently remark to the Sisters.

Sometimes she would spend several consecutive hours before the Blessed Sacrament. If she had an obstacle to surmount, a perplexity to unravel, a difficult question to resolve, she at once repaired to the chapel, and there besought counsel of Him Who is the Eternal Wisdom. However long was the time thus spent, she remained upon her knees, and so absolutely motionless was she that not even one single fold of her mantle was stirred. A priest who had for many years directed Mother St. Euphrasia, remarked upon one occasion as follows: " Her whole manner and bearing whilst assisting at the Holy Sacrifice showed the intensity of her faith, and when she received Holy Communion she appeared to be in an ecstasy. Again and again has she said to me with childlike simplicity: 'I will consult our Lord concerning this affair during my thanksgiving to-morrow morning.' At such times I was certain that her doubts would be quickly dispelled, and her footsteps guided by the Light which shines from Heaven."

Each year when the festival of Corpus Christi drew near, Mother St. Euphrasia reverted, in her addresses to the Sisters, to her favourite topic, the love of our Lord in the Blessed Sacrament. She warmly exhorted them to keep their minds fixed, as far as possible, on the Mystery of Love they were about to commemorate, and to celebrate in spirit the day specially set apart for its observance, although, as is well known, the festival is in France transferred to the following Sunday, in accordance with the terms of the Concordat. The Mother General much deplored that it could not be solemnized as she would have desired, on the day appointed, the more so since the obligation of transferring it imposed an unwonted privation on the German and Italian Sisters. We give a few extracts from her instructions on the subject of this mystery, her devotion to which was the mainspring of her spiritual life.

"Endeavour, during these days of benediction, to keep your heart fully recollected. Put on the spirit of Jesus Christ: imitate His life of silence, of sacrifice, of zeal; His life of obedience, of poverty, of humility. Let your hours of adoration be marked by the utmost attention and fervour. Avoid making the slightest noise, out of respect to Almighty God, and be careful not to occasion any distraction to those of your Sisters who may feel drawn to unite themselves more closely to Him by abandoning themselves to the delightful intercourse of mental prayer.

" You are all deeply interested in the various undertakings of our Institute, and you are anxious for their speedy extension ; but if rapid progress is desirable, how much more is solid progress desirable. And where shall we find the power to give to our works that stability which is essential to their well-being? We shall find it at the foot of the altar; by asking it of God in the quiet of meditation, beneath the shade of the tree of life. There we shall derive all the strength we need. The mistresses of the classes ought above all to have recourse to this fount of grace : they have indeed trying times to pass through ! ' "

" I do not like," she said on another occasion, " to see people generally preferring to go and pray before a statue of our Lady rather than before the Blessed Sacrament. What I say applies chiefly to the younger novices, who, without taking account of it themselves, fall into this habit, though it is one by no means pleasing to the Blessed Virgin. Our devotion to her ought rather to spring from our devotion to the Holy Eucharist. It is the same in regard of St. Joseph and the other Saints. You ought to pay heed to the difference that exists between the figure of anything and the reality, and not lose sight of what faith teaches us to believe, that the Son of God is really and corporally present in the Holy Sacrament of the Altar, true God and true Man. Whereas Mary, Joseph, and the other Saints, are, on the contrary, in nowise present in the statues or pictures representing them.

" You know well that the prayers we address to our Lord in the Blessed Sacrament, imploring grace of Him

W

as the Supreme Dispenser of every good thing, are of quite a different nature from the prayers we address to the Saints, entreating them to be our intercessors with God, to obtain from Him the graces we desire. Yet we ought greatly to venerate the images of the Saints; the sight of them incites us to invoke the protection of these friends of God, and this is so well pleasing to Him that He rewards it with countless miracles. Far be it from me to discourage you from so pious a practice; my intention is to place your devotion to the Saints on a firmer basis when I urge you to cultivate greater love for the Blessed Sacrament. It is at the feet of our Lord that you must strive to imitate Mary and Joseph, that you will learn how to honour them aright; for He above all others loved and honoured them, as you know full well.

" Let me, therefore, often see you praying before the statues in our chapel. They were placed there in token of our gratitude for the innumerable benefits we have received from our Lord through the intercession of Mary, our dear Mother, whom we regard as the real Superior of our Order, and of St. Joseph, whom we elected to be our Guardian and chief director. Never will you show as much honour to these glorious patrons as our Lord used to show them, and as He does still show them. Go frequently then to pay them homage; let it be your joy to see them occupying a commanding position, and do not omit, when passing before them, to pay them the tribute of respect and affection which is their due.

" The sight of one of these statues or pictures used to fill St. Teresa's heart with rapture. She would have liked to have had them everywhere. 'Upon what object more precious, more attractive, can our eyes rest,' she would say, 'than upon the portraits of those whom we dearly love? How the misguided heretics are to be pitied, who by their own perverse will, deprive themselves of this as well as other consolations that they might enjoy.' When she went on a journey, that great Saint always took with her, besides other pious images, a small statuette of the Child Jesus; this she generally carried in her arms, to serve as a reminder for herself and her companions of the presence of God. And yet, in her instructions to her spiritual daughters, she says: ' Be careful never to leave our Lord in order to gaze upon His image, above all after receiving Holy Communion; you will understand that, supposing some one of whom you were very fond came to see you, it would be the greatest folly on your part to leave him alone that you might go and talk to his portrait.'

" You know how zealous the excellent Superior of our convent at Oran (Algeria) is for the glory of God and the salvation of souls. You heard her talk about her mission, and could see for yourselves that, although naturally of a timid disposition, she rose superior to herself, and conquered every obstacle in her way when there was a question of good to be effected. Whilst she was here she edified us all; on her departure yesterday, she asked me to bid you all pray for her, and for the success of the important business which called her away so suddenly. She had taken steps to obtain an audience of Her Majesty the Empress Eugénie; yesterday she received a telegram informing her that it would be granted to her to-day at eleven o'clock. Although she was delighted to hear this, our poor Sister felt appalled at the prospect before her, and I, knowing her character, did not wonder at her agitation. But her courage rose at the thought that this might perhaps be an occasion of placing means at her disposal for the salvation of souls; 'If I do but get a small sum,' she said, 'it will at least provide for one or two penitents.' This audience will probably not last more than five minutes at the most, and she will not be a moment alone with the Empress. That is the way with the great ones of the earth; such ceremonial is not needed when we would enter the presence of our God. There is no time at which He is not willing to receive us; no limit is placed to the length of our visit. Let us, therefore, go to Him for all that we need."

If such was her reverence and respect for the King, can we wonder at the dutiful homage she gladly and constantly paid to His ambassador? *Ubi Petrus, ibi Ecclesia*, was her motto from her earliest until her latest breath. Never was there a more humble and submissive subject of the Vicar of Jesus Christ, never did any one cherish a more ardent and whole-hearted love for Holy Church. It was her delight to believe, her joy to obey. The Saints never inquired, "What *must* I believe, what am I *compelled* to do?" And Mother St. Euphrasia showed herself their true follower. Had her lot been cast in the evil days in which it is our misfortune to live, how deeply would she have grieved at the half-hearted, unfilial attitude of so-called "Liberal" Catholics, at the flippant spirit of men of science, who come forward with their vaunted discoveries, and weaken the faith of the unstable, giving grievous scandal to the little ones, for whom Christ died! Even as it was, she had much to suffer from her compassion for the sorrows of the Church, more especially in her later years, when matters were approaching the climax which they reached so soon after her death.

And her devotion to the Supreme Pontiff was no feeling of personal gratitude or affection for any special Pope, on account of the benefits her Order had received from His Holiness. The homage she paid to Gregory XVI., she transferred to Pius IX. Nor did she content herself with praying for the Holy Father, and bidding her children also pray for him. She sent him solid proofs of her sentiments, in the shape of large contributions to Peter's Pence. In 1866 she sent £140, and in the next year, although the price of provisions was unusually high, she sent £120. But she shall speak for herself on this subject, in some extracts from one of her instructions to her daughters.

"Never can I cease from speaking to you of the Church, the Mother of us all. We are bound to love her, we are bound to pray for her. And no Religious Order ought to outdo us in loyalty and attachment, for not one can owe her more than we do, and none surely can stand so greatly in need of her help and protection. Let her find ever in you affectionate and submissive children ; when you are sent to make a new foundation, feel that she it is who has sent you, and if you feel thus, you will meet your dear penitents in a truly apostolic spirit, and will win their souls to God.

"The Church is the ship which bears within it the treasure of our faith and hope. This vessel, which can never perish, has been tossing on the waves for more than eighteen hundred years, carrying its riches to all the nations of the earth. Jesus Christ Himself is at the helm, He steers the bark of Peter amid all rocks and over all quicksands. At times He seems to sleep, and then the raging storms break forth, and all the powers of Hell appear to be unchained. Persecution rages, and the fatal wreck seems to be not far off. Cries of distress are heard, and the Divine helmsman with one word allays the tempest, so that the ship may continue her triumphal progress throughout all ages.

"And now, dearest children, I will conclude as I began, by exhorting you to pray without ceasing for the holy Church of God, which is so sacred, so dear to the hearts of us all! Pray that she may go on, conquering and to conquer, until the dawn of the happy day which shall witness her final triumph and that of her glorious Head, *cujus regni non erit finis.*"

The reader will easily picture to himself the joy with which the proclamation of the dogma of the Immaculate Conception on the 8th of December, 1854, filled the heart of Mother St. Euphrasia. For several years she had entreated God that she might live to witness the definition. She had caused to be erected, some time previously, a statue of our Blessed Lady under this invocation, and during many years the Little Office of the Immaculate Conception had been daily recited in the Convent of Angers. On Sunday, the 30th of December, 1854, all the churches of Angers were illuminated in honour of the dogma so recently proclaimed. To the west of the city, on the slope of the hill which leads down to the Maine, lines of light were to be seen, shining out against the dark sky. Transparencies suspended from the windows of the vast pile of buildings, proclaimed to all the passers-by the names under which her children delight to invoke our Blessed Lady. Thus did the very walls of her convent celebrate the festival so dear to the heart of the foundress. She taught all who came under her influence to feel as she did, and can we wonder at this?

For who can truly love thy Son,
Sweet Mother, if he love not thee?

It was always a joy to Mother St. Euphrasia to
relate instances of help afforded by our Lady in seasons
of distress. Such an instance is the following. During
a time of drought, vegetables, and indeed provisions of
every kind, had become very dear at Metz. The
Superior of the house purchased what was needed for
the few next days, with the small sum which remained
to her. The convent was at that time so extremely
poor, that even the few half-pence needed to pay the
postage of a letter from Angers were not forthcoming.
In her deep distress, the Superior threw herself at the
feet of our Blessed Lady, and trusting in her kindness,
resolved to borrow £40, if she possibly could. She at
once wrote a letter with this object. She had not
finished her epistle, when she was asked for in the
parlour. She found there a lady who had brought her
an offering of £20. In the evening another visitor
presented herself, bringing a present of a second £20.
The next morning M. Chalandon, the Reverend Superior
of the convent, came to pay his respects to the Superior,
and ask her acceptance of another £20, which had been
given him for this purpose by a benefactor who wished
to remain unknown.

Another anecdote illustrative of the same subject
may be given here. At the period when Mgr. de
Cosnac, Archbishop of Sens, requested that a foundation might be made in his archiepiscopal city, the
Mother General was occupied with the arrangements
for several new houses in various places. Her funds
were at a low ebb, and his Grace offered very little in
the way of pecuniary help, so that she felt a fresh
attempt at such a juncture might be tempting Provi-

dence. One evening, when the nuns were taking their recreation in the garden, she left them, and repaired to the chapel of the Immaculate Conception, which had been built by this time. There she knelt at the feet of Mary, and told her all the doubts, fears, and anxieties which were oppressing her mind. When she rejoined her Religious, she said to them : " The Blessed Virgin has signified to me, by means of an interior voice, that she will be pleased to be at Sens, in the hearts of my children." Without delay Mother St. Euphrasia wrote to the Archbishop, accepting his proposals. When the Sisters reached Sens, they found only a shabby little house, totally without furniture. On the morrow of their arrival, a workman engaged in doing some repairs, brought them a large picture representing Our Lady of the Immaculate Conception. " It is the likeness of some lady, I suppose," he said. " I found it in the garret, and I am just going to fasten it up on the wall, to hide a place where the paper is torn." " Why, it is our Blessed Lady ! " the Sisters exclaimed. " I never heard of any such person," replied the workman, greatly astonished. Without delay the picture was placed in the chapel, as an augury of future success !

Another way in which Mother St. Euphrasia manifested her devotion to the Queen of Heaven, was by means of what she termed *La Bourse de Marie.* It had been originally founded by the pious M. de Neuville, of whom so much has been related in an earlier portion of this work. One day he wrote to the Mother General a note, in which he enclosed three louis d'or, and expressed himself as follows : " I do not know wherefore, but I feel myself to-day to be interiorly urged by our Lady to send you three louis d'or." The contents of Mary's purse (as it was familiarly called) consisted of presents offered by visitors which were placed in it, when the sums could be spared from the ordinary funds of the house. They were never spent except in cases of real necessity. On the day in question, the purse had been completely emptied in order to meet an urgent demand. "My dear children," Mother St. Euphrasia said, as she gave them the last of the coins which the purse contained, "tell the Blessed Virgin that I am only lending you this money, and implore her to replace it." The very same evening arrived the note from M. de Neuville, which we have just mentioned.

It would not be possible to exaggerate the affectionate devotion to our Blessed Lady, which filled to overflowing the heart of Mother St. Euphrasia. In her instructions she spoke constantly of her virtues, and strove to excite in the hearts of her hearers feelings equal to her own. Let us listen to her for a few brief moments:

"It is impossible to have too ardent a devotion to the Holy Virgin, to love her too ardently. Her help will never fail us, and our Lord delights to receive from her hands the humble petitions we venture to offer to Him. St. Bernard has assured us that a true servant of Mary can never be lost. But you, my dearest children, know better than to forget that the worship paid to Mary must never surpass, or even equal, that which is due to her Son. He is the Lord of Heaven and earth. Moreover, devotion to Jesus Christ and devotion to Mary are closely joined together. The more one loves Jesus in the Adorable Sacrament of the Altar, the more one loves Mary: and, the more one loves Mary, the more heartfelt is the homage we pay to the Most Blessed Sacrament."

Mother St. Euphrasia was very careful as to the recitation of the Rosary, and taught this devotion to those under her, both by word and deed. Often whilst walking up and down the cloisters of the convent, saying her beads, she would stop some novice or postulant, who might happen to be passing, in order that the two might join in the recitation. As a matter of course, it was considered no small honour to say one's beads with the Mother General, whose manner and bearing on such occasions were indescribably impressive and edifying. She addressed our Lady as if she were actually present to her eyes, and the accent of her voice when repeating the words *Ave, Maria*, had something peculiarly touching about it. Every now and again she would go down into the kitchen, and, seating herself among the lay-sisters who were preparing the dinner, say her beads with them. So thoroughly did she succeed, by means of her example, in spreading a love for, and devotion to, the Holy Rosary among all classes of the Community at Angers, that no Religious was to be seen, traversing the corridors and garden paths of the convent in pursuance of her appointed occupation, without her beads in her hand, which she was telling with pious recollection.

During the year 1844, ten years before the dogma was proclaimed, the fact that a Protestant minister had opened a place of worship at Angers reached the ears of Mother St. Euphrasia. She further learned that he had, in profane and blasphemous words, dared to attack the virginity of our Blessed Lady and her Immaculate Conception. The heart of the saintly foundress was filled with grief and horror. For many weeks she organized processions in the convent, as an expiation of the insults which had been offered to the beloved Mother of all Christians, and in honour also of her Immaculate Conception.

It will be readily believed how deep and how sincere was the reverential love and respect entertained by the Mother General towards St. Joseph. In 1862, she caused a statue to be made in his honour. While it was preparing, a shrine, or miniature chapel, was built to receive it. In the foundations were placed glass bottles containing petitions to St. Joseph, not only from the Mother General and her children at Angers, but from various houses of the Order, the names of which were all inscribed on a roll of parchment and laid on the spot where the feet of the statue would rest. Mother St. Euphrasia also placed a penny there, as a token that she desired the Saint to undertake the care of the pecuniary affairs of the house. On the 22nd of August, the statue being duly placed in the niche prepared for it, the Bishop of Angers, accompanied by a numerous body of his clergy, came to bless the whole. It was a day ever to be remembered at Angers, for the Mother General made it a very happy one for all classes of her Community. She nominated St. Joseph Superior General of her house, and many were the benefits she received from him, especially in regard of pecuniary aid. Among numerous instances we may select the following.

On one particular occasion, Mother St. Euphrasia was entirely at a loss how to meet a certain payment, which would fall due in a few days. She had recourse to St. Joseph as the head of the Holy Family. She caused a novena of Masses to be celebrated in his honour, and ordered a novena of prayers to be said by the Community. The day after this double novena had come to an end, she was asked for in the parlour early in the morning. She went down at once, and found a woman about seventy, who was totally unknown to her. This woman presented her with £32, begging her not to ask the name of the sender. " For," continued the strange visitor, " by receiving this gift graciously, you will confer as great a favour upon the giver as you would bestow upon a starving man by furnishing him with a meal. I was so strongly urged to bring you this sum, that I have walked more than twenty miles to place it in your hands. I wished to delay my journey, but had I done so, I should have been unfaithful to a Divine inspiration." It immediately occurred to Mother St. Euphrasia that the number of francs (800) comprised in this gift, coincided exactly with the eight hundred individuals contained in her Community. She was deeply touched. The mysterious visitor took leave at once, repeating as she did do, " Pray for me, pray for me!" Nor was it ever ascertained who she was and where she came from.

Great was her love for all the Saints of God, but we must place in the foremost rank her veneration for the Seraphic Saint of Carmel. From her earliest youth she had studied the works of St. Teresa, and so thoroughly was she acquainted with them, that she scarcely ever gave an instruction of any length without introducing some quotation from them, or relating some incident illustrative of the virtues of the Saint. St. Francis of Sales, St. Jane Chantal, St. Philomena, the Blessed Germaine Cousin were among her special favourites. Constantly and profoundly did she honour the Church triumphant in Heaven, the Saints of God and the nine choirs of Angels. We have seen how incessant and how arduous were her labours on behalf of the Church militant, whose members are still struggling here upon earth, bowed down by sorrow, harassed by temptation, uncertain as to their eternal salvation.

Tender as was the charity of her loving heart for all her fellow-creatures, wherever they might be found, not less tender and solicitous was this eminent Servant of God for the needs of the suffering Church. Her generosity was nothing short of sublime. On the day of her Profession, she, by means of a solemn vow, abandoned, on behalf of the faithful departed, all the Indulgences she might gain, without the least reservation on her own behalf, or even on that of her relatives. This generous devotion, known among us as "the Heroic Act," has recently been widely spread by means of the late revered Father John Morris, S.J., to whom we owe so much, and whose memory can never cease to live in the hearts of those who were privileged to know him.

Mother St. Euphrasia frequently made the Way of the Cross for these suffering souls, she said the Office of the Dead for them, and tried by every means in her power to alleviate their torments. She used to entreat her children to do the same, and never to forget the Holy Souls, whom Divine Justice keeps, for a season, far from the abode of the blessed in Heaven. She would often request them to pray very specially for persons whom they had known, or who were likely to be forgotten after their death.

Since the Holy Sacrifice is the surest and most efficacious means of aiding and relieving the souls in Purgatory, she had frequent recourse to it. She was fond of repeating the saying of St. Francis Xavier: "Devotion to the souls in Purgatory and zeal for the salvation of those yet on earth are inseparable." She desired to show her children that her affection for them followed them beyond the grave, and whenever there was any special day of recreation in the Community, she had Masses said for those Sisters who might be in Purgatory on account of having come short in their observance of their vows, more particularly those of obedience and poverty. " Oh ! " she was frequently heard to exclaim, " how pleasing to Almighty God is devotion to the souls in Purgatory ! " On the 13th of March, the feast of St. Euphrasia, when all her family was rejoicing around her, she did not forget the beloved departed members of it. " I wish," she used to say to those around her, " that while you are enjoying yourselves on earth, my children who are in the solemn place of expiation should have some pleasure also. Let us procure at least a degree of refreshment for them."

With Mother St. Euphrasia's gift of foretelling future events, we have already made the reader acquainted in the cases of both Cardinal Mastai, afterwards Pope Pius IX., and also of Mlle. Marie Verger, who is at present the revered Mother General of the Order of the Good Shepherd. We will now introduce two examples of the marvellous—we had almost said miraculous—power of reading the thoughts of others, which was one of her most remarkable gifts. Both this, and also her power of prophecy, formed part of the reward bestowed by God upon His faithful servant, in return for the perfection with which she did His will and maintained a constant sense of His presence and of union with Him.

Never, except in cases where it was absolutely necessary, did she break the great silence, which lasts from the first stroke of the bell which calls to Matins, until the conclusion of Prime on the morrow. Now it happened that one day, during Matins, a young novice was greatly troubled in mind. No sooner was the Office finished, than to her unspeakable surprise the novice felt the hand of her beloved Mother laid upon her shoulder, while she whispered in her ear, "My child, you have something to tell me." The novice followed the Mother General in a state of complete bewilderment. No sooner were they alone together, than Mother St. Euphrasia addressed to her some gentle exhortations which had the effect of restoring peace to her troubled spirit. Fifty-seven years have passed since that day, yet the impression made upon the mind of the Sister whose secret thoughts were thus wonderfully read, remains as fresh and as vivid as ever.

The next incident we will relate shows, not only her power of reading secret things, but also her supernatural charity. In this story all names, whether of persons or places, are for obvious reasons, suppressed. One day a Jesuit Father presented himself at the convent at Angers, and asked to see the Mother General. He introduced to her a lady, belonging to a family of distinction, who, having strayed from the paths of virtue, had fallen from one misfortune to another. He added no further particulars, but took his leave. No benefactress could have met with a warmer welcome, and the new-comer was entertained with every attention and hospitality. Some time afterwards, Mother St. Euphrasia learned accidentally, that her guest, who had run away from home in company with a lover, had done everything in her power to ruin one of the houses of the Good Shepherd. When this fact came to her knowledge, she saw in it an explanation to her of the unaccountable feeling of joy with which she had received her unknown guest, and furnished her with a reason for treating her with even greater courtesy and kindness than before. She paid her a visit every day, she sent to her room a remarkably comfortable chair and sofa, besides several other ornamental articles. For her the most delicate fare was provided, and if any dish was found to be particularly relished it was certain to appear again. The heart of the unhappy recipient of all this Christian charity was at last softened and subdued. She was tortured by remorse, but she could not find courage to tell her pitiful tale.

Thus months went on until one morning Mother St. Euphrasia sent her a message that she very much wished to speak to her. As soon as the lady entered, the tender Mother said, " My poor child, it is useless for you to remain silent any longer. I know every detail of your sad story." The unhappy sinner burst into tears, and fell on her knees before Mother St. Euphrasia. The latter raised her up, and said: " My dear child, it is because I know all about you that I am so drawn towards you, and feel so deeply for you. I long to save your soul. Please remain under our roof." " But I am afraid I shall not be able to pay for my board much longer. My relatives threaten to forward me no further remittances," replied the lady, with a fresh burst of tears. " Do not speak of such a trifle, dearest child," was the answer, " but stay on quietly where you are. We all love you, and do not want to hear one word about payment." At a subsequent period the penitent said to one of the nuns: " Your Mother is a saint; she has told me many things which I have never breathed into any living ear, and that she could not possibly have learnt by means of any human agency." Strange to say, the very next day, Mother St. Euphrasia, who did not know that this conversation had taken place, said to the Religious to whom the lady had addressed her remarks: "It is certain that, for some weeks past, our Lord has vouchsafed to give me special lights with regard to our unhappy guest." This lady made rapid progress in virtue. Her devotion to the Sacred Passion was so great, that she made the Way of the Cross every day, her passage from Station to Station being marked with her abundant tears.

But at last she was compelled to return to her family, who earnestly desired her to go back to her home. Mother St. Euphrasia, who had never received even the smallest sum for her board, carried her generosity so far as to furnish her with the means of defraying her travelling expenses, and of purchasing some fresh clothes, suitable to her rank and position. Many years later, the object of all this charity found herself, through the death of all the members of her family, quite alone in the world. She requested to be allowed to come and end her days beneath the roof of the Good Shepherd at Angers, where she had been sheltered in her dire extremity. But the Mother General deemed such a step to be undesirable, for many reasons. She therefore advised her correspondent either to remain in the world, or to enter some convent in her native country.

We have frequently had occasion to speak of the foundress' trials, and of the heroic patience and resignation with which they were borne. We cannot more fitly close the present chapter, than by introducing a short address in which she expresses the spirit in which sorrows should be borne.

x

"Do not be afraid of a few little trials. The trees which the forester prunes and lops with his axe are the finest trees in the plantation. Be not pusillanimous and faint-hearted; trample self-love under foot, and when occasion offers itself, do not shrink from performing acts of virtue which require real heroism. Our hands will never be clean if we content ourselves with just wetting the tips of our fingers, or wiping them daintily with a sponge. In order to learn to swim, one must throw oneself headlong into the water, not slip in gradually. The more we do violence to ourselves, the more richly will God reward us. We read how saints, who felt the strongest repugnance to being with the sick, used to kiss the most revolting sores, and after doing so used to find pleasure in what before inspired them with the greatest disgust. Others overcame temptation and recovered their peace of mind by throwing themselves upon a bed of thorns, and rolling their bodies upon the sharp points. St. Jane Chantal, who for a long time was subjected to formidable temptations against the faith, had, when most sorely tried, recourse to expedients of a very extraordinary nature. One day, for instance, she took a red-hot iron and branded the names of Jesus and Mary upon her heart. We have abundant examples to prove to us that there are no temptations which it is beyond our power to withstand, provided our will is steadfast, and that we are sustained by the grace of God. I must, however, warn you that without permission, mortifications such as we are speaking of must never be practised.

"Never lose heart, my children, never allow yourselves to fancy that you would accomplish your salvation more easily if you were in the world; you should rather think, on the contrary, of the great dangers that would beset you in the world's unrest, and of the unhappiness to which you would fall a prey. Do not imitate the example of the novice mentioned in the history of the Fathers of the Desert, who, tired of battling against spiritual trials and aridities, said to himself: 'I will return to life in the world, since I have found the practices of the religious life so wearisome.' It pleased God to correct this young man after a very peculiar fashion. He permitted the devil to appear to him, and deal him three heavy blows with a large iron-bound cudgel, saying, 'There, that is the way I treat those who enter my service!'

"Only at the cost of some sacrifice can one expect to taste the happiness of being a nun. Prepare yourselves for trials, my dear daughters; it may safely be said that he who has never been tempted knows nothing of the spiritual life. St. Gregory says there is the morning devil, the mid-day devil, the evening devil; that is to say, he tempts us at the outset, in the middle, and at the end of our lives, and of all our undertakings. He tempts the novices, he tempts the recently professed, he tempts the older nuns; he tempts the novices with great persistence and extreme cunning, because he thinks that, if he can but succeed in turning his victim aside from her vocation at the threshold of her religious career, all is won, that soul is his. He makes a point of tempting those who have grown old in religion, because he knows not how soon they may be removed beyond the reach of his snares; while to those who stand half-way he pays less heed, for he reckons on having plenty of time before him, and thinks too, that the instability of human nature may perhaps do his work for him."

CHAPTER XX.

ONE very striking, we had almost said the most striking, feature in the character of Mother St. Euphrasia, was her genius for government. This included, as it always must do, whether in man or woman, a great amount of tact and diplomatic skill. Had the subject of the present biography been a man, she would undoubtedly have made her mark in the world, probably as Prime Minister, Secretary of State, or in some other of the highest and most influential offices connected with whatever Government might have been fortunate enough to retain her services. She would have ruled over distant provinces with the same firm hand with which she held sway over her numerous convents, situated in all the quarters of the globe. Her keen eye detected the least sign of disaffection or individualism, both which are fatal to a Religious, and, indeed, to any other Community. She held her children united together by the bond of true Christian and fraternal charity, making them feel that she was indeed their Mother, tender and loving, yet supreme, and implicitly to be obeyed.

Born as she was to command, this natural gift was perfected and brought to maturity by the action of Divine grace. When we remember her ardent and impulsive temperament, we must acknowledge that in the school of Christ alone could she have acquired that unruffled calmness of bearing, that even and dignified demeanour under the most vexatious, trying, and provoking circumstances, which was one great cause of her marvellous influence over persons of all ranks and all ages. The atmosphere of the lofty mountain peaks, where her soul perpetually dwelt in close union with her Maker, and an abiding sense of His presence, was far above the clouds and misty vapours of this lower world.

We are told that the Mother General rarely, if ever, failed to conquer undisciplined characters, and to subdue the most violent and furious outbursts of temper. One day a couple of policemen brought to her a poor unhappy girl, whom they had been obliged literally to drag along the streets, so great was her excitement, and so determined the resistance with which she accompanied her loud and passionate declarations that she would never enter the Refuge. Mother St. Euphrasia addressed her for a short time, and before long the culprit became as quiet as a lamb, burst into tears, and expressed her deep regret for her unseemly and unwomanly behaviour.

Such instances as these were by no means infrequent while Mother St. Euphrasia was Mistress of Penitents. Her kind and gentle words poured oil upon the raging sea, and the billows subsided forthwith.

Another secret of her power was her keen insight into character, and the rapidity with which she formed a judgment, almost invariably a just one, in regard of her postulants and novices. She knew how to draw conclusions from the smallest signs. No intellectual gifts, high rank, or brilliant fortune, could ever induce her to receive as a member of her Order any one whom she saw to be wanting in the qualifications and virtues required for an efficient member of it. She knew, moreover, that however necessary the repression of external faults, such as a hasty temper, a haughty demeanour, an indiscreet tongue, may be for every one, it is doubly so in the case of the Religious of the Good Shepherd, who, although cloistered, are the subject of incessant criticism on the part of the penitents, and are, moreover, compelled to hold frequent intercourse with the parents and other relatives of the children committed to their care, as well as with various persons belonging to the outside world.

With respect to the influence she exercised upon all around her, we may here suitably give the testimony of a consecrated penitent. What these consecrated penitents were, has already been explained, and needs no description here.

" Whenever our dear Mother came amongst us," one of the consecrated penitents relates, " her mere presence seemed to electrify us, and change us for the better. Nor was this a transient impression, it was permanent, and produced a lasting effect. Many a one of us owes her perseverance in the right way to her alone. Our Mother always spoke to us in the kindest manner possible, never did she utter a word that could wound or humiliate any one. On the contrary, she strove to elevate and encourage us, to make us respect ourselves more, and place greater trust in God. Again and again would she assure us of the tender love she felt for us. 'You are my own dear penitents, why should you mind being called by this name? Am not I myself the first of penitents? Yes,' she would add, in accents of the deepest humility, 'I have offended against my God; I, too, must therefore do penance.'

" The knowledge of souls possessed by our Mother was really marvellous. How often one or other of the penitents went to her, and besought as a favour to be allowed to return to the world, urging this request not once only, but repeatedly. Our Mother would not give her consent; gently and firmly she represented to the poor girl that her only chance of safety was to remain here; that were she to leave, she would infallibly lose her soul. Her words never proved wrong. Those who listened to her kindly warning, found her prediction come true; some died a holy death, others are still amongst us, having consecrated themselves to God for the remainder of their days.

" On other occasions, however, our dear Mother acted in a contrary manner. Sometimes, as soon as her penetrating gaze rested on the countenance of the suppliant for dismissal, she would say to the mistress: ' Let her go, immediately, Sister; she will do more harm than good to the others.'

" But Mother St. Euphrasia's chief characteristic was her inexhaustible kindness, her tender compassion for the needs, spiritual and corporal, of her beloved penitents. To procure them some alleviation, some little pleasure, was her greatest delight. She could not bear to hear anything against them; and if, when she went amongst them, the good mistress in charge tried to edge in a few words of complaint, which their disregard of the rules fully warranted, our dear Mother would lay her finger upon her lips, and look at her beseechingly. Then turning to the penitents she would say: ' Now, dear children, you will not do that any more, will you ? Yes, you promise me, I know you

do; there is an end of the matter. All is forgiven;
you must never vex Mother St. Vincent again, nor me,
for you know how much I love you!'"

Nor must we fail to remark, that another secret of
the venerated foundress' eminent success, and power of
influencing all around her, was her thorough compre-
hension of the importance of little things in daily life.
Nothing was so small as to escape her scrutiny, or be
considered unworthy of her attention. It is surprising
to find how, in the midst of her numerous, unceasing,
and important duties and pre-occupations, she found
time to go down into the kitchen and see that the food
was of good quality, well cooked, and served up hot.
Now and again she would herself lend a helping hand,
and add to the various dishes some condiment or
ingredient, in order to render them more appetizing.
"This is our dear Mother's soup," was the universal
verdict, whenever it happened to be nicer than usual.
Nothing rejoiced her more than to see an air of health
and cheerfulness on the countenances of those around
her.

She was extremely careful to instil into the minds of
the young girls who composed the classes under her
care, ideas of economy and order. In order to accomplish this, she had established in each class a separate
fund, under due regulations. Each member of the class
had to try and earn her living by contributing to the
common purse. At the end of each month, the mistress,
whose business it was, defrayed out of its contents the
necessary expenses. A certain percentage was set aside
for times when work might not be forthcoming, and
also for the removal or repair of furniture, clothing, &c.
This plan worked admirably. Sometimes there was an

overplus, and one class had the pleasure of offering to another a present, such as new lamps, &c.

Occasionally, Mother St. Euphrasia associated the penitents with herself in some work of charity. She would ask each one for a trifling sum, to be earned by working overtime. She left to the head of each class great liberty in the direction of everything connected with the well-being of those under her care. This mark of confidence aroused her zeal, and gave her increased authority as far as those under her were concerned.

Another instance of the manner by which the Mother General gained influence, through the employment of means which to undiscerning persons might appear mere trifles, unworthy of notice, was her habit of giving presents. We read in Holy Scripture that, "A man's gift enlargeth his way, and maketh him room before princes,"[1] and never was this saying more fully proved than in the case of Mother St. Euphrasia. Not only did she delight in giving, but her wonderful tact enabled her to bestow on each person the very gift which that individual had desired, even though Mother St. Euphrasia had never even seen him or her. On one occasion, for instance, after a long cold night's journey, she arrived at some religious house, which had offered her hospitality, while she was arranging a foundation of the Good Shepherd in the city. She made her appearance earlier than she was expected, but positively refused to allow the Sisters, who were engaged in arranging the kitchens for the coming day, to disturb the Superioress or any of the nuns. Walking straight into the kitchen, she threw off her travelling wraps, seated herself by the newly

[1] Prov. xviii. 16.

lighted fire, and entered into conversation with the Sisters, whom she fascinated by her indescribable charm of manner, and kindness of expression. She wound up by giving to each of the Sisters a little present. Singular to narrate, this gift proved to be the very thing for which the recipient had for some time secretly longed, although she had never even breathed her wish to one among those by whom she was daily surrounded.

While discoursing of matters, small in themselves, but yet important when taken as a whole, we must not fail to say a word concerning the great attention which Mother St. Euphrasia paid to her correspondence. She was uniformly accurate and careful in fulfilling this duty. She would curtail her hours of sleep, nay, she was even known to sit up for a whole night, when letters had to be written which no one could write except herself. Never, through carelessness or forgetfulness, did she allow epistles to lie on her table unanswered, when a prompt reply was required, or had been specially asked for by the writer.

Regarding her truly Christian charity and forgiveness of enemies, much has already been said. But the following example cannot be omitted from this record. In a certain diocese where a Convent of the Good Shepherd had been established, a gentleman of high social position had allowed himself to be influenced by an enemy of the Order, and had so far forgotten himself through these misrepresentations, that he actually addressed several insulting letters to Mother St. Euphrasia. Three weeks afterwards he suddenly expired. A near relative of his wrote as follows to one of the nuns at Angers: "My beloved cousin has been removed from our midst after a very brief illness.

Happily there was just time to administer the last rites of the Church. My grief is very bitter. Dare I hope that the Very Reverend Mother General will have the great charity to remember the departed in her prayers after the painful circumstances connected with him?" The Religious at once took the letter to Mother St. Euphrasia, asking her what she was to say in reply. Tears rolled down her cheeks while the letter was read to her. "Oh, my dear child," she exclaimed, when the perusal was finished, "I remember absolutely nothing against the departed. I always entertained a high esteem for him. He was the victim of deception. Pray write at once to his relatives and assure them of my deepest sympathy. Tell them that the whole Community shall to-morrow offer their Communions for the relative they have lost." Then, after pausing for a moment, she added, "But your letter would arrive too late. It could hardly reach its destination to-day. It shall be despatched by express, in order that the relatives of the deceased may be all the sooner relieved from their apprehensions." The epistle was sent off accordingly, and the charity of the Servant of God was keenly appreciated by the family of the deceased. As they were highly placed in the world, they had, on subsequent occasions, several opportunities of obliging and aiding Mother St. Euphrasia. Of these they never failed to avail themselves.

The ardour of her love for souls never failed for a moment. She made it a rule that every class of her Community should make a yearly retreat, and she took care that each class should have its own preacher. She never spared expense when the spiritual good of her children was at stake. One day a young Irish girl, who was altogether ignorant of French, confided to her mistress that she had upon her conscience a grievous sin, adding with many tears, that she greatly desired to go to confession, but could not do so, as there was at that time no priest in Angers who understood English sufficiently well to hear confessions in that language. Mother St. Euphrasia, hearing of this, made inquiries in all directions, and discovered that at Saumur, about fifty or sixty miles from Angers, there lived a priest who possessed the requisite knowledge. She forthwith despatched a Sister in a carriage to fetch this priest. He went back at once in the carriage, while the Sister stayed in the convent at Saumur. The young girl made her confession, and recovered her peace of mind.

One year, when the Mother General had more funds than usual at her disposal, she showed her care for the Sisters, by ordering that the outer scullery, where they prepared the vegetables for use, should be thoroughly roofed in, in order to protect them from the inclemency of the weather. However the price of provisions might rise, she never allowed either the quality or quantity of the dishes served to the Community to be altered in the least degree. In order to afford the sick more light and air, she added a new room to the infirmary. In a word, she was not only the head of the convent, she was also the tender and thoughtful mother of every inmate of it. She loved each one as her own child, and watched over them all, in order to satisfy herself that the wants of both soul and body were amply provided for.

She cherished a supernatural love for holy poverty, as being the object of one of her vows. She refused to allow her habit to be made of better material than that worn by the other Religious. Several times some of her children, in the course of an especially hot summer, begged her to accept a habit made of finer and thinner substance, more suitable to the extreme heat. She invariably denied her consent. " Why do you try and lengthen my Purgatory?" she would ask. She habitually wore her garments until they literally dropped to pieces. The Sisters used to repair them unknown to her, and often sat up at night for the purpose. No stranger could have distinguished the Mother General from any ordinary Religious, except perhaps by remarking the greater shabbiness of her habit.

Nor did she give evidence of the spirit of poverty in her dress alone. She showed it in everything appropriated to her use, as, for instance, the furniture of her room, and the books she used. Her very bed was harder and smaller than those of her children, the only seat in her cell was a common straw chair, and in order still further to mortify herself, she refrained from leaning against the back of it. The water-jug of which she made use was cracked, and, when writing, she employed a small desk of common wood, which she rested upon her knees. In vain did her children press her to accept an arm-chair in which she might seat herself while she delivered her long addresses to the Community. During the dark winter evenings, while spending many consecutive hours in transacting necessary business, and in despatching answers to the almost innumerable letters she received, she never employed any light but that afforded by tallow candles. One day a Religious offered for her acceptance a Breviary bound in crimson velvet with gilt edges. The present was gently, but firmly declined.

One of her principles was not to lay by any money for the future, nor to spend any in unnecessary ornamentation. On one occasion £4 was spent, with her

permission, on planting several of the flower-beds with
edges of box. These edges served, of course, a useful
purpose, by preventing the mould from falling on to
the paths. Yet for a long while she habitually accused
herself in confession of this outlay, as a sin against holy
poverty, and, while conversing with the Sisters, she
often used to say, "Oh, my dear children, let us not
do such things any more."

When Mother St. Euphrasia chose humility as the
theme of her discourses to her daughters, she spoke with
more than her usual animation, and in her own clear,
simple, almost familiar language, she urged them to
strive after the highest standard.

"The chief benefit I desire you to derive from these
holy exercises," she said to them at the close of one of
the annual retreats, "and the one which I would exhort
you to preserve with the utmost care, is the virtue of
humility, the virtue pleasing above all others to our
Blessed Lord, for it is the basis of our spiritual
perfection. Let it be your principal object to keep this
great virtue firmly rooted in your soul, for without it
no others will flourish there, only the delusive appearance of virtue, unable to stand the test of trial or
temptation. One might as well attempt to build an
edifice in the air, without resting the walls on any
foundation, as to practise virtue and attain perfection
unless one commences with humility. This is why we
unhappily see so little solid virtue, so little sincere
piety.

"Humility, my dear daughters, is the key of the
treasury of God, for nothing is more dear to the Heart
of God than the truly humble soul, utterly devoid of all
feelings of self-love. And yet how rarely is this virtue

met with, for it is fundamentally opposed to human nature, a nature steeped in pride, so to speak, from its very birth. This is why Holy Scripture says: 'Pride is the beginning of all sin.'[1]

"Pride caused the fall of the angels; pride was the ruin of our first parents; pride is the perdition of a vast number of Christians, not only of Religious. And how can we account for this? Because pride is a poisonous plant of subtle growth; it draws its nutriment both from the sins we fall into and from our apparent practice of virtue. How many persons delude themselves in this respect, how many are blind in this matter of vital importance, and thus finally incur terrible chastisements. I assure you I would rather see a company of demons walking about our enclosure than proud Religious. At least the demons would leave us in no doubt as to their being demons.

"Pride advances by leaps and bounds, and the havoc it works is terrible. You know there is a kind of coarse grass which when once it gets into a field or garden, springs up everywhere: so it is with pride. Two or three proud persons are enough to cause discord in a whole community. 'He that puffeth up himself, stirreth up quarrels,'[2] says the Wise Man. I beg and entreat you, therefore, my dear daughters, strive to become humble. 'Be not wise in your own conceit.'[3] 'Pride goeth before destruction.'[4]

"We read that one day our Lord showed St.Anthony the face of the earth overspread by the devil so completely with snares, that it seemed almost an impossibility for any one to avoid falling into them. St.Anthony trembled at the sight, and exclaimed: 'Who, O Lord,

---

[1] Eccles. x. 15.
[2] Prov. xxviii. 25.   [3] Prov. iii. 7.   [4] Prov. xvi. 18.

can escape dangers so innumerable?' Then a voice answered him: 'He alone can escape them who is truly humble.' Our holy Rule does not impose great austerities upon us, but it requires from us great humility. Suppose one of you should appear gloomy or out of temper, or be distant in her manner after her Superior has had occasion to rebuke her, does that show much humility?

"Who can say: 'My heart is clean, I am pure from sin'?[1] Truly no one can say it as long as he lives in this world. If we look into our own hearts, we shall find many evil tendencies there. The Venerable Mother Anne of St. Bartholomew, the companion and fellow-worker of St. Teresa, one who was specially favoured by God from her earliest years, believed herself to be an abominable sinner, and bitterly bewailed her wickedness, which she thought to be the cause of all the misfortunes which happened at that time to fall upon the town where she was. 'My dear Mother,' one of her nuns said to her, 'you must know quite well that there are many far greater sinners than yourself in the world. Why then should you consider yourself responsible for these calamities?' 'I am aware,' she replied, 'that there are many far greater sinners; but that does not prevent each one of us having to carry her own sins before the tribunal of God, like a bundle of wood to be burnt; and who can say but that our transgressions may be more displeasing to God than those which others have committed!'

"Take care lest you think yourself better than any one else. To what, in fact, is it owing that we are not numbered amongst the enemies of God, if not to His grace, whereby we have been preserved from the

[1] Prov. xx. 9.

dangers of the world, and hidden, so to speak, under His wings. If we had had bad parents, or had lived a life of misery, perhaps we should have fallen into the sins so many people fall into! Our Lord Jesus Christ has vouchsafed to shed abroad upon us His gifts and graces; let this be an incentive to greater thankfulness, greater humility on our part, not to a greater esteem of ourselves; besides, the uncertainty of our final perseverance ought to keep us ever watchful, ever fearful.

"If our Lord had known any surer way to Heaven than that of humility, He would have taught it to us. Never shall we reach the point to which He attained. Who amongst you was, like Him, cradled in a manger? Who has been calumniated as He was? Who has been condemned to the ignominious Death of the Cross? 'The disciple is not greater than his Master.' I have often told you, my dear daughters, that humility alone, apart from all other mortifications which your Rule enjoins on you to practise, is sufficient for the attainment of a high degree of virtue.

"Observe that I am not speaking of that weak humility, that ought rather to be called cowardice, which, under the specious pretext of avoiding pride, deters one from useful enterprises, and engenders a state of general indifference. In a Community there is little difficulty, if such be your choice, in becoming a useless member. But you must not forget that God knows all things, that He will punish those who neglect their duties, and omit the good they might do. One who is truly humble is firmly convinced that no merit belongs to her; she is conscious that of herself she can do nothing, and yet she can do everything with the help of God. Knowing this, she throws herself with her

Y

whole heart into the work appointed for her, nor does she allow herself to be discouraged whatever the results that may ensue."

"Oh, my dear daughters, if you were truly humble, you would indeed be valuable Religious, your price would be beyond gold and silver. Humility is the best means of preparation for the conquest of souls. The acquisition of this virtue will render you worthy to become the missioners of Jesus Christ. Those whose talents are not of a high order will yet, provided they are but humble, be found capable of great things with the help of God. Let me urge upon you, therefore, to love humility ; love to be the least, love to be forgotten. If to the consciousness of your own misery you add unlimited confidence in the goodness of God, all difficulties will disappear before you. Humility will be your sure anchor in the midst of storms. You will not allow yourself to be daunted by contradictions, by labours, nor even by the faults into which you may perchance fall ; you will be strong in God's strength, and day by day you will increase in union with and nearness to Him."

The reader who has followed us in the foregoing account of Mother St. Euphrasia's life, will not need to be told how fully she applied to herself the counsels she gave to others, how diligently she practised the virtue she inculcated upon her spiritual children in such persuasive language. From the moment she entered the Order of the Good Shepherd until the hour when the painful malady, borne so long and so heroically, put an end to her manifold and multiplied labours for the salvation of souls, never did the astonishing success which attended those labours, the attention and praise

she received from persons in high positions, the supernatural gifts and favours bestowed upon her by God,
awaken in her the least movement of pride or self-
esteem. We have several times in the course of her
story seen her opposed, calumniated, slandered, treated
with great unkindness and crying injustice, yet we have
never seen her otherwise than humble and resigned
amid trials of this nature. Truly did she walk in the
footsteps of her Divine Master, following the example
of Him Who is meek and lowly of heart. When by
the blessing of God her foundations spread and
flourished beyond her fondest expectations, she took no
credit to herself. " God and my Superiors," she would
say, " have directed all these circumstances. I have
only been a worthless instrument in the hand of
Omnipotence. It was wished that I should take the
title of Mother General, but what is there in that ? I
am none the greater for it."

She invariably gave all glory to God, and attributed
every fresh success to the wisdom and zeal of one of
her subordinates rather than to her own. Ever ready
to ask help and advice from her inferiors, she wrote to
the Superior of a house as follows : " You will help me,
will you not ? I have so much need of counsel and
aid ! I am destitute of all virtue, and in myself I
possess nothing except God and His grace." Again
we find her thus expressing herself: " In spite of my
baseness and unworthiness, God graciously deigns to
make use of me, the vilest instrument, to further and
accomplish His designs."

How truly she meant what she said was proved by
the readiness she evinced to receive humiliations. On
one occasion M. Régnier came to the convent early in
the morning. He found the Mother General with her

Council, which she had convoked on account of some urgent business matters. " Reverend Mother," he said, "you have broken the great silence, kiss the ground at once." She promptly did as she was desired, saying humbly as she did so, " Yes, Father, I was certainly to blame." The members of the Council, feeling that M. Régnier had exceeded his rights, were distressed on account of their beloved Mother. But her countenance remained perfectly undisturbed, and neither then, nor at any other time, did she betray the least sign of vexation or annoyance.

Nor was she humble for herself alone. In regard to her Community she carefully concealed anything which might have the effect of drawing public attention to it, in a way which might prove undesirable. She desired that it should remain humble. In the early days of the convent at Angers, several persons who were living in the city, went from time to time to pray in the cemetery beside the graves of the first Religious who had been buried there. By means of these prayers, extraordinary graces were obtained. Mother St. Euphrasia, in order to preserve in her Congregation the desire to be unknown, asked of God that these striking manifestations should not be renewed. Her prayer was heard.

CHAPTER XXI

THE reader will doubtless remember the carriage accident which Mother St. Euphrasia met with in October, 1842, when she was leaving Angers for the purpose of inspecting a house at Augoulême, which, to judge from all accounts, seemed suited for a new foundation. Every one knows that if the immediate results of such an accident do not appear to be serious, the ultimate results are none the less to be dreaded, since they may prove to be dangerous, or even fatal. Such was the case in the instance to which we are now referring. A blow on the side, which the venerated foundress received through the overturning of the coach, originated the cancerous tumour which for a series of years caused her acute suffering, and finally brought her to the grave. She was herself entirely convinced of this, and mentioned it to the doctor, when in her last illness she consented that he should be called in. Her constitution had never been very strong, and during the last twenty years of her life, she had much physical pain to endure. The gradual growth of the terrible tumour caused the distressing symptoms which defied medical skill, whenever it was appealed to, since the true source of those symptoms was concealed by the sufferer. By affecting the action of the liver, the cancerous growth impeded the exercise of the digestive organs, and produced the constant and distressing attacks of sickness from which she had so much to endure. Moreover, the irritable condition of the stomach prevented her from taking any but very small quantities of food at a time. Yet with more than Spartan heroism, she kept entirely secret the tortures she endured, as far as such a thing was feasible, and abstained from telling any of her children the true source of the ailments it so grievously afflicted them to witness.

Half a century of labours and sorrows such as hers had been, might, by themselves, have broken down the most vigorous constitution, even without the ravages of a cruel malady. During the three last years of her life, her strength gradually but visibly gave way. She made a point of being present during the recreations of the Community, and occasionally consented to take a short airing in the garden. This, however, she did rather in order to give pleasure to those about her, than with a view to any personal gratification, for she could no longer walk, even the shortest distance, and was drawn along in a wheeled chair. Her sleeping apartment was on the second floor, and in vain did the Sisters beseech her to change it. She continued to rise at the usual hour, and spent the day in a room contiguous to the parlour, in order that she might be ready to receive strangers, and transact necessary business. She was accustomed to return to her own room about four o'clock in the afternoon, not in order to obtain some rest, as might be imagined, but to finish the day's correspondence in concert with her secretaries. In the midst of her increasing physical weakness, her mental powers remained absolutely unimpaired. Her intellect was as clear as ever, and we shall see, when we come to speak of her holy death, that she retained full possession of her senses up to her latest breath.

The year 1868, in the course of which she was to be called to receive her eternal reward, dawned sadly for her children. Although she had apparently recovered from the attack of inflammation of the lungs which in May, 1867, had brought her to the very gate of the grave, since that time she had never been able even to move about the house without leaning on the arm of one of the Sisters. It was distressing for them to behold her altered appearance, and watch the gradual decay of her strength, while they remained powerless to aid or relieve her. She continued to bear up until one day, on re-entering her own room, she dropped into an arm-chair which had been forced upon her acceptance, in a swoon so deep and so prolonged, that it appeared almost like death. As soon as she came to herself, the infirmarian, who had been present during this alarming seizure, implored permission to acquaint the Sisters with what had occurred, and to send for the doctor. This, however, she would not allow, but compelled the infirmarian solemnly to promise that she would not even hint to any one what had just happened, and positively refused to have recourse to medical aid, saying that she trusted to St. Joseph and St. Euphrasia to help her. But as the 13th of March, the feast of her patroness, drew near, she abandoned all hope of being able to celebrate the anniversary as she had been wont to do. Yet the evening before she felt somewhat better, and conquering the pain which she now habitually endured, she went down to the community-room. Her deep affection for her children, which continued in full force up to the very last, made her unwilling to deprive them of the pleasure they had hitherto experienced, in offering her their homage of love and respect. She did her utmost to cheer and encourage them, but do what she might, it was only too apparent that she was suffering intensely, and all who saw her felt the cruel presentiment of an approaching separation steal into their souls. The Magdalens, the Penitents, in fact all the various classes were obliged to come in turn to the community-room, since their beloved Superior General was no longer able, as in past years, to go from one portion of the establishment to another, and see with her own eyes how each had vied with the rest in preparing for her the prettiest decorations, the most ingenious devices to do her honour. On this mournful occasion, however, joy had fled far away. Every one tried to smile while in the presence of their beloved Mother, but tears were very near the eyes of all.

The next day, the feast of St. Euphrasia, she expressed her wish to visit the refectory. She could not walk thither, but two of the Sisters wheeled her along the cloisters in her little chair. It was the last time she sat at the head of the table, and we may almost add, the last meal, properly so called, of which she ever partook. Those present were delighted to see with how much relish she ate her meal, but alas! the sole cause was that her joy at finding herself once more in her former place, acted as a temporary stimulant to her failing appetite. The Superiors of six houses had come to Angers on this occasion, in order to congratulate their beloved Mother on her feast-day. When the hour came for them to return, each to her own convent, one of the number, kneeling at Mother St. Euphrasia's feet in order to receive a parting blessing, said: "Dear Mother, I may soon come and see you again, may I not?" "My child," she gently

whispered into her ear, "you will indeed soon come
again, but it will not be necessary for you to ask permission." The Religious to whom these words were
addressed, could not at the moment understand their
import. At a subsequent period she perceived them
to have been prophetic.

The weather was unusually fine for the season of
the year; clear and sunny, yet without the cold winds
for which the month of March is proverbial. During
the afternoon of the 14th, it was proposed to her that
she should take a little airing in the grounds. She
seemed delighted at the idea, and said how much
pleasure it would afford her to make her favourite
pilgrimages. She paused at the Calvary which stands
at the end of the garden. When she reached the chapel
of the Immaculate Conception, she said: "I wish to go
and pay a visit to our Blessed Lady on foot." With
immense difficulty she left her chair, and dragged
herself to the foot of the altar, where she remained for
some time on her knees. She made a brief halt
also before the altar of St. Euphrasia, and that of
St. Geneviève, the patron Saint of her friend Mdme.
d'Andigné, to whose liberality she owed the chapel.
She wound up her little excursion by pausing before a
statue of St. Joseph. "St. Joseph, royal and powerful
Protector of the work of the Good Shepherd," she said
in a clear, distinct voice, "pray to Jesus and Mary for
us." This was the last time she went out of doors.

From that day forward her weakness visibly and
rapidly increased. Her children begged her to try
what complete rest would do, but she persisted in
remaining at her post, and would not even see a doctor.
"St. Joseph can cure me," she repeated. "I know that
nothing short of a miracle would be required for the

purpose. But what does that matter? I pray to the holy Patriarch, and I hope for this favour from his hand during the month which is dedicated to him." When entreated not to rise at so early an hour, she replied: " Would you deprive me of my only privilege, that of receiving Holy Communion? It is, as I have often told you, the Life of my life. There I obtain light, strength, and courage to contend against the difficulties which assail me on all sides. Alas! what would have become of me during the last two years, forsaken as I have been, if I had not been sustained by the Bread of the strong!"

On the 25th of March, the Mother General could not make up her mind to allow a little colony of Sisters, who were on the point of setting out to make a foundation in Switzerland, to leave Angers without herself presiding at the ceremony of their protestation of fidelity to the Mother House and to the Institute. It cost her an almost superhuman effort to lead them from her place to the altar of our Lady at the end of the community-room. Measuring with her eye the space which had to be traversed, " Oh, my dear children," she exclaimed, " you might as well ask me to go to St. Nicholas." In order to reach this latter establishment, it was, as the reader already knows, merely necessary to pass through the convent grounds, under the tunnel, and across the garden on the other side. All who were present felt that the terrible blow which was about to fall upon the Order would not be long delayed. Until that day the courage and heroic powers of endurance shown by their beloved Superior had blinded them as to her real condition. The scales now fell from their eyes, and they found themselves face to face with the heart-breaking reality.

Four days later, on the morning of Passion Sunday, Mother St. Euphrasia got up at five o'clock, in order to hear Mass and receive Holy Communion, although she was in a very feverish condition. It was the last time she was to kneel in her appointed place in the choir, where she had spent so many hours in fervent adoration and lowly supplication. Suffering and exhausted though she was, she made her appearance at the mid-day recreation. Never once had she failed to do this, in spite of all her affectionate infirmarian could say, because she held very much to this point of the Rule. During several weeks past, her children had noticed the loving, lingering looks she cast around her, as if, conscious that the hour was approaching when she would be called to bid them a last adieu, as far as this world is concerned, she was endeavouring to imprint on her memory the faces she had loved so fondly. She experienced so much pleasure in the society of her Religious, that she used to say whenever any attempt was made to induce her to remain away from them: " Do not try to prevent me, my only enjoyment is the company of my dear children." On this particular day she was more vivacious, more charming, more expansive than ever. She surpassed herself in the bright attractiveness of her conversation, and seemed to make an effort to show some special mark of affection to each one who was privileged to be present. She afterwards dictated the letter in which she sanctioned the foundation of St. Paul, in the United States, the last house which was to owe its origin to her. Completely exhausted, she returned to her room on the ground-floor, and sank into a chair, exclaiming as she did so: " O Jesus! Jesus! I have seen my dear children for the last time! May Thy holy will be done!" She soon went upstairs to her cell, never to leave it again. In the evening she grew much worse, and the next day all the Sisters were seriously alarmed about her. March was drawing to a close, and according to the promise she had made to St. Joseph, she had steadily refused to have recourse to medical science.

On the 31st, however, those who surrounded her could no longer bear to witness her agonizing suffering, and in the hope of procuring for her some alleviation at least, they sent to Dr. Farge, the kind and skilful practitioner who was in the habit of attending the invalids of the house, and asked him to come and see the Mother General as soon as he could. This he did without delay, and was not a little shocked at the change in her appearance. He pronounced her state to be extremely critical, and held out but slight hopes of recovery. Amongst other remedies, he prescribed a blister to be placed on her side, in order to reduce the inflammation of the liver and stomach. But the patient declared that she would not hear of such a thing, alleging that she had extreme aversion to such a method of treatment, and would on no account submit to it. She was not actuated by a dread of pain. Her delicacy and modesty were so great, that she could not bear to have her person touched, even by the Sisters who attended her. For the same reason she had concealed the existence of the cancerous tumour, which we have mentioned above. The doctor, ignorant of the real motive which dictated her refusal, insisted very strenuously on the use of the blister. He even went so far as to remind her that it was not in vain that God had instituted the healing art, which is referred to in Holy Scripture in such eulogistic terms. When at last she gave way, it was only because her ingenuity had discovered a method of cutting the knot.

Later in the day she lay down in bed, and put the blister on with her own hands. But it was an absolute impossibility that she should do this properly. Hence the blister slipped, and adhered to the swelling caused by the tumour. Words fail to describe the agony thus caused. Suffice it to say that the torture reached at last such a pitch, that she could no longer conceal her wound. She still refused to allow the doctor to investigate it, but she consented to have it dressed by a Sister belonging to the Congregation of St. Mary, who was considered very clever in the treatment of wounds.

She had passed a sleepless night, enduring constant and terrible pain. At half-past five o'clock in the morning she asked to receive Holy Communion. As it was not possible for her to leave her bed, she received It sitting up on her couch, with clasped hands, and an expression upon her countenance of such intense recollection and ardent love, that all who were privileged to be present were deeply touched. Although burning with fever and parched with thirst, she had refrained from even moistening her lips with a little water, in order that she might receive our Lord fasting. The days went by and her sufferings increased, while her physical weakness became intense. Yet she interested herself none the less keenly in the work of the Institute; she gathered round her bed the Council of the Mother House in order to consult about some matters relating to the foundation of Aden, and chose three professed Sisters to be sent thither. She also selected two Sisters who were to proceed to Vellore, and made arrangements for several other houses.

On Friday, the feast of our Blessed Lady's Compassion, the patient was evidently very much worse. The disease was making rapid progress, and her strength was failing fast. It was a day of agonizing sufferings, which her children were all the more pained to witness because they were so impotent to relieve them. She received Holy Communion as Viaticum, and in spite of all she was enduring, she was soothed and cheered by some good news which arrived regarding the house at Algiers, which had lately passed through a most critical phase of its existence, and had occasioned her no little anxiety. "You have no idea," she said to one of the Sisters, "how much I have endured on account of this house! I really believe it is costing me my life! Were I not so great a sinner, I should be tempted to believe that our Lord has chosen me as an expiatory victim. But I am not worthy to be made a victim for so great a work!" Towards evening, it was evident that she imagined her end to be approaching, but she was careful not to allude openly to the subject, in order to spare the feelings of those about her. In the midst of paroxysms of excruciating pain she constantly repeated: "May Thy will, O my God, be done in me, and through me, and by me, for ever! That is my sole desire!" Her calmness and resignation were a source of much edification to her children, as they knew that she had, until then, been habitually oppressed by a dread of death.

She had always felt a special devotion to the feast of our Lady's Compassion. "It is a singular thing," she sometimes used to say, "Our Lady of Dolours generally brings me consolations, while on the contrary, on the glorious festival of the Assumption, the Queen of Heaven bestows upon me nothing but crosses, sorrows, and bitterness of soul." On this day, however, in the midst of the agony she was undergoing, she could only say: "This is a true Passion week, my dearest Sisters! It is evident that our Lady wishes me to stand beside her upon Calvary! *Fiat!*" Another time she said: "I feel that I am gradually passing away, I can take nothing but iced water. But of what consequence is all this? I am standing on Calvary, and then I shall die. It is my desire to die there, whenever our Lord shall see fit! It distresses me to think how you all suffer with me. May God's will be done!"

Saturday morning brought no relief to the invalid, but rather an aggravation of her pain. Lying on her bed, racked by torture, violent attacks of retching, and spasmodic convulsions of her whole frame, made it impossible for her to do anything but endure. About six o'clock in the evening she grew fainter, and being conscious of extreme exhaustion, she begged that the last sacraments might be given her. After receiving Extreme Unction, she appeared so much relieved that the chaplain thought he might safely administer to her the Holy Viaticum. The Community pressed around the door of the sick-room. Mother St. Euphrasia noticed this. "Come in, my dearest children, come in, all of you," she exclaimed. Before receiving the Sacred Host, she held up her hand, as a sign that she wished to speak. In a low but clear voice she renewed her vows, and then continued: "I ask pardon of the Community and of the Congregation for the subjects of complaint and the causes of scandal I have given. I forgive with all my heart every one who has ever given me pain. My Community has always afforded me the greatest satisfaction." The sobs of those present cut short her words. Could such expressions, in the mouth of one who had always been an example of virtue, do otherwise than provoke an uncontrollable outburst of feeling? Desirous of imitating to the very last the illustrious Saint of Carmel, whom she had, as we have seen, all her life long so profoundly admired, she added, as soon as she could again make herself heard: "I declare that I die a child of the Holy Catholic Church, Roman and Apostolic." After Holy Communion had been given to her, she remained for some time motionless with closed eyes. Ever thoughtful as she was for others, it suddenly occurred to her that the Sisters who were with her, might fear she had lost the power of speech. She therefore opened her eyes, and said with a quiet smile: "I am making my thanksgiving." A respite from pain seemed to be granted her, and she took advantage of it in order to deliver her last instructions to her children. "Cultivate unity among yourselves," she said to them, "and if you have little differences, try to forgive and forget. Love your Institute, do all in your power to extend and strengthen it." Mother Mary of St. Peter, who was extremely attached to the Mother General, could not help exclaiming in the bitterness of her grief: "Oh, my dearest Mother, what will become of us, now that you are about to leave us? What shall we do without you?" "Do not disquiet yourself," was the gentle answer, "I shall be able to help you more effectually when I am in the immediate presence of God, than I could ever do while on earth. But before I depart, let me exhort you to be ever loyal to Rome, to the Holy Father, to our Cardinal Protector. Tread in my footsteps. My devotion to Rome has cost me many trials and crosses, it has involved me in many difficulties, but now that I am dying, how do I rejoice to think that I persevered in it. Love Rome: there is the centre of light, there is the pillar of fire which enlightens the whole world. You will find no better Father than the Sovereign Pontiff, and after him, our Cardinal Protector." Then raising her feeble hands to Heaven, she blessed all her convents and all her children, in the warmest and most affectionate terms. "Tell all who are absent and far away that I bless them all, and embrace every one with the fondest affection. Not one has been forgotten by me in this supreme moment."

The next day was Palm Sunday. The respect she had felt all her life for the ceremonies of the Church did not desert her now. She asked for her palm, and held it for some time in her hand.[1] Later on she said: "To think that only a week ago I was able to be with you all! But it was my love for you which gave me strength . . ." Her voice failed, and large tears rolled slowly down her pale, thin cheeks. Erelong she resumed: "It was a moment of weakness. It is because I love you all so much."

Throughout the day she remained tolerably free from pain, and many consolations were vouchsafed her. At four o'clock in the afternoon a telegram arrived from Cardinal Patrizi, announcing that the Holy Father sent his blessing to the invalid, and was praying for her. On hearing the news, she crossed herself devoutly, and expressed her gratitude and joy, as well as her unworthiness of the favour thus conferred upon her. She

---

[1] This palm, which was planted by one of the Sisters in the garden, close to the chapel of the Immaculate Conception, took root and grew. Several cuttings taken from it were planted in the enclosure. Others were sent to some of the foundations.

z

kissed the telegram, and then caused it to be placed under the picture of the Holy Family which was in her room, and beneath which she had so often knelt in prayer. Two hours later, his Lordship the Bishop came to see her, accompanied by the Vicar-General. "My child," he said, on entering her room, "I have come to bring you my blessing. I have already remembered you at the altar of God, and also during my visit to the Blessed Sacrament." Every one withdrew from the apartment, with the exception of the Vicar-General. Mother St. Euphrasia never made the slightest allusion to what passed during the brief interview which followed.

It was the will of God that she should linger almost three weeks longer in agonies which baffle all power of description. As day after day crept heavily by, it is heartrending to read the recital of what she suffered, and the tale must awaken the deepest compassion in every heart. Like the three children, she "praised, glorified, and blessed God in the midst of the furnace, saying, 'O ye fire and heat, bless the Lord : praise Him and exalt Him above all for ever.'"[1] Like them also, there was One with her in the fierce flames, and He was none other than the Son of God. In her moments of extremest suffering, she constantly acted out her own resolution: "I desire to fall into no sin of imperfection during this illness." Such words as the following were frequently on her lips : "My God, Thou art my All! O Jesus, be Thou the breath of my life! Thou art my strength, I look to Thee alone for support! 'I bear the marks of the Lord Jesus in my body.'[2] Suffering has been offered to me, and I have accepted it. I am covered with wounds, but in these wounds

<hr>

[1] Daniel iii. 61, 66.   [2] Galat. vi. 17.

I have found life. My soul is at peace, for I feel that my God is within me, and suffering with me."

From her pious mother, who had herself, as we have seen, borne with exemplary patience so many, and such heavy sorrows, Mother St. Euphrasia had learned that lesson which is so absolutely necessary, and at the same time so difficult to acquire, namely, the love of the Cross. She had remembered the lesson and acted on it throughout the whole of her, life. Most sincerely would she have re-echoed the words of the old writer, who says: " If you find that there are no crosses in your path, fear lest you should have taken the wrong road." And now, when lying upon her death-bed, she could adopt the words of the Apostle, and say: " I now rejoice in my sufferings for you, and fill up those things that are wanting of the sufferings of Christ, in my flesh, for His Body, which is the Church."[1] How many blessings must she not have earned] for the foundations which were so near her heart! How many gifts of true contrition for the Penitents! How many graces of perseverance for the Magdalens!

While we so deeply sympathize with her who moved, with unflagging patience and true Christian resignation, from one station to another along her *Via Crucis*, it is impossible not to feel deeply also for those who watched around her. They knew now that nothing short of a miracle could keep her in their midst, they were fully aware that God was calling their venerated foundress to receive her crown. Like the Prophet of old, they beheld her ascending to Heaven in a fiery chariot, and they had to endure, what we all know to be one of the keenest and most piercing forms of human anguish, that namely of witnessing the

[1] Coloss. i. 24.

sufferings of those whom we love, and feeling ourselves at the same time impotent to relieve, or even mitigate them. And it must have intensified their grief to see how their beloved Mother cared for them, thought for them, loved them to the last. For instance, after an unusually rough and stormy night, she sent a Sister to go round the grounds, and see if any harm had been done in the garden, or any trees uprooted, or branches torn off. Another day she directed that some sums of money should be enclosed in envelopes, and addressed to the Superiors of houses which she knew to be in straitened circumstances. These gifts were not to be forwarded until after her death. From a feeling of delicate consideration for her children, she never used the word *death*, in reference to her end, which she herself, in common with all who were about her, imagined to be much nearer than it really was. Desirous that her final resting-place should be within the enclosure, she one day said to the Sister Assistant: " My dearest daughter, when it shall have pleased God to call my {spirit to Himself, I wish my mortal remains to be placed in the chapel of the Immaculate Conception. I am very fond of that chapel, and I shall, when there, be in the centre of our various establishments. The Magdalens, the Penitents, and the children will be able to go and pray there." While refusing actually to name her successor, she allowed it plainly to be seen that her choice was fixed upon Mother Mary of St. Peter de Coudenhove. During the past nine years this excellent Religious had, in her capacity of first Assistant General, rendered very great services of Mother St. Euphrasia, and had been admitted to her closest confidence. In a time of comparative immunity from suffering, she had a private interview with her, and delivered to her some final instructions regarding the Order. When Mother Mary of St. Peter had quitted her room, she called to her bedside two Sisters who had just entered, and said to them: "Do not disquiet yourselves. Sister Mary of St. Peter has never done anything to vex me. On the contrary, she has been my stay and support. She will be yours also."

Every day a sense of her own deep unworthiness seemed to penetrate further and further into the soul of the venerated foundress. She sincerely believed herself undeserving of the services which were rendered her. She thanked those who waited upon her in terms of gratitude so touching that they were filled with confusion. And such was the perfection with which she had learned the art of self-mastery and self-control, so difficult of practice even to those who are in health, that amid the abnormally severe sufferings which she was called almost constantly to endure, her habitual charm of manner never forsook her. Gracious and attractive as ever, she always found something pleasing and suitable to say to the Sisters who approached her bed. She would send affectionate messages to one or other of the novices, to show that she had not forgotten them, and to assure them that had the dimensions of her room permitted, she should be only too delighted to have them around her once more.

Nor must we fail to remark, how perfect a Religious she showed herself, even to the end. In respect of the virtues of chastity and purity, it is sufficient to say, as we have already done, that from motives dictated by extreme delicacy, she concealed even from those of her Sisters who were in her closest confidence, the existence of the malignant tumour which brought her at last to the grave, and must have caused her, for a long series of years, constant and daily increasing pain.

Her spirit of mortification never forsook her. When some one expressed pity for her, because she could take nothing except water and ice, she answered: " Remember St. Francis Xavier: he had no clear cold water to drink, on the scorching plains of India." Rather than disturb her infirmarian during the night, she remained absolutely without refreshment, even when the fever was at its height. And it was only three or four days before her death that she allowed the hard mattress on which she had slept for many years, to be exchanged for one more suited to her condition.

Never for a moment did she relax her vigilance, as to the exact observance of the Rule. In the midst of her acutest sufferings, she followed the actions and exercises of the Community, as if she had been still in their midst. If speech was not possible to her, she yet, each time the bell rang, made a sign to those of her children who were with her, to go where obedience was calling them. The minutest points did not escape her. On Wednesday in Holy Week, she sent a message to the Community, telling them that she should unite herself with them in spirit throughout all the Offices, at which it had hitherto been so great a joy to her to be present. She added an injunction to observe every detail marked in the directory hung up in the choir. Then she asked to see the Superior of the house, and charged her to take good care of the Sisters, and not allow any one to over-tire herself. She ordered the dinner of the Community for Holy Thursday, and desired that some extra dishes should be served at collation, on account of the watch to be kept throughout the night. Although she evinced the greatest pleasure at the presence of the numerous Superiors of houses who came to pay a last visit of love to her whom God was calling to Himself, she desired them, as Easter drew near, to return, each to her own convent, in order to keep the Feast there in the midst of her Community. "Go, my dearest Sisters," she said to them, "and thus show yourselves worthy of the office you hold. God will reward your sacrifice and mine. Perhaps you may come and see me again later on."

But we are anticipating. There remains yet much to be told concerning the Servant of God, who glorified in the closing scenes of her life, in so striking a manner, Him Whom she had faithfully served from her earliest childhood. May we not say that she glorified Him most of all, when nailed to her cross of pain? It is more difficult to suffer well, than to work diligently, especially to an ardent and active temperament like hers. She had long shown how ably she could work, and when the hour came, she proved how perfectly she had learned the manner in which the followers of the Crucified should accept suffering. Many and severe had been the trials she had met with during her life, but the manner in which, now that her physical powers were reduced to their lowest ebb, mind still conquered matter, and grace still triumphed over nature, is surprising indeed. Never did a single word, or even gesture, of impatience escape her, all the weary weeks during which our Lord delayed His coming to release her. How many times must she not have exclaimed in the depths of her soul with the mother of Sisera: "Why is his chariot so long in coming? Why are the feet of his horses so slow?"[1]

[1] Judges v. 28.

CHAPTER XXII.

DEATH.

DESIROUS of leaving no means untried, which might possibly avail to preserve the precious life which appeared to be ebbing fast away, the Superioresses who had come to the Mother House from so many various localities, proposed to their beloved foundress, that they should make in her name a pilgrimage to Saint-Joseph-du-Chêne, a Vendean sanctuary situated near Beaupréau.

"Alas! my dearest children," she replied, when the project was unfolded to her, "so many prayers have already been offered up, so many Masses said, so many novenas made, that I cannot and do not believe it to be the will of God that I should recover from this illness. His holy will must be done! Nevertheless, I do not desire to oppose your kind plan. Follow, therefore, the inspiration of your hearts, prayers can never be lost. I shall gain from yours, patience to endure the martyr-dom which I have to bear without intermission, by day and by night. Make your vow, but remember at the same time that I have no will but God's." All the Superiors who were present made a solemn promise, and three of them were deputed to go to the sanctuary in order to receive Holy Communion there. They took with them a silver heart, containing a written copy of their vow. During their absence, the members of the

Community at Angers were unceasing in their petitions
to the Patron of the Universal Church. A considerable
number of the Religious remained constantly in the
choir, engaged in prayer.

When the three travellers returned from their
journey, it was late in the evening. They went straight
to the foundress' room, and gave her an account of their
mission. With the closest attention she listened to
every detail, and then said: " God will reward you for
this act of devotion, this proof of attachment to me. I
am very grateful to you, but you must recollect that
St. Joseph, mighty and powerful as he is, can only
carry out the will of God. As for myself, I have told
you over and over again that I desire only that the will
of God should be done in me."

Many were the consolations vouchsafed her in the
midst of the furnace of affliction. The love and devotion of her children was in itself an immense support
and comfort, showing itself as it did in a thousand ingenious ways. Every post brought tender and soothing
letters from those who could not visit the sick-room in
person. Each of these letters was read to Mother
St. Euphrasia, by her special desire. She followed
every word, entered into every particular, and then
dictated her reply in terms so clear, so touching, and
so beautifully expressed, that the Religious who wrote
them down at her bedside were often almost blinded
by their tears. Her style had, moreover, lost nothing
of the terse precision, and happy choice of words and
phrases which had distinguished it in her days of health
and vigour. She was as able as she had ever been, to
dictate business letters, and answer applications concerning pecuniary concerns. As an instance of this we
may mention that on Good Friday, when her attacks

of pain were even more severe than before, a letter was read to her from the Superior of the house at Loos, stating that she had a considerable sum of money at her disposal, and that she solicited permission to build a chapel. The invalid was much pleased and interested. "Tell her," she said, "that I most willingly grant her the authorization for which she asks. How fortunate I am, in being able, on such a day as this, to raise a new temple to the glory of my Lord!" She was greatly delighted with a fragment of the sash of Pius IX., which one of the most devoted of her children sent her from Rome. In the letter which accompanied it, it was spoken of as a relic, and the hope was expressed that it might be the means of effecting a cure. "What pleasure this gives me!" Mother St. Euphrasia said, whilst respectfully kissing it. "I am suffering so much just now from pain in my heart, I shall place the relic there. I wish never to be separated from it. Please do not take it off until the very last."

We have already said that Cardinal Patrizi had sent her the blessing of the Holy Father. But yet another favour awaited her from the same source. As her illness went on, the Cardinal wrote to the Mother Assistant, assuring her of his prayers on behalf of the suffering foundress. "I rejoice," His Eminence went on to say, "that the blessing of the Holy Father afforded her so much consolation. May I ask you to have the goodness to tell her that His Holiness constantly remembers her in his prayers?" When Mother St. Euphrasia heard this, she was filled with joy. Devotion to the Vicar of Christ and to the See of Rome had always been a marked feature of her character, and she delighted to feel that the Successor of St. Peter was aiding her with his intercession during her last hours

on earth. Numerous Bishops and prelates likewise
sent her their blessing, with expressions of interest and
sympathy which greatly soothed and cheered her.
Among them we may mention the Archbishops of
Cambrai, Aix, and Westminster; the Bishops of
Poitiers, Orleans, and Arras. Among the last wishes
of the invalid, was that of seeing Father Roux once
more. One of her secretaries proposed to summon
him. " No, my child," was the answer: " I have made
the sacrifice of this final consolation, and I trust that
God will accept it. Write and tell Father Roux how
sincerely grateful I am to him for all the good he has
done me, and tell him that I will not fail to pray for
him when I get to Heaven. Henceforth I desire God
alone!" But as in the case of Abraham, so was it in
hers also. God was graciously pleased to accept His
servant's sacrifice, without requiring that it should be
fulfilled. Father Roux had been detained at Rennes
by his ministerial duties, but as soon as the Easter
confessions were over, he determined to carry out his
own great wish to have a parting interview with the
venerated foundress. He quitted Rennes at six o'clock
on the morning of Easter Monday, and had only time
to reach Angers and pay a brief visit to the Good
Shepherd, before taking the next train in order to
return home the same night. It was five o'clock in the
afternoon when he rang at the door of the convent.
The Mother General was comparatively free from pain,
so that he was able to see her at once. She expressed
in the warmest terms her gratitude for the trouble he
had taken in order to come and visit her, and then
requested all present to withdraw, in order that she
might make her confession. When the Sisters had
been recalled, she said: " Now I am not going to talk

any more. It is your turn, dear children, to speak, and
to tell our kind Father all that is going on. Tell him
that we have two new houses, one at Aden, the other
in Switzerland." When Father Roux rose to say farewell, she took up a cross, brought from Jerusalem,
which had been on her bed throughout her illness. She
kissed it, and handed it to him as a parting *souvenir*.
He was deeply touched, and thanked her over and over
again. Then he once more gave her his blessing, and
left the room. Before quitting the convent, he exhorted
the Sisters to submission, in view of the heavy blow
impending over them. At the same time he congratulated them on having had so highly gifted a mother
and foundress, one distinguished alike by the virtues
and talents wherewith God had endowed her. As for
the invalid herself, she could speak of nothing but the
consolation this visit had afforded her. "How good
and kind Father Roux is!" she repeated several times.
"What light one gains from him! Until my latest
breath, I shall never cease to be grateful for the wise
advice and prudent counsel he has imparted to me."

But it is time for us to take our place once more
beside the bed of death, and trace the closing scenes of
the holy and useful life the course of which we have
been engaged in tracing. For nearly a fortnight after
Palm Sunday, frequent and violent attacks of retching
made it impossible to give her Holy Communion.
Keenly as the sufferer felt the privation, she submitted
to it with perfect resignation. "Dear children," she
would whisper, with tears in her eyes, "God is puri-
fying me. I unite my will to His. I adore His all-wise
purposes. In His justice He is laying a cross upon
my shoulders." Whenever she was conscious that a
terrible spasm of pain was approaching, she would

cross herself with holy water, invoke our Blessed Lady, and then lie motionless until the paroxysm had passed away. Those who watched her sometimes heard her moaning feebly in the extremity of her tortures, but no one ever surprised from her parched lips a single expression of anything like impatience. It was natural that she should feel the privation to which we have just referred in a very special manner on Maundy Thursday. "Since I entered upon the religious life," she said, "this is the first time I have been unable to receive the Bread of Angels on this day. It is the sole consolation I desired, and God denies it to me. It is a terrible sacrifice, but I submit to it with my whole heart. *Fiat!*"

On Good Friday her sufferings became yet more agonizing. She ardently desired to consummate her sacrifice on this solemn anniversary. "How thankful I should be to Almighty God, if He would be pleased to call me to Himself on this day. Alas! I am too unworthy! I cannot be present at the Offices of the Church, but will you please remind me of each hour as it passes, in order that I may follow our Lord in His Passion step by step, and be the companion of the Mother of Sorrows. She has intimated to me her wish that I should remain close beside her during the Dolorous Passion. She has given me a very bitter chalice to drink. I must drain it to the dregs." She then sank into a death-like swoon, which lasted for some length of time. When she came to herself, she said: "If we die with Jesus Christ, we shall rise again with Him." She spoke little throughout the day, but the fragmentary sentences which dropped from her lips, showed that she was following our Blessed Saviour in spirit, from one scene of His sufferings to another.

Frequently she quoted the words of Isaias, and once she said: "He has always been my favourite among the Prophets, because he has said more about our Lord's sufferings than any other." On the morning of Easter Sunday she said to a Sister who was with her: " Our Lord has risen again, and I am still left standing upon Calvary! What an Easter morning for me! I cannot even receive Holy Communion! But may God's will be done!" Later on she resumed: " What a blessed vocation ours is! It has always been very near my heart. I can think of nothing to be compared to the mission with which God has entrusted us, and the favour He has conferred upon us, in permitting us to co-operate in the salvation of souls. Learn to prize your vocation aright, my dearest child, and never allow your love for it to grow cold." Later on, she again fell into so prolonged a swoon, that the Sisters feared her last hour had come.

These fainting-fits became more frequent and more severe as her end drew near. They amounted, in fact, to what may be termed " a rehearsal of death." Almost a fortnight, however, had yet to elapse before her soul was released from its prison-house. After one of these seizures, she all at once opened her eyes, and said, smiling pleasantly at the anxious faces around her bed: " A few moments ago I believed myself to be dying. Our Blessed Lady keeps me in safety, she never leaves me. I can see her with the eyes of the soul, though not with those of the body. Oh! how happy I am in the protection of Mary! What would become of me without her! Just now I seemed to be tossing in a frail boat on a rough lake, I was afraid of being wrecked! But the Queen of Heaven watched over and guarded me. On the right side of the lake I beheld our Lord surrounded by an innumerable crowd of His elect. The left side of the lake was thronged with devils, hideous and repulsive to behold. They swam out into the water, and tried hard to submerge my little boat. But Mary put them all to flight. I have still far to go in this mysterious vessel before I reach the haven of eternal rest, and you must all pray a great deal for me."

The next day, April the 19th, was Low Sunday. Unparalleled sufferings were the portion of the dying foundress. " I do not know how it is that I continue to live amid such tortures," she said. " I am enduring a real martyrdom. I incessantly invoke our Lady, for if she were not with me, I should lose all patience. How kind she is! What consoling thoughts she suggests! How grateful I ought to be for all the favours she has bestowed upon me during my long illness. She has given me the assurance that her Divine Son has forgiven my sins, but I do not yet know when I shall be promised to behold Him in Heaven." The next day, to her intense delight, she was able once more to receive our Lord in Holy Communion. The relief she experienced was so great and so apparent, that when the doctor paid his usual visit shortly after- wards, he said to her: " It is easy to perceive that another and a greater Physician has been here before me." On the 22nd she was again permitted to com- municate. In the course of the day, however, she experienced so agonizing a seizure, that her watchful Sisters thought her to be already in the arms of death. In the extremity of torture, she said to one of her secretaries: " Beg of God in His mercy to call me away. I can bear no more!" She then fainted, and on recover- ing possession of her faculties, spoke in the same strain as she had done before about our Blessed Lady. It is

worthy of note how, through the whole course of her
tedious and cruel illness, she clung to her who is so
truly described as *Consolatrix afflictorum*.   Her early
devotion to Mary, the love which had induced her to
bestow that sweet name, so dear to every Christian
heart, upon each and all her children, did indeed meet
with their reward, even in this life.   In her case the
promise was signally fulfilled : " I love them that love
me, and they that in the morning early watch for me,
shall find me."[1]   "And in thy latter end thou shalt
find rest in her."[2]

The hour of deliverance so long desired by Mother
St. Euphrasia was now close at hand.   On the 23rd she
received for the last time on earth Him Who was soon
to be in Heaven her reward exceeding great.   In the
course of the morning, she asked to see the English
Provincial, who had arrived the evening before with
one of the Sisters, and whose devotion to the work of
the Good Shepherd was known throughout the Order.
No sooner did the two visitors make their appearance
on the threshold of her room, than she stretched out
her arms to receive them.   " Come in, come in, my
dearest children," she exclaimed; "love is stronger than
death.   God has preserved my life a little longer in
order that I may have the consolation of once more
beholding you, and of clasping you to my heart.   Come
close to me, you are my joy and my crown.   Your very
presence seems to infuse new life into me."   Then
turning to the Provincial : " My dearest child," she
said, " I commit England to your care.   Keep up the
foundations.   Let Angers be in England, and England
at Angers."   This effort proved too much for her exhausted frame, and brought on one of her worst attacks.

[1] Prov. viii. 17.   [2] Ecclus. vi. 29.

Ever thinking of others rather than of herself, she feared lest the Sisters who were in attendance upon her should be over-fatigued, and begged them to go and take some rest. "I have given you a great deal of trouble," she said, in a tone of gentle apology, "but you may be quite sure that I shall not forget you when I get to Heaven."

The night which followed was one of the acutest suffering, which nothing could relieve. When the doctor paid his accustomed visit, early in the morning of Friday, April the 24th, he gave it as his opinion that the Mother General could scarcely live through the day. A few moments subsequent to his departure, Mlle. Louisa Masson, the chief benefactress of the house at Cholet, arrived at the convent, accompanied by a friend of hers, and asked if Mother Euphrasia could receive them. Consulting only the dictates of her heart, and of her habitual sense of gratitude, she instantly consented. Although her condition was so distressing that even the lightest touch caused her excruciating pain, she begged that her linen might be changed. She welcomed her friends in the warmest manner, kissed them affectionately, and made them sit close to her bed. Then she reminded the Sisters who were present how much the foundation of Cholet owed to Mlle. Masson. "My dear friend," she continued, "this is your house also. You must always regard the Mother House at Angers as a home of your own, and you must come and stay here whenever you like. You will always be received as one of our best and dearest friends, and the foundress of the house at Cholet. Thanks to you, it is in every respect a most satisfactory foundation. How can I ever suitably express my gratitude for all the benefits you have bestowed upon me!"

AA

Then taking a small cross which was lying on her bed :
" Please accept this," she said, " as a remembrance of
her who can never forget you. Here is another cross
for your friend. You will both pray for me, will you
not ? " Mlle. Masson and her companion kissed her
hand, and retired with every sign of deep emotion.

Although the shades of death were already stealing
over her, the beloved invalid showed no sign of intellectual weakness. In the course of the morning she
sent for several of the Superiors of houses who were
then at Angers, and addressed suitable exhortations to
each one of them. A Sister whom she intended to
place over the second convent about to be founded in
Algeria, she especially requested to come to her room,
in order that she might notify to her the post she was
destined to fill. " I am so glad to see you, my child,"
she said. " I was waiting for you to come. We have
elected you Superior at Oran. I entrust that house to
you." She next expressed her desire to see the Sisters
who were to proceed to Aden, and those who were
before long to embark for India. She spoke to each by
name, addressed a few kind words, suited to the occasion, to them all collectively, and then dismissed them
with her blessing.

This was her final effort, and it left her in a state of
such utter prostration that she begged to be left alone
with the infirmarians. Her power of speech began to
fail, her feeble remnant of strength was visibly ebbing
away. Yet about three o'clock, the dying foundress,
whose attachment to her Order seemed to increase with
her sufferings, roused herself yet once more, and in a
voice which was scarcely audible, asked to see some of
the Sisters. But while she was speaking, a sudden
faintness overpowered her. She could only just articu-

late, "Farewell! Farewell! Farewell, my dearest children! Farewell to the Institute!" These were her last words.

Erelong she entered upon her agony. Closing her eyes and mouth, she remained absolutely motionless for upwards of two hours, her slow and laboured breathing being the only sign of life which she gave. The Assistant Sisters, kneeling at each side of her pillow, uttered from time to time the names of Jesus, Mary, and Joseph, and sundry pious ejaculations, as she had beforehand so frequently requested them to do, in view of her last hour. They all repeatedly held to her lips a crucifix which had come from Jerusalem and which she greatly valued. When six o'clock drew near, and the *Angelus* was about to be rung, she rendered up her pure soul to God. So sweet and gentle, so quiet and peaceful was her departure, that of all those who were gathered in her room, watching her every breath, not one could detect the exact moment when she uttered her last sigh. It was the evening of Friday, April 24th, and the following Sunday, the 26th, was Good Shepherd Sunday, the special feast of the Order she had founded. She had been called *ad Cœnam Agni*, she was to keep the feast in that eternal and celestial city, of which we are told that "the glory of God hath enlightened it, and the Lamb is the lamp thereof."[1]

> Oh, what the oy and the glory must be,
> Those endless Sabbaths the blessed ones see;
> Crown for the valiant, to weary ones rest;
> God shall be All, and in all ever blest.[2]

---

[1] Apoc. xxi. 23.

[2] O quanta, qualia sunt illa Sabbata
Quæ semper celebrat superna curia,
Quæ fessis requies, quæ merces fortibus,
Cum sunt omnia Deus in omnibus!

It would be useless indeed to attempt to describe the grief of those who knew that they had lost a mother, a counsellor, a ruler, upon whose like they could never hope to look again. But as we read the pathetic story of their irreparable bereavement, it is impossible not to mingle, if we may so speak, our tears with theirs. Especially poignant must have been the anguish of the Sisters belonging to the Mother House, when they entered the refectory on Sunday, and sat down to the repast, every detail of which had been carefully planned and arranged by their dearly-loved foundress, while she was lying on her dying bed. Her obsequies were celebrated with as much external ceremony as is consistent with religious simplicity. On Saturday morning, her remains were carried down to the community-room, which had been arranged as a *chapelle ardente*. The walls were hung with black, and the windows draped with funereal crape so as to exclude all light except that afforded by a large number of wax candles. In the centre of the apartment, on a *lit de parade* covered with white flowers, reposed the foundress and first Superior General of the Order of the Good Shepherd of Angers. Clothed in her Religious dress, and barefooted, according to the custom practised in the Institute, she wore on her head the wreath which had been presented to her on the 9th of September in the preceding year, when she attained the fiftieth anniversary of her Religious Profession. In her clasped hands she held her favourite Jerusalem crucifix, and a copy of the vows which she had observed with such perfection. The silver heart she wore around her neck contained the names of all the convents, the Religious, and the various establishments which had been subject to her sway. Her gracious and charming countenance had regained all the smooth freshness of early youth, so that those who were privileged to gaze upon the calm beauty of her face, might easily have fancied that she was about to awake from a sweet and refreshing sleep. A crowd of persons passed during the day, with recollected and reverential mien, through the chamber of death, carrying rosaries, crucifixes, and other objects of piety, with which they touched the hands of her whom in life they had so deeply venerated. Every class of society, in fact, vied with the Religious in offering their tribute of sorrowful gratitude to her whose sympathy had been so freely given to all who claimed it, and whose truly maternal heart had known how to feel for each and all of the bitter sorrows which, woven together, form the web of human existence. Countless bouquets were laid on her hands, or placed at her feet, those feet which, as it was aptly remarked, " no suffering could ever turn from that path of duty in which flowers are so rare and thorns so numerous."

Mother St. Euphrasia remained thus exposed from Saturday the 25th, until Monday the 27th, the day after the feast of the Good Shepherd. Her limbs had lost nothing of their flexibility, and in spite of the extensive and terrible wound in her side, not the slightest sign of decomposition had made its appearance. Indeed, a lay-sister, Sister St. Euphemia, who helped to place the cherished remains in the coffin, noticed that the Servant of God opened her mouth, out of which emanated a delicate perfume. The obsequies were solemn and impressive. At least sixty ecclesiastics, many of whom belonged to various Religious Orders, assembled in the choir, with a view to being present when the body was borne from the mortuary chapel into the church. First walked the Sisters belonging to the Community, to the number of three hundred and forty, clothed in their mantles, each one with a lighted taper in her hand. The out-of-door servants and workmen belonging to the house had asked, as a great favour, to be allowed to carry the coffin. They now stepped forward, and respectfully kissed the feet of the venerated foundress, after which they bore her into the choir, and placed their burden on the catafalque. The composed and placid countenance was still visible, and the beautiful smile which hovered over the marble features seemed to speak to all present of the ineffable blessedness the holy foundress was enjoying in the presence of God.

When the Mass was finished, and the absolutions had been pronounced, the Community took up their places in the splendid avenue of limes which leads from the outer choir to the chapel of the Immaculate Conception. There, in virtue of a special permission granted by the Mayor of Angers, and in accordance with the wish she had herself expressed before her death, Mother St. Euphrasia was to be laid to rest. The Magdalens, the Penitents, and the various classes to which the Mother House gave shelter, occupied the paths which led out from the principal avenue. They were all veiled, and dressed in deep mourning. There were, besides, deputations from numerous Religious Communities. The Prioress of the Carmelites, and the Superior of the Visitation Convent, deputed their out-Sisters to attend. The clergy moved on to the chapel, where, on the left-hand side, near our Lady's altar, a grave had been prepared to receive the coffin, which was of lead, with an outer one composed of oak. As soon as the final prayers had been uttered, the clergy withdrew. Then the Sister Assistant removed from the hands of the revered foundress the crucifix which had come from Jerusalem, and which, as we have seen, she so greatly valued, replacing it by her own crucifix. The Religious took their last farewell of the Mother whom they so deeply mourned, and their eyes remained riveted upon her beloved form, until the lid of the coffin in the first place, and then the stone slab that covered the grave, hid her from mortal gaze.

The grave was of no great depth, thus the coffin was almost on a level with the ground. The monumental stone that covers it is of the simplest description : a slab of black marble, the only ornament of which is a cross of white marble. On the four ends of the cross are engraved in gold letters the words : Poverty, Chastity, Obedience, Zeal for Souls. The inscription, carved upon a white marble tablet let into the wall of the chapel, runs thus :

HERE LIE THE REMAINS OF

OUR VERY REVEREND MOTHER

MARY OF ST. EUPHRASIA PELLETIER,

SUPERIOR GENERAL

OF THE CONGREGATION OF OUR LADY OF CHARITY

OF THE GOOD SHEPHERD OF ANGERS.

SHE WAS BORN ON JULY 31ST, 1796 ;

FOUNDED THE GENERALATE JANUARY 9TH, 1835,

AND DIED IN THE PEACE OF THE LORD, APRIL 24th, 1868,

AGED 72 YEARS.

REQUIESCAT IN PACE !

THE LAW OF GOD IS IN THE MIDST OF MY HEART.

THE ZEAL OF THY HOUSE, LORD, HATH EATEN ME UP.

SHE BUILT A TEMPLE TO THE LORD, AND LOVED

TO MAKE BEAUTIFUL THE HOUSE OF GOD.

CONCLUSION.

IT has already been said that during her lifetime the exalted virtues of Mother St. Euphrasia caused her to be greatly revered and beloved by all who knew her. In every quarter of the world also, wherever the Order was established, the name of the venerated foundress was held in the highest esteem. And yet her death does not appear to have attracted as much general notice as one might have expected, deeply as her loss was felt in all the houses under her sway. Not many months, however, were allowed to elapse before God was pleased to make known the sanctity of His servant, not merely by the extraordinarily rapid growth and development of the Order of the Good Shepherd, but by special and signal favours obtained through her intercession. The first instance occurred at the Convent of St. Louis, Missouri.

A young girl named Mary had been placed, contrary to her will, in the convent by her father, to whom she was a source of constant trouble. Resolved to regain her liberty, she had not been there a fortnight, before she contrived, while her companions were asleep, to throw herself from the dormitory window, a height of some forty feet. She was found by the Mistress of Penitents lying on a heap of rubbish, insensible and apparently dying. On being removed to the infirmary and examined by the doctor, she was discovered to have fractured her spine, and no hope was entertained of her recovery. For three months she lingered, being kept absolutely motionless; at the close of that time two other members of the medical profession declared that ultimate cure was impossible, and that she could not live many months longer. On hearing this, Mary felt inspired to make a novena to Mother St. Euphrasia, promising that were her life spared she would become a Magdalen. Several Religious and some of the Penitents joined in this novena; the sufferer experienced no benefit until the last day, when she suddenly rose from her bed, dressed herself without assistance, and ran downstairs, crying out that she was cured, all traces of the accident having disappeared. No doubt was entertained of the miraculous nature of the event. Shortly after a relative of one of the Religious in the same convent recovered her health through the application of a portion of the dress worn by the late Mother General; this was the first of a series of cures effected by the same means both in North and South America.

As it was on the other side of the Atlantic that the exterior glory of the departed Servant of God was made manifest, so it was her daughters in Chili who took the initiative in compiling and publishing (in Spanish) a little volume entitled: *The Spirit of Mother Mary of St. Euphrasia Pelletier*, consisting chiefly of extracts from her instructions and addresses. At their suggestion, when the General Chapter met at Angers in 1886, it was determined to publish this work in French under the title: *Miroir des Vertus de la R. M. Marie de St. Euphrasia Pelletier, Fondatrice de la Congrégation de N.D. de Charité du Bon-Pasteur d'Angers.*

At that same Chapter, after the general elections of 1886, all the Provincials and Superiors of Houses who were assembled at the Mother House, signed a petition, entreating the Superior General to solicit the

Holy See to allow the cause for the beatification of Mother St. Euphrasia to be introduced in Rome. This request was supported by Mgr. Freppel, and two Religious were sent to Rome for the purpose of presenting .it to the Holy Father. They met with every assistance from the Cardinals and several ecclesiastics of high position, and were received with paternal kindness by His Holiness Leo XIII., who gave his blessing to the cause they had come to forward.

As soon as the Process was commenced (February 24, 1887), letters, not unfrequently accompanied by medical certificates, flowed in from all parts of the world to the Mother House, communicating details of wonderful cures and remarkable graces obtained by the medium of prayers addressed to the late Mother General. It is said that of all the causes introduced during the course of the present century, not one could show such numerous and striking instances of thaumaturgical powers as that of Mother St. Euphrasia.

The preliminary investigation was brought to a close n September, 1890, and the report laid before the Sacred Congregation of Rites in December of the same year. Numerous petitions have been sent in to the Holy See that the time for the introduction of the cause may be accelerated. On all sides earnest hopes are expressed that the heroic virtues which distinguished Mother St. Euphrasia, her untiring, life-long labours for the good of souls, may speedily be publicly recognized. Truly it may be said of her as of her Great Exemplar, that she gave her life for the sheep. May many hear her voice, for she "being dead, yet speaks."

QUARTERLY SERIES.

1, 4. **The Life and Letters of St. Francis Xavier.** By the Rev. H. J. Coleridge, S.J. Two vols. 10s. 6d.

2. **The Life of St. Jane Frances Fremyot de Chantal.** By Emily Bowles. 5s.

3. **The History of the Sacred Passion.** By Father Luis de la Palma, S.J. Translated from the Spanish. 5s.

6. **The Life of Dona Luisa de Carvajal.** By Lady Georgiana Fullerton. Small Edition, 3s. 6d.

7. **The Life of St. John Berchmans.** By the Rev. F. Goldie, S.J. 6s.

9. **The Dialogues of St. Gregory the Great.** An Old English Version. 6s.

10. **The Life of Anne Catharine Emmerich.** By Helen Ram. 5s.

13. **The Story of St. Stanislaus Kostka.** Third and enlarged Edition. 4s. 6d.

15. **The Chronicle of St. Antony of Padua.** "The Eldest Son of St. Francis." Edited by the Rev. H. J. Coleridge, S.J. In Four Books. 5s. 6d.

18 **An English Carmelite.** The Life of Catherine Burton, Mother Mary Xaveria of the Angels, of the English Teresian Convent at Antwerp. Collected from her own writings, and other sources, by Father Thomas Hunter, S.J. 6s.

22. **The Suppression of the Society of Jesus** in the Portuguese Dominions. From documents hitherto unpublished. By the Rev. Alfred Weld, S.J. 7s. 6d.

23. **The Christian Reformed in Mind and Manners.**
By Benedict Rogacci, S.J. The Translation edited by
the Rev. H. J. Coleridge, S.J. 7s. 6d.

24. **The Sufferings of the Church in Brittany**
during the Great Revolution. By Edward Healy
Thompson. 6s. 6d.

25. **The Life of Margaret Mostyn** (Mother Margaret
of Jesus), Religious of the Reformed Order of Our Blessed
Lady of Mount Carmel (1625-1679). By the Very Rev.
Edmund Bedingfield. 6s.

26. **The Life of Henrietta D'Osseville** (in Religion,
Mother Ste. Marie), Foundress of the Institute of the
Faithful Virgin. Arranged and Edited by the Rev. J.
G. MacLeod, S.J. 5s. 6d.

30. **The Life of St. Thomas of Hereford.** By
Father L'Estrange, S.J. 6s.

32. **The Life of King Alfred the Great.** By the
Rev. A. G. Knight, S.J. 6s.

33. **The Life of Mother Frances Mary Teresa Ball,**
Foundress in Ireland of the Institute of the Blessed
Virgin Mary. By the Rev. H. J. Coleridge, S.J. With
Portrait. 6s. 6d.

34, 58, 67. **The Life and Letters of St. Teresa.**
Three Vols. By the Rev. H. J. Coleridge, S.J. 7s. 6d.
each.

35, 52. **The Life of Mary Ward.** By Mary
Catherine Elizabeth Chambers, of the Institute of the
Blessed Virgin. Edited by the Rev. H. J. Coleridge, S.J.
Two Vols. 15s.

39. **Pious Affections towards God and the Saints.**
Meditations for Every Day in the Year, and for the
principal Festivals. From the Latin of the Ven. Nicolas
Lancicius, S.J. 7s. 6d.

40. **The Life of the Ven. Claude de la Colombiere.**
Abridged from the French Life by Eugene Sequin, S.J. 5s.

41, 42. **The Life and Teaching of Jesus Christ**
in Meditations for Every Day in the Year. By Father
Nicolas Avancino, S.J. Two vols. 10s. 6d.

43. **The Life of Lady Falkland.** By Lady G.
Fullerton. 5s.

47. **Gaston de Segur.** A Biography. Condensed from the French Memoir by the Marquis de Segur, by F. J. M. A. Partridge. 3s. 6d.

48. **The Tribunal of Conscience.** By Father Gaspar Druzbicki, S.J. 3s. 6d.

50. **Of Adoration in Spirit and Truth.** By Father J. Eusebius Nieremberg. With a Preface by the Rev. P. Gallwey, S.J. 6s. 6d.

56. **During the Persecution.** Autobiography of Father John Gerard, S.J. Translated from the original Latin by the Rev. G. R. Kingdon, S.J. 5s.

59. **The Hours of the Passion.** Taken from the "Life of Christ" by Ludolph the Saxon. 7s. 6d.

62. **The Life of Jane Dormer, Duchess of Feria.** By Henry Clifford. Transcribed from the Ancient Manuscript by the late Canon E. E. Estcourt, and edited by the Rev. Joseph Stevenson, S.J. 5s.

65. **The Life of St. Bridget of Sweden.** By F. J. M. A. Partridge. 6s.

66. **The Teachings and Counsels of St. Francis Xavier.** From his Letters. 5s.

70. **The Life of St. Alonso Rodriguez.** By the Rev. Francis Goldie, S.J. 7s. 6d.

71. **Chapters on the Parables.** By the Rev. H. J. Coleridge, S.J. 7s. 6d.

73. **Letters of St. Augustine.** Selected and Translated by Mary H. Allies. 6s. 6d.

74. **A Martyr from the Quarter-Deck.** Alexis Clerc, S.J. By The Lady Herbert. 5s.

75. **Acts of English Martyrs,** hitherto unpublished. By the Rev. John H. Pollen, S.J. With a Preface by the Rev. John Morris, S.J. 7s. 6d.

77. **The Life of St. Francis di Geronimo, of the Society of Jesus.** By A. M. Clarke. 6s.

79, 80. **Aquinas Ethicus; or, the Moral Teaching of St. Thomas.** By the Rev. Joseph Rickaby, S.J. 2 vols. 12s.

81. **The Spirit of St. Ignatius, Founder of the** Society of Jesus. Translated from the French of the Rev. Father Xavier de Franciosi, of the same Society. 6s.

82. **Jesus, the All-Beautiful.** A Devotional Treatise on the Character and Actions of our Lord. By the Author of *The Voice of the Sacred Heart* and *The Heart of Jesus of Nazareth*. Edited by the Rev. J. G. MacLeod, S.J. Second Edition. 6s. 6d.

83. **Saturday Dedicated to Mary.** From the Italian of Father Cabrini, S.J. With Preface and Introduction by the Rev. R. F. Clarke, S.J. 6s.

84. **The Life of Augustus Henry Law,** Priest of the Society of Jesus. By Ellis Schreiber. 6s.

85. **The Life of the Venerable Joseph Benedict Cottolengo,** Founder of the Little House of Providence in Turin. Compiled from the Italian Life of Don P. Gastaldi, by a Priest of the Society of Jesus. 4s. 6d.

86. **The Lights in Prayer** of the Ven. Louis de la Puente, the Ven. Claude de la Colombière, and the Rev. Father Paul Segneri. 5s.

87. **Two Ancient Treatises on Purgatory.** A Remembrance for the Living to Pray for the Dead, by Father James Mumford, S.J. And **Purgatory Surveyed,** by Father Richard Thimelby, S.J. With Introduction and an Appendix on the Heroic Act, by Father John Morris, S.J. 5s.

88. **Life of St. Francis Borgia.** By A. M. Clarke, author of the *Life of St. Francis di Geronimo*. The first Life of the Saint written in English. 6s. 6d.

89. **The Life of Blessed Antony Baldinucci.** By Father Francis Goldie, S.J. 6s.

90. **Distinguished Irishmen of the Sixteenth** Century. By the Rev. Edmund Hogan, S.J. 6s.

91. **Journals kept during Times of Retreat by** Father John Morris, S.J. Selected and Edited by Father J. H. Pollen, S.J. 6s.

92. **The Life of the Reverend Mother Mary of** St. Euphrasia Pelletier, First Superior General of the Congregation of Our Lady of Charity of the Good Shepherd of Angers. By A. M. Clarke. With Preface by His Eminence Cardinal Vaughan, Archbishop of Westminster.

WORKS ON THE LIFE OF OUR LORD.

BY THE REV. H. J. COLERIDGE, S.J.

Published in the Quarterly Series.

INTRODUCTORY VOLUMES.

19, 20. **The Life of our Life.** Introduction and Harmony of the Gospels, new edition, with the Introduction re-written. Two vols. 15s.

36. **The Works and Words of our Saviour,** gathered from the Four Gospels. 7s. 6d.

46. **The Story of the Gospels.** Harmonized for Meditation. 7s. 6d.

THE HOLY INFANCY.

49. **The Preparation of the Incarnation.** New Edition. 7s. 6d.

53. **The Nine Months.** The Life of our Lord in the Womb. 7s. 6d.

54. **The Thirty Years.** Our Lord's Infancy and Early Life. New Edition. 7s. 6d.

THE PUBLIC LIFE OF OUR LORD.

12. **The Ministry of St. John Baptist.** 6s. 6d.

14. **The Preaching of the Beatitudes.** New Edition. 6s. 6d.

17. **The Sermon on the Mount.** To the end of the Lord's Prayer. 6s. 6d.

27. **The Sermon on the Mount.** From the end of the Lord's Prayer. 6s. 6d.

31. **The Training of the Apostles.** Part I. 6s. 6d.

37. **The Training of the Apostles.** Part II. 6s. 6d.

45. **The Training of the Apostles.** Part III. 6s. 6d.

51. **The Training of the Apostles.** Part IV. 6s. 6d.

57. **The Preaching of the Cross.** Part I. 6s. 6d.

63. **The Preaching of the Cross.** Part II. 6s.

64. **The Preaching of the Cross.** Part III. 6s.

HOLY WEEK.

68. **Passiontide.** Part I. 6s. 6d.

72. **Passiontide.** Part II. 6s. 6d.

76. **Passiontide.** Part III. 6s. 6d.

78. **The Passage of our Lord to the Father.**
7s. 6d. Conclusion of *The Life of our Life*.

---

38. **The Return of the King.** Discourses on the Latter Days. By the Rev. H. J. Coleridge, S.J. Second Edition. 7s. 6d.

44. **The Baptism of the King.** Considerations on the Sacred Passion. By the Rev. H. J. Coleridge, S.J. 7s.6d.

55. **The Mother of the King.** Mary during the Life of our Lord. By the Rev. H. J. Coleridge, S.J. 7s. 6d.

60. **The Mother of the Church.** Mary during the first Apostolic Age. By the Rev. H. J. Coleridge, S.J. 6s.

The Prisoners of the King. Thoughts on the Catholic Doctrine of Purgatory. By the Rev. H. J. Coleridge, S.J. New Edition. 4s.

The Seven Words of Mary. By the Rev. H. J. Coleridge, S.J. 2s.

www.ingramcontent.com/pod-product-compliance
Lightning Source LLC
Chambersburg PA
CBHW021330110726
47900CB00005B/1414